SONG FOR A LOST KINGDOM, BOOK I

Music is not bound by time

STEVE MORETTI

SONG FOR A LOST KINGDOM

READER COMMENTS

"What a page-turner..." - *Lily Marcus*

"A melody which can span space and time, a Cello which plays that haunting music, and a character who stands up strong in both times - this trio makes this story a mystical fast read." - *Shalini*

"I can't recommend this enough." - *Keith Oxenrider*

"A great first read of the series. I would love to read more of Moretti's work in the future." - *Amy*

"This is one of the best fantasy fiction that I have ever read! Not just Adeena, even I felt transported to the magical and mystical world." - *The Book Decoder*

"*Song For A Lost Kingdom* swept me away. I was instantly drawn into this plot. I love the back and forth between present day and 1700s Scotland. It was always compelling." - *Jessica Rachow*

"If you're a fan of time travel or fantasy books, you should check this one out." - *Powisamy*

"A cosy way to pass an evening." - *The Book Worm Drinketh*

"A fun time-slip adventure with some pretty badass moments..." - *The Star Jar*

"Once I got the hang of it after a few chapters, I wasn't able to put it down. I spent hours awake at night reading chapter after chapter." - *Erica Mae*

"The most soul stirring part of the book is the music itself. The world of musical instruments, of musicians and of haunting melodies came alive for me." - *Read Write Live*

"This was a fantastic historical fiction! It had great characters and a great storyline." - *Dani Pirok*

"I had not really planned to read this book right away, but once I began, I could not put it down." - *Musing Crow*

"Wow, I loved this story!" - *Raewynn*

Song for a Lost Kingdom
Book I
Music is not bound by time

by Steve Moretti

Published by DWA Media
OTTAWA • CANADA

DWA Media

PO 493, Richmond, Ontario K0A 2Z0

stevemoretti.ca

For Pam and Keera

Song for a Lost Kingdom

Novel and Audiobook series

The Prequel: *A kingdom is lost, a song is born*
eBook, Audiobook

Book I: *Music is not bound by time*
eBook, Paperback, Audiobook

Book II: *Love never surrenders*
eBook, Paperback, Audiobook

Book III: *The heart beats in time*
eBook, Paperback, (Audiobook coming)

Join my mail list
and read the SFLK Prequel for FREE

Get updates, links to free books, contests to win gift cards and FREE books and much more!

CHAPTER 1

OTTAWA, 2018

Adeena tried to adjust her eyes against the blinding spotlights. She sat alone with her cello on the main stage of Southam Hall, a monstrous space meant to accommodate the entire National Arts Centre Orchestra. The burning white lights felt like they were searing her corneas. Beads of sweat slid down her forehead.

Adeena had thought of nothing else but this audition since she began practicing four months ago. Now she was about to perform, almost blinded and drenched in her own perspiration. How could she possibly handle the two contrasting movements from Bach's *Cello Suite No. 4* in E-flat major if she had to look at the surface of the sun the whole time she was performing? How would she even hold the bow in her hand if she was dripping wet?

The curtain in front of her was meant to ensure she would be judged only by her music. But the six-foot high wall of opaque black cloth seemed like its real intention was to separate her from her lifelong ambition of joining the orchestra.

"How you doing, Adeena?"

The familiar voice jolted her.

It came from the silhouetted shape of the tall man who

walked toward her on stage. Walter Leo was her dad's oldest and dearest friend. He had arranged this audition for a rare opening in the cello section of the orchestra where he had worked his way up to principal cellist over the past decade.

"I can't see anything with those lights!" Adeena whispered, not wanting to be heard by anyone on the other side of the curtain.

Walter moved closer and touched her shoulder. "Just turn your chair a little and look at me over at the side," he said softly. "Take a deep breath and play the way we practiced. You'll be fine Pumpkin, really!"

Pumpkin. Walter's nickname for her. Even at twenty-nine it felt good. Maybe it was because her father was the only other person who called her that. She associated it with the classical music that had filled her home as a child, especially when Walter and her father spent spirited evenings deconstructing the tiniest biographic details of renowned composers and their world-shattering compositions.

Adeena knew the history of the Cello Suites and the theory that Bach's wife, Anna Magdalena, composed whole sections of it. Walter was certain that Anna was more than just a simple transcriber. This inspired Adeena's own dreams of composing, which seemed to her to be principally the domain of old dead men. Okay – old, dead and very *gifted* men.

"Are you ready?"

The disembodied request came from the other side of the curtain. Although she could not see his face, she knew it was Friedrich Lang, the orchestra's temperamental music director and conductor.

"Yes, I am Sir," Adeena replied, hoping to project a calm professionalism that would mask the terror she felt inside. "Thank you for this opportunity. I'm very honoured."

Her eyes turned to Walter, watching from the side of the stage. He gave her a thumbs-up and a reassuring 'You can do this!' smile. She nodded and tried to relax as she realized months of preparation were over.

It was time to perform.

More than thirty cellists from around the world were competing for this one opening with the NAC Orchestra. This was something Adeena had dreamt about since she was a kid. Nothing had the potential to alter her life more wondrously, or more devastatingly, than how she performed in the next forty-five minutes.

"Wait! Just hold on," the conductor called out from behind the curtain. Adeena was alarmed when she saw two men walk on stage. They lifted the curtain wall up and carried it away, revealing an acre of empty red velvet seats. It was both terrifying and exhilarating.

"I hope you don't mind, but I hate that thing," the tall, sour-faced conductor announced. She knew Lang had a reputation as being unpredictable. The curtain provided anonymity to the candidates, but the music director had final say if it was to be used.

Was he testing her?

"It's fine," Adeena replied. "Shall I begin?"

"Please do," Lang said, looking at his watch.

Adeena felt her heart thumping softly in her ears, like a personal metronome, as she positioned the cello between her stockinged legs. She presented a fetching sight on stage. Her copper tinged hair cascaded down to her shoulder blades, with one curl falling rebelliously over the side of her forehead.

But this was not about how she looked. It was about the music. She took a deep breath and exhaled slowly, feeling her heartbeat finally reach a steady rhythm, as if signalling her to begin.

Very slowly at first, she drew the bow across the strings of her cello, the first heroic notes of Bach's grand prelude taking the perfect form she had laboured over with Walter. A pair of E-flat notes, two octaves apart, filled Southam Hall with the rich rumbling timbre of her cello, setting the tone for a continuous flow of warm eighth-note arpeggios that resonated triumphantly. She extended her left hand gracefully as she played in the demanding E-flat key.

Adeena handled the *allemande* section with careful pacing in duple rhythm – four beats to a measure. She knew her playing was technically perfect, remembering Walter's advice. 'Practice the way you want to perform and perform the way you practice.' She handled the difficult flowing quaver movement followed by the cadenza with precision and absolute accuracy.

As Adeena progressed through the series of notes, keeping her elbow raised high to reach the C-string, checking her rhythm and tempo, getting ready for the next thumb position and all of her fingering combinations, she realized she had stopped breathing, something her tutors had warned her *not* to do when playing a difficult piece.

Was she that tense? Was she focusing too much on technique?

Adeena heard Walter again in her head.

Feel the cello. Let the sound flow through you.

She felt a wave of panic wash over her, before she finally let her breath out completely. She was almost at the end of the prelude now, and the final four-note E-Flat major chord. She finished with a flourish and let her bow drop dramatically to her side.

Adeena looked up at Walter who seemed pleased, then over to Friedrich Lang, the man who would decide her fate. He showed no expression. Was she hoping he would start clapping with effusive praise and encouragement?

Nope.

Lang simply looked again at his watch, and then at the program of selections she was to cover. It was almost time for lunch and he looked like he was hoping this would soon be over.

AFTERWARD, ONLY WALTER GAVE HER ANY FEEDBACK.

"Adeena, you belong with us on the stage," he said, beaming as she packed her cello into its weathered black case. "I almost felt like Anna Magdalena was there, composing through your fingertips. Your playing was flawless!"

"Really?" she scowled. "Is that why Lang left before I got to my Mozart solo?"

"The music director... he's hard to read," Walter said softly. "I've known him for a few years now, and I still don't know what makes that man tick. But I do know this. You can't let one old conductor stop you from reaching your dreams."

She finished packing her cello, bow and sheet music into the old case. She fastened the lid and hoisted it up. "Walter, I don't know. Maybe it's just too hard and I don't have it. Dreams are great for little girls, but I'm almost thirty. Maybe it's time to move on."

He leaned in and embraced her. "Don't talk like that. I've watched you since you could barely hold a bow. You've always had talent. But you know what matters even more than that, Adeena?"

He let her go and stepped back. She stared at him with a blank deflated expression.

"Your playing. It comes from a place deep inside of you, a place most people don't even have. Don't give up. Music is who you are."

She started to walk away, but he wasn't done.

"And you know it."

THE BACK OF TARA KORMOS' NEW AUDI A4 CONVERTIBLE WAS the ideal spot for Adeena's cello. With the top down, the sporty cabriolet seemed tailor-made for carrying the bulky instrument, the old black case snugly filling most of the beige leather back seats.

Tara, her boss at the National Gallery, was also her closest friend and advisor on matters of the heart. As Adeena collapsed onto the front seat of the silver Audi, she was glad Tara had insisted they keep their hot yoga session, though Adeena had come to work dressed for the audition in high heels and a black chiffon dress. She would be glad to ditch that for her yoga pants and tank top.

"Soooooo?" Tara inquired curiously as the brilliant August sun sparkled off the Rideau Canal behind the National Arts Centre.

"Drive," Adeena replied, putting on dark sunglasses to block out the bright sunlight and hopefully, Tara's impending interrogation.

AFTER AN INTENSE WORKOUT, ADEENA FINALLY FELT RELAXED enough to rejoin the human race. She had sweated out all the tension and anxiety from the audition, detoxing the demons of self-doubt with fifty minutes of high-energy yoga that felt almost metaphysical.

Following a quick shower, and a change into Capri pants and a summery blouse, she sat with Tara at one of the outdoor cafés in Little Italy. After their sweatfest, the women had no appetite, but they eagerly downed glasses of iced chai tea.

"So how do you know he doesn't want you?" Tara finally asked after she emptied her glass.

"Because Friedrich Lang is an eeeevil man, Miss Tara," Adeena droned in her best Bela Lugosi voice. "He lives in a dark room and is afraid of the light!"

"Very funny, Miss Professional Musician Born to Suffer," Tara responded. They played this game whenever Tara tried to get her to be serious about her career or her love life, or anything else Adeena didn't want to talk about.

Adeena looked down at her sandalled toes. She took a long

sip of her iced-tea. "I practiced four damn months for one forty-five minute audition," Adeena finally said. "You think maybe he could have at least stayed until the end?"

"Maybe he decided you passed the audition, and he just wanted to get lunch."

"Yup. His blood meal, in the basement!" Adeena snorted and shook her head, looking up to the sky and closing her eyes. Tara would never understand the part of Adeena that suffered for the music that felt like it was trapped inside of her. Only Walter seemed to have any sense at all of her creative passion that longed for release.

Adeena looked at Tara, stylish as usual in her Yves Saint Laurent tortoise shell sunglasses. They were both the same age and had gone to most of the same schools, yet they were worlds apart. Tara's Greek father Mikos and her Indian mother Pia had given their daughter not only classic beauty – a smooth olive complexion, high cheekbones, long straight black hair and piercing blue eyes – but also a driving work ethos.

In high school, while Adeena was hanging out with the wrong crowd, starting an avant-garde rock band with her bad-boy boyfriend Kurt, and generally being a jerk, Tara was leading student council, organizing the prom and making sure she graduated as an Ontario Scholar with a 93% average. As if that weren't enough, whenever Adeena fell apart, Tara was always there to pick up the pieces.

"Dee – you give up too easily," Tara began with a tone somewhere between motivational lecturer and counsellor of the mentally deranged. "You've played the cello since, well since as long as I can remember. I never understood why, but I actually admired how insanely... insane you were."

"Gee, that's sweet Tar," Adeena said, taking a lemon slice from the table to squirt her therapist in the face. Tara ducked, and seemed unfazed.

"So what's the deal? You're giving up because some old guy

went for lunch? Is this what you want to do with your life or not Dee?" Tara liked to cut to the chase quickly.

"I think so, but ..." Adeena sighed, struggling to finish her thought. "You probably won't understand this Tar, but – I didn't choose the cello. It chose me."

Tara's furrowed brow was obvious, even through her giant sunglasses.

"When I was five I went to my first symphony concert. My parents took me to Montreal and after I watched Maya Beiser's solo on the cello, I bawled my eyes out for two days."

"What?" Tara looked confused. "Um, why?"

"Because I wanted to *be* her. That was supposed to be *me* on stage at Place-des-Arts. And I was only a little kid."

Adeena realized she had never told this story to Tara before.

"My mom was great. She put me in Suzuki music school right after that. But my parents never made me practice. They didn't need to. My dad would tell me stories about the history of the cello and the composers. When I started to play a new piece, he would give me the whole story of the composition – the composer, what he went through to write it, when it was first performed, what people said about it, that kind of stuff. I was a junkie for those stories."

"And here I thought you were just a snob back then, or maybe really weird at least," Tara mused. "You always said it was your parents who made you practice. Liar!"

"It was easier to blame them," Adeena responded, lost in thought for a moment. "I should probably call them, or send them a note about the audition. My dad's in Scotland right now and my mom is on her way there tonight. My grandmother's not doing too well."

"Oh, sorry to hear that," Tara said, her tone softening.

The two women sat in silence, admiring the magnificent late August weather, the sun radiating pure joy from an impossibly blue cloudless sky. Summer was a time to savour to the fullest for everyone who had survived a long Ottawa winter. It was easily one of the world's coldest capital cities, and once the icy grip of the dark winter months receded, bicycles appeared from hibernation and cafés overflowed with pale sun-starved patrons who relished every second of a bright, sunny afternoon.

Although Tara was Adeena's boss, the two behaved more like sisters, neither of them having any female siblings. Adeena knew that Tara, now the assistant curator at the Gallery, had given her a research position to help her out while she struggled with her on-again, off-again music career. Adeena's minor in art history had been a handy way for Tara to justify hiring her best friend. In fact, Adeena was an excellent researcher thanks in part to growing up as the daughter of a published history professor.

Tara pursed her lips in thought, and Adeena knew more probing was on the way.

"Dee – you've got to *commit* to this, or you have to let it go," Tara said, lingering on the word *commit*. "Anyone can see that you'll never be satisfied doing anything else. What does Philippe think about the whole thing?"

"That I'm nuts. Can't understand why I spend so much time practicing when there's so little chance of making it."

"I understand why he is saying that. He thinks you're going to get hurt," Tara said, reaching for Adeena's hand. "Well if you're not sure about music, are you at least ready to commit to him?"

"Oh sure. I commit sins with him every weekend," Adeena joked with a goofy smile. Then her smile turned as she bit her lip and brushed her long hair back from her face. "Damn! I forgot. He's taking me out to Le Café tonight for dinner. Not sure I want to go back to the NAC so soon."

"Le Café?" Tara sighed. *"Ooh-la-la!"* She looked at her watch. "Oh my, we've got to get back to work. The pieces for the new exhibit are in, and I need you to get started on them. Today!"

When Adeena finally arrived back at work, she felt like the day had already lasted a week. The audition had ground her down, and while yoga had provided a rebound of sorts, she was still exhausted. That all changed when she went to the receiving room in the basement of the Gallery to get the curator's binder and research notes for the new exhibit Tara wanted her to begin researching and documenting.

There were twelve crates in the basement of the gallery that had just arrived from the National Museum of Scotland in Edinburgh. They comprised a touring exhibit Tara was advertising as the *Art of Rebellion*. It featured paintings, journals, prints and artifacts. The star attraction however, was the Duncan Cello, the oldest surviving cello made in the United Kingdom.

Adeena read the packing slip, as well as the summary notes on the exhibit. She stared transfixed at the large sticker on the wooden crate:

EXTREMELY FRAGILE – # 3212-11
MUSICAL INSTRUMENT

"Please take that up to my office," she told the young clerk after signing the forms.

He looked down at his sign-out sheets. "That piece is supposed to stay down here in the secure storage area," he said hesitantly.

Adeena thought for a moment, before addressing the boy, who wore a loose fitting T-shirt and baggy jeans. She knew she was breaching protocol, but a private look at the cello? Rules or no, she had to see it. "You're new here, right?"

"Yup. Started this week," the young man replied. "It's a summer job, working the graveyard shift most nights, at least until school starts again. Then I'll be here part time."

"Oh, very nice. Welcome to the Gallery uh... Michael," she said looking closely at the ID badge around his neck. Listen, you're doing a great job, but I really need to have that crate sent to my office. I'll bring it back myself, later tonight."

He looked at Adeena in confusion. She smiled at him and raised her pencil-thin eyebrows in friendly fire. Her piercing green eyes and long coppery hair came in handy at times like this, as Michael took in all five foot nine inches of her shapely outline and inviting face.

"Let me sign for it, and I'll get it back to you before your shift is over," she cooed.

He hesitated for a moment. "Well . . . okay!" he replied with a wide grin, looking down to find a pen. Adeena noticed her ID badge had been flipped over the whole time.

"Thanks, Michael," she said as he handed her the forms and a pen. She printed the name, signed with a flourish, and handed the form back to him.

He studied it for a second, and then looked back up at her eagerly.

"I'll have it sent it up right away, Tara!"

CHAPTER 2

William Stuart should not have been lost.

With his new GPS steadily blinking at him, his oversized *Ordance* map of Dundee and Montrose spread out on his lap, and SIRI on his iPhone offering suggestions, he had every possible aid to find his mother's cottage at the eastern edge of the North Sea.

Yet he sat grumbling to himself in his little red VW electric car, hopelessly lost. And totally confused. He wished that his wife was here with her natural gift for direction. Jackie was landing in Scotland tomorrow, but that didn't help him today.

William was parked on the side of a country lane that struggled valiantly to accommodate the width of two cars as it wandered through the hillside pastures. He was a few scant miles from the coastal town of Arbroath. A frizzy-haired, bubble-gum blowing teenaged girl from the information centre there had explained how "totally easy" it was to find Usan – the closest village to William's mother's cottage.

'Easy for her,' he muttered, getting out of the car so he could flatten the map on the hood, fighting against a stiffening breeze. The archaic place-names and ancient landmarks filled the colourful map with an almost mythical imagery that the historian in William would normally relish. But this afternoon it just added to his growing web of confusion.

Was it Usan? Or the *Maine* of Usan? Maybe the *Scotson* of Usan?

William was so engrossed that he did not notice the flock of Soay sheep slowly surrounding his car. In their meandering curiosity, they inched nearer and nearer, seemingly unmoved by his dilemma in their search for the tastiest bits of heather.

"Could Ah offer ye some assistance, sir?"

William looked up startled. He now saw the sheep and a rugged young man in denim overalls and knee-high black rubber boots standing beside them.

"Oh, I'm sorry!" William exclaimed, feeling somewhat embarrassed. He studied the grazing sheep that appeared to have adopted him as their new shepherd. "I'm not much good at herding," he said, looking over the animals for a moment. "But they do seem a lot like my first-year students!"

One of the larger ewes eyed him with a blank stare. William smiled before turning back towards the young man. "Hello. I'm William. I had no idea I drove into your pasture."

"Donnae worry about that," the man said, stepping closer and offering his hand. "I'm Murdo," he said warmly. "And Ah see you've met my flock!"

The sheep continued to gather from all directions and seemed determined to find something particularly appetizing growing just under the hood of William's automobile. He smiled at their single-minded determination.

"I didn't even notice them! I'm so lost and can't figure out how to get to my mother's place." he said. "My mother says 'I'm near the sea, close by Usan. But there is no road that I can find to get to her cottage from here, and I'm not sure which 'Usan' she even means."

William studied the wrinkled note he'd received from her last week, made damp by hours of frustration and the humid sea air.

Murdo took a few steps closer to try and help make sense of it. "Who's yer mother?"

"Margaret Rose," William replied, "Margaret Rose Stuart."

"Maggie?" Murdo chuckled.

"Yes! You know her?"

"Course Ah do! Her place is next tae mah farm!" Then he grew serious. "She ain't well though. Yer her son?"

"Yes, from Canada." William replied. "I knew she was sick. I was coming in October. But when I got this note last week, I changed my ticket and flew here right away."

Murdo frowned. "What did she say?"

William read over his mother's words again. There was as odd sense of urgency in them. Margaret Rose always had a flair for the dramatic, but something in the tone of this letter was different from anything he'd heard before. And he had heard *a lot* before.

He looked up at the tall blue-eyed Scot in mud-caked boots staring at him intently. Murdo was about the same age as Adeena and seemed to know Margaret Rose. For some reason William had a good feeling about him. He decided to read directly from the letter.

"Come at once William, I am not well. We need to go to Kinnaird for Adeena."

"Adeena?" Murdo asked.

"My daughter, back in Canada. She and Mum are close," William explained. "They're a twosome, always playing games with each other."

"If she's anything like Maggie," Murdo grinned, "I have tae meet her!"

"Actually, Adeena's quite normal."

Murdo chuckled like he had spent some time with Margaret Rose. He thought for a moment and then turned serious. "And Maggie wants ye to take her to Kinnaird Castle?"

"Castle?"

"If that's the Kinnaird she means in 'er letter," Murdo answered. "It's close to here, quite near Montrose."

IT WAS ONLY AFTER WILLIAM FOLLOWED THE BACK LANE – A well-travelled sheep path really, directly through Murdo's farm, that he was able to finally locate the tiny cottage where Margaret Rose had decided to live out her life. He was curious why there was no actual road to the cottage.

Murdo was puzzled by the inquiry. "A road? We've a perfectly guid lane through mah farm!" he explained "All property in our bonnie land is open. There's nae such thing as trespassin' through a field."

William was still smiling as he parked near the cottage and took in the spectacular view. It was a breathtaking panorama of sea and sky, palettes of translucent blues contrasting with dark earthy browns. A pasture of tall grass extended all the way to the water, where crashing waves pounded against boulders that had challenged the surf for eons.

William was awed by the horizon that appeared stacked with mile-high swirls of cotton-candy clouds. Pity he had not found the opportunity to travel here before. He really should have visited his mother after she had returned to Scotland from her four-year sojourn to Canada. His relationship with her was decidedly difficult.

His entire life he'd rationalized his mother's actions. He knew he could never fully appreciate the suffering she endured after the loss of his father in a fatal car accident when he was two years old. She had been left to raise William on her own as a penniless, unemployed, single mother in Perth. He knew she was battling depression when she finally sent him to Canada in 1961 to live with his Uncle John, who became the closest thing to a father he would ever know. Her motives clearly stemmed from a desire to protect him from her own crushing poverty and debilitating personal demons.

Although he understood all this as a university professor approaching sixty, William still wrestled with childhood wounds. No matter how legitimate her reasons may have been, deep down inside, he still felt like she abandoned him.

As he climbed onto the porch he saw his mother through the front screen door. When she saw him, her eyes lit up and she waved him inside.

"Hey Mum! I may have a new career tending sheep," he joked as he entered the tiny cottage, and then added tenderly, "I've missed you. How are you doing?"

"William, thank God ye made it," she replied, rising slowly from her chair.

William embraced her warmly but was alarmed at how frail her thin frame felt. He noticed a pile of pills on a plate sitting next to her tea cup, and then somewhat startled, saw a plump middle-aged woman smiling at him from the corner of the kitchen.

She wore a silk bonnet that struggled to contain her greying curls, and a pale blue apron wrapped tightly under her bosom. Together with white suede pumps that appeared two sizes too small for her feet, she gave the appearance of a poorly cased sausage. But she moved towards him with the grace and lightness of a Highland dancer.

"I'm Fay, Mum's nurse," she offered cheerfully.

She turned to Maggie and addressed his mother as one might a rebellious toddler. "He's 'ere now, Maggie. Go and take yer meds, like a guid girl," the nurse said firmly, and then turning to William added in a softer voice, "Been trying for the last hour."

"Piss off and die!" Margaret Rose volleyed back to her nurse. William was afraid how Fay would react, but her smile only widened.

"Aye, soon enough," Fay grinned, coming closer and pushing

the pills toward Margaret Rose, and then commanded firmly: "Take these now, please."

This seemed like a game both were used to playing. His mother finally took the pills with a glass of water that Fay handed to her.

Satisfied that her patient was okay for the time being, Fay gave his mother a hug and gathered her bag to leave.

"Good luck, William. She's a pistol today!"

THE WORN FLOORBOARDS OF THE OLD COTTAGE CREAKED AS Fay saw herself out. The room was still until the slam of the screen door startled both William and his mother.

Margaret Rose reached for a dark wool cardigan as she rose from her chair. Although frail, she was a strong, wiry woman always ready for battle. She had been born at the start of the Great Depression, grown up during World War II and lost her husband as a young bride in the fifties. Now as William helped her with her sweater, he couldn't help but admire her fighting spirit. Her hair was completely white, but she wore glasses only for reading and preferred corduroy slacks and leather boots to pajamas and slippers.

William offered his arm to support her when she announced she wanted to go outside for a walk.

"I'm dyin' but I'm no a cripple," she rebuffed as they made their way down the steps of the porch.

He looked over at the long grasses that mixed with the purple thyme and red clover in the pasture that extended all the way to the green sea. Along with the layered shades of a blue sky, the view seemed like it had been lifted right off the canvas of an impressionist masterpiece. William understood why his mother would choose to live here. And at eighty-five, she had earned the right to select any place she wanted to spend her last days on earth.

"Ye got my letter, then?" his mother asked, as she walked beside him on the path that led to the rocky seashore, now exposed by the receding tide.

"Yes Mum, but I don't understand," he countered. "You're not well, you should be resting. Maybe we can find another doctor?"

"Nothin' can save me now, Will." She stopped walking and looked directly into his blue eyes. "But ye can help save our family."

William weighed his response carefully. His mother had struggled for years with depression and mental illness. Doctors and specialists had never agreed on a diagnosis. Her insistence that a dead relative talked to her on a regular basis was something every psychologist interpreted differently. They all agreed however, that his mother was 'troubled'.

"Mum, let's not go there again. Why don't we just enjoy the time we've got together?"

"William Stuart! Why do ye still fight me? I've so little time left!" she snorted, and then turned to walk again toward the shore with William in tow. She said nothing as they marched. The crashing waves punctuated the silence, as crescendos of salt spray shot high above the granite boulders.

"Jackie dinnae come then?" Margaret Rose finally said without slowing down on her relentless journey to the sea.

"She's on her way. Landing in Edinburgh tomorrow," William responded. He thought about his wife, a psychologist at the Ottawa Hospital, and how Jackie always advised him to handle his mother's delusions.

Don't argue. Let her talk.

"An' how's mah Adeena?" Margaret Rose asked as they neared the coast and the grass gave way to exposed slates of black rock. The breeze lifted a soaring gull, its white wings contrasting with the sapphire sky as it glided over the beach. "She still wants to be a musician?"

"Actually, she has an audition with the National Arts Centre

Orchestra," William responded, looking at his watch. "It was supposed to be today. My friend Walter, you know the one who plays cello with the orchestra? He helped her rehearse."

"Ye think she'll make it?" she asked with unusual doubt in her voice.

Her tone surprised him. His mother adored Adeena. Actually 'adored' wasn't quite the right way to describe it. Margaret Rose and Adeena had an understanding to which no one else was privy. Particularly, William.

Their connection developed during the time his mum had come to live with them when Adeena was about nine years old. Margaret Rose and Adeena would talk together in ways that William could never fathom. He knew that much of what they discussed involved the dreams that his mum had been having since his father died. She claimed the same woman was always in her dreams, a distant relative who needed help.

Adeena was completely enthralled and insisted on knowing everything about the woman in her grandmother's dreams. He and Jackie had tried to put a stop to these conversations, for fear they were making Adeena's own struggles worse. But there seemed to be no way to curtail the two.

William thought about his daughter's chances of making a spot on the orchestra. Not very good, considering the fierce competition that Walter warned him Adeena would face. "I don't know, Mum," he said, not wanting to falsely raise his mother's hopes. "It'll be tough. She's so good, and it's always been her dream, but I don't know if she's, if she is..."

He paused, thinking about his daughter.

"If she's what?" Margaret Rose demanded.

"I'm not sure if she's competitive enough. Well, not competitive, but you know, focused enough? Walter told me the music director, Lang, I think it was, yes, Friedrich Lang. He's apparently a real son-of-a-bitch."

Margaret Rose took hold of her son's arms and looked at him intensely. "Ah can help 'er," she said. "Ah have something for

Adeena that was taken from us a long time ago. Ah finally think I know where it is."

"Finally found it? Found what?"

"Ah saw it in mah dream, Will," she said to him, still holding both his arms. "When Jackie gets 'ere, we're going to Kinnaird tae help Adeena."

She turned away and looked out to the sea before adding quietly, "And hopefully, change our history."

CHAPTER 3

Philippe Levesqué reached into his suit pocket again, feeling for the velvet case. It held the diamond ring he bought that afternoon. As he crossed Sussex Drive towards the National Gallery, he wondered what Adeena's reaction would be tonight. He was sure she would have only one.

About time!

He crossed the street in front of Notre Dame Cathedral and gazed up at the colossal bronze spider sculpture gracing the Gallery's front entrance.

"Salut Maman!" he sang out cheerfully to the towering arachnid, noticing for the first time its sac of white melon-sized marble eggs suspended high above his head in a braided nest.

Maman indeed. He smiled reading the sculpture's official name carved onto a metal sign at the front of the Gallery. Maybe not that many, but a few eggs would be perfect. He chuckled wondering if he would prefer a boy or girl first.

Inside the Gallery, Philippe impatiently showed his ID and got a visitor's badge. What a lot of bother! Adeena could just as easily have met him in the foyer after he texted her when he left his office:

On my way. Been thinking about us all day.

Her response had left him deflated.

OK

That was it? "Ok?" Shortly after she had added:

In my office working

Romance wasn't Adeena's thing, Philippe rationalized, but she was dedicated to her work and she'd make an amazing wife. He admired her passion for music, art and history. Yes, they were very different and their relationship often stormy, but Adeena's creative side inspired him and drew him to her, almost it seemed, against his own will.

"Philippe!" a cheerful voice rang out as he clipped his visitor badge to the lapel of his silky Italian suit. He recognized the voice and immediately felt better.

"Tara!" he responded, looking up at the woman in the tight-fitting skirt and stylishly cut matching linen blazer. They hugged warmly and kissed each other on both cheeks. He pulled her aside into a vestibule beside the coatcheck area. He wanted her opinion on his choice of diamond.

Philippe pulled the velvet ring case out of his pocket and held it before her.

"Ohhh... at last!" Tara exclaimed with a dazzling smile. "I had such a good feeling when I introduced you two, I knew she wouldn't be able to resist your French charms." Then her face tightened. "Adeena's had a bad day you know. The audition was rough. The *big kahuna* didn't even stay until the end," Tara sighed. "Hope she's okay."

"Yeah, me too."

He had been telling Adeena not to get her hopes up too high.

He knew how difficult it was to get a spot on the NAC Orchestra. As a reporter at the *Ottawa Citizen*, he'd written a background piece on the music director, Friedrich Lang, and found him arrogant, calling Ottawa a "pretentiously dull little city". Lang later asked not to include that in the story, and while he complied, Philippe kept the whole recording anyway.

"Thanks for the heads-up," he said to Tara handing her the ring that had cost him three months' salary. "I knew this might be a bad day for her. That's why I planned to give this to her tonight – so she could forget all about Monsieur Lang."

Tara opened the velvet-lined case. The one carat diamond shimmered brilliantly, reflecting the overhead tungsten lights in a thousand different directions. The flawless jewel was surrounded by a double halo of sparkling diamonds encrusted delicately on an 18-carat platinum band.

Tara's face flushed and her eyes grew wet as she closed the ring case and placed it back in Philippe's hands. She gave him another kiss on the cheek.

"Go give this to your wife."

CRATE NUMBER 3212-11 HAD BEEN CAREFULLY PACKAGED IN Edinburgh four days ago for shipment to Ottawa. The logo of National Museums Scotland, a stylized interpretation of St Andrew's Cross, had been burnished into the thick plywood lid. A carpenter at the museum had finished work on the crate only last week, and the sweet aroma of freshly cut pine filled her office as Adeena carefully used a screwdriver to undo the long blue wood screws that held the lid firmly in place.

Like a child opening a Christmas present while everyone was sleeping, she lifted the heavy wooden lid, looking around to make sure no one was watching through the glass doors of her office.

She knew Tara would have a fit. Rare artifacts, especially those that formed the showpiece of a heavily promoted Gallery exhibit, had a long list of security and handling protocols. Still, Adeena felt compelled to do this.

She just had to see this piece.

She set the lid down on the floor and looked at the tightly wrapped contents of the crate. A large manila envelope was taped on top of the foam packing. The envelope was labeled: *Duncan Cello – Documents.*

The wretched audition she had endured earlier in the day faded away as she opened the envelope and began to read the papers inside. Robert Duncan had created this instrument in his workshop near Aberdeen, Scotland in the 18th century. The fact that it was the oldest surviving cello ever made in the UK, and that it sat only a few feet away from her, about to be seen in North America for the first time, filled her with a sense of nervous anticipation.

Adeena studied a glossy black and white photograph of the nameplate:

Robert Duncan. *Maker.*
ABERDEEN, 1736

SHE PORED OVER THE CELLO'S HISTORY AND ORIGIN. MOST fascinating were theories of why it was made in the Italian style of Antonio Stradivari, better known by his Latinized name – *Stradivarius*. The documentation theorized that Robert Duncan travelled to Italy and may have learned his technique in Florence or Cremona, home of the Stradivari family, before returning to Scotland to set up his own workshop in Margaret Leith's Court, Upperkirkgate.

She gathered the papers and photographs together and looked over at the open wooden crate. A yearning she hadn't felt in a long time swept across her. What would it be like to play this cello?

Except for few minor alterations over the centuries, it was the same instrument created more than two hundred and seventy years ago: the same thick canted neck and fingerboard wedge, and decorative white lines scratched around its edges. It was even the same ink purfling on the belly and the back that Duncan himself added when he triumphantly completed his finely crafted creation so many years ago.

Adeena stood up. She had to see this for herself. The cello was still carefully wrapped and wedged inside the wooden crate. It was nested inside thick foam padding.

As she bent over and prepared to remove the top layer, there was gentle tap on her office door. She froze then looked over to see Philippe smiling through the glass.

Shit.

He opened the door, beaming like a school child as he bounded into her office.

"Ready to go babe?" Philippe asked, as she stood up and stiffly received a hug from him. She felt guilty for acting so cold, but the gears in her brain were moving in a completely different direction.

"Yeah," Adeena responded, glancing down at the wooden crate holding the cello she wanted so badly to see and to touch, if only for a second. She stepped back from Philippe and pointed to the crate.

"You know what's inside there?" she asked.

"No. What?"

"It's the star of our new exhibit," she said as if announcing a winning lottery ticket: "The Duncan Cello!"

"Cool," Philippe replied, reaching into his suit jacket to check on something in his pocket. "Our reservations are for seven-thirty. We really gotta run." He kissed her cheek. "C'mon, let's go!"

Adeena was frozen to the floor.

She wanted to lecture him about this instrument, and its role in the musical renaissance of 18th century Scotland. Where had it been played? Pubs? Royal halls? Castles? Who played it, and what music did they perform?

But he wouldn't really care, she thought. And they were already late. "Okay, fine."

She grabbed her jacket and followed him out the door. As she turned off the lights and locked the door, she took one last look at the open wooden crate through the shadows in her office.

The treasure inside would have to wait a little longer.

PHILIPPE HAD CHOSEN LE CAFÉ FOR THE ATMOSPHERE AND ITS cuisine that highlighted flavours from across Canada. He had even reserved a table with a panoramic view of the Rideau Canal. But the fact the restaurant was inside the National Arts Centre, and that to get there they had to walk past Southam Hall where she had auditioned this morning, left Adeena feeling like she'd been punched in the gut.

Again.

It felt wrong to be back here so soon after the morning's debacle. The Duncan Cello had worked wonders in changing her mood, and now Philippe had dragged her back like his own little cavewoman, to the scene of the slaughter.

"I love the way they do the beef tenderloin here," he crooned, looking over the menu.

She thought she might actually start screaming.

What was she doing with him anyway? She couldn't make it as a musician and she only had her job at the Gallery because of Tara. And the 'love of her life' had no idea of who she was, or that she felt like crawling inside a hole at this very moment to die a slow painful death, decaying into rotting flesh as birds pecked her eyes out.

A smiling waiter arrived with a chilled bottle of Moët & Chandon and poured them both tall glasses of the French *cuvée.* Philippe lifted his glass to propose a toast.

"To us!" he offered.

Adeena glared at him.

As she struggled to raise her glass, the voices in her head began to scream. Should she throw the champagne at him, or smash the glass on the marble floor? What would he do if she hurled it against the picture window that looked out on the Rideau Canal?

Instead, still holding the champagne flute in her hand, she started to cry, releasing a swollen river that had finally breached its dam.

A THIN-CRUST PIZZA BAKED IN A WOOD-FIRED OVEN UNTIL THE crust was slightly burnt, topped with ripe tomatoes, tender basil leaves and fresh *bufalo* milk mozzarella was a simple meal. Served at an opportune moment with a bottle of French champagne, it could be the catalyst for lasting peace between the bitterest of warring nations.

Philippe knew he had been a fool.

No, a complete asshole. He had gotten so caught up in the engagement ring, reservations at *Le Café,* and trying to turn Adeena's failed audition into one of the most memorable nights of her life, that he never stopped to think about what *she* was actually going through.

His Italian suit jacket lay draped over an office chair, its precious diamond cargo still secure inside the front pocket. He had removed his tie and undone the top button of his shirt as he looked over at Adeena, happy to be back in her office, reaching for a second slice of the pizza he had picked up at the ByWard Market.

She grinned at him as she washed down the pizza with more champagne from a plastic glass.

"Thank you," she said to him after she drained the glass in two gulps. Finally, she was looking like the Adeena he had fallen in love with.

"You're welcome," he replied. "I'm really sorry, babe. I thought I could help you forget the aud—"

"Shhhhh," she interrupted standing up and coming closer to him. "It's over. Let's not talk about it." Adeena had cried as they had walked along the canal, up Mackenzie and back to the Gallery. Every time she began to beat herself up he stopped her, and told her how special she really was.

Philippe stood up and pulled her towards him, wrapping her in his arms. He could feel her breathe deeply, her full breasts swelling against him. His passion was growing as he pulled her close. Their faces met. He wanted her now, to consummate this evening right here in her office.

But he wanted it on her terms. "You were going to show me that cello?" he said, struggling against his own desire.

"You really want to see it? Now?" she asked doubtfully.

"Yes," he lied, trying to conceal the lust building inside him.

She gave him a light peck on the cheek. "Alright!"

ADEENA GINGERLY LIFTED THE FOAM PACKING FROM THE wooden crate. She had read that the Duncan Cello was still used by members of the Ancient Music Ensemble of Scotland, and was played at important recitals. The tone was said to be truly exceptional. She removed the last of the packing material and set it aside.

There it lay before her, a simple wooden instrument, created three centuries earlier. It seemed to call out to her.

Adeena looked over at Philippe, sitting on the couch.

Somehow he always managed to redeem himself. It had been

three years since she met him at a party Tara arranged to celebrate Adeena's newly minted Masters' Degree in Musicology. Philippe had walked her home in the rain, her head spinning from mixing beer, vodka and tequila. Just as they reached her place around 3 AM, completely drenched, she felt her stomach retch and she vomited uncontrollably on the street. Philippe didn't flinch. He helped her make it up to her apartment, cleaned her up and tucked her safely into her bed.

She looked back again at the cello.

"Well? Are you going to play for me?" Philippe asked.

It was breaking every protocol Tara had given her about handling museum artifacts, but this *was* a working musical instrument. Adeena just wanted to be sure it had survived its transatlantic journey in good shape.

"Yes I am," she finally responded as she carefully lifted the cello out of the wooden crate. "Do you like Bach?"

After getting a bow from her own case, Adeena sat on a chair beside Philippe and positioned the Duncan Cello between her legs. With no endpin, it took a little bit of an adjustment from the way she held her own cello. But it was completely comfortable. It even felt strangely familiar, like an old acquaintance. As her bow touched the strings and she began to play, a feeling of joy enveloped her.

Adeena closed her eyes. She could feel the music flowing through her. Bach's timeless creation filled her small office with a haunting echo. The cello responded to her as though she were making love with it, effortlessly creating layers of colours, tones and shades that she had struggled to find with her own instrument. She saw Magdalena's score in her head, the individual notes rushing past her like stars on a clear night, each one flowing through the cello, brought to life by her fingers and bow.

When she was done, Philippe stared at her transfixed. A passion she had rarely seen in him burned in the wells of his eyes.

"Are you an angel, Adeena?" he whispered. "Your music, you... is it from Heaven?"

Philippe took the cello from her, wrapped Adeena in his arms and raised her to him, bringing their faces together. He kissed her deeply and she hungrily accepted all that he offered.

CHAPTER 4

The eight miles from Usan to Kinnaird was a fairly easy drive if you knew where you're were going. Jackie Stuart had been in Scotland less than twenty-four hours, but she was happy to be back in her familiar role as navigator for her directionally challenged husband. William was a brilliant history professor at Carleton University, but he had trouble finding the house across the street, never mind something as obscure as the castle his mother had arranged for them to visit this weekend.

"Turn left here – Southesk Place," Jackie told William as he ran out of road and appeared about to drive straight into the frigid green waters of the North Sea.

William smiled. "You don't want to see if this thing will float?"

Jackie squeezed his leg. "Not with these heels on, darling," she joked, sizing up the oncoming roundabout. "Take the first turn, the A92, right here."

She looked over her shoulder to the backseat where Margaret Rose sat clutching her purse ready for battle. "William says we've got the Macduff apartment for the whole weekend, Mum?"

Jackie asked, hoping to understand what her mysterious mother-in-law was up to. "Apparently it's the best set of rooms at Kinnaird?"

"That's right Jacqueline," she confirmed, adding after a pause, "Gonnae be busy though. Workin'."

Jackie looked at William. He shrugged. Although Jackie was a psychologist at the Ottawa Hospital and accustomed to the delusions of older patients, this was indeed a special case. "Busy doing what, Mum?"

"Findin' somethin' that belongs to us. Somethin' lost a *lang* time ago," Margaret Rose said, drawing out *lang*. "And I'm gonnae need yer help, dealing wi' the soldiers, Jacqueline."

Jackie searched for the right response. "Something inside Kinnaird Castle?"

"Aye. 'Twas hidden a lang time ago by a Carnegie in our own family, the same who stole Kinnaird from his cousin's widow," Margaret Rose spoke with a level of determination that belied the fragility of her cancer-ridden eighty-five-year-old body. "Mah grandmother Faith told me stories, and now finally I know from mah dreams, where the bastard hid it."

Jackie and William sighed together. They drove in silence, William gripping the steering wheel tightly.

"Mum. Really?" he asked finally, glancing at the rear view mirror at his mother. Her wide eyes danced with a faraway look as she gazed out at the Angus county scenery.

"This is it, Will. Right here" Jackie motioned in the direction of an upcoming intersection.

William turned the little red car onto a tree-lined lane. They soon arrived at the main entry gate of the walled estates of Kinnaird. They stopped in front of the imposing structure.

Jackie noticed a stone guardhouse, nearly as big as her mother-in-law's cottage, on the other side of the closed gate. There was no one in sight.

"Ye'll need this tae get in," Margaret Rose said. She passed

Jackie a hand-written note with numbers scrawled in the middle. "To unlock th' gate."

"Did you get that from your dream too, Mum?" William chuckled, as Jackie rolled down her window looking for a place to punch in the code.

"Nae, William. They emailed it to me."

Jackie found a keypad and typed in the numbers. A series of beeps began to sound and the heavy gate slowly opened. William inched the car forward between the towering pillars that guarded the estate.

"Finally," Margaret Rose whispered from the back seat, "I can help her."

NO ONE SPOKE AS THEY DROVE TOWARD THE CASTLE, WHICH lay nearly a mile ahead, nestled in more than a thousand acres of pristine forest and sprawling parkland. Something about the majesty of the sunlight filtering through ancient oak trees reduced the Stuart party to an awed silence.

In the distance, a herd of Highland cattle grazed in open pasture while fallow deer roamed freely. Pheasants scurried past the side of the road, their plumage becoming brilliant rainbows in the soft afternoon light. As the tiny vehicle approached an opening in the trees, they caught their first glimpse of Kinnaird Castle, rising majestically over the Angus Valley as it had done since the beginning of the 15th century.

The castle's stone-constructed conical turrets, steep copper-covered roofs and armorial carvings seemed out of place in a world of electric cars and smartphones.

But as the view of the massive structure overwhelmed them, time itself seemed frozen forever.

JACKIE FOUND THE LUXURIOUS MACDUFF APARTMENT IN THE castle to her liking.

After unpacking her clothes, including the outfits she bought with Adeena on their last trip to Montreal, she explored the three-bedroom apartment. The ornate dining room could comfortably accommodate twelve guests. The cozy panelled living room, with its old stone hearth and split firewood at the ready, was the perfect spot to enjoy a glass of *chardonnay* in front of a roaring fire.

The view from the front windows of the formal gardens looked like something out of the pages of *National Geographic.* When she opened the lead-cased windows, the fresh scent of the countryside filled the room with pine and lavender. She used her phone to get a picture of the front gardens with their ornamental hedges and the sweeping front lane that led to one of the walking paths crisscrossing the estate.

She sent the picture to Adeena with a text message:

Our castle in the Scottish countryside.

Jackie and William also enjoyed a leisurely riverside stroll. They avoided the private area directly around the castle. This was reserved for the use of the castle's current inhabitants, the Earl and Countess of Southesk.

Now sitting in the finely appointed dressing room, adjoining the master bedroom with its dominating four-poster bed, Jackie admired her reflection in the smoky Victorian mirror. The faded surface softened her features with a dreamy sepia effect, hiding the imperfections of her fifty-three-year-old face.

This is a perfect mirror, she thought with a smile.

"Lady Stuart, your laird awaits," William announced from the bedroom in a rolling brogue.

"Almost ready, my liege," she responded playfully, putting the finishing touches on her mascara. The black satin blouse topped with sheer lace and thin straps that Adeena had picked out for her in Montreal was almost too daring. It reminded her of something she would wear during her 'wild days' as a single woman, when every man seemed to be a pawn in her own private chess match. That was before she settled down, got her Ph.D, got married, got old...

This was going to be fun, elevating her husband's blood pressure, just a *wee* bit.

William did not disappoint her.

His eyes could not get any wider, as he took in the complete picture of his alluring French-Canadian wife – from her vermilion red four-inch heels to her high-split skirt showing a bare leg, to the thin blouse highlighting her ample curves. She smiled wickedly as he admired the view and finally looked her directly in the eye.

"Let's just stay in tonight," he growled. "Forget the ball!"

"My laird!" she squealed, just as they heard a knock on their bedroom door. It opened slowly and her mother-in-law stood before them decked out in a plaid sweater, long skirt and blue beret.

"Are ye ready Will and. . ." Margaret Rose inquired and then stopped, looking at Jackie. "Oh! Yer gonnae catch the eyes of a few soldiers tonight, Jacqueline Stuart!"

AS THEY STOOD OUTSIDE UNDER THE IMPOSING ARCHWAY, waiting by the front doors of the castle to open and let them inside for dinner, Margaret Rose pinched herself to be sure she was awake. She touched the rough granite surface of one of the stone pillars. Only last week, the young woman in her dreams had stood in what looked like this exact spot, crying for help.

She called the woman in her dreams 'Ashlyn', though she didn't know if this was her real name. The woman had first appeared to Margaret Rose in a dream after the death of her husband Robert, who had died in a car accident when William was a toddler. In Margaret Rose's overwhelming grief, the dreams were meaningless flashes of faces and images. She thought the dreams came from the stories her grandmother Faith had endlessly told her while she was growing up near Perth.

But as the years progressed, and the pain of losing Robert receded, the dreams and the voices became clearer and more focused on this woman and her agony. Mixed with Margaret Rose's own despair as a young, destitute single mother, Ashlyn's suffering was often too much to handle and Margaret Rose would sink into long bouts of depression. When she finally sent William away to live with her brother in Canada, she felt almost incapable of going on with her life.

"Mum, you okay?" William interrupted her thoughts.

"Aye, William," she replied gently, returning to the present. She took hold of his arm firmly and whispered, "Stick wi' me when we go in. Ah'm going to need yer help, dear."

William was about to protest when the heavy wooden doors of the castle opened.

THE DINING ROOM OF KINNAIRD CASTLE WAS SOMETHING IN which any professor of history, particularly one specializing in the cultural origins of Europe, would find a delight of the highest magnitude. As William soaked in details of the room, he was glad his mother's usually nonsensical ramblings had gotten them a seat for this dinner. The towering portraits that stared down at them each seemed to hold a captivating story behind their stern faces. He was eager to learn more about the lives of each of these characters.

"Lairds and ladies. Welcome to Kinnaird Castle," a young man announced. He was dressed in a traditional black barathea jacket with a dark bow tie and kilt. He stood at the end of the long, formally laid table covered in white linen. Jackie, sitting beside William radiant in her finery, touched his leg and smiled at him. William imagined he might be a duke sitting in his castle, having captured the heart of a beautiful duchess.

"The Earl and Countess of Southesk welcome you to Kinnaird's August Dinner Tour organized by *Alba Aismhor,* Historic Scotland," the man said to the two dozen guests gathered. "As it happens, the Earl and Countess are abroad this month, so you'll have to suffer through the evening with me, Charles, your humble servant."

Gentle laughter filled the room as two waiters appeared with bottles of wine and began offering the red or white to each of the twenty-four guests dressed as though they were dining with royalty. Soon afterwards an elegant scotch broth was served, with a piece of tender lamb shank in each bowl. The first course was just enough to whet their appetites for the feast ahead.

Margaret Rose sitting across the table caught William's eye. She tilted her head to the left, as if she was trying to get him to look at something at the end of the room. He noticed an archway leading up to a wooden staircase.

"What is it, Mum?" he whispered.

"Ah need the loo."

As he weighed his options, Jackie intervened. "I'll take you," she offered.

"Both of you come, please," Margaret Rose said, rising stiffly. "I'm feeling a wee dizzy. I donnae know why."

She stood up and left the table, walking slowly toward the staircase, with Jackie hurrying to help and William not far behind.

Upstairs, Margaret Rose led them into Kinnaird's library. The tall shelves were filled with rare books, maps and original documents. The tapestries on the walls seemed familiar to her.

"Where are we going Mum?" William asked with growing alarm. "The toilet's not here."

Margaret Rose was searching one of the bookshelves in the middle of the room and was about to respond to William, when a man, dressed in a tight-fitting doublet, tartan waistcoat and kilt joined them.

"Is everything quite alright?" he asked.

"Mum's not feeling well," William replied as Margaret Rose moved closer to a section of the bookshelf with a small neatly handwritten card over one section that read: *Peerage, Earls of Southesk*. She reached for a volume, the thickest in the section: *Sixth Earl of Southesk* and handed it to William.

"Should I call for the nurse?" the man asked, and then added in a concerned voice: "Sir, please be careful with those volumes. They are extremely fragile. Would you mind putting it back?"

Margaret Rose looked over at her daughter-in-law, dressed like some kind of bewitching French harlot. She tried to catch her eye.

Time to play your part Jacqueline, Margaret Rose thought to herself, nodding at the middle-aged man in the kilt, hoping Jackie would get her subtle message. Jackie looked at her. Their eyes locked as she nodded and smiled.

Smart girl!

"I think she just needs some air," Jackie said, turning to the man and placing a hand on his shoulder. "Sorry, I didn't catch your name?"

"Angus, ma'am. Angus McDonald."

"Well, Angus, would you mind escorting a lady to dinner?" Jackie purred

He hesitated a few seconds until William slid the volume back into its place on the shelf.

Jackie touched Angus's shoulder and interlocked her arm through his, turning him towards the stairs leading back to the dining room. "So, will you?" she asked.

"Indeed ma'am! I'd be honoured," Angus replied as they walked away.

WILLIAM WAITED UNTIL THEY HAD DISAPPEARED DOWN THE wide staircase. He reached again for the heavy leather-bound volume.

"Open it. Quick!" Margaret Rose whispered to her son. He was after all, a history professor and a Stuart. He ought to be of some help.

"It's the diary of Sir James Carnegie, Sixth Earl of Southesk," he read to her.

"Aye. Look up 1745, August Ah think," she whispered.

William turned the pages carefully. "3 June 1745... wait, 12 July... Okay here, 'Kinnaird, 6 August 1745'. Is that the 'mystical' date you dreamed about?"

There was no time to fight with him. "Read it tae me!"

William adjusted his glasses and read to her in a quiet voice:

> "Kinnaird will soon be mine. Arrangements now in progress are going well. Tonight I returned from my glorious dayes in Flanders with the officers in my regiment and we were welcomed by my brother George, who arranged a feast of mutton and ale.
>
> Sister Katharine travelled from Aberdeen to play for me on a new cello from maestro Duncan of Upperkirkgate that George was able to secure through his merchant associates.
>
> But that she, a woman and mine own sister too, would play an instrument clearly in the domain of men, was scandalous.
>
> The song Katharine played seemed to intoxicate my men. It was the most seditious song I ever heard and played on such a lewd instrument too! Katharine said it was a composition that she composed. She sang as though possessed by spirits that

talked directly of the Jacobite traitors and their young Pretender king.

I scolded her forthwith afterward - for my men were transfixed of a spirit that frightened me. I confiscated her score and hid it in my keep. I warned her never to perform it again, lest it embolden the traitors amongst us who would destroy the Union. I also forbade her from ever playing that instrument again and to find something more suitable for a lady, such as a cittern."

MARGARET ROSE STOOD TRANSFIXED, STARING AT WILLIAM. He was holding a time capsule that had just opened a world that she had never completely understood - until now.

It wasn't 'Ashlyn' but 'Katharine'. And just like in the dream, Katharine's brother was her tormentor.

"We need tae find the keep, William," she said as she took the leather volume from him, glancing over the pages that made everything so much clearer. "And Ah think Ah know where to look."

IT HAD BEEN QUITE A WHILE SINCE JACKIE HAD BEEN THIS coquettish with another man. Over thirty years, she thought to herself, adjusting the thin strap holding the lacy edge of her tight sleeveless blouse.

Men were such simple creatures, driven by the primitive urges of their brain chemistry, Jackie mused as she smiled at Angus. She had persuaded him to sit in the seat across from her at the dining room table.

"My husband just texted me," she said looking down. "He's taking his mother back to her room."

"Oh. I do hope she's alright, Mrs. Stuart," Angus replied with concern.

"It's Jacqueline," she said, pursing her lips slightly and looking up at him innocently through her lashes. Just like riding a bike, she thought as she turned her charm offensive up a few notches. "Angus, tell me more about yourself..."

In her dreams, Margaret Rose suffered alongside 'Ashlyn', who she now knew was Katharine Carnegie. Katharine searched everywhere for the musical score deliberately hidden by her paranoid brother, Sir James Carnegie, 'the Captain'. The fuzzy outlines of years of misty dreams were snapping into focus, sharpened considerably by a few paragraphs of hand-written text.

Margaret Rose searched for the stairwell that she thought must be somewhere near the library. She felt certain this would lead to the alcove she had seen so vividly in her dreams.

"Mum, we'll never find the keep. It could be anywhere," William protested.

Then she noticed long shadows in the corner, near the end of the wall of shelves.

"Follow me," she said marching towards the dark shadow.

William followed behind slowly. The shadow in the corner was actually the opening of a tiny arched staircase that led down four steps to a small alcove. Above the alcove door was a round stone plate inscribed with a crest – a pair of wings overlaid with four jagged arrows and two crowns, one above and one below what looked like a barbershop pole.

Above the crest in large letters were the words:

DRED • GOD

Margaret Rose gasped when she saw it. "This is it! Ah keep seein' that in mah dreams!"

William studied it. "It's the Carnegie clan crest and their motto. I've been reading about the history of this place. This castle is ground zero in Carnegie history."

Margaret Rose peered inside the dark alcove. "See if ye can find a light, Will."

William felt around and found a switch just inside the alcove entrance. He flicked it on and two incandescent lights in metal caged enclosures lit up, throwing a soft glow throughout the tiny space.

Margaret Rose entered first, and studied the shelves that were literally carved into the thick granite walls. On one side, the shelves were at least three feet deep, holding wooden, plastic and cardboard containers of all shapes and sizes, each neatly labelled.

"We need tae find Katharine's music," Margaret Rose urged her son.

William scanned the boxes in sheer amazement. His mother realized this must be like finding the Holy Grail for him. A student of history, standing in front of a treasure of original documents, manuscripts and journals that had been rarely seen and most likely forgotten by just about everyone else, this was a rare treat indeed.

He looked at the labels carefully and read them quietly to her. "Look at this, *1647, Journale et papiers: Marquis de Montrose,"* he whispered in excitement.

"Nae son, yer a hundred years early!"

He walked slowly calling out the years to her. "Okay, *1692 - Charter of Sale, Master of Carnegie, 1702,* oh and look at this, *1713, James Carnegie, Fifth Earl of Southesk and Lady Margaret Stewart, Marriage Contract,"* he read to her, his voice reverberating in the small stone alcove.

"Keep goin' son," she urged him.

JACKIE WAS HAVING FUN AND ANGUS WAS AN INTERESTING study.

His receding hairline was tinged with the grey onset of middle age. After many years of menial jobs and a protracted divorce, he had gone back to school and graduated from the University of St Andrews in Fife with a degree in mediaeval studies. He was uncertain of his job prospects, but for now he was enjoying a summer placement with Historic Scotland, the government agency.

As a psychologist, Jackie had an unfair advantage. She regularly used techniques to draw out the inner feelings and emotions of her patients. And as a well-preserved woman in her early fifties, already dressed for seduction, this was almost too easy. In just ten minutes, Jackie had gotten Angus to open up about his life's passion and what he would consider to be the *perfect* companion.

"Jacqueline, I've never talked to a woman like you before," he stammered, leaning in, unable to take his eyes off her. "I hope you don't think me a complete dolt."

"Maybe no one's figured out what makes your engine roar," she teased, taking a sip of her wine and licking her lips.

"Nae, you're right about that," he responded. "Mah motor's barely ever been started!"

WILLIAM COULD BARELY CONTAIN HIMSELF.

The items in this little ancient library were an intoxicating elixir of artifacts that connected him directly to the people and events of Kinnaird over the last five hundred years. As he read the list of documents, journals, letters, wills, deeds and maps, each in their own boxed container, he fought against his desire to study them all. He bent down to examine the label of a flat box labeled *10 May 1525 - James Strathauchan of Monboddo* when his mother shrieked loudly.

"Will, over haur! Look!" She pointed to a clear plastic container. It was labeled *1765 - Sir James Carnegie, 3rd Baronet.*

William rose stiffly and peered up at the container. It looked heavy, and was loaded with papers and books.

"Hurry," his mother urged him.

He knew he shouldn't be doing this. These were fragile, important documents that should be carefully handled and preserved. They were rare 'primary sources' to an historian, akin to a perfectly preserved fossils for a palaeontologist.

"Mum, this is wrong. We should be getting permission to do this, maybe talk to the owners and do this in a proper way. I don't know if I can be part of this."

He expected a blast back from his mother. But rather than fight, she dropped her head. He could hear her breathing, shallow and strained. Suddenly she seemed small, fragile.

He rested his hand on her shoulder. She placed her hand on his and looked at him. A long moment of silence followed, before she spoke. "Can't you help me?"

He hesitated thinking about all she'd been through in the course of her life. Was she going to die with her heart broken by her only son?

"Okay, Mum," he said, studying the box that might bring his mother some resolution.

William hoisted it from the highest shelf in the alcove and sat it down on the tiled floor. He opened the lid carefully and set it aside. The documents were divided in two sections. He began looking through them carefully, starting to wonder if this was going to end badly.

She seemed to sense his doubt. "Ah know it's there, Will. Ah seen it in mah heid."

He kept searching, getting near the bottom of the first stack. And then he saw it – a thin cloth-stitched notebook with faded lettering and an amateur looking rendering of what looked like a stringed instrument. In the corner of the cover page was scrawled lettering:

Seventeen Hundred and Forty-Five

William picked it up gingerly and opened the notebook to the first page. It was a handwritten musical score, some of the ink smudged slightly, as if it had been written quickly. He turned a couple of pages and then handed it to his mother, amazed that she had been right all along.

"I think we've found it."

CHAPTER 5

There was a knock on the glass door of her office. It opened before Adeena could get up.

"Dee, drinks after work..." Tara had a way of commanding, even when asking a question.

Adeena was not as much of a 'Thank God It's Friday' girl as her colleagues were. Although she loved weekends, she didn't normally see the last day of the working week as a cause for special celebration. But this week was shaping up to be one where she could use some alcohol therapy.

It had been four days since her audition for the NAC Orchestra. If not for the Duncan Cello and Philippe's love-making heroics in her office, this would go down as a week to blot from existence.

"Yup, I'm down for it," Adeena said. "Should I ask Philippe?"

"Sure. Mercury Lounge on the market, after..." The phone on Adeena's desk rang, interrupting Tara. "After work," Tara said completing her thought. She spun around to leave. "Tell Philippe."

"Okay, see you later," Adeena said, picking up the phone. "Research Services."

"Adeena?" It was Walter.

"Hi Walter, how are you?" she asked, worried what news he might be bringing.

"I'm okay," he responded. "How are *you* doing?"

"I'm fine. So what's the deal, Walter?"

There was a long pause. "Well... you didn't quite..." he hesitated. "You didn't quite make it."

Adeena froze.

"It wasn't your playing. That was perfection. Friedrich admitted your technique was good, even excellent. But he's not looking for just *any* cellist. He wants someone to groom – a soloist, to show off his compositions."

"Compositions?" Although she could barely talk, this surprised her.

"Yeah – supposedly. But his work hasn't been well-received, to put it mildly. He told me on our tour of the UK last year that he spends all of his spare time working on something he thinks is going to be huge."

"Really? I wouldn't have guessed," Adeena replied, thinking she might have misjudged the stern-faced conductor.

"Yup. But to tell you the truth, anything he's brought to the orchestra has been... well, embarrassing."

"Did he say anything else, Walter?" She hesitated, "anything else, about me?"

Silence. She could almost see Walter organizing his thoughts for another one of his *Pumpkin* pep talks.

"He did like your outfit," he finally responded. "And . . ."

"And what? What did he say?"

"He just, well, he thinks you're a little too cute. He said that you're more about 'perfect hair and a perfect smile' and playing Bach in E Flat to impress him," Walter finally blurted out, as if he needed to purge the poison inside. "But, Adeena, he doesn't know you the way I do. I tried to tell him he was wrong, dead wrong. He's very stubborn. He's decided on two candidates from Europe for the short list."

As she listened, Adeena felt her senses numb. Her dream was

being crushed and buried. Lost forever. All her hopes for becoming a professional musician were being exorcised from her soul. As she glanced at her tear-stained reflection from the mirror on her desk, she vowed that it was finally, completely, once and for all, over.

The dream was dead.

AS TARA WALKED BESIDE HER LEAVING THE GALLERY, TALKING incessantly about plans for the weekend, Adeena thought she finally understood the whole TGIF thing. But shouldn't it be TGIF-F?

Thank God It's Fucking Friday.

Tara finally paused long enough to notice Adeena was not listening. "Didn't you hear me Dee?"

"What?"

"This weekend? Montreal? You? Me? Shop till we drop?" Tara was staring intently at her as they waited for the light on Sussex Drive to change so they could cross the street to the ByWard Market.

"Not sure about that, Tar."

"Be–cause?" Tara asked, stretching the word over three paces as they crossed Sussex Drive.

"I'm planning on canoeing over Niagara Falls."

"You're so melodramatic my dear," Tara replied. "I'm surprised you chose music and not acting."

Adeena stopped when she reached the sidewalk. "I'm not a musician anymore. I'm not really anything. Just your galley slave working the nine-to-five, doing my job while the whole fucking world passes me by."

"Would you chill, please?" Tara was getting impatient. "What are you talking about?"

"It's over, Tar. I'm giving up on music, putting away my cello.

Maybe Philippe will marry me and I'll produce a family of fat sheep to graze away their lives, waiting for a fun afternoon at the abattoir."

Tara winced. "He's a good man, Dee. Why can't you see that?"

"It's not him, Tar. It's *me*. I'm the one who's completely fucked up. I don't deserve to be with him, let alone be his wife. I don't think he would want to marry someone who spends all their time trying to get perfect fucking hair anyway!"

Tara took her hand and started marching down George Street towards the market. "Adeena Stuart, you're coming with me and I'm getting you piss drunk!"

THE MERCURY WAS A CLUB PHILIPPE ALWAYS ENJOYED WHEN he had the chance, particularly after a day of wrestling with politicians and their minions on Parliament Hill.

As a relentless investigative reporter, he had developed a homing instinct that could smell shit from ten thousand feet. His sources on the Hill respected him, and while they did their damnedest to protect their political masters, he always found a way to extract truth from the thin gruel of PR pabulum they tried feeding him.

Adeena's text to meet her and Tara at the Mercury was perfect timing.

He had just filed a story on a government minister who had been handing out favours to his buddies in Toronto. Over three million dollars in contracts for "web-development, social media strategies and communication infrastructure options." With no deliverable other than a five page PDF report with some pie charts, the Minister knew he was in for some tough sledding.

Philippe smiled as he walked through the doors of the club, looking for the ladies. Levelling a crooked politician with the truth was an art form all its own. And Philippe had mastered it well.

Now, if only Adeena was as easy to understand.

He had put the diamond ring away for now, waiting for the right time to pop the question.

Maybe this weekend?

TARA SPOTTED PHILIPPE WALKING TOWARDS THEM UP ON THE second level. The House DJ was getting warmed up with ska and reggae, easing the happy patrons slowly towards the house rhythms that would rock all three levels of the club as the evening progressed.

"Philippe!" Tara sang out above the music as she saw him looking around. He raised his arm and smiled.

Adeena watched him walk towards them and noticed the grin on Tara's face. Why are people so damned happy all the time, she wondered.

"Bonsoir!" Philippe greeted them as he reached the table. "I love this place!" He gave Tara a hug and pulled a stool beside Adeena, placing a light kiss on her lips before sitting down.

"You got to help me with this one," Tara said, leaning in towards Philippe and pointing to Adeena, who scowled at them like Winston Churchill without a cigar. "She needs to get happy!"

"I absolutely agree," Philippe nodded as the waiter arrived with a tray of colourful martinis.

Tara raised her glass and Philippe stood up holding his drink. Adeena reluctantly picked up her own.

"To the most beautiful women in Ottawa," Philippe toasted the women, clinking each of their glasses, "who dance better when drunk!"

Adeena raised the glass to her lips and let the sweet mango martini begin working its magic. The vodka raced to her brain with a pleasure bomb of welcome relief. In one long gulp she finished the drink and sat back. A smile fought with the frown etched across her face.

The music was just the right mix of walking bass line and smooth guitar. Philippe seemed so relaxed and Tara was just being herself – glowing like a heavenly body on a starry night. Oh, to be just like those two – ready for the cover of *People*.

Adeena's phone interrupted her thoughts, vibrating on the table. She looked at the name on the display:

Dad

She grabbed it, got up and walked away from the table.

Adeena had a hard time hearing anything her father was saying. She shouted into the phone as she walked towards the exit, trying to get away from the background noise. She finally left the club and moved out onto the street.

"Give me that again. What did you just say?"

"We found something here that your grandmother wants to you have," her father explained again. "It's a piece of music that's been lost. Lost for quite a while."

There was a pause as Adeena processed this, looking over at the fruit and vegetable vendors packing up for the evening.

"It's a score that your grandmother and I found at Kinnaird Castle here in Scotland. It was written more than two hundred years ago, and hidden in a wall in the castle. Until this week."

She listened to the words, still not understanding.

"But Adeena, your grandmother is delirious about it. She insisted I send you the music, by courier."

Adeena had a flashback of being in her backyard playhouse as a kid drinking tea with her grandmother. She remembered listening in rapt attention to the details of poor Ashlyn from Grandma's dreams. Adeena shivered listening to the stories, like someone was walking on her grave.

"Really? Why?" she finally responded.

"I have no idea. I don't get it. But she's not doing well, and getting worse by the second. She's so stubborn! I had to agree to send this to you before she would even let me call the doctor."

"Is she going to be okay?"

There was a long silence. "I don't know, but there's something else, Adeena. I called Walter and told him about the music that I found and said I was sending it to you. He got pretty excited and he had an idea."

"Really? What?"

"He's going to call Friedrich Lang, you know, the conductor? Walter thinks he can persuade him to let you audition the music for him next week. Maybe give you another chance!"

A SECOND ROUND OF MARTINIS SAT ON THE TINY BAR TABLE. Classic style – Tanqueray gin with a splash of dry vermouth, and a ripe olive on a toothpick. Shaken, not stirred please.

Tara sipped her drink slowly, feeling her normal sensibilities of order and control being subsumed. She leaned in toward Philippe. "So, you didn't give her the ring?"

"No. I couldn't," he responded, shaking his head.

"Why? I don't get it."

Philippe sighed and took a sip of his martini. He set it down on the table and moved his head toward her a little, encouraging Tara to do the same. "Because," he finally replied, "I realized I was only thinking about myself. You know the kind of day she had, with that bastard Lang? And she was so absorbed with that old cello."

"The Duncan Cello? Oh shit! I asked her to start researching it right after yoga," Tara said, resting her face on one hand. "I should have just told her to go home and relax. She spent four months rehearsing for that audition. She must have been bagged. What was I thinking?"

"Actually, you did her a favour. You should have heard her play that cello. It was magical."

Tara's eyes widened. "She played it? She played the Duncan Cello?" Tara bristled, sitting straight up and crossing her arms. "Oh my God! I absolutely need to kill her!"

"Why? She said it should be played every day. Isn't it a working instrument?"

"Philippe, do you know how much insurance we had to arrange to bring that cello to the gallery for just three months?" Tara asked, trying to focus against the martini's dulling effects on her normally razor-sharp mind.

He shrugged his shoulders.

"Five million dollars!"

"It's worth that much?"

"Damn right! I had to submit a security plan, find a carrier that would give us a policy, even send a letter from the Deputy Minister to Scotland. This is no regular old cello you can just pick up on Rideau Street!" Tara fumed, shaking her head in disbelief.

"Tabernac!" Philippe exclaimed, taking a sip of his drink.

As if the DJ knew that his patrons needed to forget the working week, the music began morphing. He started a mix with a heavy backbeat, sampling a range of past and present vocal gems, from the Fine Young Cannibals to Junior J. The change came with a sharp increase in volume. The pounding bass, mixed with familiar notes from the old pop song 'She Drives Me Crazy,' began coaxing folks out of their seats and onto the dance floor.

Tara was silenced for the moment. Further talking was useless, unless she wanted to shout like a complete maniac. She sat drinking her martini, her mind racing, wondering how she would deal with Miss Adeena.

Philippe sat looking at her. She wondered what he was thinking and why this fine male specimen was still a bachelor. If only, she mused, he wasn't in love with my best friend.

If only *she* had the slightest idea of how to find a man like this, a guy who didn't come straight from the factory where they made an endless supply of jerks so stupid they challenged the theory of evolution. Maybe we've reached our peak as a species, and we're devolving back into apes she thought, draining the last of the martini. She popped the olive into her mouth.

"Dance?" Philippe shouted standing up, reaching for her hand.

Tara smiled. "God, yes!"

MUSIC IN THE MERCURY POUNDED THROUGHOUT THE THREE-level club. It lifted anyone entering the lounge, washed with colour in waves of fluorescent light. Tonight the music was so loud, it blew right out the front door, assaulting anyone walking by.

Adeena stood under the deserted stall of a fruit and vegetable vendor directly in front of the club, still absorbing the news from her father.

Her grandmother was sending her a lost musical score hidden in a castle in Scotland. It hadn't been seen by anyone for three centuries. And maybe, just maybe, she would get to play it next week in a private audition for the music director of the National Arts Centre Orchestra.

As the music from the club washed over her, Adeena felt herself come alive again. Black thoughts vanished. Maybe there was hope after all. She could almost hear her grandmother urging her to perform again, her face creased in solemnity.

She smiled and let out a wild whoop. Then closing her eyes added softly, "Thank-you."

Adeena had to share the news. The loud pounding music was exactly what she needed, and it sucked her back into the club. When she got up to the second level and the empty table, she was puzzled at first.

Then she saw them on the dance floor as a robotic remix of a

Flaming Lips song began. Tara was jumping to the music and Philippe was close to her, perfectly in sync. They seemed completely lost in the moment.

Adeena wanted to join them.

She took a drink of her martini, watching Tara laugh at Philippe, who was displaying moves that Adeena had never seen before. He was after all a slightly crazy downhill skier who liked to push himself to the extreme. Now, he was doing his best to defy the laws of gravity.

Adeena snaked her way through the pulsating dance floor. She started to move to the beat as she got closer to Tara and Philippe, who finally noticed her and waved her over.

Adeena raised her arms again as she reached them shaking her head to the music as the bright lights danced over her coppery ringlets. Philippe put his arm around her waist and pulled Tara closer. They were all laughing as they started to dance arm-in-arm.

"What happened?" Philippe shouted over the music.

"I've got another chance!"

THE SETTING SUN THREW LONG SHADOWS ACROSS THE PORCH of Margaret Rose's cottage by the sea. William stared out the window, knowing it would be black soon with so few outdoor lights. An old pickup truck rambled slowly down the sheep path that served as the only link to the outside world.

William looked over at his wife Jackie and the nurse Fay sitting at the small kitchen table. Jackie was about to pour tea for both of them.

"I think Murdo's back," he said quietly, walking toward the front door. The women looked up and smiled.

"Aye. He's a good lad, that one," Fay said, stirring a little milk into her tea. Jackie nodded in agreement. William opened the front door and Murdo stood before him holding two very full grocery bags.

"Thought maybe ye could use somethin' fresh," he said, handing one of the bags to William. The women looked over, their smiles brightening the room.

"Come in," Jackie said, standing up.

"Thanks. Ah was in Montrose at the supermarket and wasn't sure whit ye had," Murdo said, placing the other bag of groceries on the kitchen counter.

William looked inside the bag Murdo had handed to him. He could see eggs, bacon, cheese and a carton of milk.

"Ye like raspberries?" Murdo asked. "Just picked them myself from the garden. Ah put some of those in for ye as well."

Jackie pulled out a basket overflowing with plump raspberries. "Murdo! Thank you so much. Would you like to sit down? We just made tea."

"No ma'am. Chores been waitin' patiently for me all day," he replied, grinning. He looked at William and his smile faded. "How's she doin'?"

William's face felt heavy as he struggled to respond. After almost three days of watching his mother fade away, he knew the end was close. The cancer was winning.

"Not good," he said. "But she doesn't give up easy. A fighter 'til the very end." William's eyes were moist. He was too tired to feel much anymore, but talking like this reminded him that his mother was nearly gone.

Murdo put a hand on his shoulder. "Maggie's a good woman. Ye be proud of your mother and let me know if there is anything Ah can do," he said.

"Thanks. She told me how you took care of her when she was sick last time, and how you took her to the clinic in Dundee. Thank you, Murdo. We appreciate it. Very much." William was having a hard time now keeping his eyes from filling with tears.

There was complete silence in the little cottage as the evening light faded. A feeble voice finally broke the stillness.

"William? Ye still here?"

MARGARET ROSE LAY IN HER BED, FEELING THE DARKNESS closing in. She knew her body was weak and her time was near. She felt a strange calm, but there was one last thing to do.

"William?" she said, looking up and seeing her son. She felt his hands holding both of hers.

"I'm here Mum," he whispered. "I love you."

Margaret Rose felt his devotion flowing through her. She had not been a very good mother, but she had never stopped loving him. Sending William to Canada broke her heart, but it gave him the chance to have a real life. And now he would be able to fix everything.

"Faith was right," she said slowly, taking a deep breath.

"Your grandmother?"

"Aye. Ah didn't understand before... but now Ah do." She squinted through her eyelids, and let out another long, laboured breath. "Ye sent it to Adeena... the music?"

"Yes, Mum. It was delivered today."

"Thanks," Margaret Rose said slowly, closing her eyes again. Then she pointed to the night table beside her bed, her eyes still closed. "Look."

William glanced at the night table, covered with old black and white photographs. "The pictures?"

"No," she whispered. "The drawer."

William opened the night table drawer and gasped. "Mum! You took this?"

William picked up the leather-bound volume. It was the diary of Sir James Carnegie. Margaret Rose had taken it from Kinnaird castle.

"Help her," she gasped, barely able to speak.

Her eyes were closed tightly. William put the diary down and put his arms around his mother. She could feel him close to her. She had so little energy left, barely any breath inside of her.

“Adeena... needs...” Her breathing was laboured, struggling as she fought to continue, “needs to...”

Her head fell to her chest.

Margaret Rose was gone.

CHAPTER 6

Adeena and her grandmother skipped through a field of golden grass.

They gathered flowers, laughing like schoolgirls under a turquoise sky. They collected long stems of lavender, handfuls of tangerine buttercups and a clutch of translucent wildflowers before finally flopping to the ground to begin arranging them.

They hummed a song both instinctively knew, smiling at each other as they worked. Their heads swayed in time to the music as they admired their floral creation.

It was a simple arrangement her grandmother placed in a delicate crystal vase that appeared out of nowhere. Then she stopped humming and with a blinding sun behind, stood before Adeena. The light formed a halo of dancing sunbeams around her grandmother's head.

The heat of the morning sun touched Adeena's face, and she woke with a start. With a half open eye she peered at the clock radio:

7:44 AM

Adeena could still see her grandmother's face and the translucent flower arrangement. She laid her head back down on the pillow and closed her eyes with a sigh.

She wanted desperately to return to her dream.

An hour later her father called. "Adeena? You awake?"

She held the phone to her ear, her eyes closed, and her mind only half-conscious. "Dad? What? What is it?"

"Grandma," he said in a quiet voice. "She's gone."

There was a moment of silence between them before Adeena gasped. "Oh God."

"She loved you, very much."

Adeena could barely talk. "I loved her too."

Her dad listened for a few moments, feeling her pain all the way across the Atlantic. "Adeena?"

There was no response. She had dropped the phone and was sobbing like a little girl.

Adeena cried for a long time, draining all the hurt until her eyes were red and burning. When the deluge finally ended, she lay gasping on the bed. Fighting for breath, she felt like she had run a marathon.

When she felt calm enough to sit up, she got up and shuffled over to the kitchen. She sat at her little glass table staring out over the ByWard Market and the city. She slowed her breathing with deep, deliberate breaths. A sense of calm was fighting to replace the grief.

She wanted to be strong to honour her grandmother.

Adeena gazed out the window and began humming to herself. It was the melody from her dream.

And then she stopped.

There was something familiar about it. She had heard it before. With a jolt, she realized it was the opening to the unfinished composition she had been struggling to complete for so long.

It had first come to her as a teenager, waking up one morning with the notes etched into her head. She had started transcribing, working out the notes and chords on her dad's piano. She got the first eight bars down and then drew a blank.

She was going out with Kurt at the time, and they were working on a couple of songs. But this one was different, less pop, more symphonic, for piano and cello rather than guitar and drums. She had planned to share it with Kurt when she finished it, but they broke up and whenever she returned to the composition, she felt unable to complete it.

Adeena's thoughts returned to her grandmother. Was she still with her? Adeena had never lost someone so close before. But somehow she still felt connected.

Yesterday had also been difficult. Tara had convinced her to go shopping in Montreal, and most of the two-hour drive was tense.

"Your job at the gallery is to be a researcher," Tara began as they took the 417 out of the city, heading east. The top was down on the Audi and Tara had to strain to make herself heard above the wind and road noise.

"Yeah, I know that," Adeena shouted, a little puzzled as she sipped her latté.

"So darling, you don't go around busking with a five-million dollar cello!"

Adeena nearly choked. "It's worth that much?"

"According to our insurance agent it is!" Tara responded, moving into the passing lane and leaving the slower moving cars behind. Although she was a stickler for details, she had no patience for anyone driving at the ridiculous 100 kilometer per hour speed limit.

"But it's a working instrument, Tar," Adeena pleaded, raising her voice. "It is a cello that needs to be played on a regular basis. And I am a cellist! Doesn't it make sense for me to be the one who plays it?"

Tara's Audi zoomed past the city limits of Ottawa through open pastures. There was a long pause. A gale force wind blowing through the women's hair was the only sound to be heard.

Finally Tara shouted above the roar. "No. It does not!"

ADEENA THOUGHT BACK ON THE DAY, AND THE LONG FIGHT that followed Tara's pronouncement. It was quite a show of force. They were both still a little hung over from the night before, racing down the freeway with the top down, engaged in an all-out scream-fest.

Tara hated anything that wasn't by the book, especially the book of protocols she lived and breathed as the assistant curator of the National Gallery of Canada. Adeena on the other hand, had no use for rules generally, and particularly not in this case.

"Why can't you just trust me?" Adeena yelled. "No one can take care of that cello better than me!"

"You can't even take care of yourself," Tara responded. "You never have! You can't *not* be in trouble and I'm not going through Grade 8 again."

An image of bright red oil paint spilling all over Tara's white-satin dress flashed through Adeena's mind. The dress was a treasured family heirloom from Greece that Tara wore for a class presentation. "That wasn't my fault," Adeena responded. "I got pushed by the boys who were teasing you. Blame them for wrecking your stupid dress."

"You were spitting at them, calling them pussies," Tara shot back. "That was my mother's wedding dress!"

Adeena recalled the day. "Sorry. It was an accident."

"You're an accident! An accident magnet, and you never

change," Tara continued. The dress incident was a sore spot that always got her fired up. "And now you're going to blow it again, with Philippe."

"What's he got to do with this?"

"You don't even know he's alive," Tara said. "The poor guy should be sainted."

"Thanks! Guess I'm just a total bitch. What could he possibly see in me?" Adeena screamed over the howling breeze.

"Sometimes I wonder," Tara yelled back. "At the rate you're going, he'll never marry you."

"Holy shit! You take a fucking hate pill this morning?" Adeena shot back. "At least I *have* a boyfriend."

From here the conversation degenerated even more. They accused each other of assorted crimes, sins, vices, and indiscretions, swearing that the other lacked good taste, moral judgment, honour and intelligence of any kind. It was cathartic for both of them, purging all the little annoyances they kept inside. The relationship-cleansing therapy continued to build as they sped down the highway.

By the time they crossed the Quebec border and were approaching the bridge toward the island of Montreal, all the poison had been drained. Their voices were hoarse from shouting as they finally began to negotiate a peace treaty, from sheer exhaustion. Or maybe it was from a sense that neither of them was perfect.

Their friendship had survived worse.

In the end, Adeena agreed to get Tara's signature when she checked the Duncan Cello out of security to do her research. However, Adeena could not play it until she got a security clearance, and then only under strict guidelines, including the need for a gallery technician to be present every time it was removed from its case.

Adeena thought it was all pretty dumb, but she agreed to the 'rules' as long as she got to play the Duncan Cello.

"But once the exhibit opens in October, you'll have to leave it be," Tara concluded. "Now, let's talk about shopping? Where do you want to start?"

IT WAS ALMOST MIDNIGHT WHEN ADEENA GOT HOME AND flopped down onto her bed up on the fourteenth floor of her condo. She passed out and slept deeply until the dream about her grandmother and the bright sunlight woke her up and she had received the horrible news from her father in Scotland.

Now, hours later, she lifted herself stiffly from her small table to make coffee. Her phone rang and she reached over to where it lay charging on the counter.

"Good morning Ms. Stuart," a cheerful voice on the other end announced. "This is the front desk calling. We have a special delivery that arrived yesterday. Can you come down and sign for it?"

MARGARET ROSE HAD INSISTED THAT THE PACKAGE BE SENT across the Atlantic by courier – RUSH DELIVERY.

As Adeena opened the flat FedEx carton, she wondered why her grandmother wanted her to have this music. Why was it so important that it needed to be sent across the ocean in such a rush? And what does this have to do with me?

As she slid the document out of its cardboard sleeve she noticed a handwritten note from her father clipped to the top:

Pumpkin:
Your grandmother insisted I send this to you!
She said you would understand.
Love, Dad

Adeena carefully removed the score from the clear plastic

bag and set it down on her table. There was no title on the document. Only the outline of a poorly sketched cello on the cover gave any hint of the personality behind the composer.

She delicately opened the faded sheaf of papers and laid the first two pages flat on the table. The paper had long ago faded to a sepia colour. The ink used was a rich shade of burnt chocolate and the lettering a fine example of 18th century calligraphy. The words were drawn with a flourish of upper case characters, with elegantly curled ascenders anchored by descenders with exaggerated bowls.

Adeena traced the inscription at the top of the first page with her finger:

Cantata No 1 a Voci Soprano, Alto Tenore Basso,
Acompagnate di violini, Violincello e Piano Forte

To the left of the ledger lines were neatly written inscriptions: *Violini, Violincello, Basso, Piano-Forte, Soprano, Alto.* Adeena read the music, humming to try and get a feel for it. As she continued to hum out loud, working out the melody in her head, she suddenly stopped with a gasp.

Was this the song that she and her grandmother hummed in her dream last night? The same notes that Adeena had written as a teenager in a fit of inspiration after waking one morning from a restless sleep?

Adeena looked again at the score, focusing on each section, and sounding the notes out loud to herself. She froze, covering her mouth with her hand in shock.

It was the same music.

LATER THAT AFTERNOON SHE GOT A CALL FROM PHILIPPE. SHE told him about the passing of her grandmother.

"I'm sorry," he said quietly. "I know how close you two were."

"Yeah, we were," she replied, fighting to keep her eyes dry. "We really understood each other. And I know this might sound weird, but I think she was thinking about me," she paused, "right until the end."

Philippe listened to her breaking voice and quiet sobs. After a moment he asked gently, "Are you okay?"

She wiped her eyes. "Yeah, yeah. I'm fine." She blew out a deep breath, trying to be strong. "You're in Toronto?"

"Yup. Just landed to do some more interviews. I can't believe what I've unleashed," he said. "My story in the *Citizen* created a buzz. Everyone's running it – CBC, CTV and all the papers – *Globe & Mail, National Post*, even the *New York Times*. They're all poking fun at the government paying three million dollars for a five page PDF. Three hundred thousand dollars a page!"

Adeena could hear his excitement. "You're a bloodhound for the truth, no matter who you piss off."

"Yup. The PMO is lining up their heavy hitters as we speak. They've already got hacks on all the talk shows trying to protect their asses."

"The Prime Minister's Office?" Adeena whistled.

"Oui, mademoiselle," Philippe replied with glee. "But the real fun is just getting started. I'm going to be working from Toronto for a few days chasing the story a bit more. I want to see how deep the shit is really piled."

He paused for a few seconds. "I miss you, and..." he hesitated, unable to finish his thought.

"Me too," Adeena said softly. "And what?"

"And, well, I have something. Something for you. I'll be home Friday. I love you."

"I love you too."

"Have to run, babe. My taxi's here." The line went dead.

She laid the phone down, wondering what he had for her. She saw the score on the table and picked it up again. It was almost as if her grandmother was here, talking to her through the pages of this composition. Could she have known that Adeena had actually started to write this score herself?

She was sure they were the same notes. She dug up her old composition from her closet, and laid it down beside the yellowed notebook from across the sea. She carefully compared the two works. The first five bars were note-for-note identical!

She stared out the window, watching dark clouds gathering over the Ottawa River, a sheet of rain falling far off in the distance. Her mind wandered, trying to make sense of the music. Who had written it – this score that completed to perfection something Adeena herself had never been able to finish?

And it was a 'cantata,' meant to be sung. But there were no lyrics in these ancient sheets. As she went through the rest of the score, Adeena saw how the opening phrases were used in a type of 'ritornello' form. Her university music professor would have loved this, as he used to lecture incessantly about how Vivaldi and Bach used the technique of including recurring variations of the same musical passage in their Baroque masterpieces.

She closed her eyes a moment, trying to play the whole score in her head. She needed other musicians to hear how it all came together.

I wonder if Walter is busy, she thought as she looked up his number on her iPhone.

ADEENA WAS ENRAPTURED BY THE MUSIC.

Walter had gladly agreed to work with her and even found a space for them at the home of Maria Valenzuela from the National Arts Centre Orchestra. She gladly volunteered to join them. Maria was a dark-haired virtuoso violinist in her late thirties who lived alone in a new upscale home near Island Park Drive.

Over the next four days, the three musicians explored the lost score. Each contributed ideas about style, texture, and pacing. The more they played, the more they were taken by it, as they discovered little nuances and made adjustments to their performances.

Lyrics came to Adeena the more they played. She would sing them to herself as she played, beginning with the phrase 'Gone is my heart...' The words began to take form in her head, and she jotted bits down after each session.

As they were setting up to play on Thursday evening, Maria turned to Adeena. "This music, it's inside of me now," Maria said. "The structure is so simple, but it has so much emotional depth. There's such longing and yearning and..." she paused, studying Walter settling at the piano, "and loss," she said finally, finishing her thought looking down at the floor.

Adeena reached for her bow. "I know what you mean. It's almost like," she paused searching for a way to express her feelings, "like liquid sadness. It seems to pour off the pages as we play."

Walter seemed oblivious to the women's analysis as he took a sip of water, put his glass down near the piano and pulled up his stool. "Ready, ladies?" he said.

As Walter began on the piano, Adeena felt the effects of the music again, the electricity of creation arcing through the circuits of her mind. These sessions had become one of the most powerful creative experiences she could ever recall. Only one other time could compare to these sessions of musical conception.

As a teenager, Adeena and her punk-rocker boyfriend Kurt had gone to her parents' cottage on Wolfe Lake for the weekend while her folks were out of town. Besides smoking pot and having sex on every piece of furniture, Adeena and Kurt shared one desire – to make music.

They created a composition they christened *Lake Nights.* As Kurt worked out chords on his acoustic guitar, Adeena wrote the lyrics and composed the chorus on the portable piano her dad kept at the lake. She remembered how Kurt, a manicured city boy, had found her dad's loon whistle shortly after they arrived at the cottage.

"What the hell is this?" he said, picking up the ivory-coloured, porcelain flute. It had an adjustable wooden stick inside of it, marked with tiny black lines on the outside to indicate the correct positions for creating various loon calls.

"It's for calling loons," Adeena laughed, as she watched him bring the flute to his lips and pull the wooden stick all the way out. Kurt blew it tentatively, making a strangely captivating wailing whistle on his first attempt.

"Cool!" he smiled and then tried it a few times. Adeena thought it perfectly mimicked the cries of the black loons that were always on the lake in the summer. Kurt was thrilled with his discovery. "We can use this!"

The plaintive tones of the loon whistle added a mystical sense to their finished composition. They recorded it on Kurt's laptop and the act of creating and then listening to the final mix under a cloudless night sky, bursting with twinkling stars and an explosion of constellations, was a profound experience for Adeena. It was on par to seeing Maya Beiser's solo on the cello as a young girl.

Now, as she started to move her bow across the strings of her cello, Adeena again felt the same intoxicating rush. She was giving life to a composition that had remained silent for nearly three centuries, a composition that completed a musical idea that she herself had begun. Together with Walter and Maria, they helped release notes confined for so long to the pages of dusty parchment.

After they finished playing, there was a long moment of silence from the three musicians. Each was lost in their own thoughts, flushed from the emotions their performance had stirred within. Walter spoke first. "Adeena," he said with an unusually serious tone, "this music is going to change your life. I hope you're ready."

Maria, still holding her violin, stood up and she too seemed overcome. Her eyes were moist as she spoke her mind. "Walter's right, Adeena. This music needs to be performed. Share it with the world," she said, touching Adeena's shoulder. "I'm honoured to have been a part of its re-discovery. Thank you."

DRIVING HOME THAT NIGHT, ADEENA REFLECTED ON HOW THE music had affected Walter and Maria. An emotion came over them, almost like a spell, each time they began to play. She thought about Maria's moving performance, her long dark hair cascading in waves, moving slowly from side-to-side as she was drawn into the depths of the music.

Adeena thought again about the missing lyrics. There was no indication of the libretto for the *Voci Soprano* section. It was like they were playing the music from a Beatles song without knowing the words. As powerful as the piece was as an instrumental, Adeena wondered what effect the vocals would add.

She flashed back to the words she had written herself, when this music had first come to her one night. She smiled thinking about that day, getting her tongue pierced and fainting, and then riding home in the backseat of her mother's car, working out lyrics in her head, pretending to be asleep.

Had she written them down? If so, they were long gone. Kurt had insisted on her helping him with his own song, and nothing more became of her back seat masterpiece.

As she drove she tried to remember those words. Were they still inside her somewhere? Could she find them again?

Maybe she mused, I just need get my tongue pierced again and they'll all come back to me.

Pulling into the parking garage, she wondered what was next. Walter was still pleading with the music director at the NAC to let them perform the composition for him. The director said he was curious about the work, and wanted to see the score. Walter agreed, but only if they could perform it for him first.

She pulled into her parking garage, found her spot and turned off the ignition. She closed her eyes and her grandmother's face flashed before Adeena.

Was she still guiding her, reaching out through this music?

FRIEDRICH LANG GLARED AT HIS COMPUTER SCREEN THROUGH gaunt, hollowed eyes.

He scratched his hand across his unshaven face as he watched the cursor mindlessly follow the progress of the musical notes that filled the room.

It was just after 3 AM.

An empty wineglass sat on top of his keyboard. Sheets of paper were strewn over the floor of his studio and torn pieces of paper were taped to the walls. Most of the lined score sheets had notations in red ink; many scratched out with notes off to the side in German.

"Christ!" he moaned as he listened to the playback in anger. He'd had enough and could no longer focus. He stood up, stopped the playback with a disgusted grunt and turned off the light.

The moonlight peeked through the windows and cast a soft glow on the portrait of Ludwig van Beethoven that dominated Lang's work area. He studied the portrait for a moment and shook his head in disgust.

"Fuck you!" he said as he walked away and shut the door on the torture chamber that was his music studio.

CHAPTER 7

The loud chirp from Walter's Chevy Camaro confirmed it was armed and locked. The sound boomeranged off the concrete walls of the NAC's underground parking lot, where he had found an empty oasis near a back wall. There, his precious could hide, protected from being accidentally scraped by the rusted cars of the proletariat.

His new toy gleamed proudly in its blue velvet metallic paint. Only Walter's red '67 Corvette Stingray, carefully stored in a garage all winter, was dearer to him.

He looked at his watch and then checked the Camaro one more time. Its menacing look reminded him of his boss, Friedrich Lang - ready to roll over anything in its path.

Walter turned away and strode toward the lobby, thinking about Adeena. What a day this must be for her! He was so relieved when Friedrich agreed to give her another chance. Thank God William had found that score in Scotland. It seemed the music was really the conductor's main interest. But if it gave Adeena an opportunity, so be it.

By the time Walter had walked through the parking garage and into the flood of daylight pouring through the gracious modern architecture of the National Arts Centre, he still had ten minutes before the two o'clock audition. Maybe "audition" was the wrong word. This was something a little different - a musical premiere?

As he sauntered past Southam Hall on his way toward Friedrich's office, Maria, carrying her violin case, came speeding towards him. Her face was contorted in displeasure.

"What's wrong?" he asked.

"Lang! I don't get that guy."

"Why? What is it?"

"He's in there with Adeena. She got here early."

Walter was confused. "Okay, and so? What're they doing?"

"Not sure, but Lang said he didn't need us. He is a great violinist after all," Maria replied in resignation. "He started fooling with the piano part of the score as soon as Adeena showed it to him. He asked me to leave and shut the door. Said he would be fine and just to leave them alone!"

"Really?" Walter said with a peevish tone. "He *is* a nut!"

He looked at Maria, her sequinned black dress sparkling like a perfectly buffed Cadillac.

She shrugged her shoulders. "Let's go get a latté. We can come back later, in case he changes his mind."

"Good idea!" Walter smiled as they turned and left together.

ADEENA WASN'T SURE WHAT TO MAKE OF HER SITUATION.

An hour ago the music director of the National Arts Centre Orchestra was almost a stranger to her, more mythical creature than real person. Now, as she stood beside Friedrich Lang, with the pages of her score spread all over his piano, they were like old comrades.

She surveyed his private practice room. Baffles made the acoustics rich and pure. A row of spotlights lit a line of framed photographs highlighting Friedrich's career, conducting and performing on stages around the world. One dramatic series of black and white photos captured him in performance at Carnegie Hall, dripping in sweat, entranced in what must have been a sorrowful violin solo.

"Ja! Ja! I see how this will work," Lang shouted as he played parts of the score on the piano, getting a feel for the tone and tempo and muttering to himself.

Adeena began to worry that his interest was only in the music she had brought him.

"Would you like to hear me play, Mr. Lang?" she finally asked tentatively.

He suddenly stopped, looked up from the piano and stared at her, as if seeing her for the first time. "What?" he asked, focusing on her and then at her cello case, propped up in the corner. "Yes, of course! Bring your cello over here. Let's try playing this through, together."

Adeena felt relieved as she unpacked the cello and lifted it carefully from the case. He stared at the old instrument.

"That's your cello?" he asked. "No endpin? Where did you get it?"

Adeena felt her heart pounding through her chest like it might expose her at any second. She took a deep breath and spoke carefully.

"It's the...the Duncan Cello," she said matter-of-factly. "I work at the National Gallery and I have, uh, well...I have special permission to use it."

Lang studied her carefully and Adeena wished she could read his thoughts.

"Really? I just saw a story about it on the news." He examined it more closely and slapped his hands together in hearty approval. "Five million dollars? *Scheisse!* Okay, you've got my attention young lady."

Lang stood up and moved a wooden stool near the piano. He motioned for her to sit.

"Let's play, my dear. See what we can do with this piece!"

As the conductor focused on her music, Adeena glanced toward the open cello case and the original copy of the score, sealed in a plastic bag. An image of her grandmother flashed in her mind. She mouthed a silent "thank you" to her.

It had not been easy to "borrow" the Duncan Cello from the National Gallery. Indeed it had required a certain degree of deviousness on her part. But for the moment, cello and musician were together. At last, she could perform the music that seemed a part of who she was with an instrument that felt like it had always belonged to her.

Adeena listened to the opening bars of the music coming from the piano. The conductor was astute. He understood this music instinctively. The effect on his face was clear and his focus profound as his fingers touched the keys. Lang's head began to sway, directing an invisible orchestra in front of him.

Adeena sat watching him on a wooden stool. She pulled the Duncan Cello between her legs. It somehow felt naturally comfortable. This instrument was her voice, its haunting timbre was able to bestir her nethermost emotions with a depth she had never experienced. It brought release to the creativity imprisoned within her. As she traced her fingers along the smooth wood grain of its weathered fingerboard, a rush of blood pounded within her trembling hands.

Lang looked up from the piano. He seemed entranced as well, as he gave a slight nod of his head for her to begin, closing his eyes to better concentrate on the music.

Adeena tightened her grip, ready to start the dark, timeless tango of cello and cellist.

Slowly, she began to play. As the strands of her taut horsehair bow glided across the strings of the cello with a lush friction, an odd sensation swept over her. The harmonics of cello and piano combined to create a sense of yearning, enveloping the windowless chamber in a wave of sound that focused the emotions rising within her.

Adeena closed her eyes and felt her head spin. It was like a drug-induced high, but more potent than anything she had ever felt. The lost score had found its true companion in this cello and she was simply reuniting two lost lovers separated by time.

Clouds began to swallow her consciousness.

The conductor's studio faded and a blinding ray of light filled her eyes. She was floating, looking down at a ghostly representation of herself and Friedrich Lang, both lost in the music. The light flared brighter, eclipsing the images in the conductor's practice room until it pulled her into a symphony of light and spectacular colours. A piercing sound bored through her head as she felt an impossibly heavy pressure pushing down on her. It felt like every atom of her body was being flattened between slabs of granite. She tried to breathe, but could draw no air. The sense of motion, of being pushed faster and faster, continued to increase exponentially until suddenly she felt it release.

Then she felt nothing at all. Whiteness followed by blackness and then - total emptiness.

And then all her senses awoke at once. She gasped, desperately trying to fill her lungs. A volley of stars spun around her head. She felt a cool draft and shivered, still fighting for breath, as a fierce pain gripped her head, then relaxed.

Had she just fainted? Or had some kind of seizure? If so, what would Lang think of her now? Unable to withstand the pressure of playing great music, most likely. How could she explain this to him?

And then faintly at first, she heard the music again. Was someone playing Maria Valenzuela's violin part? Was that the smell of burning candles?

She opened her eyes. The conductor's tiny padded studio was gone, replaced by a massive stone chamber. Her eyes focused on a performance hall illuminated by candles and torches. The chamber was packed with wide-eyed men and women.

Adeena and her gleaming Duncan Cello were on a stone floor, playing as if she had been here all along. She sat on a wooden stool, performing with a small group of musicians.

Directly beside her, a man wearing tartan and lace was playing a violin, in much the same style as Maria, with similar passion. Off to the side, a tall man played on a small boxy-looking piano, while a young lady wearing a collar of white ribbons ruffled together like flower petals, played a pear-shaped instrument Adeena recognized as an English guitar, or as it was more properly called, 'a cittern'. Finally, a young man played on a viola directly beside Adeena.

It all felt so real, and yet so impossible. Her dreams were usually just emotions, vague images. But now her senses were alive with all the textures of this real world. The glowing heat of a nearby hearth felt warm against her face.

Where am I?

Though she was disoriented, she continued to play, taking in the details of the spacious cavern around her. The stone walls stretched high above her head, framed with ornate wooden inlaid corners and rails. A series of framed portraits formed a noble backdrop for the performance. Regal ladies and gentlemen, painted with the same dark oils she recognized from the National Gallery, looked down at the proceedings in solemn countenance. This was some kind of reception, she thought, as she continued playing the lost score that she had rehearsed all week for Friedrich Lang.

Her mind was racing. Is this all real? Did somebody slip something into her smoothie this morning?

A group of about twenty-five men and women watched her and the other musicians. The men were dressed in jackets and kilts, as if they were part of the Highland Games she had seen down in Maxville south of Ottawa. The women wore wide bell-shaped satin and damask skirts, stretched over stiff petticoats. Each woman seemed more striking than the next, wearing an array of white, mauve, and wine coloured skirts, trimmed with linen and lace at the bodice. Adeena noticed many wore a white rose.

She absorbed every detail. She was in a trance of some sort, aware of who she was, but at the same time, playing the part of someone else who belonged in this strange world.

The music came to a transition in the piece where the cello was picked up by another instrument. The man on the viola took up the cello lines and Adeena found herself setting the Duncan Cello aside. She stood up and began to sing the words she had worked on for the last week and could no longer contain.

Gone is my heart without you,
Now I am lost once again.
Praying for life that grows within,
All I can ask is when?

When will the sword meet the sky,
To show where I belong?
Forever, I will wait for you
Even after I'm gone.

As Adeena continued singing, her haunting voice filled the space with an outpouring of longing and promise and mostly, of hope. The small audience listened transfixed. She finished again on the cello with a solo that echoed her voice.

And then she was done.

She breathed heavily, still disoriented at what was happening to her, but glowing with satisfaction.

Boisterous applause and cheering erupted. A tall young man with long hair, dressed in a dark waistcoat, approached her and lifted her from her chair.

"Rise, Lady Katharine," he said as he pulled her up and embraced her warmly. Then holding her hand and raising it with his over both of their heads, he turned to the cheering group.

"My sister, Katharine Carnegie," he proclaimed. "She gives new meaning to our cause. We have found our voice!"

The reaction was deafening and Adeena was overwhelmed with confusion. What was happening? Where was she? What happened to the conductor and the audition?

An older woman approached them and the man was quick to introduce her. "Katharine, this is Lady Jean Drummond, one of the matriarchs of our struggle," he said deferring to the older woman who carried herself with a regal air. "Her sons carry on the work their father began in the preservation of the Kingdom."

Lady Jean seemed flushed from Adeena's performance. "Young lady, you have a gift more powerful than all the swords and all the sterling being collected here tonight," Lady Jean started, her gaze intense, unwavering. "My son James has a noble title, but you dear Katharine, have reduced to him to a mumbling fool!"

There was a man standing behind Lady Jean. He was tall and fair, with blue eyes staring intently at Adeena. He was dressed differently than the others, in a flowing blue tartan cape, an officer of some sort, perhaps? Though his features were soft, almost child-like, he carried himself with a commanding air.

He moved towards Adeena and bowed his head respectfully.

"Lady Katharine, you have indeed inspired me," he said, bowing again. "James Drummond, at your service, my Lady."

Adeena wasn't sure how to respond. Was this a dream? Was she this lady Katharine Carnegie? It felt so real, every tiny detail, astoundingly vivid. She could smell the wood fire of the hearth in the distance. She looked around and heard conversations, aware that most of the room was still focused on her. Many seemed as if they waited to greet her.

This man addressing her, James, was about her age probably. Who did he think she was?

"Thank you," she whispered. None of this made sense, but words came out of her mouth anyway, almost like someone else was speaking for her. Her voice echoed strangely in her ears. Was she speaking with a Scottish accent?

The young man who had introduced her, apparently her brother, stood beside Adeena and seemed breathless to join the conversation. She heard someone address him as George. His features seemed familiar.

"Katharine, you know that James, the Duke of Perth, is here at Kinnaird with purpose. His father died fighting, as did our uncle, the Earl Carnegie, to return the King to his rightful place as our true sovereign," George summarized with deadly earnest. "They pledged on the day Union was declared with England, that Drummond and Carnegie would be united forever against it."

Lady Jean took hold of Adeena's arm firmly.

"My son rallies men to ride with Bonnie Prince Charles, who has returned to lead us against our captors," she said. "But your brother, the Captain with the Union, is a traitor to our cause."

Adeena was beyond confusion now. She stared blankly at the group before her.

"And what o'clock will the Captain arrive?" James interrupted.

"He lands at Montrose this very eve," George replied. "He was summoned to return from Flanders. Seems we're more important than fighting the French."

"What business does he have here at Kinnaird?" James asked.

"He is heir to the estate, and covets to recover it from attainment, even though Lady Margaret contests him," George responded. "But his main purpose, I am sure, will be to convince me to renounce my support for the Jacobite King.

George paused and looked directly at Adeena. "Our brother, no doubt, wants us to join him in preserving the Union."

Adeena knew that none of this was real, but she couldn't explain it. For now, she could only play a part over which she seemed to have no control. This man, George, looked to her for some kind of reaction. All she could manage was confusion.

But George was certainly fired up. "James, my brother and I

have sworn allegiance to opposing kings, but we agreed to meet here, at Kinnaird – the home of our dear uncle, a great ally of your father."

Lady Jean sighed at the mention of her husband. "Will you stand against your own brother, George Carnegie?" she asked in a tone that sounded more like a command. "And will you follow Prince Charles to wrest our kingdom from the crown in London?"

She stared at George with a fire in her eyes so intense Adeena could almost feel the heat from her inquisition. "Or will you join your brother and fight against us? Against your fellow Scots?" she challenged him angrily.

"Never!"

Adeena was lost, swimming in a sea of confusion. She noticed for the first time that she was dressed in white ribbons and silks herself and that she wore a heavy necklace. She touched the jewel hanging from her neck, and then looked up as she felt all eyes turned toward her.

"And you, Lady Katharine?"

It was the young tartan-clad officer, James, asking her. Maybe this was all a set-up, a National Arts Centre theatre production that she had wandered into by mistake. Was it possible? Maybe it was being staged in conjunction with the new exhibit at the Gallery she had been researching, *The Art of Rebellion.*

"Sorry," she replied finally, "I don't know the lines for this scene. I'm just a musician . . ." Adeena paused, unable to finish her thought.

Lady Jean and her George looked at her oddly. James however still seemed enraptured. "And your music powers our imagination of what can be. Your passion leaves us breathless, my lady."

Adeena studied the tall man bestowing this flattery on her. James, was it?

"Thank you," she whispered, trying to get the words out even as she felt her voice fade. Her head suddenly exploded with pain and she was overcome by darkness.

FRIEDRICH LANG STARED AT ADEENA WHO LAY MOTIONLESS IN her chair.

They had just experienced a remarkable session of musical union. She had even sung to him, like some kind of creature possessed, with words from another realm. The cello solo that followed her singing had filled him with ideas for a sweeping arrangement with various sections of the orchestra. This was the work he had been searching to create, unable to bring to life through his own powers of composition.

"Adeena?" he called out to her.

He stepped from behind his piano and walked towards her. He glanced over at the cello and caught sight of the plastic bag in the open case. The brown parchment and faded lettering could mean only one thing – the original copy of this miraculous work.

There was a knock on the door.

"Friedrich?"

It was Walter Leo, his principal cellist, who had arranged this session.

"Just a minute," Friedrich responded.

ADEENA TRIED TO FOCUS. THE WORLD WAS FUZZY. DISTORTED. Sounds were muffled.

"Ade-e-e-e-e-e-n-a," The words swirled surreal around her, trying to connect.

Her head felt tight, like she was being constrained in a vise.

"Adeena?"

She suddenly opened her eyes and saw a familiar face staring at her.

"Walter?" she said, confused and staring through a haze.

"You okay? What happened?" Walter asked. She could see the conductor behind him in the distance and Maria standing nearby.

"You passed out Adeena," Lang said softly. "Does that happen often?"

Adeena was finally able to focus clearly. She sat upright. "No, not really," she replied. "Was I out long?"

"Just a few moments," Lang said from his position behind Walter and Maria. He moved forward. "I thought maybe you were overcome by the music."

He paused a moment before continuing. "Ms. Stuart you are a gifted musician. I would very much like to offer you a position playing here with us, as a member of the National Arts Centre Orchestra."

She froze, looking at Walter, who was beaming at her.

"You would? Oh my God! Thank you, sir!"

CHAPTER 8

Philippe filled a flute of champagne for Adeena as they sat at her dining room table, gazing over the sparkling lights of the Ottawa skyline.

He had prepared his signature *filet mignon* dish, flambéing lobster tails with cognac as a finishing touch. "To you, my dear. You did it!" he said, handing Adeena her the bubbling glass.

"Thanks to my grandmother," she replied, feeling her eyes well up. She raised her flute and nodded to Philippe through impending tears.

"To your grandmother then," he offered quietly.

Adeena took a long sip, thinking back on all that had happened in Friedrich Lange's practice studio this afternoon.

"You know, I passed out during the audition," she said, treading slowly, to gauge the resistance ahead. "It was really weird. As soon as I began playing, I went into some kind of a dream. But, it was soooo real. Completely real. It was like..." she paused, trying to explain to Philippe, and to herself, what had happened. "It was like a daydream. And I went into some kind of other world. I've never felt anything like that before." She hesitated a moment. "I think somehow, maybe, it *was* real."

Philippe eyed her, one brow raised.

Putting down his empty flute slowly, he finally responded. "You've had an awfully stressful time lately, getting ready for that audition. Probably even dreaming about it. Then, your grandmother dies, and you get that lost music from Scotland," he continued, sequencing the events. "Finally, you get to play alone with the conductor of the NAC himself, on a five-million-dollar cello no less." His face lightened and his tone warmed. "I am sure you felt like you dreamed and went into another world!"

Adeena knew he didn't believe her. How could he? She didn't believe it herself. She felt a lingering ache from the experience, but aside from that, wondered if she hadn't created the whole thing in her mind; maybe some kind of migraine that had built up over the last few weeks?

But every second of it, the sights, sounds, people – even the odours of the wood-burning hearth, the perfumed ladies – all lingered vividly.

"Tara knows you took the Duncan Cello, right?" Philippe asked, changing the subject.

She paused a second at his inquiry. Philippe and Tara were both such sticklers. "Yes," she answered, stretching the truth like a tightwire over the Grand Canyon. She took another sip of champagne. "Tara was told that the cello needs to be played every day. And well, I am a cellist."

Philippe smiled, but Adeena knew the wheels were turning in his head. She called him a human polygraph. He laughed at that label, but they both knew he could detect bullshit in any form. It was a job requirement he said, for reporters on Parliament Hill.

Hopefully his sensors were turned off now. Tara had stressed to Adeena that she could *not* play the Duncan Cello until she got a security upgrade. Paperwork, paperwork. Tara lived for it. The gallery had hired a fellow from a company that sold and repaired musical instruments and had the proper security clearance.

But the man was a simple technician, not a real musician.

This morning Adeena had asked him if he could do the tuning in her office, so she could take some pictures for her exhibit research. As he completed his work, which required him to play a short piece of music, she was struck once again by the haunting tone of the Duncan. Her audition was coming up in just over two hours.

"Can you give me a few minutes to take some more pictures?" she asked the man as he got ready to pack the cello back in its case. Adeena noticed the remnants of leftover sleep in his eyes. He had yawned throughout the tuning procedure. "I've got a meal card for the cafeteria if you'd like to get yourself a coffee or something," she offered, flashing a huge smile as she extended the charge card to him.

"Thanks," he said. "I was up all night with the new baby. I'll go get a coffee from the cafeteria and maybe soak my head in it for a while. Take your time. Just pack it up when you're done and I'll come back and pick it up later."

Adeena felt guilty about what she was going to do, but it was a risk she felt compelled to take. As soon as the man left, she took *her* cello, with its endpin removed, and packed it into the hard-shelled case used to carry the precious artifact.

Then she took the Duncan Cello, carefully placed it into her own cello case and left for her audition.

PHILIPPE WAS DOUBTFUL ABOUT THE WHOLE THING. HE TRIED to ignore his instincts that Adeena took the Duncan Cello without permission.

It wasn't that important. The moment had come that would change both their lives.

His career was taking off. He had done more TV and radio interviews than he could count since his exposé was published. He had been invited to become a regular political commentator on CBC radio. His editor was talking about new opportunities and hinting at becoming a national political columnist for *Post*

Media. He had even gotten a call from CNN in Atlanta. He knew that at last, he could be a good provider.

And today Adeena had proved to all the world she was a musician. And a damn good one!

Philippe placed the ring case he had been carrying for so long onto the glass dining room table.

Adeena froze, looking up at him with wide searching eyes.

He studied her face. Those green eyes seemed to see right into his soul. Her smouldering looks – full lips, delicate nose, high cheekbones – all were imprinted deeply inside him. Adeena's face was the last thing he saw when he closed his eyes at night.

He reached for her hand. "Adeena Stuart, will you marry me?"

She carefully lifted the velvet case and examined the diamond ring, its reflected light dancing in all directions around her. He waited silent and nervous, like a teenager asking a girl out for the first time.

She began to cry and put the case back on the table.

He took the ring from the case, lifted her left hand and placed it on her ring finger.

"Will you?" he whispered, still holding her hand. "Will you be my wife?"

Adeena drew back her hand. She was still crying. He waited. Had he overwhelmed her? Each moment of silence heightened his feeling of dread.

Finally, she spoke. "No, I can't, Philippe."

His heart jumped into his mouth.

"I'm not sure I can be your wife. Or anyone's wife."

He sat stunned, searching for words. "Adeena, I love you, more than I've ever loved anyone. I'm not perfect, I know that. But I will put you first, every single day. I want to spend my life loving you, loving..." he hesitated, "...our family."

Adeena bowed her head. "I know you do. But, it's not you... it's me."

"What do you mean?" His voice was becoming urgent.

"I don't understand it myself. Maybe I'm not ready, or maybe I never will be." Their eyes locked together. "To be married, to anyone."

Adeena looked down at the ring on her finger. She touched it, staring at the sparkling gem that graced her hand. She began to remove it from her finger.

Philippe placed his hand over hers. "No," he said quietly. "That is yours."

She closed her eyes. Her face seemed heavy and sad. Philippe had played out the scene of proposing to Adeena in his head so many times. Never had he imagined this.

"It's not right for me to keep it, to do this to you, Philippe." She removed the ring from her finger, and pain shot through him as if someone had poked an open wound.

"Are you afraid? Is that it?"

"Maybe," she replied. "Maybe I am."

"Do you love me?"

Adeena closed her eyes, another tear rolled down her cheek. Every second of silence was another moment of molten pain searing his chest. Finally, without opening her eyes, she spoke. "Of course I do."

Should he embrace her? His beloved, so close, yet so far away. Should he just leave, and take his wounded pride with him?

Maybe this is a test. If it's really meant to be, if she is the one, then this is just an obstacle to conquer. Someday, when they were looking back on years of marriage, this little drama would be something they laughed at. Just keep it in logical perspective he told himself.

Logic and love though, don't make good companions.

"Fuck," he finally said. "I'm so fucking stupid."

"What?" Adeena said, looking a little startled at his sudden change of tone.

"I thought that we could build a life together. I convinced myself that you and I wanted the same things. I fooled myself into believing that I was really it. The one for you..."

He stopped, his head swirling. The pain, the anger, the bitterness – all were getting the upper hand. He didn't want to let it all out, afraid of these feelings and how he could screw up completely.

"Philippe, you're a good man. You're not stupid. I'm not sure I know how to do it, to love someone, completely. To commit to anyone..."

He nodded. "I have to leave."

ALONE IN HER LIVING ROOM, SHE SAT STARING AT THE RING. IT represented so much, and every sparkling reflection seemed to be trying to convince her that she had made a mistake.

Was she that afraid of all that it meant? To be married, to have a family, to be someone's wife?

Or was it that unfulfilled feeling that Adeena could not shake? A sense that she wasn't complete, that she was still searching for fulfillment as a musician? Or maybe as a composer? It was desire for creation that haunted her, frustrated her and demanded she find a way to bring it to life.

No matter what the sacrifice.

"I'm so fucking stupid." Those were *his* words, but they applied more to her than to poor suffering Philippe. Did she love him? What does that kind of love feel like? Maybe the last few years, struggling to find her musical career while he took care of her, always being patient, waiting for her to really embrace their relationship, had all combined in her taking him for granted.

How could she say no to someone who loved her and probably always would?

She looked over at the case holding the Duncan Cello.

Tears welled up again, and without knowing why, she got up and unpacked the instrument from its case. She lifted it up and in a kind of stupor felt its oddly familiar touch.

She sat and drew the old cello between her legs. The notes of the lost score played in her mind, as she reached for her bow. The entire piece lived within her, as it had since she first transcribed the opening notes so long ago. She was re-discovering what had always been there.

Her bow touched the strings. She began to play the score once again. The same feeling she had experienced in the conductor's studio overcame her within a few bars. A bright light lifted her once more as the clouds swallowed her and she felt the sweeping power of the music carry her consciousness away. The piano and violin filled in the sound and another stringed instrument added counterpoint and depth.

Was she dreaming again?

Adeena's eyes flashed open to the same glimmering world of silk gowns and lively merry-making by the roaring fires. She was once again playing with the music ensemble in the great room with its soaring stone walls. Stern portraits looked down once more at the group of musicians and their enraptured audience.

She saw the man, George, from her previous 'dream', standing beside another man dressed in a red military uniform. Both focused their gaze on her, each with a deadly serious look. Neither smiled.

There was a different group of people here than from her previous performance. Almost everyone watching her now was male – soldiers or officers, dressed in the same colourful red as the man beside George.

Adeena continued playing, and once again set aside the Duncan Cello to sing. The words flowed effortlessly, ending in her final verse:

When will you turn night to day?
So hope may greet the dawn?
Forever, I will wait for you,
Even after I'm gone.

Every eye was upon her. The musicians repeated the final bar once more as her voice swelled to a crescendo.

Even after I'm gone.

When she finished, the men were more boisterous than the previous group and their applause even more thunderous. She felt humbled, still confused by what was happening. She was surprised that her voice carried so well in this medieval setting. It was not just the torches and hearth that created this warmth she had never experienced before. While she had no way of making sense of what was happening, and was as confused as before, this was something completely new – an audience connecting with her music.

George began to approach her, but another man held him back. They looked at each other sternly for a moment, as she took a bow in recognition of the continuing applause.

"My sister, Lady Katharine Carnegie," the man said in a commanding tone, directed towards the cheering soldiers. "She honours my return to the United Kingdom of Scotland and England, mighty Great Britain, ruled by our gracious King – George the Second."

Adeena stared at him tentatively. Another brother of Lady Katharine?

She walked toward him now as the men continued to cheer, many calling to her. She smiled and accepted their praises modestly. Her music had touched them, deeply it seemed.

Adeena was beginning to believe, impossibly, that this was not a dream. She tried to wake up, shaking her head, pinching her hand forcefully, trying to return to her apartment, to her familiar Ottawa surroundings. Nothing worked. She couldn't wake herself up.

For the moment, she was here – performing at an ancient concert, somewhere in the United Kingdom, probably Scotland, it seemed. The only truly familiar thing was the Duncan Cello. It was her lone connection to the world of Adeena Stuart. That and the lost score. The song connected her to this world and to an emotional centre that may have always lived within her.

Adeena bowed one more time, her cheeks glowing from the outpouring directed towards her. She had reached this audience in a way she had longed to from the very first time she had performed.

A strong grip on her arm, intended to get her attention and cause discomfort, pulled her from her thoughts. It was followed by an angry whisper, the speaker inches from her ear. "Under whose authority do you play that whorish instrument in this society?"

"What?" she responded, forcefully prying the hand from her arm.

George intervened as the soldiers continued to show their approval, chanting for more. "Could we step outside please?" he said, taking Adeena's hand and whisking her away.

The chanting and applauding continued even as George stepped quickly, hurrying through a great stone vestibule. Adeena marvelled at the walls. A massive chandelier, with dozens of burning candles, illuminated the entrance to this place.

It's a castle, she thought, as George pulled her like he might a troublesome child, and the three siblings stepped out into the crisp evening air. George marched straight ahead a few feet before he stopped and finally let go of her hand. He turned to his brother.

"James! Leave Katharine alone!" he exclaimed to the other man who stood defiantly before him.

"It is 'Sir James'," the man seethed with indignation. "You'll do well to remember that I am the sitting Member of Parliament for Kincardineshire!"

George glared at him angrily. "As if you'd ever let me forget, brother!"

"I'm also a Captain in his Majesty's service," the older brother snorted, glaring at George and Adeena. "Are you trying to deliberately undermine my authority with the officers from the Royal Twenty-first Foot? And tell me, the two of you, what in the name of our Lord God, is the meaning of this childish, seditious, *overbearing* music?"

"Childish? Overbearing?" Adeena responded. "What's your problem, bud?"

George and the Captain both looked at her with confusion.

"It is me who arranged for Katharine to play for you, *Captain,"* George responded unable to say the word without mockery. "And your men call for her still. Listen."

Adeena could hear the chants from inside the castle. She looked around at the outside of this massive structure, lit by a long series of torches. It was like castles she'd visited on her summer trips to England and Scotland as a teen. She listened to the chants coming from the open doors.

"LADY KATHARINE!"

It seemed to annoy the Captain who now turned to George.

"And was it you, dear brother, who invited the Jacobite traitor James Drummond to Kinnaird?" he sneered. "Seeking volunteers to follow the Young Pretender? I've received reports the coward was here earlier, indeed this very eve!"

George made no effort to reply. The brothers faced off, two bulls sizing each other up, searching for any weakness before charging. Adeena turned over the name in her head – James Drummond, the man from her previous dream?

Dream?

It was real, so sensory, so rich with detail. She felt the cool evening air and shivered, pulling her arms together. She breathed deeply, the savoury aroma of roasted meat filling her senses. She touched her soft hair, long and full, flowing over her shoulders.

This is not a dream. But yet, it can't be real either.

"He honours his father and our uncle, the Earl Carnegie, who made a pact on this very spot to unite our clans forever against the Union," George finally retorted. "They both died trying to preserve the kingdom of Scotland – something you seem to both forget and detest!"

The Captain seemed to weigh his response. Adeena sensed his outrage at George's comments, but he said nothing, and instead turned to her.

"As your oldest brother, the rightful heir to the estate of Kinnaird, a loyal member of his Majesty's army and the Member of Parliament for Kincardineshire, I hereby *forbid* you sister, from ever performing that seditious music again," he announced stiffly to Adeena. "Give me the script you played from, lest it become known beyond the shire."

"You can't *forbid* me from doing anything, *especially* not playing that music, which I wrote and will perform wherever, and whenever I please!"

The Captain stared in shock.

"You pernicious wench!" he fumed. "I will not allow you to bring shame on our family. I will take that music and I warn you thus; never perform it again, lest you desire to discover the full bounty of my wrath. As for that lewd instrument, it is intended for a man, not a lady of moral repute. You shan't play it ever again."

"You're not the boss of me!" Adeena shot back. "Who do you think you are jerk-off? King Kong?"

George and his brother seemed dumbstruck. They stood staring, unable to mount any suitable response to this strange outburst. There was complete silence for a few seconds, save for the background chanting that continued from inside the walls of the castle.

"I am the head of this family with charge to command as I please," the Captain responded. "With my authority as a member of His Majesty's government, and an officer in his infantry, I could have you arrested. Heed my warning sister, or presently you shall discover the consequences of your disloyalty.'

Adeena glared at him, her anger tempered only by the

ongoing backdrop of chants and applause that continued from the depths of the castle behind her.

"I don't think your men share your opinion," she said pointing to the open door. "They seem to like my 'childish, over-bearing' music."

The Captain stared at her, pursing his lips and listening to the pleas of his men. One of them appeared at the door, and he waved the man closer.

"Escort my sister, Lady Katharine, back to the hall and instruct her on the jig we dance to," he commanded to the man. Adeena and George began to walk away, toward the open door. The Captain held the officer back with his arm, and spoke to him under his breath.

"And bring her music score to me."

CHAPTER 9

The morning sun greeted the produce vendors in the ByWard Market with the promise of a warm September morning. Beneath a powder-blue sky they prepared for another hectic day of commerce. The sweet aroma of freshly baked bread and hot croissants from the French bakery filled the air. A driver unloaded overflowing baskets of the Ottawa valley's autumn bounty – butternut squash, beets, pumpkins, and Brussels sprouts.

A block away, Adeena winced at the first rays of sunlight streaming into her bedroom. She peered dimly at the light through flaking mascara as she slowly awakened.

'Thank God it's Saturday,' she thought, closing her eyes, only to immediately register excruciating pain in her head. The pounding pressure behind both eyes stretched from her temples and ran deep into her skull. She massaged her forehead, seeking relief as a familiar line from a Bruce Springsteen song surfaced through the pain. *A freight train running through the middle of my head.*

"Jesus!" Adeena cried. She lay in bed staring at the ceiling, images of her dream flashing through her mind. Something felt strange on her left hand. She reached over and touched the diamond ring on her finger.

She raised her hand to take a look and then winced, remembering the pain she saw seared across Philippe's face last night. She had hurt him with her ambivalence.

Ambivalence? Try cruel bitch. Why couldn't she say yes to a man who adored her? Yes to the man who promised to love her always, a guy that wanted to build a life together?

But no, she couldn't give him an answer. He had left, angry and hurt, with the ring still on her ungrateful finger.

She closed her eyes. But even that set her forehead throbbing. Adeena finally dragged herself from bed, her head pounding like a jackhammer on steel. She swallowed two extra-strength ibuprofen tablets with water, closing her eyes as they slid down her throat.

After the pain eased a bit, her mind wandered to the dream she experienced after Philippe left. It didn't make sense and she couldn't explain it, but she had again gone to another place, in another time and once again, become another woman – Katharine Carnegie.

She looked around the apartment, back at her life as Adeena Stuart. Her mind felt like it wanted to run in a dozen different painful directions.

She badly needed coffee.

By the time she had nursed down a large mug of a strong, dark roast, the freight train in her head had run its course, leaving only a dull ache behind.

She noticed the Duncan Cello carefully standing in the corner.

That is Katharine's cello, she thought, reliving the performance, remembering the words she'd sung so effortlessly, so powerfully. She recalled the texture of the sounds filling the ancient hall and the faces of the men and women who watched her perform.

How was it possible? Was it really her? Her words, her voice?

She looked once more at the cello and suddenly thought of Tara. Adeena glanced at the clock and realized she better get it back to the gallery before Michael, the young security guard, finished his shift at nine this morning.

Adeena took another long sip of coffee, staring out the window, and thought more about how she would get the Duncan Cello back to the gallery. Good thing Michael was such a sweet kid. He was clearly taken with her, and if she just happened to fuel his imagination with her innocent flirtations, who was she really hurting?

She noticed her iPhone on the table and thought of her own grandmother. Of all the people on earth, perhaps only she would understand. But Margaret Rose was gone. She felt very alone and wished that her parents were here with her.

She picked up the phone and touched her dad's face on her favourites list. She hoped he would pick up, even if he and mom were so far away. She waited as the circuits connected across five time zones to Scotland.

"Hi, Pumpkin," her dad's familiar voice finally greeted her.

She could almost feel his arms wrapping around her. "Hi Dad! How are you doing over there? I really miss you. Both of you."

"We miss you too," he responded. "It's been a rough couple of days. I wish you were here." He paused for a second, and then added, "Is everything okay, Adeena?"

She felt a flood of despair welling up inside her. She fought not to dissolve into tears. Every word that popped into her head seemed useless, incomplete. Her dad must have sensed something, because he broke the long silence by changing the topic.

"We've been thinking about you. How did your audition go yesterday? Any news?" her father asked with a tone of parental optimism.

Adeena had almost forgotten about the audition. She closed her eyes for a second, hoping to exorcize the sadness that seemed to possess her over her grandmother's passing. Her dad sounded so hopeful, so proud of her.

"I got it, Dad!" she said, forcing herself to try and sound cheerful. "Mr. Lang offered me a position with the NAC Orchestra, said I might even get to do a solo."

"Oh, Adeena! We're so happy for you! You deserve it!" he gushed. "So you played that music we sent you on your cello?"

"I did," she said after a moment. "But actually, I used the Duncan Cello, from the gallery, at work." She paused again, considering how much she should tell him. "Dad, there is something special about that instrument and about the music Grandma sent me." Adeena choked a little on the word 'Grandma'. But she felt an overwhelming need to tell someone about her 'dreams'.

"Something special? You mean about the music or the cello?" her father asked.

"Well both, actually. It's almost like they know each other," Adeena said her voice trailing off. "And there's something else too." She hesitated, remembering Philippe's reaction to her story. "I had the most intense dream... afterwards."

Her father didn't respond. He was quiet and she wondered if he heard what she had said. "Dream?" he finally offered.

"Yeah, Dad. Almost like a story you would tell me," she said, choosing her words carefully. "I was playing the Duncan Cello, but as another woman. She was from the past, I think."

"Really? Who? Who was this woman?"

"Katharine. I became this Lady Katharine Carnegie in my dream," she replied, wishing she could see the reaction on his face. "And I was singing, really powerfully. I, or Katharine maybe, was singing words that I had been thinking about for a long time, and..."

She stopped, wondering how crazy she must sound.

"And what?" her father asked gently. "Adeena?"

She hesitated, unsure how much to say. "And," she said doubtfully thinking this must sound so silly. "I was in a castle performing for Katharine's brother George and another brother, uh Sir James. I think he is a captain?"

"Sir James Carnegie?" he asked.

"Yes, that was it!" she replied, closing her eyes, thinking back. "It all felt so real. I've never had a dream like that, where I can remember every little detail." Her voice dropped into a frightened whisper. "Dad, I don't know what's going on. I had that dream twice. Both times I was playing as Katharine, but for different people. I think I might be losing it..." Her voice trailed off in silence all the way across the Atlantic.

Her dad was quiet, like he sensed something was wrong. "Take a deep breath, Pumpkin," he said in a comforting tone. "Start at the beginning and tell me everything you can remember about your dreams."

WILLIAM HUNG UP AFTER HIS CALL WITH ADEENA.

He stood frozen for a moment. Jackie, puzzled by the long silence, glanced up from the sink where she was drying the dishes to see William staring into the distance, lost in thought.

They had just finished lunch at his mother's cottage where they were working on getting Margaret Rose's things packed up and putting her affairs in order.

"What on earth was that all about?" Jackie inquired, having listened to one side of a very peculiar conversation. "Thank God Adeena finally got that stupid conductor to give her a spot with the orchestra. But, what did she say happened after? I didn't get that part."

William pursed his lips, still puzzled by everything he had just heard. "Yup, she got the job alright, with the NAC. She worked so hard for it."

"She did. I'm so happy for her," Jackie agreed, putting the last of the glasses and cups away. "But what was all that stuff about dreaming and singing? And did I hear, something about soldiers or a captain?"

William hesitated for a few seconds before responding. "Remember the score we sent to Adeena last week, just before Mum died? Had to arrange that overnight courier? Well after she played it for the orchestra conductor, Lang, I guess she had a couple of *very* vivid dreams."

"Dreams? Really? More than one?"

"I think so. It was after she played the score... and oh by the way, she used the Duncan Cello. You know the one I was telling you about? The one from over here in Scotland?"

His wife nodded, looking more perplexed. "Yeah. So what about it?"

"So, she says that after she played that music, on that cello, she dreamed she became Katharine Carnegie! She played for Katharine's brother George and for Sir James Carnegie and . . ."

William suddenly stopped and bit his lip, staring at this wife blankly.

"And what?" Jackie demanded.

"The diary. You know the one Mum took from Kinnaird?" he muttered, getting up from the sofa. His mind was racing. "Didn't he mention something about a brother? Wasn't it George?" He looked over at her, wide-eyed now. "Did you see it? The diary?"

"There's something on Mum's nightstand," Jackie replied. "You said we had to take it back to Kinnaird, remember?"

William hurried into the bedroom and found the leather-bound diary sitting on the nightstand. He opened it, trying to find the passage his mother had made him read to her in the library at the castle. Jackie stood in the bedroom doorway, staring at him as he thumbed through the pages.

"What was that date?" he said. "I think it was August . . . 16 or wait. Here it is, 6 August, 1745."

He slowly read the entire passage. He raced across the words in disbelief.

He whistled to himself. "Wow," he said quietly. "Oh my God!"

"What? What is it?" Jackie demanded.

"You better listen to this," he said, adjusting his glasses and reading to his wife directly from the diary.

"Kinnaird - 6 August 1745.

Kinnaird will soon be mine. Arrangements now in progress are going well. Tonight I returned from my glorious dayes in Flanders with the officers in my regiment and we were welcomed by my brother George, who arranged a feast of mutton, pies and ale, along with musical merriment."

"You see! It was George!" he said, looking up at Jackie.

"Yeah okay, keep going," she replied impatiently.

"Arrogant Sister Katharine travelled from Aberdeen to play for me on a new violincello from maestro Duncan of Upperkirkgate that George was able to secure through his merchant associates."

Jackie interrupted. "The Duncan Cello?"

"I think it might be, but wait," William responded. "It gets better."

"But that she, a woman and mine own sister too, would play an instrument so clearly in the domain of men, was scandalous and altogether unacceptable. Katharine's insolence was intolerable. She told me that 'I could not forbid her from doing anything.' But alas, she is sadly mistaken in her naïveté."

William looked at Jackie. Was she thinking the same thing as him?

"Would you just keep reading, please?"

"Sorry," he said, looking down again the diary, continuing his narration.

"Even worse, the song Katharine played this eve seemed to intoxicate my officers, and she used their reaction against me. For tho' it was indeed miraculous, it was also the most seditious song ever heard, and played on such a lewd instrument too! Katharine said it was a composition that she herself wrote, and she could perform it 'wherever and whenever' she pleased. She performed and sang as though possessed by spirits that talked directly of the Jacobite traitors and their young Pretender.

We had sharp society afterwards, and her hot temper served no useful design. Her delirium was evident when she used her foul Abeerdeen dialect, calling me a 'Jerkoffe'- possibly a Jacobite curse of some sort."

Jackie smiled at this, but her face was contorted in confusion. William paused a moment. "Keep going," she implored.

"When I warned her never to perform the cantata again, lest it embolden the traitors amongst us who would destroy the Union, she refused. In her fury she inquired if I was 'King Konge' a line of royalty I am ignorant of, but I believe was meant as an insult to my person.

I forbade her from ever playing that instrument again and to find something more suitable for a lady - a cittern. I had her score confiscated and placed it in my keep, where it will remain and cause no more harm to the preservation of the Union."

"King Kong?" Jackie repeated, looking over William's shoulder at the diary. "Let me see that."

CHAPTER 10

The security clearance Tara requested for Adeena had been denied.

There was no reason provided by either the Ottawa Police or the Canadian Security Intelligence Service. There was just a simple "X" in one of the checkboxes beside the "DENIED" option on the form for *Level I Security Clearance Certificate* in regards to 'Adeena Rose Stuart'. Getting that certificate was a requirement of the insurance company for any person with private access to the Duncan Cello.

Tara had worried this would happen. She wondered what sort of a file there might be on Adeena, who had suffered more than a few brushes with the law during her stormy teenage years.

As Tara left her office to deliver the bad news, she recalled one awful summer night in particular, soon after they had both turned 18. Adeena had gone to a party that ended wildly out of control. Kurt – the boyfriend Adeena swooned over and Tara loathed - had invited his mates from the avant-garde rock band that he and Adeena had formed. They in turn invited their friends, and it seemed to Tara, most of the entire Grade 12 class at Nepean High School, to a backyard pool party at his sprawling

Westboro house. His parents, of course, were out of town for the weekend.

By the time the police arrived, the flashing lights of their cruisers washing over the whole neighbourhood, Kurt's house and the party were in shambles. There was a motorcycle in the pool, and the police arrested a couple of kids dealing drugs. Adeena was charged after getting into a nasty fight with one of the other girls, who told the police she wanted to press charges.

Tara had stood up for her friend, insisting that Adeena was acting in self-defense when she punched the 'bitch' in the head and knocked her into the pool. The fact that Adeena then jumped into the water to bite said 'bitch' was harder to explain.

Oh Miss Adeena...

Was she the sister Tara never had? She certainly created enough trouble for both of them. Tara's parents would never put up with the stunts Adeena pulled. A Greek father and an Indian mother – you just don't fuck around with them. They were results people – one a lawyer, the other a deputy minister in the government, and they made it clear they had zero tolerance for teenage nonsense.

Tara had just accepted that as a fact of Indo-Greek life.

As she strode towards Adeena's office, Tara mused how she had vicariously lived her teenage years through her best friend. She had nursed Adeena through bad relationships, lectured her on drugs, booze and sex, and helped her deal with problems that seemed to follow her around every corner. And she had been there after the prom when Adeena overdosed and lay near death in the hospital for two long days and two even longer nights.

Surviving her best friend's teenage years had been exhausting. Tara had sacrificed so much as Adeena's eternally patient guardian angel, that she never had the chance at introspection, to figure who *she* was, or what *she* wanted from life.

Maybe when I hit thirty, she thought with a smile as she reached Adeena's office, I'll quit my job, travel to Greece and track down the god of debauchery, or a rugged guy that looks a lot like him. I'll get drunk, smoke cigarettes and have an orgy for a whole month.

Tara walked into Adeena's office and braced herself. "Dee – you've been a naughty girl. I can't get your security clearance approved." She tried to strike a sympathetic tone. "I'm going to keep working on it, but I'll need your help."

Adeena sat engrossed on her computer. She didn't react the way Tara had expected. "Jerks," Adeena finally responded without taking her eyes from the computer screen.

Tara sighed. "Well, until I can find out what skeletons they've unearthed, you can't be alone with the Duncan Cello. We'll have to keep the music technician around to play it for now. You're not authorized."

Adeena looked up at Tara blankly. "Really?" she said, releasing a sigh of disgust before turning back to the screen, peering closely at the web page she had been absorbed in studying.

Tara always had a hard time understanding her friend. Why did she attract problems to her like moths to a floodlight? Why couldn't Adeena learn that dreams usually turn out to be fantasies that lead you over a cliff? Why did she always choose the rockiest road? The one that led nowhere or to a place of pain, misery?

Is that why she can't get a *Level I Security Clearance Certificate?* Tara thought. Is she just a pathological rule-breaker? Tara looked at her best friend, her 'sister' and unfortunately, the subordinate she was supposed to manage. Adeena sat reading the computer screen, ignoring Tara as if she wasn't even there.

That trip to Greece sounds really good, Tara thought. "How's your research going for the exhibit?" she finally offered. "You like the name we came up with? *Art of Rebellion?*"

There was a pause and Adeena finally turned her head and looked serious. "I do," she replied, still absorbed by the article on the screen. "Did you know the Duncan Cello had a direct role in the rebellion, the 1745 Jacobite uprising?" Adeena had a faraway look in her eyes. "I didn't really know about it before, but I'm starting to get it now. I feel very connected to it somehow."

Tara studied Adeena. She always took everything to an impossible level. "You do? Why?" Tara replied. Then she noticed the reflection on Adeena's hand. "What's this?"

"It's from Philippe."

"You're wearing it on your right hand?"

Adeena looked down and took the ring off. "I shouldn't be wearing it on any hand." She closed her fingers around it and stared at the ground.

Tara couldn't believe what she was hearing. "You said no?"

Adeena nodded. Tara moved closer and touched Adeena's shoulder. "He loves you. I thought you..."

"It's not him." Adeena interrupted. "I'm not ready, or I'm not..." She paused, looking up as if searching for an answer.

"You're not what?"

"I don't know, exactly. Maybe, not ready to be his wife," she sighed.

"Why? Is there somebody else?"

Adeena hesitated. "It's my music, Tar. I'm so focused right now. I think I've finally found my voice."

Tara bit her lip, frowning. Music was always tied to heartbreak for Adeena – from two-timing Kurt and their punkish band that went nowhere, through ten years of auditions with bad endings and projects.

"Dee, will that really make you happy?" Tara started, forming the outline of another counselling session in her head. "I thought you were paddling over Niagara Falls with this whole music thing?"

"I was. But yesterday I got invited to the join the NAC Orchestra."

Tara's heart jumped. Finally, after all these years. "What? You didn't tell me that!"

Adeena smiled and Tara leaned over the chair and wrapped her arms around her. "Congratulations!" She felt such pride for her friend. Adeena had been through so much to finally get to this day. The NAC orchestra! It always seemed like a wild dream that would end in crushing disappointment.

A tap on the open office door interrupted them. It was Tara's new assistant Pablo, on his second day at work. His wife was an old friend, and Tara had given the young art history graduate a term assignment as a favour to her.

"Ms. Kormos," he said, looking like he had important news. "They really need you to look at something for the new exhibit." Then he added with a sense of urgency. "They want you to come and see it, right now."

Tara motioned for Adeena to follow her. "Thanks Pablo, we're on our way."

TRAVELLING EXHIBITS AT THE NATIONAL GALLERY OF CANADA brought in much needed revenue to the institution. Hopes were high that the *Art of Rebellion,* featuring the Duncan Cello which had received so much media coverage, would be a smashing success, both artistically and perhaps more importantly, financially.

Adeena had managed to get the star artifact of the show back to the Gallery on Saturday morning without incident, thanks to Michael. She knew it wasn't fair to flirt with the young clerk who worked the weekend shift in security. But no crime was committed, Adeena rationalized. No one was harmed through her using an instrument that needed to be played every day and that seemed to belong to her anyway.

"Like the sign?" Tara interrupted as they approached the entrance to the area of the gallery where temporary exhibits were staged.

Adeena studied the huge hanging banner – a photograph of the Duncan Cello trimmed to the contours on the right side. It was so large that it dominated the three-storey glass atrium. An even larger version hung outside the gallery. The lettering was simple, written as if in haste, with the splotched ink drops of a sloppy quill:

Art of Rebellion - Art de la rébellion

The silhouette of a bayonet-tipped musket served as an accent under the lettering. The background imagery was a landscape painting of the misty Scottish Highlands. Adeena stared at it for a moment thinking about Katharine Carnegie and her two brothers, George and the Captain, and of course the young man James Drummond. She had just been reading about them online in her attempt to sort out the characters of her 'dream'.

The people she had met were all real. And Kinnaird was real. How could she have dreamed of historical characters and places she was completely unaware of last week? Had she heard it all before and simply forgotten?

Strange though, she had yet to find anything on Katharine Carnegie. There was nothing anywhere on her – from *Wikipedia* to the extensive subscription-only databases she had access to through her National Gallery research account.

Tara touched Adeena's shoulder, bringing her back to the present with a start.

"Let's take a look," Tara said, motioning Adeena forward.

The women, along with Pablo, walked past the signage through a wide entrance into the exhibit. One wall had been set up to resemble the exterior of a castle and two mannequins dressed as soldiers faced off against each other.

One was dressed as a Highland clansman, wearing a blue bonnet, plaid waistcoat and a tartan kilt. His sword was thrust straight ahead, threatening the other man, who was meticulously outfitted as an English Redcoat, his long red uniform covering his knees and hiding most of his earthen-coloured breeches. The Redcoat aimed his bayonet-tipped musket directly at the head of the clansman.

"What do you think Dee?" Tara mused. "Like to have these two over for drinks sometime?"

Adeena stood in silence. The English soldier reminded her of the men who had cheered on her performance. But these were lifeless mannequins, wanna-be models for 18th century military fashion.

"Is it historically accurate?" Tara asked. "You've been researching this stuff, haven't you?"

"Yes, I have. But they are *too* pretty – too clean, too neat," Adeena responded. "They didn't look like this. These guys look more like they want to pose for Abercrombie and Fitch." Adeena shuffled around the mannequins, touching the buttons on the Redcoat's uniform. "We need to give them some grit, some life. They didn't have dry-cleaning back then. Why don't we dirty them up a bit?"

Tara shook her head in disagreement. "No can do," she said. "We got these from the National Museums in Edinburgh. I believe they *are* big fans of dry-cleaning."

Adeena turned away from the mannequins. She looked around at the portraits and the paintings on the walls as Tara was called away with a question from the carpenter. He was building another wall that needed to look as though it was made of stone.

A shiver of *déjà-vu* shook Adeena's shoulders. She felt undone standing there, staring at those reflections of characters frozen in time. Their passions long forsaken, they were now reduced to stiff lifeless portraitures. Static faces masked the fiery spirit that she knew burned inside.

She looked more closely at one portrait in particular of a man who looked oddly familiar. She read the description beside the portrait. It was James Drummond, the tall man who had been 'smitten' by her first performance at Kinnaird. In the portrait, his square shoulders and stoic face belied the charm he had conveyed in their brief encounter following her performance.

Taking advantage of Tara's distraction with the carpenter, Adeena squinted and pitched her head from side-to-side, feeling the memory of James' face pulse to life. She shut her eyes to help conjure the feeling of seeing him, and then alternated opening and closing her left and right eyelids. After a moment, the eyes in the painting seemed to come alive! James was staring down at Adeena, his eyes locked on hers. She blushed as memories of the gleam of gold, the clink of glasses, twinkling chandeliers, the aroma of a wood fire and the perfumed necks of the ladies flooded over her.

He held his gaze on her, and she felt her cheeks growing warm. And then he bowed gracefully, lowering his head and his shoulders in respect. He rose from the bow and raised a hand towards her, and seemed to mouth 'my lady'.

Adeena snapped back from her haze to see James' portrait, stiff and dreary. In those few moments with him, she had gotten to know his spirit better than any art historian could ever hope.

"Dee – take a look at this," Tara called out.

Adeena looked over at the huge fresco on the opposite wall. It was a scene that featured a musical performance and what looked like a woman playing the Duncan Cello. Was it Katharine Carnegie performing at Kinnaird Castle?

Adeena froze.

Am I going mad?

There was that boxy piano and the other musicians from her dream – the violinist and the man on the viola. There was the same gathering of men and women, dressed like those she had seen. Adeena moved closer to read the description of the art:

Preparing for War: A music recital in 1745, inspires Jacobite supporters to pledge allegiance to Bonnie Prince Charles, son of the 'young Pretender' who would be King.

"This is where we'll display the Duncan Cello," Tara announced, pointing to a wooden podium that a carpenter was sanding.

Adeena nodded, still absorbed by the fresco. "You're displaying the Duncan Cello here?" she asked doubtfully.

"Yup. And see those lights in the ceiling?" Tara replied, raising her arm upward to a set of recessed pot lights aimed at the podium under construction. "It will light it up, very dramatically. And, I was thinking, maybe we need a soundtrack to play in the background. What do you think, Dee?"

Adeena frowned. Once the exhibit opened in two weeks all the flirting in the world wasn't going to help her get close to the Duncan. Only that dim-witted music technician would get to play it as part of the cello's maintenance regimen.

"Well?" Tara repeated, still waiting for Adeena's response.

"I think that for once, Tar, you need to trust me," she huffed. "I can maintain the Duncan Cello better than any jerk-off music tech guy, and we both know it."

"Can we discuss this somewhere else?" Tara responded as the carpenter chuckled to himself. Pablo stood beside her, rocking uneasily.

"I'm sorry, I didn't mean to put it quite that way," Adeena said softening her tone. "The Duncan Cello needs a professional musician to play it. Is there no way around this stupid security certificate thing, Tar?"

"Absolutely not," Tara replied forcefully. "You know Dee, I'm really tired of always cleaning up after you. It's not my job to be your fairy godmother and grant your three wishes whenever you don't get your way."

"So that's it, then?" Adeena asked. Why couldn't Tara relax for once in her life, quit drinking all that bureaucratic Kool-Aid?

"Yup. No means no. You simply cannot play that cello without a security clearance." Tara pronounced. "End of discussion."

Adeena snapped. Losing access to that cello was worth fighting for, even if it meant losing her job and her best friend. "Thanks Tara. You're a great administrator," Adeena snorted. "Protecting the government from bad girls like me. What's next?

You going to post my criminal record on Facebook? Why don't you just trust me?"

Tara glared at Adeena. "That cello is worth five-million-dollars, Adeena!" Tara replied. "It's not a matter of trust. If something happens to it and we void the insurance, then we're–"

"Fucked?" Adeena barked in a mocking tone.

Pablo and the carpenter both grimaced and looked at Tara.

"You're out of line, Ms. Stuart," Tara bristled.

"Good!" Adeena shouted. "I'm tired of being *in* line, following all your stupid rules that make absolutely no sense! You've got a cellist with the NAC Orchestra and you hire a high school dropout to play a precious instrument he can barely even tune?"

"He's a dropout with Level I Security Clearance! I'll bet he doesn't have a police record!"

"Yeah, that's because he still lives at home sucking mother's milk all day!"

"You're dismissed, Ms. Stuart," Tara said coldly. "Please leave."

"Gladly! Good luck opening your exhibit in two weeks! Your other slaves are all out getting lobotomies at the mall. I'm sure they'll make great researchers!"

THE INSTRUMENTS IN THOMAS PEETERS' SHOP IN GATINEAU, across the river from Ottawa, did not come cheaply.

For the past twenty-five years, the luthier had created nearly a whole orchestra worth of stringed instruments including reproductions of originals created by Antonio Stradivari. Thomas, who started working on violins at thirteen, studied violin-making in France and Italy after leaving Belgium and honed his craft across Europe with specialized training in the restoration of baroque-era stringed instruments.

More than a few members of the NAC Orchestra played on a

violin, viola or cello created in his small Victoria Street workshop. Thomas spent time getting to know each musician who commissioned an instrument from him. He wanted to understand their preferences regarding the tone they wanted, the comfort and playability sought, and of course the overall look of the hand-crafted instrument he would create for them. He finished each one lovingly, in the knowledge it would be played for many years and handed down from generation to generation.

Adeena had heard about Thomas Peeters from Walter, who played one of his cellos and often talked about the luthier's understanding of the relationship between musician and musical instrument. Walter said Thomas was a master craftsman, who was moved by the music that was produced by the cellos and violins he created. He even cared for each of his 'children' long after they left his workshop, with regular maintenance and ever-so-precise adjustments.

Adeena, cooling off after locking horns with Tara, was at home scowling at her computer screen. She regretted letting her temper get the better of her. Tara was a true friend that she had always relied on. Maybe someday I'll be there for her, Adeena thought.

If only she could get that broom out of her ass.

Tara needed something or someone who would sweep her off her feet. Somebody who showed her that ecstasy doesn't come from balancing a budget or writing another fucking report.

Trying to stay focused, and put Tara out of her mind, Adeena continued to browse Thomas Peeters' website. She read about his background and training. His workshop blog was full of detailed accounts about the instruments he created or restored, and the musicians he had worked with over the years.

She read how Thomas sometimes replicated instruments that inspired him, such as *The Lady Tennant,* a violin crafted in 1699 by Antonio Stradivari. The original survived dozens of owners, numerous wars and ended up in Scotland where Sir Charles Tennant gave it as a gift to his wife Marguerite, an amateur violinist. It was sold in 2005 for over two million dollars and was loaned to the Belgian violinist Yossif Ivanov. Apparently Thomas was so moved by the story of the violin's journey to his fellow countrymen, that he devoted himself to a painstaking recreation of the baroque-era instrument as a kind of homage to his craft.

Adeena picked up her phone to call him. She had a very special assignment for him.

One she hoped he would not be able to resist.

THOMAS PEETERS' WANTED TO GET TO WORK A LITTLE EARLIER than usual this morning.

He swept a hand over his receding hairline as if stroking his shock of chestnut-coloured hair would somehow propel him more quickly down the street. Thomas had an extra jump in his forty-five-year-old legs today. He touched his glasses as he caught sight of his quaint two-storey red-bricked shop, which lay just ahead of him. He was more eager to be at work than he had been in some time.

His workshop, home to many of the same tools used by stringed instrument makers for the last three hundred years, took up the first floor of a renovated two-storey house on a little street near the Canadian Museum of History. As he turned the key and opened the heavy wooden front door, he wondered about how he should handle the strange request he had received yesterday afternoon.

The National Gallery of Canada needed a replica of the Duncan Cello, and they needed it *fast*. He had been dying to see it since he learned it was in Ottawa, and now in a few minutes, a woman from the gallery was bringing it for him to see firsthand. She was a friend of Walter Leo, one of his oldest and most loyal customers.

While a pot of his aromatic loose-leaf English breakfast tea sat steeping near his workbench, he scanned his email and opened a web browser. Within a few minutes he had found the Duncan Cello and begun reading about its history, and its creator Robert Duncan of Aberdeen. Thomas studied pictures of the cello closely. He guessed that its creator had spent time in Cremona, Italy. Robert Duncan might have even worked with Antonio Stradivari himself, he thought adjusting his reading glasses.

Thomas sat back and poured himself a steaming mug of tea. As he stirred in a little sugar, he wondered what it would have been like for the young Scottish craftsman to apprentice with the master himself. What secrets had he learned? What insights had he gained into the acoustics, the varnishes, and a hundred other tiny details that only someone who created an instrument from bundles of raw wood could truly appreciate?

A knock on the front door startled him from his thoughts. As he set his mug down, the front door opened slowly. He stood up from his stool.

"Hello?" a woman called out. She stepped inside, holding a large Bam cello case, usually reserved for shipping instruments overseas. He knew the hard shell case was designed to protect its precious cargo suspended snugly inside on plush cushions.

"Hi!" he responded, stepping closer to greet her. "Thomas Peeters. Let me help you with that." He took the cello case from her and stood it beside him.

"Thanks. I'm Adeena. We talked yesterday on the phone?" she said. "Thank you so much for making time to see me."

Thomas looked at the young woman standing before him. Her long copper-tinged hair and green eyes were striking. Somehow she had the look and carriage of a classical musician, the featured virtuoso.

"No problem. Thank you for calling me," he replied. "Come in, come in. I was just reading about your cello. Fascinating!"

Adeena's eyes lit up and the force of her smile almost

knocked him over. What was it the Borg used to say to their victims before they were absorbed into the collective?

Resistance is futile?

A beautiful classical musician carrying a five-million-dollar baroque instrument could have just about anything she wanted in this workshop.

"Let's take a look at your cello," he smiled, as Adeena took off her jacket and placed it over a chair. He laid the case down on the floor. She leaned over and unfastened the latches of the Bam flight case, revealing another cello case nested inside. Gingerly she opened the second case and stood back, unveiling the prize he had been so anxious to see.

"The Duncan Cello," Thomas said reverently, absorbing the full majesty of the old instrument. He sighed in appreciation. "Oh! Verrrry nice. Yes, I can see he must have learned his craft in Italy. I think he apprenticed in Stradivari's workshop."

"Robert Duncan? The man who built the cello?" Adeena asked.

"Yes. His style is definitely influenced by Stradivari, and from what I've been reading, he likely spent time in Cremona, perhaps even working with him," Thomas replied. He carefully lifted the cello from its case and laid it on the blanket that covered his workbench.

Adeena sat down on a stool beside Thomas as he delicately examined the cello, like a jeweller inspecting a precious gem. He used a lamp attached to a hinged arm positioned over his bench to illuminate the instrument, studying every edge and groove of the antique subject that lay before him.

"Can you do it?" Adeena finally asked. "In a week?"

Thomas looked up and studied the young woman sitting beside him. This was no government bureaucrat. There was a fire inside her that could melt stainless steel.

He thought for a moment before responding. "The replica you need, it's for display only? No one will play it?" he asked.

"No *musician* will play it," she said, with what sounded like a hint of sarcasm. "It's really just for display, but it has to look exactly like the real Duncan Cello. We need a kind of 'stunt double' to fill in for the exhibit, whenever the real one is . . ." she hesitated for a moment. "You know, removed from the exhibit. The real Duncan needs to be played every day."

He nodded. It did make sense, and he knew that if this was essentially a prop, he could meet the deadline, as long as he dropped everything else.

"You play, right, Adeena? Did I hear you say you're with the NAC Orchestra?" he asked.

"Yes, I just got offered a position. We're starting rehearsals this week," she replied.

Thomas smiled and offered his hand to her. "Congratulations! I knew there was an opening. That's quite an accomplishment." He offered her his hand. "Would you do me the honour of playing for me? I'd love to hear the tone of this cello. I've been wondering about it since you called me yesterday."

"Oh," she hesitated, and Thomas wondered if he was being too forward. Some musicians didn't need much coaxing, especially when he created the companion so integral to their artistry. But not all musicians felt that way.

"Yes, certainly. It's so special to play," Adeena said, lifting the instrument from its case. She looked up at Thomas. "I have some music that was first performed on this cello in the 18th Century."

Thomas took a step back and sat down as she got ready to play for him. This was turning out to be quite a morning.

CHAPTER 11

Adeena drew the cello closer to her, like an old friend. Thomas watched her intently as she prepared to play. He was someone who truly appreciated the Duncan, but even he did not realize its significance. And as with Walter, she felt a sense of trust for him. Here was a craftsman who devoted himself to the relationship between musician and instrument – the personalities of each fusing to create texture, tone and, if both had it within them, the expression of human emotion.

Adeena closed her eyes, focusing on the lost score. She had come straight from the National Gallery to this little shop a few blocks away, not knowing how things might unfold. She looked again at Thomas, who sat transfixed. He was waiting for her to bring the Duncan Cello to life.

She began to play, unable to resist its pull for another second. Thomas' face lit up as she lovingly coaxed the first dark, sweet tones from the old instrument. Her head began to swim again as the music poured from her, like a river racing to the sea. She was on a mystic journey, her bow revealing the path forward.

Adeena felt the warmth of sunlight streaming onto her, brilliant and strong. She opened her eyes and was back in the castle.

Kinnaird? But now it was daytime, and she sitting on a wooden chair, playing the cello as if she was practicing by herself. She was in the same physical space, the same room as last time. But it looked nothing like before.

The furniture in the room was covered in cloth, pushed together in the middle of the open space, as if it was being stored. The area felt abandoned. No matter, she was alone with a cello that responded to her thoughts as naturally as when she curled her toes or opened her eyes.

Adeena found depth in every note and chord in this ancient place. The tones seemed at home with the oil paintings and wool tapestries on the wall behind her. A soft ray of sunlight illuminated her from behind, as if a lighting director from the heavens had focused it upon her.

As she reached the section where the vocals were about to begin, she saw a man in the corner she hadn't noticed before. It was George, Katharine's brother. He smiled and nodded his head. This all felt so natural, and as she began to sing, the power of her voice was reflected on George. His eyes, his mouth, his dream-like expression, even his posture seemed captivated.

After she finished he approached. "Katharine," he called out, as he made his way closer to her.

Why did this all seem so real? Was she actually Katharine Carnegie or was she just in a very real hallucination? George approached and touched her shoulder. "Katharine, your music feels like salvation," he whispered. "It is as if I am lost in a dark sea when a ship made of stars lifts me from the depths and carries me upward."

She studied the serious look on his face. She felt a tear forming. "Thank you, George," she replied. "This cello and I have a connection. It inspires me each time I perform with it."

George's serious look softened into a smile. "Maestro Duncan knows you well."

Adeena stared at George, her brother – or at least

Katharine's brother. "Robert Duncan, the cello maker? He knows me?"

"Aye, he does indeed, darling sister! You performed with his quartet and he told me he would create a bespoke instrument for the only lady, indeed the only musician, he had met that truly understood the voice of a violoncello."

'Violoncello.' The original name for the cello and still a name many preferred. But wait, the Duncan Cello was created for her? For Lady Katharine?

Adeena looked down at the cello. It did seem to fit her. The grip of the fingerboard and the neck, the width of the body, even the placement of the F-holes and the finishings, the scroll, the pegs, all felt as naturally suited to her as her own skin. And it wasn't just the physical features that seemed made for her. It was the tone and the harmonic resonance – almost as if there was a music box inside of it connected directly to her mind.

"You are aware too, that your music has given our cause new inspiration?" George said, his tone changing.

"Our cause? The rising?"

George looked at her curiously. She had spent the last few days reading about the 1745 Jacobite rebellion in Scotland or the 'rising' as it came to be called.

"Yes, of course, sister!" he replied. "The plans are becoming somewhat urgent. I received a request from the Duke of Perth for you."

"Duke of Perth?"

"James Drummond, the leader who saw you perform here three nights past," George said, looking over his shoulder. He began walking towards the door. "I think he may be here now. Will you see him?"

Adeena set the cello aside and looked towards the door where George was headed. She heard the sounds of a horse approaching, hooves clattering heavily on the stones. Suddenly the rich aromas of the castle – the smoke of a wood fire and the fragrance of lavender wreaths – caused her nose to twitch. She looked down at her earthen dress, simple but elegant in its fullness. Her long hair was gathered to one side and she pulled a lock down to see it was the same coppery colour she was used to.

"Come, Katharine," George called from just outside the door.

Adeena hurried towards it and heard George greeting someone. As she approached the entrance, she recognized the massive wooden chandelier that held dozens of thick, sooty candles, now long extinguished. She walked outside under the stone archway and saw George standing near the tall man who had been so taken with her performance.

James Drummond – the Duke of Perth, she thought as he turned to her, still holding the reins of his chestnut brindle stallion. The muscular horse turned towards her, as if he needed to size her up for himself. His wet nostrils flared widely, and he lowered his head slightly. Their eyes locked together briefly and she felt a kind of understanding sweep between them.

She saw her own reflection in the panorama of the horse's immense brown eyes and wondered what he was thinking. The stallion raised its head, then shook a fly from one ear with a massive shiver. He lowered his whole head in the direction of his master and gave a loud snort.

The man grinned. "My lady! You have even charmed Balgair, and he has yet to hear you play." He bowed slightly, still holding the reins of his horse. "James Drummond, at your service Lady Katharine. I have ridden from Perthshire to ask a favour."

She stared at James. He was a curious mix of soft features drawn over a hard frame. Tall and sturdy with a few days growth of beard, long sandy hair and a plaid cape, Adeena thought he would have no trouble passing for a rock star in her world.

Balgair snorted and tried to lift his head, pulling against the reins.

"Whoa!" James exclaimed, holding on tightly as the horse turned towards the stables off in the distance. "Will you walk with me?"

Adeena looked at George. He said nothing, but his smile seemed to convey approval. She turned toward James, holding the reins to his horse, who clearly had designs on the prospect of a meal after the long ride.

"Sure," Adeena finally responded.

James smiled as George looked towards the stables. "Take your horse there," he said pointing to the grey barn far off in the distance. "Use all the water and oats you require."

JAMES DRUMMOND HAD CAREFULLY PLANNED FOR THIS moment.

Lady Katharine was all he had thought of the past three days. Her music had touched him, inside a place he did not know even existed before he heard her perform at Kinnaird. She had swept him away and inspired his imagination.

He had also seen the effect her music had on his men – men he would soon lead into a battle that many would not survive. The rebellion to restore King James was just beginning, and although he had his own dreams about a future transformed by science and discovery, he knew his obligation was to lead his clan in support of the restoration of the Scottish nation.

He glanced at Katharine on one side of him and at Balgair on the other, walking with his usual sense of equine independence. The three found a natural synchronization as they made their way towards the weathered grey stables that lay across the meadow.

"Lady Katharine," he began, having rehearsed his speech during the long ride from his home at Drummond Castle.

"James," she responded. "Just call me..." There was a hesitation as he noticed a thoughtful manner come over the lady. "Katharine?" she said finally, with an air of uncertainty.

"Katharine, my lady," James repeated. "You have made a great impression on me, and those who follow me and pledge allegiance to our Bonnie Prince, Charles Edward." James was aware of the stiff manner of his speech, and that the lady probably thought him foolish beyond reproach.

"Thank you," she responded.

Balgair lowered his head a little as they continued to walk across the field. James hoped the stallion was not too embarrassed by his master's clumsy conversation. He had told his speedy mount all about her during their three-hour ride this morning through the lowland forests, pastures and bogs of the Angus countryside.

"Your music speaks to me," he continued, "I have never before in all my two and thirty years experienced that kind of poetry and musical composition. But even more than that..." James stopped walking as his horse tugged at the reins.

"You might think me a fool, Katharine," he said turning towards the lady now. "But alas, I am fool that has been shown light to guide me through the darkness. It has given me a desire, that I did not know existed within me."

Lady Katharine looked at him with a perplexed countenance. Her emerald eyes stared through him. The sun danced in the shiny copper locks flowing over her shoulders.

"I mean not to be bold or offensive with my words, my lady," he said, thinking suddenly that he had gone too far with his speech. "Please accept my apologies if you think my intentions unworthy."

"James, relax," Katharine smiled. "I'm really glad that you like my music."

He felt his tension disappear. "You speak plainly, Katharine," he replied with a smile. "You have an air about you that is refreshing, a tone that sets you apart."

Balgair seemed to tire of the conversation. He made his feelings known by a loud *neigh* and began to jerk his head back and forth.

"I think he's hungry," Katharine laughed. "Let's find him something to eat!"

"Aye! He grows tired of his master's sorrowful tongue." James looked at the stables, far off in the distance. "Katharine, ride with me to the Kinnaird stables? Until Balgair is served his oats, we will not know peace."

She looked up at the towering horse and the rider before her. Her eyes seemed to consider the proposition a moment. "Yes. Of course."

James smiled and mounted Balgair first, before taking Katharine's hand to help her up behind him. As Balgair started to trot, she wrapped her arms around James to steady herself.

It had been a long time since he had ridden thus with a lady. Not since he and Rosalyne had spent the summer of his eighteenth year together in France, had he felt the pleasure of a woman on his mount.

"Are you all right Lady Katharine?" he asked, as Balgair's trot quickened suddenly.

"Yes, I'm good," she responded, tightening her grip around him as he gave the horse a kick of encouragement.

As they rode across the lane and on towards the stables over a mile away, James patted Balgair's sturdy neck. He had earned a few extra apples this afternoon.

ADEENA LOVED HORSEBACK RIDING.

As a child, she and Tara had spent time with Angela, a classmate who had her own horse and spent most weekends on the farm with her mother. Adeena had learned about grooming, riding, feeding and generally everything related to horses. She had discovered much about their behaviour from Angela – and was impressed that horses naturally sensed a person's fears and according to her friend, their intentions.

As she held on to James, riding on his powerful stallion across a pasture of golden grass under a clear blue sky, she wondered again what was happening. It seemed clear that she and Katharine Carnegie were connected. The Duncan Cello and the lost score belonged to both of them. Or was she really Katharine herself?

"My lady. Your instincts are correct about Balgair," James shouted as the horse began to gallop. "Hold on!"

All four of the horse's legs seemed to leave the ground simultaneously, as Balgair pushed with every muscle in his massive frame to reach top speed. A knot of fear dropped to her stomach, and she gripped James' chest tightly. She could feel him inhale and exhale more and more as they thundered towards the stables.

The countryside flew by her. She saw a kaleidoscope of towering trees, rolling hills, moors, pastures, herds of cattle, and stone houses. All these flashed by her as she clung to James while Balgair took them on a wild dash, faster than any horse ride she had ever been on at Angela's ranch. She felt exhilarated as the stable drew closer and the powerful beast finally began to slow.

Balgair came to a stop in front of the door to the grey barn. Adeena tried in vain to catch her breath. She was winded.

"I'm sorry, Katharine," James said, turning his head to look at her. "His stomach is a force of nature, much beyond being tamed by a mortal such as me!"

"It's fine," she gasped. "Wow! That was totally... totally awesome!"

James laughed out loud. "The lady is pleased?"

"Oh yeah!" Adeena panted trying to catch her breath. She realized he was confused by her modern words. "It was exceptionally divine," she said, feeling slightly foolish.

He laughed once more. "Direct your thanks to my noble beast who believes he is a mighty eagle, not just a horse. His appetite is the one thing I can truly rely on each and every day." James turned to face her. "Here, let me help you down," he offered.

He kept a hold on one of her hands as she completed the dismount. She looked up from the ground at him still sitting in the saddle. The sun shone directly into her eyes, creating a silhouette of the tall rider before her, and his even taller four-legged companion.

AFTER THEY HAD ATTENDED TO BALGAIR'S MOST URGENT needs for oats and water, James set him free in the pasture. Adeena didn't see a fence or anything to prevent the horse from running away.

"You're not afraid he will run away?" she asked James.

"If he wanted to leave, no wall in Scotland could hold him," he responded. "He is free to stay with me or to find sweeter heather elsewhere."

Balgair a few yards away, turned and looked at both of them for a second, before continuing his quest for the tender shoots of tall grasses around him. Adeena nodded her head in understanding. She had always admired the bond between rider and horse, but had never seen it demonstrated quite like this.

"James, you told me there was something you wanted to ask me?" she said as they walked, following the grazing horse ahead of them.

"Indeed I do," he replied. "Katharine, would you honour our cause with a recital of your music at Drummond Castle? Prince Charles himself makes his war council there on Saturday, and has asked my mother Lady Jean to host a ball to celebrate his landing in the Highlands and his recent proclamation of the King."

"A ball?"

"Aye. The Prince wishes his subjects to regain their pride now that he has declared Scotland a Kingdom once more and proclaimed his father, King James, our Catholic sovereign. We no longer need pledge allegiance to the Protestant rulers in London. The English time in our land is coming to an end. Will you help us celebrate?"

"I'm not sure if I can," Adeena said. "How would I get there?"

James seemed relieved with her weak but nevertheless positive response. "Your brother George travels to Perthshire in a few days," he said. "Come with him and stay at Drummond. I have talked to the Prince about you, and he thinks you may be a sign, an omen of success to come. He is planning to march on Edinburgh very soon."

Adeena looked over at James. She might be Katharine Carnegie to him, but she was still Adeena Stuart inside. She weighed the implications of all this and how she should respond.

"Will you honour us with your music?" James pressed her. "You have a voice and a tone in your violoncello that strike deeply. Your words and your music stayed with me long after I left Kinnaird last week. Indeed, I have thought of little else since."

Adeena felt her cheeks flush. He seemed to have been captured by the music she had created and performed as Katharine. It was the kind of creation she had always longed to find. All her life she had been searching for the keys to unlock the music in her head, music that longed for release.

"Thank you, James," she finally responded, as they meandered through the long grasses, following behind Balgair. "I have wanted to be a musician and to perform all my life. But more than that, I have wanted to compose, to create music that..." she paused, reflecting on what drove her in such a maddening way, "...music that truly connects with others."

"You have succeeded," James replied. "You have connected with me. It feels like your music comes from a place deep inside of you."

Adeena stopped walking. He seemed to understand everything even if he had no idea of what was really happening to her. He was staring at her, waiting for an answer.

"I would be honoured to perform at your ball."

George seemed anxious when Adeena made it back. She had walked slowly back to the castle after James had departed. His words echoed in her mind as she approached the archway.

"Katharine," George shouted. "Come here!"

She hurried the final steps up the cobbled lane and stood near George.

"What is it?"

"You are coming with me to Perthshire?" he asked.

"Yes. Yes, I am."

"Thank you, sister. I was not sure that I should be the one to respond when James solicited my advice," he said. "We shall leave Kinnaird on Friday, at first light."

The loud crack of gunfire in the distance startled both of them. Moments later, from around the back of the walled garden, their brother, the Captain in the British army, approached on his white mare. He brought the horse towards them and pulled the reins tightly to an abrupt halt.

"We saw the traitor," the Captain shouted.

"Traitor? Who?" George asked, raising his voice to the same level as that of his inflamed brother.

"James Drummond, from Perth," the Captain seethed. "One of my officers saw him leaving Kinnaird, but was unable to apprehend him." The Captain dismounted quickly, anger in his eyes. "There is a thirty-thousand-pound bounty on the head of his 'Young Pretender' master, the so-called 'Bonnie Prince'. But I will satisfy myself with Drummond for his treason in the Highlands assisting the Jacobites."

"You'll never catch him," George sneered. "The Duke rides a beast that the devil himself has no dominion over."

"If you support Perth, you are a traitor too!" the Captain exclaimed, spitting in disgust. Then he turned towards Adeena.

"I may not be my brother's keeper, but I do control you," he warned. "I forbid you from having any society with that Drummond scourge who will soon hang from the highest gallows in Edinburgh."

"You're not my keeper either," Adeena shot back. "You don't *control* me."

"Do not test me Katharine," the Captain threatened. "You will lose."

"Chill!" she retorted, suddenly feeling dizzy, bending over in pain, and lowering her tone. "Oh God! I think I need to sit down."

Adeena felt the world growing darker. Her head tilted back and she felt herself grow weak as George rushed closer.

"Katharine, what is it?" he asked.

Adeena could not speak as all the light disappeared from her world and she fell into George's waiting arms.

CHAPTER 12

It was just like Adeena, Walter mused as he hurried toward the cello maker's shop in Gatineau. She always took everything to the extreme. It had been like this since he had watched her first perform as a little girl – her tiny hands barely able to grasp the bow and reach across the fingerboard.

Even back then, Walter thought she had a musical gift. He warned her father that true artists usually suffer. But as he and William watched young Adeena sawing away with determined ferocity on her child-sized cello, they both knew nothing would stop her.

Walter parked his gleaming Camaro on a side street near Thomas Peeters' shop, leaving lots of space between it and the mud-caked van in front of him, glad there was no other vehicle behind. He hurried over to see what in the world was happening this time. The call from Thomas this morning had been troubling.

"Thank God you're here," Thomas exclaimed as Walter opened the front door.

Adeena sat hunched over in a wooden chair. She seemed to be asleep, head down, body sagging.

"Adeena?" Walter called out to her. He touched her shoulder lightly. "Adeena?"

"She played the most amazing piece I've ever heard. Ever!" Thomas exclaimed as Walter studied her. "She brought me the Duncan Cello, and she even sang, I almost cried listening to her, and then..."

Thomas paused and Walter looked over puzzled. "And, then... what?"

"She seemed to go into a trance and then she just kind of passed out," Thomas replied. "Does she have narcolepsy or whatever you call it when someone just falls asleep?"

Before Walter could reply, Adeena took a deep breath and opened her eyes. She stared at them, disoriented.

"You okay, Adeena?" Walter asked, lightly touching the back of her head.

"Ohhhhhh..." she moaned. "Ohhh my..."

Adeena looked at Thomas and then over at the Duncan Cello, which he had laid carefully on his workbench. Suddenly she cried out in pain.

"Jesus!" she cried. "My head feels like it's going to explode!"

She tried to stand and Walter helped lift her from her chair. She stood, wobbly and took a deep breath. Thomas appeared with some water and Adeena took a sip.

"I'm sorry," she said weakly. Then she turned to Walter. "I don't know why this keeps happening."

Walter studied her. Her parents were still in Scotland and while he wasn't any kind of relation, he felt a sense of duty. And rehearsals had now been moved up a day for some reason. He needed to get Adeena to a doctor.

Today.

WILLIAM AND JACKIE HAD SPENT ALMOST TWO SOLID DAYS cleaning out the little cottage Margaret Rose had called home for the past eight years.

Husband and wife differed greatly in their approach to the task. Jackie, although sensitive to William's passion for history and old documents, valued task completion over sentimentality. She had grown up in a family with five siblings, where turmoil was the natural order. It actually felt strange to her as a kid when things were quiet. It always felt like the calm before the storm, chaos in waiting.

Her French father and her English mother had a tenuous hold on order in their home at the best of times, but more often, a hurricane raged inside their suburban Montreal split-level. Maybe because she was the oldest, and constantly struggled to keep her brothers and sisters from killing each other, she now valued order.

"Look at this!" William called out from inside Margaret Rose's bedroom. Her husband was obsessed with the 'treasures' he had found in his mother's closet. Boxes of old letters, journals, and documents. He was like a little kid.

"Really?" Jackie called out. "We've got to get rid of stuff. You know Murdo's coming over with his truck at noon, right?"

William popped his head out the door. He held a stack of old envelopes long faded to a musty brown.

"You can't keep everything, Will," she responded, dragging the heavy plastic bag she had filled up with old newspapers and magazines.

"No, this is important, Jaq; letters from my grandmother, Faith. I didn't know she went to University."

"Yeah, okay. So?"

"She sent these letters to Mum. I think she needed to get the old stories down – she may have dictated them to someone. This stuff is incredible!" William whistled as he shuffled through the letters. "They're even typed up."

Jackie knew she wouldn't be adding anything to her garbage

bag from the pile of envelopes in her husband's grasp. "Okay, lay it on me," she said with resignation.

William looked up with a smile. She knew he would be happy to stay here for months and read every word on every piece of paper, from every drawer and cabinet in the cottage. Jackie on the other hand, needed to get back to work and besides – something wasn't right with Adeena. She didn't like being so far away from her.

"Most of it is Faith telling Mum about the history of our family. I don't think anything ever went right for anyone on her side for the last three hundred years, if you believe all this," he said, shaking his head.

"Well, they certainly had a flair for drama," Jackie agreed. "And you believe everything in those letters?"

William took the envelopes and sat down on the sofa. He had opened one and was still absorbed in reading it. After a long silence he put the letter down and rubbed his eyes. He bit his lip, processing what he just read. "Remember the lady that Mum always said she saw in her dreams?" William asked looking up at Jackie. "The one who wrote the score that we sent to Adeena?"

"Yes, wasn't it Katharine, the one in the diary your Mum 'borrowed'?"

"Yeah, Katharine Carnegie wrote a piece of music that my grandmother says was very popular in its day, but she says it was also the beginning of the troubles for her family."

Damn! Why did she let William suck her in? "Troubles? What kind of troubles?"

"Katharine got pregnant and had a 'bastard' son. Apparently, they were on the wrong side of the risings and lost everything, living in shame and poverty until Katharine died, leaving the child an orphan when he was still a boy," William said, still holding the letter in his hand.

Jackie looked at her husband. The story echoed his own childhood. She studied his face. He looked out the window towards the sea and a blackening sky.

"So if Katharine was an ancestor on your mother's side, I guess that would make the boy your great, great... well, *uber* great, grandfather?" she mused.

"It would indeed," he replied and walked back into the bedroom lost in thought.

ADEENA STOOD ON THE STAGE OF SOUTHAM HALL, VERY unsure of herself.

She had arrived early for her first rehearsal as a cellist with the National Arts Centre Orchestra. She liked the sound of that, but it would take some time before it felt real.

The other musicians were unpacking their instruments. She hoped Walter and Maria would show up soon. Adeena wasn't sure of the protocol for rehearsals, or on which side of the stage the conductor positioned the cello section. Likely the opposite of what she would expect.

It had been a difficult forty-eight hours. She had managed to get the Duncan Cello back to the Gallery thanks to the help of Michael in security. She handed it off just before Tara came to see her about completing the research for the exhibit. She asked meekly if she still had a job after their blowout the other day. She did. After a lengthy scolding, Tara told Adeena to finish up her research. The exhibit was opening next week.

Adeena had also gone to see her family doctor, who squeezed her into his evening clinic. He was an older doctor but didn't provide much insight into passing out and migraines. He wrote a referral to a neurologist at the Ottawa Hospital. Adeena mused she could have gotten that from her mother. Hmmm, what would *she* say about all this? Mom was the medical type. She would want to find a scientific explanation, or worse, tell Adeena she was imagining the whole thing.

"Adeena! How are you feeling?" It was Walter at last, and

Maria not far behind. The two walked onto the stage carrying their instruments.

"Much better, now. Thank you for your help," she replied. Maria stepped forward and offered her hand.

"Congratulations Adeena," Maria said. "Welcome to the orchestra. I'm so glad you're here!"

"Thank you. And thanks so much for rehearsing with me. It really made a difference," Adeena said.

"It was an honour. That music of yours is still in my head. I'd love to play it again."

Adeena looked up as Friedrich Lang walked on stage with his usual stern expression, holding an open cardboard box.

"That would be great, Maria. I would really like that," Adeena replied, watching Lang walk to the front of the stage. She turned to Walter. "Where are the cellos?" Before he could respond, a young woman in a long black skirt, with a dark jacket and high heels, strode on stage carrying a narrow case. The woman approached the music director and his face lit up.

"Adeena, we're over here. Lang likes us close, to his right," Walter replied. She followed him and found her chair, near the back, just in front of the bass players.

The woman with Lang opened the zipper for the case and pulled out a rectangular object about four feet wide. She set it down and pulled up a cloth banner rolled inside. Using a pole she snapped together, she stretched the banner to its full six-foot height.

Adeena watched the scene from the corner of her eye as she unpacked her cello. The tall banner was turned towards Lang who studied it, nodding his head in approval. He pointed to the corner of the stage, indicating where he wanted it placed.

"What's he up to?" Walter whispered to Adeena as the two took their seats, waiting for words from the conductor, and curious about the banner that was being set up. Finally, the woman, the orchestra's publicist no doubt, stepped away and the banner was visible to everyone in the room.

It featured a stylized silhouette of a classic sailing ship, set on what appeared to be the fabric of a sail. Adeena read the wording:

Voyage of Destiny
A new work by
Friedrich Lang

A black and white photo of Lang lost in thought was inset dramatically behind the wording.

"He finally finished it," Walter said. Adeena was excited to see what the music director had created. She had a deep affection for composition and composers. She knew the blood and tears required to create anything with emotional resonance.

Friedrich Lang picked up a stack of papers from the box beside his desk and began handing out a booklet to each musician. Adeena waited breathlessly for her copy. The conductor seemed to wait until just about everyone had one before he moved to the cello section.

Lang handed a copy to Adeena and looked at her for a moment, before turning away without a word. She thought he might have offered some form of welcome, but apparently not. He gave a copy to Walter and the other cellists and then strode away quickly to the front of the room.

Adeena studied the cover page with its huge letters: *Voyage of Destiny,* by Friedrich Lang. There was a note about copyright and some legal warnings in a small font near the bottom of the page. She set the cover aside and arranged the first two pages of the music on her music stand. She studied the opening notes, and the arrangement of the instruments.

"Oh my God!" she whispered to herself, as she continued to read the music. She picked up the rest of the papers and started looking through it – quickly, furiously – shaking her head the whole time and muttering: "No! No! No!"

She looked up, holding her hand to her mouth in shock, and

turned her head towards Walter. He too looked perplexed, biting his lip and looking back at her in anger.

The music the conductor had just distributed to the orchestra was the lost music that her grandmother had sent to her.

It was note for note, bar for bar, an exact copy of the score.

FRIEDRICH LANG'S PRIVATE STUDY WAS A PLACE ACCUSTOMED to drama.

He had fought here many times with the NAC Orchestra management – dim-witted bureaucrats always complaining about funding, low revenues, high costs, audience expectations, etcetera, etcetera, etcetera . . .

Who cares? Why should he be distracted by their issues? His only focus was music.

Eternal. Passionate. Timeless.

Now finally, he would join the ranks of the legendary German composers, as he brought this lost music into the world, under his careful guidance. He already had a sense of the power of the music, but it was nothing without him. While technically he had not written it, he had discovered it and would bring it to life in the 21st century.

Just need to deal with these two first, he thought, staring over at Walter Leo and young Adeena Stuart. He thought he should have a word with them before the rehearsal. Should have known they would make trouble.

"This is NOT your music!" Walter started. "How can you dare make such a claim?" The anger on his face was clear. Lang had never seen him this agitated.

"I know the origin of this piece," Adeena added. "It was written by Katharine Carnegie in the 18th century. You can't just steal it like this and claim that *YOU* wrote it!"

Lang said nothing. He was used to negotiating. He had realized early on it was always simply a question of leverage – measuring your assets against your opponent's, calculating your liabilities against theirs.

What did they have to offer? Nothing. What did they have against him? Nothing. What did he have on them? Everything!

"It was lost, and I found it," Friedrich retorted. "I will bring it to life for the whole world, crafting it into a piece that will stand the test of time." He spoke coolly because he knew his emotions could work against him.

"You didn't find it! You stole it!" Adeena half-shouted, her voice rising. "You stole it from me when I passed out – in this very room!"

"I seem to remember it a little differently," he smiled. "Didn't you steal something yourself, from the National Gallery of Canada?"

Adeena's shoulders sagged.

"Friedrich, please," Walter began. "I rehearsed that score with Adeena for nearly a week. You've copied it, note for note. How can you even think about telling the world that you composed it?"

Friedrich looked at his principal cellist. He was a good musician, reliable and talented, if not innovative. Alas, he was a family man first and foremost, with a loving wife he adored.

"Walter, you and I can speak privately if you want. I'm not sure Ms. Stuart here would like to hear about London?" Friedrich purred, "London, England?" He waited to see the reaction on Walter's face.

There was nothing but a stoic look, a clenched lip. Silence fell over the room, save for a few deep breaths from the two cellists lost in their own thoughts.

"Mr. Lang, please," Adeena started. She looked like she was going to try a new tack. "I know this music, it's deeper inside of me than..." she hesitated. "Deeper than I can explain. I am glad you want to bring it to the world, but you can't take credit for composing it. It has its own history."

"I can do what I please, Ms. Stuart," Friedrich responded. "You have joined the National Arts Centre Orchestra solely at my discretion. It was my decision alone to hire you. And I can dismiss you, just as easily."

She winced at the threat. But he could tell this one was a fighter, not easily dissuaded.

"My grandmother and my father found that score in Scotland. They sent it to me, and I have the..." her words trailed off.

"The originals?" he smiled. "No my dear, I have the original, unsigned score. I have it stored away, quite safe."

Adeena's face hardened as both she and Walter glared at the music conductor. They could still make trouble for him. He had used the stick perfectly.

Now did he need a carrot?

Or a bigger stick?

As Adeena punched the button for the fourteenth floor of her condo, she let out a loud sigh. She wanted to kick something. Or someone. She had gone from hot rage to quiet simmer over the last two hours.

What a day! She had not had the chance to reflect on her latest adventure as Katharine Carnegie, because she had focused completely on her first rehearsal as a member of the NAC Orchestra. She only had so much space in her brain to deal with issues. As the elevator started to ascend, she mused that a glass of wine and a hot bath might be about the only thing she could handle tonight, even though she was as hungry as a horse.

A picture of James Drummond and his headstrong stallion, Balgair, flashed through her mind. She wondered what they were doing right now as she reflected wistfully on the image of horse and rider and the promise she made to James to play at the 'ball' he had referred to at Drummond Castle.

I want to perform there, she thought as the elevator reached the fourteenth floor.

When she turned the key and opened the door to her condo, she was surprised to find lights on. She looked over to see Philippe sitting at her dining room table

"Hi," he said, getting up and walking toward her. "I still have a key, and wanted to see you. Hope you don't mind"

"No, it's fine. I'm surprised you're still talking to me."

"Well, I've done a lot of thinking," he said. "You've been through a lot, and maybe you're just not ready, with everything that's happened. And everything that's happening with you."

He stepped forward and gathered Adeena in his arms. They said nothing as they both closed their eyes and held each other.

"Thank you," Adeena said, as she looked up at him. "I must be the worst..."

"Shhhhh," he said, putting a finger to her lips. "Don't. Don't put yourself down. You're my inspiration. My suffering artist, the musician who stole my heart."

"You're not mad at me? Are we still a..."

"Yes. I'm mad at you. But I'm more mad at myself for not understanding you. I still want you, still want us. I want a future with you, hopefully as my wife."

Adeena nodded. Maybe he did understand her, and could give her the space she needed. "Thank you, Philippe. I'm sorry I'm not easy to be with, or easy to..."

"Stop, babe!" he said with a smile. "Can we just focus on tonight? You must be hungry after the day you've had."

"Starving." It was then she noticed a spread of takeout food containers on the counter from the Thai restaurant they liked. "Oh, nice."

Philippe released her and moved to the counter. He poured her a glass of wine and she took a long taste. "That's just what I wanted. God, I just want to crawl into a hot bath and escape. What a strange day."

"Strange, good?"

She took another sip. The dry, slightly fruity flavours of the wine lingered on her tongue. She closed her eyes for a second as she savoured the taste. "Not sure about *good*. More like *holy crap!*"

Philippe grinned.

Adeena wondered if she was a little too coarse for his refined sensibilities. If so, he made no protest, but just smiled, nodding his head as he reached for the bottle and refilled her glass.

"Sit down," he said. "Relax." She sighed and flopped down onto the sofa as he walked away.

"Where you going?" she called out.

"To run your bath," he responded heading for her ensuite bathroom. "Go ahead. Tell me all about your 'holy crap' day."

PHILIPPE LISTENED TO ADEENA'S STORY CAREFULLY AS THE deep tub filled with steaming hot water. He nodded at the details while he brought her a plate of crispy Thai spring rolls stuffed with shrimp. She dunked them in the plum sauce and launched into an animated recounting of her encounter with Friedrich Lang.

Philippe was intrigued. As a Parliament Hill reporter, he was used to the games played by people in authority. He liked bringing them down with the power of his pen. The credit though, really went to the contacts he had nurtured over the years. Secretaries, chauffeurs, executive assistants – all trusted him to keep their identities anonymous as they shared details of the damaging indiscretions of their bosses. Once he could substantiate a claim, he moved in like a leopard, methodically stalking its prey.

"So let me understand this," he summarized, carrying Adeena's empty plate back to the kitchen. "Lang takes the original copy of the score your grandmother sent to you, transcribes it as if it's his own, and now threatens to fire you and tell Tara you've been using the Duncan Cello, if you say anything?"

"Yup, that's pretty much it."

Philippe turned it over in his head.

He spooned some of the red curry shrimp dish Adeena liked so much over a mound of sticky rice. He added a few of the pineapple and peppers from the sauce, and as he carried the plate over to her, he knew this had all the trappings of a great story. Too bad it was outside his beat. He could try pitching it to the City Editor, or maybe someone on the entertainment desk. "Lang's taking an awful chance," he said handing her the plate. "If this got out, he'd be ruined."

Adeena took the plate and nodded her head in agreement and then looked away, seemingly lost in her own world. He had a feeling there was more to her story, something she wasn't telling him.

He studied her. She was everything he had ever wanted in a partner. A radiant beauty with a gift for music and a love of art. Yes, she also came with a huge helping of stubbornness, a feisty attitude that bordered on insulting. And she had turned down his marriage proposal. At first he thought they were through. But he wasn't ready to give up so easily.

He and Adeena had been intense lovers at first, but it had mellowed over the past year and he wasn't really sure why. Was it him? Was he too focused on his career? Was he taking her for granted?

Philippe poured more wine into Adeena's glass. She looked up at him with a worried expression, biting her lip. "There is something else, something I need you to understand," she said.

He reached for her hand, pulling her up off the sofa and leading her toward the open door that led to the bath he had drawn. "Go ahead. I'm listening."

As Adeena slipped into the hot bath she felt the world fade away. Soothing warmth enveloped her, relaxing every strand of her aching body. She slipped deeper into the tub, warm pleasure flowing right up to her chin. She closed her eyes. She wanted to purr.

"Feel better?" Philippe smiled, watching her from the corner of her bed.

"Ohhhh, yes..." she sighed. Her clothes lay on the floor of the ensuite bathroom connected to her bedroom. Philippe had silently watched her undress and she sensed his arousal as she slipped naked into the bath. He had a coy look in his eyes and a smile that could be seen from space.

"The view from here is spectacular," he grinned. "Now, what was it you were going to tell me, anyway?"

Adeena didn't respond. She was floating. Serene, warm, weightless.

She looked over at Philippe. "Come here."

He pointed to himself. *"Moi?"*

"Oui, monsieur."

Philippe slid off the bed in one move. "You're too far away," she whispered.

He rolled up the sleeve of his shirt and sat on the ceramic tiles on the edge of her oversized Jacuzzi-style bathtub. He began to massage her head, slowly working his fingers through her hair.

"Mmmm," she moaned. "That feels good." Adeena closed her eyes and felt the last vestiges of tension evaporate. He massaged every inch of her head and the small of her neck, and then slowly caressed her cheeks with the back of his hand. "Ahhh..." she sighed.

His hands drifted lower into the warm water. He moved his hands over her breasts rubbing her nipples with his finger. She raised her arm out of the water and brought it to his face, tracing her fingers over his mouth.

"I want you," he whispered.

She wrapped her arm around his head and drew him close. He bent down and kissed her tenderly. She responded willingly, exploring his mouth with her tongue. Their faces remained locked together a long time before he reached around, scooped her up to a standing position and carried her to the bed.

Their foreplay continued until she just had to have him inside of her. Adeena wrapped her legs tightly around him, urging him on with uncharacteristic ferocity until finally her screams echoed throughout every space of her apartment.

AFTERWARD, SHE LAY ON THE BED LISTENING TO PHILIPPE'S breathing. He was recovering from the most intense lovemaking they had experienced in months. The pent-up tensions from the last few days were gone.

Adeena stared up at the ceiling and then toward the window at the twinkling lights of the Ottawa skyline. It reminded her of the candlelight ambiance of Kinnaird. Images of her musical performances in the castle flooded over her. She closed her eyes. She had to make sense of what happened when she played the Duncan Cello.

"I need you to understand something – to help me figure it out," she said, reaching over to touch Philippe's bare chest.

"Of course," he replied. "Adeena, that was truly amazing."

She turned her head towards him and looked at him in the soft light. She turned over the details of her journeys to Kinnaird, not sure what they represented, how it was possible or if perhaps she was losing her mind. But she needed to talk to someone about it. Someone who would just listen.

"You know that I've passed out every time I have played that score my grandmother sent me – every time I've played it on the Duncan Cello," she started.

"Every time? I know it happened once. I didn't realize it was *every* time you play." He seemed confused. "Is that what you're saying?"

"It's every time I play that music on the Duncan Cello. I've performed it three times. Each time I passed out."

Philippe sat up on the bed. "What? What are you saying, babe?"

Her eyes grew teary. "I don't know. I *really* don't know!" she half-sobbed, sitting up. "I need to understand what's happening."

He put his arms around her. Her bare skin against his felt good. After a few moments Adeena pulled away and looked at him.

"Okay, now you have to listen, please." She stared into his eyes. They were wide open, clear, and she hoped – understanding. "When I pass out, I go into another world, and I . . ." she paused, looking away, and then back at Philippe. "I... become someone else. Someone in the past I think, in Scotland."

Philippe stared. He raised his eyebrows and pursed his lips. "Who?" he finally said, forming the words slowly. "Who do you become?"

"Katharine . . . Katharine Carnegie, the sister of George and his brother the Captain. They're on opposite sides of the Jacobite rising of 1745," Adeena replied, studying his expression carefully.

He stared at her, confused. His eyes darted back and forth. He said nothing.

"I don't know what it means," she continued softly. "It's like Katharine and I are... well, somehow, we are the same person, only living in different times. I perform her music, music that I started to compose years ago, and I even sing, words that have been in my head for years." She looked away. "I sing music that feels like it has always been inside of me. Music I've been searching to complete my whole life."

Philippe released his hold on her. He studied her without saying anything.

"What?" she pleaded. He just stared. The silence was deafening. "For God's sake Philippe, say something!"

"I'm sorry, Adeena," he finally replied. "I don't know . . . I just don't know what to say."

"Tell me you believe me," she said her eyes desperate. "Tell me I'm not bipolar, schizophrenic, or just plain fucking crazy."

"Babe," he put his arms around her again, trying to comfort her. "Maybe we just need to find some help."

"Help?" she sobbed. "What do you mean?"

"Passing out like this, I think there's something very wrong. Didn't you say your grandmother had issues, and she used to tell you all those stories when you were a kid?"

Adeena pushed him away and moved backwards on the bed. She wrapped her arms around herself, covering her breasts and holding herself tightly. "You think I'm going crazy, don't you?"

Philippe hesitated for a moment. "No. I didn't say that. But I am worried about you passing out. Are you having migraines?"

"I don't need medical advice, Philippe," she said, staring out the window. "I just need you to listen, to help me understand what's going on."

"Adeena, please. Maybe you're just having some kind of, I don't know, some kind of intense dream. You're a musician and you finally made it with the NAC Orchestra. That's all you've talked to me about for years. Maybe this is all coming from the stress you've been under, with your grandmother passing away and Lang stealing the music?"

Adeena gripped her arms around herself even more tightly.

He would never understand.

She shook her head, wondering if everyone would have the same reaction. "I knew you wouldn't believe me," she muttered. "The one person I needed most in the whole world to just listen and try to understand." Her eyes were dry now, her resolve stiffening.

She climbed off the bed and stood naked, staring out at the city through her window.

"Babe, wait," Philippe looked up at her imploringly from the bed.

"You think I'm a nut job, right?" Adeena replied. She suddenly felt exposed, standing before him undressed. She crossed her arms, wanting to hide herself from his gaze.

He didn't reply. She turned and walked into the ensuite bathroom and closed the door.

"One thing I can try to do," Philippe said raising his voice so she could hear him through the door, "is to help expose Lang. I know how to deal with his type." She said nothing, and waited until she heard him in the kitchen running the water, before she opened the door to her bedroom to get dressed.

She pulled on a baggy sweat shirt and flannel pyjama bottoms. "And for the record, I am not crazy," she said, walking out of her room. Her tone was cold. "I don't know what's happening, but I do need to find someone to talk to."

"You can talk to me," he replied in a hurt voice.

"Wrong! You might be a good reporter. But you're a lousy counsellor."

"I'm sorry. I am having a hard time understanding how you can become another person when you play that music. You might feel like you're this Katharine woman, but..."

"But what?"

"Adeena – you don't go anywhere! You pass out and it must be that your mind takes over when you do. It probably feels like you've gone back in time or become another person, or whatever it was you told me," he said.

"Did you even listen to me?"

"Yeah, you go to a castle in Scotland in the 18th century, right?" Philippe said defensively.

"You're mocking me now. Thanks a lot for the support!"

"Adeena, it's all happening in your mind. You don't actually *go* anywhere. You think you're travelling somewhere, becoming someone else and it feels like it's really happening. I get that."

"No, you don't understand shit!"

"Adeena, please!"

"You think I'm a fucked-up space cadet, right? A strange

little girl who goes on mind trips without drugs, because she's half cuckoo."

"I never said that! Why are you getting so mad at me for trying to help you?"

"Help?" she shouted. "Help me? Right! Your idea of help is taking me in for shock therapy at the Royal Ottawa nut house!"

"I just said you needed to see someone," he retorted. "You think it's normal to pass out and have hallucinations where you think you become another person?"

Adeena stared at him. He was making sense.

And that pissed her off even more.

CHAPTER 13

Thomas Peeters had outdone himself this time. Recreating a faithful reproduction of such a rare and precious instrument was not just a job. It was a love affair.

The passion that drove him was something only another luthier would understand. For almost a week he had laboured over the re-creation of an instrument that needed to look exactly like the cello Robert Duncan had brought to life in his 1736 workshop. And not just because Thomas had been hired to do this; it was more about honouring the ancient craft and the original craftsman.

Ms. Stuart had let him photograph every detail of Duncan's ancient instrument. He got the photos printed as large full-colour matte prints which he taped onto the walls of his workshop.

No detail of the Duncan Cello was too small to escape inspection. The thick canted neck, attached with a rectangular-headed nail, had been a challenge. He had discarded a few attempts before he was satisfied that he had created an exact duplicate. He carefully matched the colour of the nail with a dab of stain mixed with some rusty shavings.

The fingerboard, which reached about halfway to the cello's upper corners, was surprisingly easily to build. The wood seemed to understand his intentions as it yielded to his skilled hands. But the problem became the two decorative white lines scratched around the edges. For hours he studied the photos, peering through the jeweler's loupe he kept around his neck. As he studied the detail, Thomas marvelled at Duncan's workmanship.

The cello's one-piece back was a completely different challenge, covered with intricate inked purfling, also applied on the belly. He tried over and over without much luck, to recreate the effect, getting more frustrated with each attempt. Late into the night he finally left it to work on the tailpiece. Its unusual trapezoidal shape curved in slightly and was attached to the spikeless end button by a wire gut.

Thomas finally went back and finished the purfling using a stencil he created to guide him. He practiced applying it to some scrap wood first until he got it right. Finally, he stood back and nodded his head in satisfaction after three hours of detailed, precision painting.

Perfection.

As he applied the coloured varnishes, after much experimentation, and tightened strings around the pegs, he admired what he had created. Not having to worry about the tone and timbre of the cello had let him focus solely on the look. His array of electronic toys for measuring every aspect of vibration, frequency, volume, tonal range, and a dozen other aural elements had not been needed.

This was a 'stunt double cello' that belonged in Hollywood, not Carnegie Hall.

As he packed it carefully for the short drive to the National Gallery, he smiled thinking about how Ms. Stuart would react when she saw what he had created. Somehow, getting her approval was worth just as much as his five-thousand dollar fee.

Adeena felt giddy as she walked through the exhibit hall.

The clone of the Duncan Cello had turned out even better than she had expected. It was almost unreal. After Thomas had delivered it to her office yesterday, they compared the original to the copy, examining them side by side. She, marvelling at the precision of Thomas' work, he, smiling and pointing out intricate details she had never noticed before.

Michael, her 'boyfriend' from Gallery security, had brought the real Duncan Cello up to her office one last time, before it was due to go on display that day. "When you're done with it, Adeena, I need to take it downstairs. They're setting up this afternoon for the new exhibit," he explained after he delivered it to her.

Michael was a sweet kid, she thought. True she had tricked him the first time they'd met – signing her name as Tara. But he got it over it quickly when she later explained she often signed for her boss. He had stood staring at her in the doorway and she finally gave him a hug and a heartfelt peck on the cheek.

"Thank you, Michael," she told him. His mouth dropped a bit before he turned and left, a huge grin covering his young face.

Now as she carried two large banker's boxes of research files about the exhibit, Adeena knew the moment of truth was at hand. When Michael had returned to her office to pick up the Duncan Cello, she had substituted Thomas Peeters' lovingly crafted copy for the real instrument, which she discreetly placed in her own empty cello case.

Michael unknowingly delivered the replica to the exhibit. Now he stood by the instrument, in its padded case, as if some masked cello thief might suddenly appear from behind the imitation castle walls to snatch it. He scrutinized the assortment of Gallery staff to see who might pose the biggest threat to the precious cargo he guarded.

As Adeena set down her banker's boxes, she felt a tinge of nerves at what she was doing. She saw Tara strolling up the outer walkway approaching the exhibit entrance.

Showtime, Adeena thought, trying to project a calm exterior.

"Dee, everything looks fantastic!" Tara beamed as she strode in with her assistant Pablo. "I love the changes you made with the candles and the women's outfits."

"Thanks, Tar," Adeena smiled. "I wanted it as authentic as possible."

"I think you've succeeded," Tara said, looking at the paintings, the placards and the new scene around the podium that would hold the centrepiece of the show – the Duncan Cello.

Adeena had the idea to set up a group of mannequin musicians, both male and female, who looked as if they were getting set to perform. The idea was to highlight the cello and recreate a setting where it would be used in performance. She dressed the two female musicians in black velvet blouses trimmed with gold lining and puffy elbow accents. Both wore white roses, the symbol of the Jacobite rebellion.

One of the female mannequins held a cittern, the other was positioned as if she were looking up at the Duncan Cello, literally reaching for it. The men were dressed in the same fashion as those she had performed with at Kinnaird, wearing full flowing coats and white lacy shirts. They held the same instruments that Adeena had seen them use – viola and violin.

"Well, let's get our star out and I'll take some pictures. We're posting these online and Pablo's going to tweet them out," Tara said, after she adjusted one of the mannequins ever so slightly. "Mike, would you get the Duncan Cello, please?"

Michael grinned at the request. He carefully opened the case, reverently lifting it up and bringing it forward. Adeena flinched as Michael carried the imposter towards Tara, who looked it over carefully. "It's such a beautiful instrument," Tara said. "Amazing that it's over two hundred and seventy years old. It's in such good shape too. It looks like it was made last week!"

Adeena held her breath. Tara touched the cello, feeling the smooth varnish features. She gingerly touched one of the strings. "This is what they're all coming to see."

Michael handed the cello to the waiting technician. He took it and looped a nylon cord around the neck. It would be used to suspend it above the podium, designed to look like a section of the castle wall. The thin black wire would be invisible as it held the cello in mid-air so that visitors to the exhibit could walk around the instrument, examining it from all angles.

"I think this is going to work," Adeena said as the two women watched the cello being raised into place. When finally set up, and the spotlights focused on it, the effect was stunning.

"Whoa!" Tara whispered. "Perfect. Visitors can walk right around the whole set-up, as if they were one of the musicians about to perform. Nice work!"

Adeena nodded her head. Thomas had created a replica that somehow, looked more authentic than the real instrument. Tara stood staring at the display. She reached for her phone to take a picture, but she was too close. She took a few steps back but was still too close. She took a few more steps, and then knocked over both of the banker's boxes stuffed with Adeena's papers and notes.

"Oh shoot. Sorry, Dee," Tara exclaimed, almost falling over herself. The boxes lay on the floor, with their contents spread all around – photos, papers, coloured index cards, files and assorted scraps of paper. "Those are your notes? For the exhibit?"

"Yeah," Adeena responded. She bent over and started gathering the papers.

Tara bent down too. "Here, let me help you." She grabbed some of the index cards and notes, and then picked up an invoice. It was from 'Thomas Peeters, Luthier.' She stood up, reading it and looked at Adeena curiously. "Five thousand dollars for 'professional luthier services'?" she asked. "What's a luthier? I should know that, but remind me."

Damn! Adeena froze. Had she gone too far this time, even for Tara to keep her out of jail?

"Luthier? Uh, they fix and build stringed instruments," Adeena said, fumbling for an explanation. She looked at the mannequins and then back to Tara, still holding the invoice. "Thomas had instruments that I wanted to use, things he could adapt to be historically accurate."

Tara looked at the mannequins, each with a different stringed instrument. "Oh, you mean for the display?"

"Yes, yes. Exactly! He makes copies of old instruments. He made the cittern that woman's holding," Adeena said pointing to the mannequin with the pear-shaped guitar.

Tara looked at the invoice again. "Hmmm, this stuff doesn't come cheap, does it?" She handed it to Adeena and walked towards the mannequin holding the cittern. "It's a good thing you found someone who could make such authentic looking pieces. I thought for sure they were real."

Adeena smiled weakly as Tara turned her gaze to the fake Duncan Cello and studied it carefully. Adeena's blood pounded in her ears. It was deafening – she might need to shout to make herself heard. "Tar, now that the exhibit's ready, I'm going to take some time off," she called out, hoping no one would notice the thumping inside her chest.

Tara took one last look at the suspended cello, and walked towards Adeena. "Yeah, I figured that was coming. You do have another job now."

"Another job?"

"The NAC Orchestra. *Duh?* You know, that little gig you landed?" Tara smiled.

Adeena felt a sudden release of tension. "Oh yeah, that job."

"You've started rehearsals, I guess?"

"Yes, had the first one two days ago."

"How'd it go?"

Adeena looked at Tara, her childhood soul-mate, and still her closest friend. Why couldn't she just tell her what was happening? Get advice from her, the kind she always gave whenever there was some crisis in Adeena's life. But this was different. Tara would be about as much help as Philippe.

Tara was still waiting for a response.

"Oh, yeah, well, you know, it was pretty good," Adeena finally managed.

"Pretty good? That's it?" Tara laughed. "Dee, this is your chance girl. Don't blow it! You need to put your heart and soul, and everything else you might have, into this. You need to nail it – completely. Otherwise, you'll end up with me as your wicked boss until you're an old lady."

Adeena smiled. The Tara pep talk. *Get it done. Get off your ass. Work hard. Focus!*

"You're right Tar, I wouldn't want that, and neither would you," Adeena laughed. "You know what? I'm going to go up to the lake for a while, stay at my parents' place so I can really focus on the music and my technique. You're right, I need to nail this!"

Tara leaned in and gave her a hug.

"Do it, Dee. You are now a cellist with the National Arts Centre Symphony Orchestra. Make your dream a reality."

PHILIPPE KNEW A THING OR TWO ABOUT THE INGREDIENTS OF a good front-page story.

Greed. Deceit. Lust. Revenge.

When committed by a public figure, the deadly sins were irresistible to readers.

"I got something," he offered at the weekly story meeting, which included most of the *Ottawa Citizen's* editors and senior reporters. "You know Friedrich Lang, the NAC conductor and music director?" he began. "Well, he is beginning rehearsals this week for a new work that he claims he composed himself."

The arts and entertainment editor, Peter Smithson, looked up from his laptop. "Oh yeah. We just got a release on that from the NAC." He clicked a few times on his track pad. "Here it is, *Voyages of Destiny,* a new work by Friedrich Lang. World premiere, December 9, 2018, Southam Hall, Ottawa."

"Lang didn't write a single note of it," Philippe said. "The music was composed in the 18th century. My girlfriend's a cellist with the orchestra. Her grandmother found the score in a castle in Scotland and sent it to her. Lang stole it, note for note. And if she says anything, she'll get fired."

All eyes turned towards Philippe. This sounded like it had a bit of everything. Peter Smithson sensed the interest and saw an opportunity for an Arts story to get onto the front page – for an extended run.

"Will she talk about it? On the record?" Smithson asked, peering over his glasses from behind his laptop.

Philippe hesitated. "Hmmm, no. Probably not."

"Okay. Well, it sounds like a great piece," the arts editor said, looking back to his laptop. "Keep an eye on it, and let us know if you get something we can use."

THE SHORT DRIVE TO THE ANGUS ARCHIVES, JUST OUTSIDE THE county town of Forfar, had given William and Jackie a much-needed change of scenery after their days of being cooped up in Mum's little seaside dwelling. The archive housed historical records for all the tiny burghs of the county known for centuries as Forfarshire, but now referred to as 'Angus' – familiar around the world for its prized black cattle.

After reading about the letters, photographs, military records, death warrants, journals and old census documents housed in the Angus Archives, William knew he had to make a visit. With a little luck, it might help him make sense of the puzzle pieces that his daughter, mother and grandmother had thrown his way.

Pieces that so far didn't add up.

He turned over the clues in his head as he and Jackie made their way through the Scottish countryside in companionable silence. They were content to simply admire the scenery and enjoy the serenity. The open pastures shimmered a verdant green in the early September mist. The changing colours of the autumn leaves, the deep reds and brilliant oranges of the century-old trees lining the rural roads, framed the scene to pastoral perfection.

They slowed down as they approached an imposing structure.

"You see that?" William asked, pointing to the impressive landmark beside them. Jackie looked across the open pasture at the square stone tower. The ancient looking three-storey structure was topped with an octagonal spire visible for miles in all directions.

"Neat. What is it?" she asked.

"Restenneth," he answered. The history professor in him had been dying for an audience. "Probably built by the Picts and converted in the 12th century into an Augustinian priory."

William stopped the car by the side of the road so they could get a better look. "It's mostly just a stone shell now," he continued and then paused, somewhat dramatically, "but, it is the last resting place of Prince John."

Jackie strained her head around to see more of the structure. He had her hooked now. "Oh Professor, who was Prince John?" she sang out in a mocking tone, as if she was a starry-eyed first-year student in one of her husband's medieval history classes. His lectures were not just full of facts. William made an effort to weave mystery and suspense into everything he taught. He wanted to inspire his students to be detectives. His aim was to capture hearts as well as imaginations.

"I thought you'd never ask! Prince John was one of only two of Robert the Bruce's legitimate sons," William began. "Unfortunately, John, beloved as he was by his father, maybe the greatest Scottish king of them all, died as an infant. But his twin brother

David, succeeded his dad and became King of the Scots when he was only five – 1329, I believe."

Jackie whistled. "I'm not sure what's more impressive. The history lesson, or the fact that you remember all this."

"I just read about this place yesterday, when I Googled how to get to the Angus Archives," he replied. "I have a thing for dates and for Scottish kings."

"You certainly do! Uh, Professor Stuart, I have one more question," Jackie said playfully. "How many children did Mr. Robert the Bruce actually sire? Is that the way you say it?"

"Yes, we do. Although in Britain, 'to sire' is usually associated more with horses," he responded. "Well Miss, Robert the Bruce was a busy king, but he did find time to 'sire' eleven children – five boys and six girls. And of the kids, six of them were as they say, 'bastards' from unknown mothers."

"I guess he travelled a lot on business?" she giggled. "But why did he bury his son John, here at..." she paused, trying to remember the first part of the lesson. "What was it?"

"Restenneth. And that's a very good question. Unfortunately, I don't know, but, maybe we'll find out in about two minutes."

He put the car in gear and they slowly rolled the remaining few yards ahead on the road to the adjacent Hunter Library, home of the Angus Archives.

WILLIAM PULLED THE CAR UP TO THE FLAT-LOOKING entrance of the building. Inside the unassuming structure, forgotten stories of knights, princes, ladies, villains and plain ordinary folk, awaited discovery by local historians and visitors from around the world who came here to trace their Scottish roots.

The archive was housed in a simple one-storey flat-roofed brick structure trimmed with wooden beams stained dark brown. Rectangular windows placed just below the roofline, provided natural light on most days.

Inside the archive, William headed for the search room. He was mindful to turn off his mobile phone, as per the regulations he read on the archive's website. Jackie lingered at the front desk, talking to an imposing looking grey-haired woman, apparently the librarian on duty. Jackie wanted to know more about Prince John, buried nearby, and why his father, Robert the Bruce, had chosen Restenneth as his infant son's final resting spot.

William was hoping the archive would help him unlock the mystery of Katharine Carnegie. He had been unable to find any reference to her online. There was plenty of information about the Captain, Sir James Carnegie and his brother George. But nothing on their sister Katharine.

He glanced at the signs describing the types of resources available in the search room including parish registers, a collection of gravestone photographs with monumental inscriptions, and online databases such as one dedicated to Angus burial records.

Just as he started looking through the gravestone photographs, Jackie appeared with the librarian, an old battleship of a woman wearing thick glasses. She didn't look like she ever had much fun, on or off the job. Her stern face would make a mean dog whimper.

"Your wife says ye search for a local Carnegie lass?" the woman said, her friendly tone in sharp contrast to her threatening demeanour.

"Yes, that's right," William replied. "She apparently was the sister of Sir James Carnegie of Pittarrow. She must have been born around 1720 I think, possibly around Kincardineshire."

"Why do ye have such an interest in her, if I may be so bold as to ask?" the librarian inquired. "Is she an ancestor? Are ye workin' on a family history?"

William looked at Jackie. They both smiled and nodded their heads, almost in unison. "Yes, it's sort of a family history I guess.

I think this woman might be some kind of distant relation. I know she spent some time at Kinnaird with her two brothers," William said.

"Our not-so-famous castle," the librarian said, squinting as she considered the research task at hand. She made some notes and went to check something on a computer terminal, under a hand-lettered sign that read 'Archive Indexes'.

William got up to follow her, but Jackie stopped him. She pointed to the journal that sat on the desk beside him.

"Is that the journal Mum took from Kinnaird?" she whispered.

"Yeah. What about it?"

Jackie looked around and saw the librarian was completely engrossed on her computer. "You might not want to let *her* see that," she said quietly, tilting her head in the direction of the librarian sitting at the desk in the corner. Jackie pointed to the journal. "She might wonder how you ended up with it – or think it's part of their collection."

William studied the journal lying on the table. She was right. He should probably keep it in his backpack for now. He was about to put it away, when Jackie reached for it.

"Wait, can I see that entry you read to me the other day?" she asked him as she opened the journal. "What was that date again?"

As Jackie flipped through the pages, William tried to recall the entry. He had so many dates in his head. He sifted through his mind, like a computer trying to access the right sector of a hard drive. "Uhhhhh, oh, yeah the sixth... 6 August 1745."

Jackie turned the pages, keeping her back turned to the librarian. "Here it is. Oh my..." she said quietly to herself. She started reading and turned a page, completely engrossed. "Oh. Uh oh..." She kept reading and turned a few more pages. After she finished, she looked up at William. Her smile was gone. "You better read this."

William put on his reading glasses. He glanced over at his wife. "Read!" she admonished.

"Kiinaird, 9 September 1745

My suspicions have all been confirmed.

As I made final preparations to join gather our forces, I was infuriated with news that the rapacious knave from Perth, the traitor James Drummond, had returned seeking council with George and Katharine.

I have delayed attempts to secure my succession to the Earldom of Southesk, the peerage debarred from my cousin through Attainder some thirty years ago. Besides his title, he lost Kinnaird, all of which should have rightly passed to me as the eldest surviving Carnegie. upon his death in France. His traitorous support of the Jacobites in the '15 cost him everything, and casts a long shadow over this family still.

And now my own brother plots with Drummond to repeat the same misfortune and continue the plague on the Carnegies.

Worse, the overseer at Kinnaird claims he saw Katharine at midday, by the stables, in conspiracy with Drummond. The overseer watched the two for some time, and proposed to me that Katharine has developed affections for the traitor. If Drummond be a suitor for Katharine, I will be ruthless in my resolution against her.

An officer from my regiment saw Drummond on the estate as well, at about the same time and alerted me, but we were unable to capture him, even though we fired muskets and gave chase. I fear Drummond is trying to enlist both my brother and sister in support of his loathsome pretender prince.

I warned Katharine not to associate with Drummond, lest she bring more ruin to our family. Insolent as ever, she refused to obey my rule and threatened to do 'whatever with whomever' she pleases.

Katharine will know my wrath if she dares associate with

Drummond. He is headed for the gallows as surely as my cousin was attainted and died in shame.

My sister seems poison'd lately by a spirit of brazen indecency. She admonished me to chill. Her strange manner of late is troubling indeed.

I have stationed two men from my regiment to keep watch over her, lest the traitor from Perth return. My hope is that Katharine will become sensible. If not, she will be detained here at Kinnaird, or in the castle at Edinburgh, until Drummond is captured, hung and dismembered."

WILLIAM CLOSED THE JOURNAL, DEEP IN THOUGHT. HE SAID nothing as he removed his reading glasses, folded them into his pocket and slid the journal into his backpack.

He whispered to Jackie, "*Chill?*"

"Yeah, I saw that," she responded quietly.

The librarian, who had been working off in the corner, approached them. "I think I've found something that might be of help to you."

She held a dark burgundy leather-bound volume. The cover was trimmed with a gold embossed border. The centre was adorned with a family coat of arms, also embossed in gold. She handed the volume to William. He put his glasses back on and read the inscription inside the coat of arms:

DRED GOD

William turned to the librarian, who had indeed found a volume of interest.

"I think ye may find what ye seek in this history," she said. The grey-haired librarian reached over and opened the book to the title page. Jackie, standing close by, looked over William's shoulder so they could both read the page:

HISTORY
of
THE CARNEGIES
EARLS of SOUTHESK
and of
THEIR KINDRED
By William Fraser

"Thank you," William said excitedly. "This is exactly what we need. Can I borrow it?"

"No, laddie. That volume and a couple of others ye might want to check, are almost one hundred and fifty years old. It's for reference only, and cannot leave the archives," she replied firmly. "But ye can use it here, as much as ye wish."

Jackie nodded her head and William turned to her as the librarian walked away. "You should probably get comfortable, dear," she said pointing to the desk and chair. "But first, you need to do something for me."

"Something for you?" William repeated.

"Yes. Book me a flight to Ottawa. It's time I went home. I think my daughter needs her mother."

CHAPTER 14

Adeena turned her father's Volvo toward Richmond, a sleepy rural village deep in Ottawa's southwest corner. As she accelerated down the long country road, tunnelling through tall September cornfields, she took a quick peek behind her at the precious cargo nestled in the back of the station wagon.

The Duncan Cello, inside her old leather cello case, and then stuffed into the Bam travel case, fit snugly in the car with the seats folded down. Sitting beside the cello was an overnight bag and a few groceries she'd picked up at the ByWard Market.

Adeena noticed a light on the car's dashboard: *LOW FUEL*. As she reached the intersection and signaled right toward Richmond, she noticed the name of the road she was turning onto – 'Perth Street,' and the name of the gas station on the corner – 'Drummond's.'

She smiled as she pulled into the station and stopped at the first pump. A young man wearing an Ottawa Senators cap popped out from the tiny shoebox of a store attached to the station. She rolled the window down.

"Regular or premium?" he mumbled.

Adeena looked at the boy, a teenager, maybe eighteen. How

much did he know of clan Drummond and their roots in Perthshire, Scotland? An image of Balgair flashed in her head, grazing in the long grass, all muscle and power. And free as the wind.

"Miss?" the boy asked again, jolting her back to the present.

"Oh, uh... premium. Fill it up, please."

"Sure."

As he started to fill the tank, she plugged her iPhone into the USB jack in the car. She searched for a playlist and thought about how good it was going to be to escape the city for a while.

As she pulled out of the gas station and headed west on Perth Street for the hour drive to her parent's cottage, she clicked on a playlist she called *Falling*. Each piece in it held special significance for her. And they all had one thing in common – the ability to touch her emotions.

First up was Brahms, her favourite of the German Three B's, (Bach and Beethoven were tied for second). Her father first told her about Brahms when she was about nine. At the time, she was learning her first really complex cello composition. She was fascinated by the story of young Brahms who, like her, began learning the cello at a young age.

Adeena found it hard to believe he composed a piano sonata when he was only eleven. Even more curious, he burned his own music because he thought it had too many bad notes. He was a performer and a composer, a soloist and basically a musical superstar. While other girls swooned over The Backstreet Boys, Adeena preferred her poster of a young, moody Johannes Brahms – teen sensation circa 1821.

She cranked up the car's rich Bose sound system as his Piano Quartet No.1, Opus 25–1 began. She'd always loved this piece, but it had taken on new relevance since she discovered Johannes composed it when he was about her age, in his late twenties. And at first apparently, no one liked it. That made her enjoy it even more.

She could feel the music lifting her. The Volvo left the road, floating as she glided on a wave of musical perfection. She was one with the players and the composer. Her head swayed as she played the cello part with her fingers forming notes on the steering wheel.

Fifty minutes later she approached Wolfe Lake, where her parents' post-and-beam cottage was located. The moody cello suites and haunting Celtic-inspired compositions she listened to as she drove, seemed tuned to her surroundings. Autumn was just starting to paint the sugar maples with dabs of bright orange, while the birch, elm and oak trees added their own butter and amber colours. The crown of a stately autumn blaze maple had turned a brilliant red and the rest of the leaves were well on their way.

As the car gracefully climbed the highway overlooking the lake, Adeena turned up the volume on violinist Nigel Kennedy's recording of Vivaldi's *The Four Seasons* that featured Charles Tunnell on cello. The virtuoso violinist's frenetic, crazed performance was countered by the measured, earthy tones of Tunnell's cello, providing a deep foundation that filled the car with a sombre contrast to the bittersweet melody.

Adeena turned off the highway towards the cottage, and as if on cue, the next movement in the *Four Seasons* suite, *L'autunno: Adagio molto* began to play. She started down the long lane that led directly to her parents' place, with Vivaldi's understated composition providing a delicious sense of anticipation. This music seemed to vocalize the quiet serenity of the autumn woodlands. *Le quattro stagioni*, was a concerto Antonio Vivaldi composed nearly three hundred years ago, yet it felt as fresh to Adeena as the day Vivaldi's quill first inked the notes to parchment.

It doesn't age, she thought.

She pulled the car up in front of the cottage and sat looking at the lake. It was late afternoon, and the loons were feeding, diving under the dark water to fish. She turned the engine off, rolled the windows down, but left the music playing. The Allegro from *L'autunno* was just finishing.

How appropriate, she thought, watching the loons feed. This movement was referred to by Vivaldi as *La caccia,* The Hunt, and although the sonnet the Red Priest wrote to accompany it talked of 'horns and dogs' it seemed to work equally well for the loons of Wolfe Lake.

ADEENA GOT A ROARING FIRE GOING IN THE STONE FIREPLACE that dominated an entire wall in her parents' cottage. She poured herself some wine and got busy making dinner for one.

Her parents had enough food in the basement freezer to survive any catastrophe. Besides individually wrapped steaks, there was a hefty prime rib, a half-dozen lamb shanks, two grain-fed chickens and a selection of frozen beans, berries and rhubarb. There were also homemade pies and maple-glazed shortbread cookies. And if that wasn't enough, a selection of one-dish meals like her mom's mini *tourtières,* along with a variety of soups and stews, were neatly stacked up on the top shelf of the freezer.

She selected a glass container filled with her dad's butternut squash soup. After gently warming it on the stove, she savoured the aroma rising from the velvety soup infused with nutmeg and cinnamon. She accompanied it with a fresh baguette, a round of soft Brie, a tangy arugula salad and a glass of cold *Pinot Grigio* – a perfect meal for a Fall night at the lake.

As she ate, Adeena browsed the web on her laptop. She had always had a fascination with history, but her recent adventures as Katharine Carnegie gave her added incentive to dig into the past.

She Googled 'Sir James Carnegie' as she had done a few times in the past week. She clicked on the second search result that came up: 'Sir James Carnegie, 3rd Baronet.' The short article gave no indication of the ruthless character she had twice encountered face to face. She noted the reference to the Battle of Culloden and that his younger brother was on the opposing side, supporting the losing Jacobites on the field of battle.

She sat back in her chair, finishing her wine and gazing out at the lake. The sky was painted blood-orange from the setting sun, and the loons were calling to each other. She thought about George, the 'younger brother' in the Wikipedia article. He was as intense as the Captain, but completely opposite in his manner toward Katharine.

She put her wine down and typed 'James Drummond, Duke of Perth' in the search box of her browser. It returned a list of references including the 2nd, 3rd, and 4th Dukes of Perth. She noticed that the first link on the list of search results was for 'James Drummond, 3rd Duke of Perth'. She clicked on the link, but the progress bar on her browser began to spin like a circus wheel, unable to load the requested page.

She checked the WiFi indicator on her laptop:

LOOKING FOR NETWORKS...

Damn!

The unpredictable satellite service was on strike again. Adeena closed the laptop.

These people didn't seem real, with their names and titles listed so neatly on the screen. How could an entire lifetime be reduced to a couple lines of text? People weren't just what they did. They were all their emotions and their passions, all of their hopes and dreams, every tear of pain and each moment of laughter.

Adeena got up from the table and poked at the fire a bit. She placed a heavy log into the fireplace and pulled the black grate closed.

The Duncan Cello leaned close by, waiting patiently.

At last they were alone together.

Adeena sat in the middle of the great room of her parents' cottage. It was getting dark, but she could still make out the outline of the shore through the floor to ceiling windows that formed a V-shaped prow reaching outward towards the lake. The view was something she never tired of – regardless of time of year or time of day.

She sat on a stool from the dining room, drawing the Duncan Cello toward her. This was her cello after all, she rationalized. She knew everyone would say what she had done was wrong. Only her grandmother would have understood. Margaret Rose would want her to do this, for Katharine.

Adeena began to play the music from the score. Again, almost instantly, clouds filled her mind. She floated among waves of raw feelings and jagged emotions. She felt the ecstasy of creation surging within her. Light and energy pulled her towards a path she could not resist.

This is my music. This is my cello.

Her head was spinning and she felt herself losing control, even as she somehow kept playing. There was a moment of complete blackness, and then she heard a familiar voice. It was close beside her.

"What did you say?" the man asked, pulling her out of the fog.

It was George. They were sitting side by side in an enclosed environment. They seemed to be in motion, bumping up and down. Her hand gripped an invisible bow as if she had been playing a phantom cello. She looked around. There was a faint light coming from a small window on the other side of George's head.

"What?" she asked.

"You spoke something, Katharine, just this moment," George replied. "I thought I heard you say, 'This is my cello.' I take it that you refer to your violoncello, the one fashioned for you by Maestro Duncan of Aberdeen?"

Adeena was still trying to orient herself. There was a hard bump, and she was thrown forward, but George intervened and prevented her from falling into the black wooden slats in front of her.

"Oh, yes. Of course," Adeena responded. Now it was clear. They were in a moving carriage, and she could hear the driver urging the horses forward, with a snapping crack of his whip and loud admonishments to *"Gie oan!"*

She looked outside through a tiny window. The light was dim, it was early morning or dusk. She sat on a wooden bench inside the carriage beside George.

"It is your music Katharine, and 'tis the reason for our journey this morn," George said. "But I fear the Captain will not be pleased, when he learns we have left without his 'royal' blessing."

"Oh yeah, the Captain," she mumbled, not sure what he was talking about.

George groaned. He glared at her as if she had hurled an insult toward him. "The *Captain*. Our brother. Your jailer. The turncoat," he growled. "If not for my deception of the soldiers he had stationed to keep watch o'r you, you would be his prisoner still."

She considered this wondering what had happened. "How... how did you do it?"

"I dispatched them to Montrose to fetch brandy and swords, arriving on a vessel that I fear will nae make port this fortnight," he laughed. "They left me to watch you, a role I performed with woeful ineptitude!"

Adeena smiled as she studied George. He really cared about Katharine. As an only child, Adeena had always wondered what it would be like to have a brother. She liked it, very much. "Thank you, George," she said, planting a gentle kiss on his cheek. "It was sweet of you to look after me."

"Sweet?" he chuckled. "You never fail to surprise me with your creativity." He looked away a moment, and then turned to her. "It's a shame. If not for our brother's polluted love for London, and his lust for Kinnaird, you would be free to pursue your music. You have a fire inside you that burns to compose, to perform. He is afraid of your gift. He seeks to douse your spirit with his own cowardice."

Adeena basked in his analysis. Perhaps she and Katharine were the same person, one spirit connected through time by the same creative struggle. Is that why she had never felt complete? Why she was always searching for something more?

They sat in a silence for a while, until the carriage hit a sharp bump and they both bounced high in their seats. George slapped his leg. "I still find it hard to fathom how our brother can turn his back on our family," he said. "He rebukes even the Countess Dowager of Southesk, Lady Margaret, even though her husband, our cousin the Earl, fought for our cause so long ago."

Adeena realized that Katharine should know who the Countess and the Earl were. Her cousin? Her cousin's wife? She was trying to put the pieces together.

"Remind me George, what year was that, when the Earl, er, that is when he fought?" she said, trying to sound innocently forgetful.

"Katharine Carnegie!" George admonished her. "You have heard me talk about the Fifteen so often, and how Earl Carnegie, our cousin, rightful Laird of Kinnaird, fought so valiantly."

"1715?"

"The year of our Lord," George said. "The Union with England was still a festering sore, and the Earl and the Countess joined with the Duke of Perth and the Master of Sinclair, and many more, to fight, even though it would cost them everything. They had been sworn to action since the day the Union was declared in Edinburgh."

"The Duke of Perth?" Adeena was confused. "But was he even born then?"

George smiled. "The Third Duke was not, but I can assure you his father, the *Second* Duke of Perth, was very much born!"

The light outside seemed to grow a little brighter. The countryside was becoming more visible. Everything was getting a little clearer. In fact, Adeena had researched most of what George had just told her. She had just not assembled the pieces in the context of Katharine. At least George had confirmed one thing, the date.

"So now in 1745, James, the *Third* Duke of Perth, fights again, like his father," she said, sorting it out in her mind.

"Just like his father, his grandfather, and his great grandfather and if truth be told, all the Drummond's stretching back o'er two centuries. All o' them who carried on the crusade for Scotland and the support of our king," George said, his tone beginning to sound like a lecture.

"Is that what drives him? His ancestors?"

"It does. But there is something else I believe, that is even stronger," George grinned.

"Something else?"

"Aye. Lady Jean, his mother."

At this Adeena needed no explanation. The brief encounter with Lady Jean the first time Adeena had played at Kinnaird, confirmed she was a woman you defied at your own risk. "I met her at Kinnaird the night I performed. She did seem like a strong woman."

"Ye have no idea," George confirmed. "Her husband, the Second Duke of Perth, died in Paris a few years after he escaped to France. Lady Jean raised the boys on her own, and she turned them into patriots, the likes of which we have rarely seen in this country."

"The boys?"

"Aye, James and little John, although not so little anymore," George said. "Katharine, rest a while. It will be some time before we come upon the gates of Drummond Castle."

"I'm not tired George, really. Tell me more about the Drummonds and the Carnegies. I seem to have missed so much."

"Yes, my sister, indeed you have. Your music was all you cared about. I used to think it had swallowed you whole!"

Adeena smiled at this assessment. She understood Katharine instinctively and had a good idea what she was doing when she was 'swallowed whole' – composing, creating, searching to find the music within her. She looked at George. "Well, are you going to tell me a story or not?"

"Aye, sister. Sit back and I will give you the whole sad, epic tale."

The driver snapped his whip again at the horses, and they responded with a burst of energy. And for the next two hours George recounted to Adeena in the most minute detail, stories of the Drummonds and the Carnegies. He took her through their adventures and misadventures, their triumphs and failures and all their loves, losses and hates. He also wove in his own personal version of the rise and fall of the Scottish nation.

Her dad would have given his right arm to hear this history lesson.

THE DAY WAS GROWING BRIGHT WHEN THEY SUDDENLY stopped.

Adeena had been so absorbed by George's stories, she had almost forgotten she was in a horse-drawn carriage. Though it was bumpy and they swayed back and forth, it was not unlike a long car ride.

"What is it?" George called out to the driver.

"Ye better get out, my laird."

George opened the door and jumped out. Adeena followed.

The carriage had stopped on a well-travelled lane, surrounded by trees. They were in a dense forest, but off in a clearing, a castle dominated the horizon. Two men on horses blocked the road ahead. They seemed to be soldiers, judging by their double-breasted red coats, blue bonnets and bayonet-tipped muskets.

"Is there a problem?" George shouted, walking towards them.

"Aye, there is," the first soldier responded. "Who are ye? And where ye headed?"

"George Carnegie, with my sister Katharine," he responded, as Adeena stepped up beside him. "I am escorting her to play for the Duke of Perth tonight, at the Prince's ball."

The two soldiers peered closely at Adeena. The second one said, "The same who performed at Kinnaird?"

Adeena looked up. "Yes, the same."

"Lady Katharine," the soldier said. "I am Andrew, and this is Ross, my cousin." He pointed to the other man on horseback. "We both had the guid fortune to see ye perform las' week. Words cannae tell all the problems ye caused."

"Problems?" George asked.

The two men smiled, nodding their heads. "Your sister's music," Andrew continued. "It's in me head. In me heart too. But alas, the Duke told the Prince that you're spoken for!"

Adeena blushed. George grinned and put his arm around her. "The Prince is here now? At Drummond Castle?"

Before Andrew could answer, there was a loud crack of gunfire.

Andrew's horse collapsed, throwing him to the ground. The two horses that had been pulling the carriage were startled and reared up wildly. One of the horse's heavy hooves came down and caught Andrew's shoulder, pinning him to the ground. He screamed in agony as his horse lay dying beside him.

George grabbed Adeena and pushed her towards the open door of the carriage. "Run!" he yelled. She scurried towards the carriage, but didn't get in. Instead, she crouched down, looking through the legs of the two startled horses still harnessed to the carriage.

George ran to Andrew, who was writhing in agony. His horse

lay beside him, dead. There was a bloody gouge in the horse's skull, and the ground ran crimson with warm blood from the lifeless animal. George moved closer to Andrew, who was bleeding badly. His shoulder was deeply gashed by the hooves of the horse that had reared up.

Another shot rang out. It seemed to come from behind a broad oak tree off to the side of the carriage. Ross, who had already dismounted from his horse, dashed towards the tree.

Adeena watched with horror, crouching down near the carriage. She needed to help. Now! She ran towards Andrew who lay screaming in pain, the eye of his dead horse following her as she fell to his side.

"His shoulder," George whispered desperately. "He's bleeding, something awful."

Adeena knew this was bad. Fatal, if they couldn't stop the bleeding. She looked around for something to use as a compress and realized that she was wearing a cape. She tore it off and managed to lift Andrew just enough to wrap it tightly around his wound. He screamed as she worked to stop the flow of blood with her improvised dressing.

"Stay with him," George said. He fled towards the tree where Ross had run.

Ross brandished the blade of his Highland dirk. He found the man who had shot at them, and in a single motion, used his blade to knock the musket from the man's hands before he could finish reloading with fresh powder. Ross pushed the man over and pinned him to the ground with his boot, thrusting his sharp dagger inches from the man's terrified face.

"Don't kill me!" the man pleaded.

"Who are ye?" George shouted as he reached the scene. The 'man' on the ground, was actually a boy, maybe fifteen at most. He trembled as Ross pushed his blade forward, touching the lad's quivering chin.

"I donnae want a die!" the terrified boy screamed.

"Should've thought of that before ye shot at us," Ross

shouted. George laid his own hand over Ross', and pulled it back an inch or so from the gasping boy's soft chin.

"You won't die, if you tell us why," George said. "Why did ye fire upon us?"

"I was told to make sure your carriage never reached Drummond Castle," the boy exclaimed. "By my laird."

"Your laird? Who?" Ross demanded. "Who is your laird?"

"Sir James Carnegie, o' Kinnaird. He makes us fight. He threatened my father who farms for him," the boy said, almost crying.

Ross looked confused. He turned toward George. "Sir James Carnegie? Do you know of him?"

"Indeed I do! He is my brother. And Katharine is our sister," George answered.

Before Ross could react, there was a loud scream.

It came from Adeena. She held Andrew in her arms, her white smock now completely drenched in his blood. Standing over her was another man, much older than the boy. The man held a musket pointed directly at Adeena's head.

George looked over as Ross kept the lad pinned firmly under his boot.

"Let my boy go!" the man shouted, his musket fixed on Adeena's head. "Or I will finish what he started."

The boy pushed Ross' boot off him and scurried away, running as though possessed.

"What do you want from us?" Adeena shouted to the man who held his musket inches from her face. George and Ross approached slowly.

"Turn this carriage around now and follow me back to Kinnaird," he said. "The lady and her brother are to be tried for treason if they take another step toward Drummond Castle."

Ross continued to advance slowly, his knife thrust before him. George followed behind.

"Stop where you are," the man yelled. He shoved the musket against Adeena's head.

"Who gives ye these orders?" George asked.

"Sir James Carnegie of Pittarrow, Laird of Kinnaird. Member of Parliament for Kincardineshire, and a Captain of His Majesty's royal regiment," the man replied.

Adeena studied her captor. He was strong and determined. He held his weapon firmly against her head. Andrew lay nearly unconscious in her arms. George and Ross stood frozen, just a few steps away.

And then in an instant there was a wild, ferocious whoop and a brindle stallion charged from the woods. The man pulled his gun from Adeena's head, and pressed his boot down onto Andrew's chest, pushing hard on both Andrew and Adeena who still held the wounded man in her arms.

James Drummond, riding Balgair, flew towards them in a fury. The musket exploded with a deafening blast, firing in the direction of horse and rider, just missing both. James leapt from his horse and onto the man, knocking him over. In a split second, James scrambled up and pressed his dirk to the man's neck. Ross and George rushed forward, grabbing the man's smoking musket.

James held the sharp blade steady against the man's throat. He yanked the man's head back, grabbing his long dirty hair. James gripped the handle of his weapon tightly, scraping the man's throat just above his protruding Adam's apple. "Prepare to die!"

"Stop!" Adeena shouted. She had never been this close to death before. She still held Andrew, gravely wounded, writhing in terrible pain and perhaps close to dying himself if he didn't get immediate attention. "We need to get help! He's bleeding, badly."

Ross crouched down, his face inches from his wounded cousin. "Andrew? Speak to me!"

Andrew moaned and tried to speak. His head fell back onto Adeena's shoulder.

"There is a surgeon at Drummond," James barked. "He will

tend to Andrew. Put him in the carriage so we can take him there now." Ross bent down and began to lift Andrew into his arms. Adeena helped as best she could, transferring the bleeding man to his cousin. Ross got his arms around Andrew, lifted him up with Adeena's help, and the two carried him to the carriage.

James kept his knife to the attacker's throat. "The Lady wishes me to spare you," James said roughly, rotating the blade to remind the man that he still controlled him and could extinguish his life in a second. George came over and looked at the man directly.

"I know this man!" he exclaimed. "I've seen him, at Kinnaird."

Adeena returned and studied the man herself, then turned towards James. "What are you going to do with him?"

"He tried to kill one of my men," James snorted. "What do you suggest, My lady?"

Adeena, her clothing still wet with Andrew's blood, felt only pity. She looked at the man, his life hanging precariously on her words, a sharp blade at his throat.

"Please. Enough James," she cried. "Let him go!"

James slowly pulled his dirk away from the man's throat, but kept a firm hold on his hair. "For you, Katharine. Only for you," James said. He let the man go, and then pushed him to the ground. He lay there a moment, before standing slowly – angry and sullen.

George stepped forward and looked at the man. "Ye work for my brother, then?"

"I have nae choice," the man responded. "He is my laird. My overseer. He gave me but one choice. Fight, or leave my farm."

"Your farm?" James intruded. "You farm at Kinnaird?"

"Aye, black cattle. And oats and barley, to pay the victual rent" the man replied. "Six bolls per quarter."

"So ye fight against your own country?" James asked. "To keep your land?"

"Aye. It's not my land, but I need to keep from starving. Nae for me, but for my wife. For my sons and my daughter," the man said.

"What name are you called by?" James asked. Adeena watched curiously, as she sensed his attitude towards the man shifting.

"We are Beattie. Finlay Beattie."

James seemed to consider this for a moment. Adeena wondered what he was thinking. A few moments ago he was ready to kill this man, and it was only her protests that seemed to save him. She glanced at James. He looked at her like he was running a set of calculations in his head.

"I will spare you, Finlay. Pray that Andrew survives or I may have to reverse that course," he said. "You fight to protect your family. We fight to save our Nation. The Prince has already conquered Perth and the Highlands, and soon all of Angus will follow."

Finlay was listening, nodding his head.

James continued, his tone shifting. "And do you know that you have a new king? The Prince has proclaimed James the Eighth returned once more, and the Union with England abolished. Scotland is its own Kingdom again, as it was when our fathers were born."

Finlay rubbed his chin. "My father hated the Union. He served Earl Carnegie. Twice the man his cousin will ever be, a black Carnegie who thirsts to regain the Earldom and all o' Kinnaird."

George stepped forward. "My brother will stop at nothing in this quest. He is using you and your son, and he will offer you nothing for your sacrifice."

Finlay sighed. "I fear you know him well."

"Join us, Finlay," James offered, "and we will protect your family. Return to Kinnaird, and tell your master that George and Katharine have fled beyond your grasp, and that you know not what became of them. Wait for us. Our cause is strong all across

Angus and Forfarshire, and soon, very soon, we will need your help."

Finlay said nothing, but Adeena could see him nodding, considering what had been offered.

James turned to Adeena. "Come, my lady. We need to get Andrew to the surgeon. And I need to get you to Drummond Castle."

CHAPTER 15

These were the kind of days that caused Tara to wake with a start, ready to pounce. The opening of the new exhibit had sparked national media attention and the guest list for today's opening was the crème de la crème of embassy row and the haughtiest of Ottawa's haughty upper crust. And she was the epicentre, the cog that kept everything moving in a synchronous orbit.

She had to admit, Adeena had done a great job getting the exhibit ready. Her research painted a compelling story of 18th century Scotland. And focusing the throes of war through a prism of rarely seen art had turned out to be a brilliant idea. Of course, Tara thought with a smile, it was mine.

She stood beside the National Gallery's director, André Borgons. He was getting set to address the dignitaries, journalists and other assorted guests who stood outside the glass walled entrance, dominated by the hanging banner announcing the *Art of Rebellion / Art de la rébellion* exhibit.

"Fantastic!" André whispered to her. "Great work."

She smiled again thinking about Adeena and the sparks that flew between them bringing the exhibit to life. 'Nothing worth having comes without some kind of fight,' she mused. The words from Bruce Cockburn were an inspiration she often drew upon. While others might seek the path of least resistance, Tara sought out challenge and never considered losing to be an option.

"Thanks André, I've got a great team," she replied. "You got my notes?"

"Yeah. Thanks, Tara," André said, stepping forward to address the group. "*Bienvenue* ladies and gentlemen, *mesdames et messieurs*, to the National Gallery of Canada," he started, projecting his voice like the experienced public speaker he had become over the last five years. "We're proud to give you a sneak peek of our new exhibit and a collection of artwork and artifacts never seen before in North America."

Tara had always admired André with his doctorate in art history and his long list of published articles.

But his real talent was as a showman. He knew how to sell the sizzle.

AS THE TOUR PROCEEDED THROUGH THE EXHIBIT, TARA TOOK note of the attendees she had invited, drawing satisfaction from the black tie, evening gown crowd. She checked them off in her head – the ambassador to Canada from the United Kingdom, the president of the Robert Burns Association of North America and the head of the St. Andrew's Society of Toronto.

They all mingled together, sipping sparkling wine or testing their olfactory glands with samples of twenty-five-year-old *Bunnahabhain* single malt Scotch. Formally attired servers offered delicate salmon canapés, miniature haggis and Angus meatballs on toothpicks tipped with tiny blue Scottish flags.

There was also a gaggle of local and national politicians, including the mayor of Ottawa, a proud Scot apparently, who arrived in full Highland attire, towing a group of TV cameraman and newspaper photographers behind him.

Perfect! Tara thought. A photo of him and the Duncan Cello would hopefully grace the front page of the morning papers, maybe show up on the late-night TV newscasts as well, and of course make for great social media feeds.

Tara looked around to see if the NAC conductor, Friedrich Lang, had arrived. He had accepted her invitation and she was curious to see if Adeena's description of him as fire-breathing dragon was accurate. She noticed a stern-looking, grey-haired man making his way through the group toward her. She studied him carefully. Maybe Adeena was right to be afraid of this old German. Where did he get his training? The KGB?

"Ladies and gentleman, I would like to present the star of the show," André called out, directing everyone to focus their attention towards him. He stood beside the Duncan Cello, shimmering in the spotlights, and floating in mid-air above a stone podium, as if held aloft by unseen forces. The tiny black piano wires that created the illusion of the floating cello were completely invisible, and Tara again admired the effect.

"The cello you see here has never been exhibited outside of Scotland," André continued. "It was built by Robert Duncan of Aberdeen, more than two hundred and seventy years ago in his workshop. He learned his craft from a young Italian, who some of you may have heard of... Antonio Stradivari."

There was a murmur as everyone tried to move a little closer to the cello suspended before them.

"I would ask that you not touch the instrument please. We've come up with a unique way of presenting it but do keep in mind what your mother told you: 'If you break it, you bought it.' And I'm not sure if you have five million dollars available on your credit card!" he joked with a grin.

There was some laughter and a female news photographer moved in, looking for a dramatic angle to best capture the instrument that seemed to levitate before her. As Tara admired the proceedings, she felt a tap on her shoulder.

"Nice work, *mademoiselle!*" It was Philippe, dressed for the occasion in a crisp black suit and sky blue tie.

"Hey! You made it!" she exclaimed. He leaned in to give her a hug and a kiss on each cheek.

"Bien sûr!" he responded. "You pulled out all the stops. Quite a gathering of Bytown snobs!"

"But of course," Tara smiled. "Dee does her thing, and I do mine. We're not just pretty faces you know!"

"And what's wrong with a pretty face?" Philippe grinned.

Tara felt a flush warming her cheeks. Before she could respond, Friedrich Lang approached them.

"Ms. Kormos," he began stiffly. "Thank you for the invitation. Remarkable display."

"Thank you, Maestro," Tara responded. She pointed to Philippe standing beside her. "Do you know Philippe Lévesque, from the *Ottawa Citizen?*

Philippe extended his hand. "Mr. Lang," he said. "I don't know if you remember me? I interviewed you when you first came to Ottawa."

The conductor did not appear to remember. His expression was somewhat puzzled as he gingerly shook Philippe's hand. "Oh? Really?" He paused a moment. "Very nice to meet you, again."

"Thank you. My girlfriend, Adeena Stuart, is excited to be working with you," Philippe responded. Tara watched to see how Lang would respond to this. Again, a puzzled look washed over him.

"Adeena?" Lang asked. "Your girlfriend?" He paused, looking at the Duncan Cello with interest. He continued without taking his eyes off the instrument, speaking in a distracted manner. "She's a very talented young lady. I believe she may go far, performing with the... the symphony..."

His words trailed off as he seemed captured by the Duncan Cello. He studied it carefully. Another photo op flashed through Tara's mind. "Maestro, let's take a closer look!"

FRIEDRICH LANG HAD AN ODD FEELING AS HE MOVED TOWARDS the Duncan Cello.

There was a sense he had, adjusting his glasses, that there was something wrong. The object the shallow Canadian bourgeoisie gathered here were fawning over, in their typical stupidity, somehow did not seem to be the same one he had seen in his studio.

He inspected it carefully, removing his glasses and taking a closer look, shaking his head the entire time.

The young lady who had introduced herself to him when he arrived as Tara Kormos from the National Gallery, and who also happened to be the boss of his new cellist, Adeena Stuart, stepped up beside him.

"I sometimes wonder about all the musicians who have played this instrument over the years," she said to him, interrupting his forensic inspection. She moved closer, together with the annoying journalist. "Don't you think it must have quite a story to tell?"

"Yes, indeed it certainly would," he replied. He noticed that Tara had dragged along a photographer and a TV cameraman with her. She knows how to play the game, he thought. He had an idea.

"It would make a very good picture if you would let me, Ms. Kormos, play something on this instrument," he suggested. "Just for the cameras of course, something very short."

He watched to see how she would react. He could tell she was a sly administrator from the way her eyebrows raised at his suggestion, while she maintained a smile and considered his offer.

"That would make good TV," she responded. "Wait here for a minute. Let me get it down for you."

WHEN FRIEDRICH FINALLY GOT HIS HANDS ON THE PRECIOUS instrument a few minutes later, his suspicions were all but confirmed. It seemed highly unlikely this was the Duncan Cello.

It was partly the wood grain. From what he could see it just seemed wrong. And also the *schnecke,* or the 'scroll' as his English-speaking colleagues referred to it, made him look twice and then a third time. The scroll was the delicate carving at the end of the neck of the cello. Its main purpose was simply decorative, but this one was too perfect. When Adeena had passed out in his office a week ago, he had studied the old instrument she had brought with her. He wanted to see for himself what made it so valuable. He had traced his fingers over the scroll and examined it closely, noticing the scar and nicks, the way the varnish had weathered, with a little black blob of it stuck inside one of its grooves.

Now as he stood smiling beside Miss Kormos, holding the bow she had brought him, thoughts raced through his mind. The scroll of this instrument, lacked the blobs of varnish, like someone had wanted to remove these blemishes, but he knew that would be almost impossible unless the scroll had been replaced.

He touched his bow to the strings and swept across them slowly. The sound was not even close. It lacked depth, tone and the haunting, sombre richness that moved him so deeply in his studio.

As his short recital proceeded, captured by the cameras, he realized this was good publicity for his own work. But was he right? Was the real Duncan Cello somewhere else? After he finished and took a short bow, he turned to thank the Gallery administrator.

"You are absolutely correct, Ms. Kormos. Indeed, the Duncan Cello would have had a grand history," Lang said coyly.

"Would have?" she repeated.

Friedrich wasn't sure what was happening here. He was

almost certain though, the instrument he just played was not the Duncan Cello.

"Excuse me, madam," he smiled. "Sometimes my English, is, well – it's not my first language."

"Oh maestro, your English is great!" she responded. "I have heard so much about you from Adeena. You know, she did all the research for the exhibit before she left." She paused for a moment and then added, "She's trying so hard to impress you!"

Friedrich looked at her blankly. "Left? What do you mean?"

"She's gone up to her parent's cottage to practice. I've known Adeena since we were kids. She's dreamed of playing with the NAC since, well, since, forever. And now you've given her a chance to live her dream, " Ms. Kormos beamed like she was Adeena's mother.

Lang smiled, nodding his head. He suddenly had an idea where the real Duncan Cello might be. "How far away is her cottage, from the city?"

"Uh... I don't know, maybe an hour or so?" she responded. "Adeena packed up, took her cello and said she needed to be alone to practice. She really wants to be ready for you!"

Friedrich nodded his head and looked down again at the imposter cello.

"Why do I get the feeling that you're... not that impressed with the star of our show?" she asked.

He considered his words carefully and nodded. "I think you might ...."

But before he could finish more, the man who had been talking previously, called out to her. "Tara? Can you come over here?" Lang recognized him from the introduction. He was the director of the Gallery.

"Excuse me, Mr. Lang, I have to go. I'll try to find you later." She turned and hurried away, leaving him alone. A staffer from the gallery took the cello from him. He watched as it was raised again to a place of honour under the lights.

He was about to leave when the annoying journalist from the

newspaper stepped up beside him. “I hear you have a new work,” the man said with a hint of sarcasm in his voice.

“Yes, that is true,” Lang responded. “Adeena told you about it?”

“She did indeed,” the young journalist replied coldly. He paused and moved in close. “And I know for a fact that you stole the music from her.”

Who the fuck is this asshole? Lang wondered. “I stole it? That’s quite an accusation...” He looked at the man’s name tag. “Mr... Lévesque?”

The din of conversation around them created a bubble that provided a sense of privacy, even in such an open public space. Friedrich sneered at the brash reporter who stood before him. “*Voyage of Destiny* is my work.”

“Too bad we have copies of the original score,” Lévesque replied.

“A photocopy proves nothing,” Lang responded. “I am giving Adeena a chance to perform with the National Arts Centre Orchestra. But if you would rather pursue this, I could easily dismiss her. And...” he paused, making sure he had the asshole reporter’s full attention, “make sure she *never* performs with another symphony orchestra, *anywhere* in the world again.”

Friedrich studied the reporter’s reaction. He was a cool customer. He didn’t seem fazed. Perhaps another approach would be more effective. “You know, my composition isn’t the story you should be investigating.”

“Really? And why is that Mr. Lang?”

Lang moved his head closer to Philippe and whispered, “Go ask Adeena. I’m sure the Gallery would love to know what she’s done with the *real* Duncan Cello.”

CHAPTER 16

Adeena opened her eyes slowly.

Her head was jackhammering pounding pain, worse than any other time she had played the Duncan. It was so bad that she wasn't sure she could even stand up. She had fallen to the floor and lay on her back, frozen on the wool carpet in the great room of the cottage, with her cello lying beside her. Her face was turned toward the fireplace, where the roaring fire she built was now reduced to a single, incinerated log over a glowing heap of embers.

She stared into the glow from the fireplace, closed her eyes and thought of Katharine.

Are we the same person?

Only her grandmother would have believed any of this – that a person could be caught between two places in two different times, unsure of whom they really were.

Adeena tried to turn her head. The movement made the pain in her skull worse, but she managed to turn slightly toward the wall of windows. She saw the moonlight reflected on strands of wispy clouds and could just make out stars in the night sky, though the amber moonlight washed most of them away.

Her mind was spinning. Do time and space matter? Is there

something that transcends them and guides a soul between two incarnations, regardless of where and when they exist? Adeena sighed with a sense of frustration, a feeling of anger.

It's just a dream, a very real dream that I'm making up inside my own screwed up head.

The fire began to crackle and a tiny flame erupted, as the centre of the remaining log finally succumbed. She felt tears streaming down her cheeks. She let them fall to her lips, the salty sting adding to her despair. She sobbed, trying to release all the frustration and anger inside her.

After a while the tears stopped. Adeena remained on the floor, breathing deeply, her eyes closed. She was not of this world. But, she was not of that other world either.

Is this what happened to my grandmother, Margaret Rose? Everyone said she was 'disturbed.' Is that my fate? Am I to become like her?

She lay on the floor thinking for a few minutes. And then gradually, ever so slowly, she began to feel a calmness settle over her. Strength from somewhere, deep within, began to take hold. She pushed herself back up into a sitting position. And then with an even greater effort and a loud groan, she heaved herself on to her feet. Her wobbly legs wavered for a moment before she could find her balance.

There was a determination growing within her. She would never give up. She would not surrender to pity. She wasn't going to blame someone else for her problems. For too long her self-doubt had been a vice grip of despair, an unrelenting demon of negativity.

Adeena reached for the Duncan Cello and prepared to play the score once more. She remembered something Margaret Rose had once told her.

Fear is for those who are afraid to live.

And Adeena suddenly felt she wasn't afraid of anything.

THE MUSIC POURED ONCE AGAIN FROM THE DUNCAN CELLO, A hypnotic elixir intoxicating the ladies and gentlemen assembled around Adeena. The other musicians followed her lead, adding harmonic counterpoints. The violins and violas picked up her cello lines in tidal waves of musical power.

Adeena looked across the gathered men, dressed in tartan colours, many in elaborate Highland garb. The ladies, in white silk gowns with fine embroidery, seemed to be as completely absorbed with her music as the men. Most wore white roses or white ribbons. She knew she was playing for what must be the grand ball at Drummond Castle. This room was twice the size of the one she had performed in at Kinnaird. A row of pewter torches and suspended wheels of hanging chandeliers with hundreds of burning candles on each one, gave the hall a glowing radiance full of fire, and life.

Adeena stood up, setting the cello aside. She closed her eyes and began to sing words that had come to her as a bewildered teenager, but that now found their purpose. Her voice resonated throughout the room finding every ear that longed to be found.

Gone is my heart without you
Now I am lost once again.
Praying for life that grows within
All I can ask is when?

When will the sword meet the sky?
To show where I belong?
Forever I will wait for you
Even after I'm gone.

Now as you raise the flame of hope
Sailing into the darkest sea
The black night is all around
You light the way for me.

When will you turn night to day?
So hope may greet the dawn?
Forever I will wait for you
Even after I'm gone.

As the music rose behind her, and she swelled with a kind of confidence she had never experienced, Adeena opened her eyes. James Drummond, standing near the front of the room, draped in a dark flowing plaid and a starched white tunic, stared sternly into her eyes.

Unblinking. Unmoving.

She felt the power of his gaze looking directly inside of her. He didn't seem to just listen to her music and to her aching words. It was more like he absorbed them in every cell of his rugged frame. And trembled in response.

When the song was over, there was a brief moment of silence. Only a crackling from two blazing fires at both ends of the room could be heard. Then the men and women erupted into cheering and applause with an outburst of chanting and shouting that threatened to wake both the living and the dead from across the whole of Perthshire.

A tall, nobly-dressed young man with fine delicate features moved forward, and the crowd acknowledged him with more chanting. He made a dashing image in his Highland coat of silk tartan, red velvet breeches and a blue bonnet trimmed in gold, topped with a large jewel and St Andrew's cross. He wore a green sash and carried himself with a regal, yet energetic step toward Adeena.

She was unsure of the protocol here. She knew that very likely this was the Prince, 'Bonnie Prince Charlie' as history knew him, but much more of a natural leader than she had expected. The stilted paintings of him always made him look like a royal fashion model, rather than a soldier prince leading his army into battle. The sight of him moved Adeena. She bowed her head and attempted an awkward curtsy, then dropped to her knee.

"Lady Katharine," he said to her in a commanding voice. "You honour my father, King James, and the Kingdom of his ancestors. All of Scotland is inspired by your music. Rise!" He offered his hand to her and she held it for a second. Their eyes met and he smiled, displaying a countenance as royal as anyone she had ever imagined could be.

Adeena stood and Prince Charles bowed his head to her. The assembly roared their approval as she stood smiling before them, waves of cheering filling her with the satisfaction that came from releasing the music within her to people who wanted it, as surely as they needed air to fill their lungs.

"Lady Katharine!" the crowd chanted. She bowed and felt her face flush, again.

The Prince stood beside her and when she raised her head, he turned to her and whispered, "You have captured their hearts. Hold them carefully." He paused a moment to acknowledge the chanting and then left her, walking to the side of the room to speak to two men who seemed the only ones in the room still serious and stern. The chanting continued and then James, who had been standing at the very front of the room, stepped forward almost touching her.

"Katharine, you honour us," he said, speaking just loudly enough over the chanting so that only she could hear him. "Your gift is rare and precious, and..." he seemed to be at a loss for words, almost nervous, "I am glad you are here tonight, with me."

She nodded in acknowledgement.

She noticed that George had also been near the front of the room, sitting next to a middle-aged woman, about the same age as Adeena's mother. She recognized her instantly – James' mother, Lady Jean. Her white rose was prominently displayed on her dark shawl. "Lady Katharine, you are as brave as you are musical," she said in a steady, powerful voice. "James told me you saved one of his young soldiers."

"I only wrapped his wound," Adeena replied. "Is he okay?" Then, seeing Lady Jean's quizzical expression added, "I mean, is he well?"

"Aye, the surgeon says he will fight again for the Prince," Lady Jean said. "Your bravery saved him. But I think it is your music that might win the battle." She looked over at George. "Your sister has a rare gift, a voice that inspires men." She turned her gaze to Adeena. "And ladies too."

George nodded. "Her song has always been strong, and her heart true. It has helped me become decided on what I must do."

James, who had been listening intently, turned to George. "You will join us then?"

"I will," George replied. "I must fight for my country and for my family. The Carnegies and the Drummonds helped build this Kingdom. I cannot turn my back on those who died for me."

"You honour them well, George," Lady Jean said. "Your uncle and my dear husband prayed they would have sons like you and like my James."

"Thank you Lady Jean," George said. "If only *all* of our family knew their duty."

"Your brother has chosen another path," Lady Jean said. "He was fed lies all his life in Glasgow, and turned away from his aunt, Lady Margaret of Kinnaird and Carnegie history. I remember how much she tried to help him after her husband, the Earl died. He refused to accept her guidance."

James looked at George. "Fighting your own brother will not be easy. But the blood our fathers shed must not have been spilled in vain."

George nodded. Lady Jean touched her son's shoulder. "James, you must give thanks to Lady Katharine."

James smiled, and looked at Adeena. He raised a hand to

quiet the boisterous men and even more boisterous women who had continued their chanting and clapping all this time. He raised his voice, booming over them. "This is why we fight!" he yelled out, extending his arm towards Adeena. "This is who we are! A nation – the Scots! We are not English. The Union is dead!"

The crowd roared its approval. The Prince, talking to two tall officers at the side of the room, looked up.

James continued forcefully. "We are each of us the descendants of our fathers, and our grandfathers – men who lived, and died, to preserve this land. And we are one with every father and every grandfather who followed their king for more than four hundred years, to build a nation and *our own* Parliament!"

The crowd cheered after every tiny pause, each single inflection in his speech. He quieted them now by raising his arm. "And now Charles Edward, our own Bonnie Prince, has proclaimed his father, James the Eighth as our true and rightful king. The King of Scotland!"

Adeena stood watching James, transformed from nervous suitor to fierce orator.

"Our Bonnie Prince has already led us to victory in the Highlands. We have routed the English dogs and their General Cope everywhere they have tried to halt us!" James shouted. "They have failed, and they will fail again! And again! And every time they dare try to stop us!"

James looked at Adeena. His eyes were wild with passion. The Prince who had been huddled with the two officers, moved towards James and Adeena. He looked out at the crowd and the room quickly grew quiet as he raised his arm.

"This man," he said, gesturing towards James, "has been a part of my most trusted counsel since I made landfall in the Kingdom, some eight weeks ago. He helped lead us with his courage, his bravery, indeed his determination. The Duke of Perth is a man that Perthshire, and indeed all of Scotland should hold in their hearts with pride."

The men and women showed their approval with applause and a toast to "The Duke!"

"And tonight, fair ladies and brave gentlemen, I appoint James Drummond, the Duke of Perth, to the rank of Lieutenant General in the army of King James the Eighth. He is a leader who I will entrust with my own life."

Adeena looked up at James. He bowed his head to the Prince and then turned toward her. Their eyes locked for a moment, and then James turned away. The crowd was still cheering at the announcement. The Prince raised his hand once more.

"Tomorrow," he thundered, "the eleventh day of September in the year of our Lord Seventeen Hundred and Forty-Five, we march toward Edinburgh. And before the week is over, the city will be restored to its rightful place as capital of the Kingdom of Scotland."

The crowd exploded and the other musicians, sensing the joyous mood, began a spirited jig. The Prince laughed out loud as the music began. He presented himself to one of the prettiest young ladies in the room with an exaggerated, playful bow. They began to dance, with the adoring approval and conspicuous envy of the other ladies in the room.

James turned and bowed to Adeena and offered her his hand. She accepted it and they joined the others on the wooden floor laid with wide beams of polished oak. She instinctively knew the dance the moment they began. Her feet and legs moved in graceful sync with James and the other couples in the room.

James took his dancing seriously. He never missed a step, never took a break and only stopped when the musicians themselves paused momentarily. Adeena was caught up in the excitement. She twirled, curtsied, laughed and felt like she was flying in the air most of the time, her feet barely touching the ground. The DJ at the Mercury Lounge was no match to the motivating power of the violin and viola, encouraged by a room lubricated with an unending supply of ale and brandy.

Adeena's only thought was to keep pace with James. They danced until she thought she couldn't possibly take another step.

And then they danced some more.

WHEN THE MUSIC FINALLY DID END, ADEENA WASN'T SURE SHE could still walk.

She was physically exhausted, but felt only joy. Any worries she might have had were vanquished. She had given the musical performance of her life, playing her own composition, which connected deeply and directly with her audience. And then she had got lost in dancing to music that felt as natural as if had it sprouted from the ground itself.

James took her hand and led her outside into the cool night air. She followed without questioning where they were going.

"My lady, you dance as one who is free, unfettered by what others think," he said as they stepped through the archway that led to a generous stone balcony. The evening air felt crisp. A nearly full moon in the cloudless sky provided a glowing iridescence to the surroundings.

"I have never danced like that before," Adeena replied. "Ever!"

They reached the edge of the balcony, a wall of stone about chest high. She looked out at the neatly manicured gardens before her, resplendent with tall flowers, carved hedges, neatly trimmed shrubbery and ornamental trees. Even by moonlight, it was impressive.

James stood near and looked out at the gardens before them, and then turned his gaze toward her. Even without looking, she could feel his eyes. She turned her head to face him.

"Katharine, I feel so young with you, never sure, of myself," he said haltingly. "I have laid out the entire town of Crieff, I have led men into battle and I have even managed to win the approval of my mother Lady Jean, but with you..."

Adeena waited for him to continue. He was over six feet tall but seemed as shy as a little boy. "With me, what?"

"With you... I feel like I know absolutely nothing," he replied. "How shallow I must seem, to you with your power to make the fiercest of men shed tears, and every woman feel one with your soul."

Adeena could hardly breathe listening to his analysis. She stared at James, unable to respond. The wind rustled across the trees in the distance. The conversation from the hall floated towards them, white noise ebbing and flowing in the background. "You are anything but shallow," she said and then looked away at the neatly laid out gardens. "I really don't understand myself, the power this music seems to have."

"It is a part of you," he whispered. "Perhaps, not meant to be understood."

The glow of the moon outlined his face before her. His features were soft and his eyes had an intensity that held her transfixed, unable to turn her eyes from his. The breeze suddenly picked up and rustled in the trees. She shivered from the frigid air, holding her arms to her chest.

James had grabbed his plaid cape on the way out of the hall and thrown it over himself. He unwrapped most of it now extending it towards her. "Come closer," he offered.

She took a step forward. He took most of his cape, still wrapped around his neck, and placed it around her, drawing her in. He placed his arms over her shoulders and pulled her closer. Adeena felt warm inside his cape, and as natural as if she had done this with him a thousand times. She placed her arms around him, his back taut and muscular. She closed her eyes and laid her face on his shoulder.

They spoke not a word.

The breeze made its own harmonies, sweeping through the distant trees. The music from the ball began again. James and Adeena unconsciously started to sway, moving together slowly, wrapped in each other's arms. Adeena felt like she was melting, becoming a part of him. They moved together naturally, drifting slowly across the balcony, floating in tiny circles.

There was no need for conversation.

After a few minutes she raised her head from his shoulder and he looked down upon her. There was fire in his eyes. He lowered his face to hers.

She parted her lips and he kissed her softly. Tentatively. Sweetly. She opened her mouth to his.

Adeena's head was spinning and her whole body wanted him. They responded to each other like lovers separated for centuries. Lights began to explode in her head and the darkness consumed her once more.

CHAPTER 17

The Air Canada Boeing 767 rolled slowly as it began its descent towards Ottawa International. Jackie gazed out the window at the quilt of narrow fields bordering the St. Lawrence River below her. If only life was so neat and tidy, she thought, draining the wine from her glass before handing it to the flight attendant making final rounds before landing.

A copy of the *Journal of Clinical Psychiatry* sat in the empty seat beside her. She studied the cover, a profile of a young woman set against a starry sky. The accompanying article, documenting the telepathic abilities displayed by autistic adults, had been a compelling read. As she tucked the magazine into her mauve laptop case, she considered the evidence of telepathy presented in the paper, so similar to the work she had done in graduate school. It suggested human thought might have an electromagnetic means of transmission, not unlike data being sent through a WiFi network.

Was it possible? She hoped it might be, although her natural reaction was skepticism. Like the journal entries she and William had read in Scotland that echoed some kind of 18th century version of Adeena, a simpler explanation was more probable. Choosing an answer with the fewest assumptions, Occam's razor, was her *modus operandi.* How could the characters in these journals be connected to Adeena?

Jackie smiled thinking about her. Why did trouble always seem to follow her daughter? There had to be a logical explanation for those journals, like the patient she helped recently. He claimed to be the reincarnation of his own grandfather who drowned on the same day the patient was born. The man had a debilitating fear of water so bad he even refused to drink it. Under hypnosis, Jackie listened to a detailed account of his grandfather's death, last seen alive sinking to the depths of a dark lake. Later, she discovered the man had almost drowned as an infant. She worked with him and eventually he was able to control his fears.

The wide-body jet bumped heavily onto the runway. The twin engines screamed in reverse to slow down the 160-ton speeding bullet. Jackie looked over at the terminal where Adeena waited and thought of a simple strategy to help her daughter.

Be her mother.

ADEENA WAITED FOR HER MOTHER AT THE INTERNATIONAL arrivals area, trying to focus on the real world again after all she had experienced as Katharine Carnegie over the last forty-eight hours.

When the glass doors unsealed the customs clearance area with a mechanical swoosh, and her mother strode forward as impeccably styled as a Paris fashion model, Adeena felt a familiar sense of comfort. Her mom had always been there for her.

"Ma petite!" Jackie exclaimed as she rolled her luggage rack piled high with suitcases towards Adeena. Mother and daughter hugged tightly, oblivious to the traffic jam they were causing as passengers tried to squeeze around them.

"How was your flight?" Adeena asked after they relaxed their embrace, with Jackie still holding both of Adeena's hands.

"Long. But I'm so happy to be home. How are you doing?"

"Good," Adeena smiled weakly. She knew her mother could always pick up on what she was thinking. She wished it was easier to hide her feelings as her mother studied her face, but she only smiled back. Maybe she was losing her touch?

They stood for a moment without words. Arriving passengers struggled to get around them until Jackie began to push her luggage down the ramp towards an open area. Adeena followed closely behind. Jackie turned and put her arms around Adeena again. "I've been thinking a lot about you."

"Me?"

"*Oui.* My musical daughter, my NAC cellist, my dreamer..."

Adeena laughed. "That's me. Always dreaming."

"Since you were truly *ma petite,*" Jackie grinned. "Where's Philippe? I thought he was coming too."

"He's working on the Hill, on deadline." Adeena's face grew pensive.

"Oh," Jackie said, her eyes searching. "Is everything okay, between you two?"

Damn! How does she do it? Adeena felt a wetness in her eyes. "Yeah." She fought impending tears. "Well no, not really."

Jackie touched Adeena's cheek softly. "What happened?"

"He asked me to marry him."

"Really? *Mon Dieu*!" Jackie beamed.

Adeena shook her head, a tear rolling down her cheek. "I said no."

Her mother searched her face. Then she embraced her again and Adeena cried in her arms feeling like a much younger version of herself.

After they loaded the luggage into the Volvo station wagon, Jackie considered her next move. Her daughter always seemed to be her toughest patient.

"Dad told me you blacked out during your audition?" Jackie began.

"Yeah, it was weird. And then I've been having really bad headaches too, almost migraines. You know, like I used to get?"

Jackie was worried. "I think we need to get this looked at. Maybe I can get you a referral to a neurologist at the Civic. They can do a CT scan and see what's going on."

"Can you set it up?" Adeena responded as she navigated the car out of the parking garage.

Jackie was quiet. Something in Adeena had changed. She looked tired. Her tears had made a mess of her mascara and Jackie's motherly instincts, together with her professional training, were giving her a sinking feeling. She had to proceed slowly to put the pieces together.

"So are you and Philippe... still together?"

Adeena said nothing for a moment. She seemed focused only on driving. "Yeah. We are." She looked at her mother with a blank expression. "I just need a little time. I'm so busy with rehearsals and my music, right now. I think he understands."

"If he does, he's a good man, to wait and stand by you. I think most would just move on."

Adeena didn't respond. She just looked over at her mother and nodded.

Jackie's conflicted instincts screamed at her to stop the car. Jackie the mother wanted to take Adeena and comfort her here and now to find out what was going on. Jackie the psychologist preferred careful probing.

"Philippe's got a big family in Quebec, doesn't he? Three brothers and two sisters, right?" Jackie said.

"Yeah, you got it."

Jackie laughed. "If you did get married, it'd be a big wedding!"

"Probably... I just, don't..." Adeena's words trailed off, like she was in deep thought. They rode in silence down the airport parkway toward the city.

"What is it, *ma belle*?" Jackie finally said. She knew it was probably time to shut up and listen. See if her daughter would talk.

Adeena sighed, as they came to a red light.

All the struggles Adeena had faced when she was younger – her rebellious attitude, the screaming and fighting, dealing with the police after drunken teenage parties, and worst of all, the drug overdose after her prom, flashed through Jackie's head. She preferred images of Adeena as a child – always making music on her tiny cello.

But now, her daughter was all grown up, strong-willed, artistically driven and frustrating as ever.

"Mom, I'm just not sure about..." Adeena volunteered slowly.

"About, what?"

Adeena hesitated for a moment. "Not sure if... " She paused, "Well, if I could be a wife. I don't think that I am cut out for marriage."

Jackie smiled. "You're worried about being married to Philippe?"

"It's not him, Mom. It's me."

"You're being too hard on yourself. You're not afraid of anything. You're beautiful. You're talented. You're musical, and you're smart as hell. You're my daughter!" Jackie mused. She looked out the window as they approached the city. "There is only one question, really. The only thing you need to ask yourself."

"What's that?" Adeena replied, glancing at her mother.

"Do you love him?"

Adeena sighed again. She stared straight ahead and bit her lip. A tear formed in her eye and rolled down her cheek. "I don't know. I really don't know!"

Another tear slowly followed the path of the first. Jackie reached over and patted Adeena softly.

"You've had a lot to go through, *belle*. Losing Grandma Stuart, the audition, and all the stress of trying to live up to your dreams. You've always wanted to make music, to be a cellist, and suddenly you're rehearsing with one of the top orchestras in the world," Jackie said in a low, soothing tone. "You look exhausted. Maybe marriage is too much to think about right now."

"It's not that!" Adeena cried. Tears were streaming down her cheeks. "Did you not hear what I just said? I don't know if I love Philippe! How can I marry someone I don't love?"

The mother and the psychologist inside of Jackie struggled for control. She weighed a range of options from both perspectives until finally the mother prevailed.

"You don't love him? Of course there are going to be doubts. I get it. You're both strong-willed, and passionate about what you do for a living. You're so busy with your own careers. I know how much he wants to be your husband. He's talked to your father and me so many times about you and about the plans he has. This is just my opinion, but I think he would always be there for you, no matter what life throws your way."

Tears were streaming down Adeena's cheeks now. "There's only one problem, Mom," she said, her voice quavering.

"What's that, *belle*?"

"I think I'm falling in love with someone else."

THE REACTION TO THE *ART OF REBELLION* EXHIBIT FAR exceeded anything Tara had expected.

The press, the public and her gallery colleagues were crazy for it. Day after day they set new attendance records. Her boss, André, gleefully sent her updates on ticket sales, along with links to news coverage, social media 'Likes' and 'Tweets,' along with notes he was still receiving from dignitaries. He praised her managerial skills and sent a stream of compliments on her organization and the unique design of the exhibit.

There was only one snag. The Duncan Cello. It was the attraction that so many visitors wanted to see with all the newspaper write-ups and the social media buzz, the photos, and the TV coverage. But something wasn't right. Friedrich Lang's comments on the night of the opening stayed with her in the days following the event.

Had she imagined his doubt about the authenticity of the instrument?

Why did he say those things and what did he know? Is it possible the National Museum of Scotland sent the wrong cello? That hardly made sense. They made too big a deal about insurance policies and required registered letters from the Minister for them to have screwed that up. She knew that while it was possible, it was extremely unlikely, given the care and protocols and all the documentation they had required before and after shipment of the instrument.

She had to get to the bottom of this.

"Pablo," she called out from her office. "Have you got a second?"

Her assistant appeared at the door, with a cell phone at his ear. He raised a hand to Tara as he finished off the call. "I've got to go, Laureen. I'll call you back."

"Sorry, didn't know you were on a call. How's your wife?"

"Great. She says hi. We're going out tonight, first anniversary."

"Congratulations, Pablo. You two are great together."

"Thanks, Ms. Kormos," Pablo replied, putting away his phone. "What can I help you with?"

"First thing tomorrow, I need you to get me all the expense claims and receipts related to setting up the new exhibit," Tara responded, looking out over the glass walls of her corner office. She turned to Pablo and added, "Particularly, anything to do with the Duncan Cello itself."

William checked his backpack one more time to be sure he had packed the diary. It was there, sitting right on top. He didn't trust his aging memory which routinely deleted the clutter of everyday details. Maybe there was only so much room for important stuff - like the history of Europe for the last one thousand years.

He and Murdo were on their way to the archives in Dundee. As they entered the outskirts of Arbroath, William reviewed what he knew of the little Scottish seaside town. It was here in 1320 that the Declaration of Arbroath was drafted and sent to the Pope, declaring Scotland independent from English rule.

As important as this declaration was, some claiming it was the model for a group of colonials in America to draw up their own Declaration of Independence, it paled in comparison to Arbroath's other gift to the world, according to Murdo, who shifted down a gear as they reached the town's old harbour.

"Ye ever had a smokie?" he asked as they parked in front of a line of weathered fishing dinghies.

"I've heard of them," William replied, glancing at the huge sign advertising *'Oor ane' - Arbroath Smokies - Sold Here!* He stepped out the car into the bright sunlight. "Any good?"

"Any guid?" Murdo replied in disbelief. "Treasure o' the sea!"

William laughed. He loved Murdo's enthusiasm, and it was nice to have the distraction. As they made their way toward the little fish house across from the harbour, William felt like egging Murdo on a bit more. "Exactly what is a smokie? An 'Arbroath' smokie?"

"Only the finest tasting fish in all the world. Ye know how they're made?"

"Smoked haddock?"

"Aye, smoked to perfection, Will. Absolute perfection! But ye need tae do it just right, or they're not worth a damn." Murdo was in his element now. "Ye start with fresh sounded haddock – put them in a salt tub to get them ready for the fire."

"Sounded?"

"Headed and cleaned. After ye salt them and wash 'em off really well, tie th'em together in pairs by the tail with some hemp twine and get your smokie pit ready."

"You've done this, I take it?"

"O' course. Worked summers here going to school. My job was to dig holes for the whisky barrels. I lined 'em with slate to make a fire in them. Then we fetched the fish on sticks and the smokie-maker took over."

"A smokie-maker?"

"Oh indeed. They know just how much smoke you need, how much to dampen the cloots depending on the day. And after about an hour, when the fish turns golden brown, we take'em off," Murdo said. "Had many a taste, straight off the barrel!"

William was taken with his description. In fact, he soon found out he could have gone further in his praise. They bought a few smokies 'hot off the barrel' and the taste was as Murdo claimed pure poetry.

Finishing off their quintessential Arbroath lunch, Murdo spotted a fellow he knew across the street. "Excuse me, Will. Need tae ask my mate about the sheep auction in Aberdeen."

"Take your time, Murdo," William said, enjoying the warmth of the sun on his face. "We've got lots of time. I'm going to get a coffee."

AS WILLIAM SIPPED HIS STEAMING 'WHITE' COFFEE HE flipped through the diary he had grabbed from the car. He found the entry for 10 September 1745 that he had skimmed a few days ago. He re-read it carefully.

> "George has betrayed me. And he draws sister Katharine into his traitorous design.
>
> The two have escaped Kinnaird by deceiving the men I had stationed to guard them, to prevent my family from making another disastrous decision. I know not where they fled, but I

have reason to believe they travelled to Perthshire and Drummond Castle.

I have dispatched Finlay, both father and son, to bring them back, and also sent a courier to warn my officers in Montrose that we may soon need to gather the regiment.

If Katharine, whom I suspect has been drawn under Jacobite influence, has developed affections for Drummond, I will deal with her sternly, and confine her if need be - until the head is torn from the body of this rising. Her petulance lately has become loathsome, and I fear she may need a long period of solitary discipline. Oh, but the Tower in London be closer, to provide its strong antidote.

As for George, all may be lost with him."

William closed the journal and looked across the fishing boats of the harbour. Except for the outboard engines, the dinghies were probably much like the boats that had plied these waters for centuries. He laid the diary on the table and considered the passage. He didn't remember mention of Katharine and George leaving. He had thought that the entry talked about how the Captain and his brother had walked together and argued about the history of the Union with England.

Or had he read that at all? If only he had taken a picture of it, he could be sure.

He took out his phone and snapped a few shots of the pages for this entry. It seemed to him that passages he had already re-read were not the way he remembered them previously. The photos would help ensure he wasn't treading down the family road of psychosis. Might be an idea to take pictures of all of the entries for the week of September, 1745. He drained the last of his coffee and flipped through the next few pages.

Had the diary entry for 10, September, 1745 changed? It now appeared that Katharine and George had fled to Drummond Castle, and that Katharine's reasons had to do with James Drummond, the Duke of Perth.

After Murdo dropped him off in Dundee, William needed to make his way to Drummond Castle.

ADEENA SETTLED INTO HER CHAIR ON THE STAGE OF SOUTHAM Hall.

This was her first formal rehearsal as a member of the National Arts Centre Orchestra. What a difference from the last time she sat on this same stage, scared and trembling that her future depended on how she performed.

My future.

She considered the phrase for a moment. Is it in the past?

Adeena looked over the pages for the cello section of Friedrich Lang's *Voyages of Destiny* suite. The music sitting on the music stand was a line-for-line transcription of the score. Katharine's music. *My music.* She studied the conductor going through his notes at the podium in the centre of the stage.

She saw Walter and Maria arrive, and wondered about their take on Lang's blatant plagiarism. Maria walked over to the violin section, waving to Adeena with a smile. She recalled Maria's passionate plea to share the music with the world. Letting Lang steal it probably wasn't what she'd had in mind.

Walter went directly to the conductor's podium. They exchanged a few words, then walked off the stage together, engrossed in animated discussion, before disappearing behind the black curtains. Maria picked up her copy of the sheet music and walked over to Adeena.

"I can't believe you're letting him get away with this," she said. "Your grandmother sent you that score from her death bed. This is not *his* music!"

"I know. I'm just not sure what I can do."

"Too bad we don't know who really composed it."

Adeena was silent, but Maria was fired up. "He's printing copies of this music like he owns it, because he knows it's never been published, never been heard before. It's a crime no one will ever know the real composer. He must have been gifted."

"He?"

"Yes, the guy that composed this work. It's a damn outrage that *Herr Lang* is going to get all the credit, instead of him," Maria said.

"What makes you think it was composed by a man?" Adeena asked, raising her eyebrows.

Maria studied her for a moment. A big grin washed over her face. "Oh! I guess it's my general bias. I suppose technically you could be right, but then women didn't generally do a lot of composing in the 18th century, did they?"

Adeena stood up and turned toward the direction that Walter and Lang had exited the stage. "They did indeed, Maria. Excuse me. I'll be right back."

ADEENA FOUND FRIEDRICH LANG AND HIS PRINCIPAL CELLIST a few yards behind the heavy black stage curtain. They were engaged in a heated exchange. She paused a moment, hidden in a dark fold, not wanting to reveal herself just yet.

"You have a choice, Walter. Play the music, or leave," Lang hissed.

"I'll only play it if you credit the real composer," Walter shot back.

"No one knows who he is, for Christ sake! I'm the one putting my career on the line here," Lang snarled.

Before Walter could respond, Adeena stepped forward. "I already told you who the real composer is."

The two men turned toward her, startled.

"What? Who?" Lang snapped.

"Katharine Carnegie, from Scotland. She wrote it in 1745 and performed it with a chamber ensemble. It was a big hit, too. Spellbinding, in fact," Adeena said.

"Can you prove that, Adeena?" Walter asked.

Lang looked at her, his face contorted in anger. She turned toward Walter, trying to deflect Lang's scorching gaze. "I don't know, maybe," she responded. "There's probably something. There must be a record of it, somewhere."

Lang grinned. "Sounds like wishful thinking, Miss Stuart. Maybe you should spend more time rehearsing, instead of threatening me. You're still on probation you know."

"You need to give the credit for this work to her, Mr. Lang," Adeena replied. She was trying to be professional.

"Give credit to who? Some fantasy woman of yours?" Lang sneered. "I'm the one bringing it to the world, arranging it for an orchestra, staking my reputation on it. I'll damn well take credit for this music. It's as much mine as it yours!"

"Wow!" Adeena said, looking the conductor straight in the eye. "And I used to admire you."

Walter stepped forward, but before he could say anything Lang interrupted. "You two have a choice to make," he started. "You can be part of the symphony, shut your mouth and play the music. Or, I can fire both of you."

Walter and Adeena looked at the conductor in angry silence.

"And Walter, before I let you go, I could call your wife if you want, to tell her about your adventures in London. I'm sure she would love to know about your evenings with Maria," he said with a wicked smile.

Walter winced at the statement. He glanced at Adeena and then looked back at the conductor. "You bastard."

Lang sneered. He seemed to enjoy the power he wielded. "I'm sure your Mrs. would love to know about the morning I found Maria naked in your bed."

Walter grimaced. "I didn't..." He looked as if he had more to say, but then seemed to decide against it. He looked over at Adeena, who covered her mouth in shock. "Oh shit! Adeena, I didn't...I didn't want it go that far. It was only once. We had too much wine. Way too much, I swear!"

Lang wasn't done. "Ah, that's not really true Walter. You and Maria still make *such* a nice couple."

"Leave him alone!" Adeena said.

"Oh yes, your highness," Lang retorted. "And let me ask you something, Cinderella, with all your high fucking moral standards. Tell me, are you taking good care of the Duncan Cello up at your cottage?"

Adeena froze. "What?"

"Oh, come on. You know what I'm talking about. You missed the grand opening of your big exhibit. Everyone was there, including me and the mayor, and a bunch of airheads from the government," Lang said. "Oh, and also someone I think maybe you might know? Ms. Tara? Your boss from the National Gallery?"

"What are you getting at?" Adeena asked angrily.

"The big group of important assholes were all there to admire the one and only Duncan Cello," he continued, his voice rich with sarcasm. "Too bad all they got was a nice fake piece of shit. Oh, it looked so much like the *real* five-million-dollar instrument to the assembled idiocracy!"

Walter turned to Adeena. "What's he talking about Adeena?"

She hesitated, reluctant to admit anything.

"Secrets," Lang answered. "All of us have a few, don't we? I think it's best they remain that way and we focus on creating music and letting our sleeping dogs lie. Unless you want them to bite you."

Adeena said nothing. She stood for a few moments in silence before letting out a deep sigh and following the two men back onto the stage.

CHAPTER 18

Adeena poured herself a glass of wine, and stood in the kitchen of her condo, looking out over the Ottawa River that kept Quebec from sliding into Ontario. She noticed there were two missed calls from Philippe on her phone and also a text message from him:

Dinner? I'm leaving in the morning. Let me spoil you

She swiped the message back and forth on her phone, as if she was toying with his offer. The glass of chilled *pinot* was calling to her and she sipped it thoughtfully, unable to form a response to the simple text message.

Who am I kidding?

Adeena was trying to think of a reason why she couldn't have dinner with him, and yet there really wasn't anything she could come up with.

Gee Philippe, I know you love me, my parents think you're amazing, you have a great family, a good job, you want kids, you love adventure, travelling and making love to me, but . . .

She poured a little more wine into her glass.

But I'd rather blackout and dream that I'm another woman from the past with another man no one else will ever meet.

Adeena typed a response:

Okay. Where?

While she waited for a reply, she got up and walked towards her bedroom, thinking about what she should wear tonight. The Duncan Cello sat in the corner, still in the special double-lined travelling case she used to transport it. She felt an almost magnetic attraction tugging at her as she tried to walk by. She wanted to ignore it.

Friedrich Lang knew she had taken the precious instrument. How long before Tara figured it out?

And now Walter knew her secret too. She thought about him and Maria, and Walter's wife Grace and their two kids, both about Adeena's age. They had grown up together. Grace had even been something of an aunt to her. Walter worshipped his wife, but Maria had a passion that must have been hard for him to resist – especially when they were alone for long stretches out of the country, making music together. Adeena didn't like what Walter had done, but she understood the emotions that drew musicians together.

Adeena touched the rough surface of the Bam cello flight case. A spike of adrenaline shot through her. It was becoming a forbidden pleasure. It felt like it was calling her. Taking the Duncan Cello had been wrong on every front, and there was no way to justify it. She realized that she could be arrested and maybe even serve time for what she had done. She might find a way to spin some kind of story about having restorative work done on it, creating a prop for security purposes, or some other lame excuse.

But deep down, she knew she had to make things right.

Even though she struggled against it, she kept her hand on the cello case, unable to escape its pull. A few inches away lay the doorway to another world, one that was beginning to feel more where she belonged than her own reality. Katharine's cello and her music were expensive artifacts, intriguing historical curiosities for galleries and museums. The Duncan Cello might be worth millions to a collector and the music might be the ticket to jump-starting a frustrated old composer's career.

But no one understood their true value.

Adeena finally found the strength to lift her hand. She knew the cello and the music were worth fighting for and that somehow they played a part in the story of her family – her grandmother, her father, and herself. If she had to be incarcerated to sort things out, well...she might just have to do that.

Her phone beeped and vibrated on the counter. It was probably Philippe texting her back. Before she could answer it, there was a knock on the door. Adeena looked over, confused. She went to the door and opened it wide.

Philippe stood in the hallway, smiling. He was dressed in a dark suit and purple tie.

"Surprise!"

Adeena laughed. "You don't give a girl a chance, do you? Come on in."

"I got reservations for a new place on the Market. It just opened," he said as he walked into her apartment. "Gourmet pasta, fresh seafood flown in every day, all with French wines paired with each course. The chef is from *Le Cordon Bleu.* He just arrived from Europe."

"That sounds good," she said. "I'm starving. Just give me a minute to put something on." She gave Philippe a peck on the cheek and turned towards her room. "Pour yourself some wine."

Philippe watched Adeena as she turned and started towards her room. Just as she approached her bedroom door he called out to her. "What's that?"

She stopped by the Bam cello flight case. "You mean this?" she said pointing to the oversized black case.

Philippe looked at her seriously. "That's not your case." His smile was gone. "I hope it's not what I think it is," he said sternly.

Adeena hesitated. Had there been a news release? Did everyone know she had the Duncan Cello? "I just, uh... I needed to have Thomas Peeters do some touch-ups on it," she said weakly. Trying to fool Philippe was like trying to swim across the lake in lead boots.

"Adeena, do you have any idea what you're doing?" he asked. "Friedrich Lang told me you took the Duncan Cello. I didn't believe him. I thought he was just trying to threaten me, that he was just an old fool! Oh my God, Adeena!" he groaned.

She turned and walked back towards him. She took his hand and held it in hers, looking up into his face. "Can I at least try and explain this to you?"

FOR THE NEXT FIFTEEN MINUTES, ADEENA TOLD PHILIPPE ONE more time, everything about her experience with the Duncan Cello, and what happened when she played the lost score that her grandmother had sent to her. He listened as she described her performance and how she became Katharine Carnegie, the composer, singer and cellist. She told him how Robert Duncan had designed the cello for Katharine, and that she had two brothers – George and Sir James Carnegie, the Captain, and how they ended up on opposite sides of the 1745 uprising in Scotland.

Philippe studied her curiously.

He said very little during her explanation. When she was finished, he moved over and sat down on the sofa. He put his head back and stared at the ceiling. He looked lost in thought as he rubbed his temples and shook his head in frustration.

"Ohhhh my," he said at last. "I can't believe this is happening."

"What's that supposed to mean?" Adeena asked.

"You! You, Adeena. You steal the cello, and now you tell me you're . . . I don't know what you're trying to say. You're time travelling?" He gazed out the condo windows towards the dark sky.

"You don't believe a word I've said, do you?" she replied.

"Adeena! C'mon!" he sang out, exasperated. "You're not *really* going back in time. You know your history, you know the music. You are just dreaming all this stuff. Do you *not* understand? None of this, all these stories you've told me, none of this is real!"

"You think I'm crazy," Adeena replied. "Don't you?"

"I didn't say you were *crazy,* but do you not think that *maybe* it's just all happening in your mind?" he said, standing up and straightening his tie. "Let's go talk about it over some wine. We'll have dinner and we can sort this out."

Adeena looked at him like he had just murdered her dog. "Philippe . . ." she said putting her thoughts together. "You have no idea what I'm going through. You're right. I might be going crazy, or, this might *really* be happening to me. Either way, I need you. I need you to really be with me on this."

Philippe was silent. He seemed to be reviewing his options. "Okay. I'll try. Are we going?"

"I need to know. Do you believe me or not?" she said, her laser eyes boring a hole through his skull.

He hesitated a long while before he answered tentatively, in a barely audible whisper. "I don't think I can, Adeena. I just can't believe that could really be happening."

She felt herself losing control. An inner tension grew from tiny pebble to blazing comet in a nanosecond. Why couldn't he just be there for her, when she needed him most? If he could not or would not, she wanted him gone. "I don't want you here. Please leave me alone."

"Adeena. You need help. Let me take you somewhere, take you to see someone. But first, let me take the Duncan Cello back to the Gallery before you get arrested."

"No! Just leave, leave me alone! I'm crazy, right? Your fucking wacko criminal girlfriend," she screamed. "Right?"

"Adeena... please."

"LEAVE!"

He hesitated and then took a few steps away from her. He stopped one more time, shook his head and walked out the door.

ADEENA SOBBED AS SHE OPENED THE BAM CELLO CASE.

Philippe was probably right. She needed help, and none of this was real.

Yes, she knew the history, and she knew the music. As she lifted the Duncan Cello from the confines of its inner case, she felt like she was losing control. Katharine was becoming stronger and Adeena weaker. She needed the oxygen that only the Duncan Cello and the lost score could provide.

Her eyes filled with tears as she began to play – a junkie unable to resist her next fix.

LADY JEAN BEFORE ADEENA, HOLDING A STEAMING TEAPOT with the same blue inlaid flowers and leaves as the cup Adeena held in her hand.

"Katharine? More tea, dear?"

Adeena looked up at her and nodded. "Yes. Please." She was seated at a wide oak table with sunlight streaming through the narrow windows that provided a view of the spectacular ornamental gardens in the castle's courtyards.

Around the table sat Katharine's brother George and James Drummond. Both ate heartily of the breakfast laid before them: thick hocks of ham and roasted pork, hardboiled eggs, toast, oatmeal cakes, marmalade and what looked like a pint of dark ale parked in front of each of their overflowing plates.

"Eat hardy. Aye, the road could be with both of ye a long time," Lady Jean admonished, and then turned to George. "Ye have chosen wisely. Your brother, the Captain, not so well."

George smiled at her analysis as he finished his breakfast. "His mind was made up years ago," George said, finishing off a thick piece of ham, "as a child it would seem. The history he learned in Glasgow was twisted to paint a glorious picture of a Union ripe with riches and opportunity. They neglected to tell him that his family fought and died for o'er two hundred years to preserve Scotland."

"Aye," Lady Jean said. "Your aunt, the Countess Lady Margaret, tried everything to give your brother a proper education, by those who knew the history of the Carnegie family. Your brother became chief of the House of Southesk when your father died, but alas, he never learned its history. Instead he developed a hatred for the Jacobites who seek to preserve it."

James listened to all of this without saying a word. He finished up his breakfast and drank deeply from the tankard of ale before him. He wiped his lips with a linen cloth and laid the empty pewter vessel on the table.

"Today, we start for Edinburgh. The capital will soon be restored," he said.

Lady Jean beamed at his confidence. "Your father, and your grandfather - the whole Drummond and Gordon clans in fact, will be watching. They are counting on you, James," she warned. "Ye must not fail them."

James nodded. "We will do them proud before the week is done. I found another one hundred and fifty men from Perthshire to march with us, along with more than two thousand who have already joined us. And now, we have support of the Farquharsons, the MacGregors, the Stewarts, the Menzies and the Robertsons. They all pledged their allegiance to the Prince last night," he paused, glancing at Adeena, "after the ball."

Adeena watched the back and forth between James and his

mother. As Lady Jean continued to talk, explaining to George how she had been praying for this day since her husband had died twenty-five years ago, James caught Adeena's eye. He seemed to be pointing his head slightly to the right, as if he wanted her to follow him. Lady Jean sat down beside George, took his arm, and began explaining how her husband had been part of the Jacobite group that had almost captured Edinburgh Castle during the 1715 rising, some thirty years before.

Adeena stood up. "Excuse me for a moment," she said. George and Lady Jean barely heard her as she left the table. James was not far behind.

OUTSIDE OF DRUMMON CASTLE, ADEENA SAW MEN PREPARING for the march. They had amassed supplies of oatmeal, cured beef, salted herring and salmon, along with barrels of brandy and ale, and were loading them onto wagons that would follow behind the men on their trek towards Edinburgh. The brindle stallion Balgair was tied to a post and she smiled at the sight of him. He glanced over at her and snorted loudly, raising his head high in the air.

"Now, you be careful what you say to her, Balgair!" James laughed as he drew up and stood beside her.

Adeena chuckled. "Don't worry. He only says nice things to me."

James gave the horse's nose a good rub. "Katharine, I may be gone for some time. I want you to know that I will watch over George. I will do my best to protect him."

"Thank you, James," Adeena said. She moved closer and scratched the side of Balgair's sturdy neck. He seemed to appreciate it and stamped his front hoof. She glanced at James. "Your mother puts a lot of pressure on you, doesn't she?"

He smiled. "Your brother, the Captain, may be fierce in battle, and General Cope may have cannon and fodder aimed at my head, but it is my own mother who truly gives me fright."

Adeena laughed. "I can see that. I guess you grew up hearing all about your duty and finishing the work of your father?"

"I did, my lady," he replied. "From the age of seven. That is when he died and I became head of my family and took his title, Duke of Perth. I've known my responsibility, and my duty to all those who came before me, for a very long time indeed."

"Is that why you fight now? Why you are leaving for Edinburgh?" she asked.

James looked at her with some confusion. He seemed to be thinking, uncertain how best to reply.

"Katharine, you have given me a renewed spirit to believe that what I do is necessary and indeed required, to help restore the Kingdom – the lost Kingdom of my father and his father, and all the members of the House of Drummond before me," he replied. He paused a moment, looking at her. "But Katharine, you probe deeply. You seek to understand me, do you not?"

Adeena studied him. His blue eyes, long hair and soft features belied the savage strength she had seen him display when he had saved her in the forest. "I guess I do, James," she replied. "I want to know what drives you to take up this fight."

He looked away. Maybe this was not the way a woman in the 18th century talked to a man.

"That is a question which I often ponder myself," he said finally. "And one which no one, save Rosalyne, has ever asked me before."

"Rosalyne?"

"My first love, in France," he replied. "We spent the summer together when I was a boy of ten and eight years."

"Eighteen?"

"Indeed. I met her as a boy. I left as a man."

"What happened? To her?"

"She was a widow, older than me, and..." his words trailed off. He turned and looked at Adeena. "My mother, my brother John and I, we all needed to return home from France, to Scotland, back to Drummond Castle where I was born. I had been away for more than ten years. I was like a stranger when I returned to this place, but alas, it was deeper inside of me than I ever imagined."

Adeena wasn't sure what he was trying to say. "What about Rosalyne, I mean. What happened to her?"

James' face tightened. "The fever. It took her, not long after I left Paris. Our letters were few, but they live sacred in my memory. After she was gone, I took to running Drummond and worked more than ten years on a plan for the township of Crieff with everything I had learned in France."

"For her?" Adeena asked.

"She was never far from my thoughts," he replied. He took his hand and laid it on her shoulder. His touch was strong and firm. "I have not talked this way before, not since I was with her."

She reached for his face and stroked his cheek. "James, you're a good man. I think I'm beginning to know your heart."

He drew her into his arms and pulled her closer. "You do, Katharine, because you are there."

She closed her eyes as they held each other. The worlds of past and present collided in her head. Whether this was real or a dream, she could not tell. But all she could feel now was James. She felt like she could hold him a long time.

"Katharine, we need to be on our way. Release your prisoner!" The voice came from George who now approached them. She smiled as James relaxed his hold on her.

"Yes, my laird," she replied. "As you command." James let her go and moved towards Balgair, checking on the fittings of his bridle and saddle. She noticed another horse, a brown mare, being trotted towards them by a soldier dressed in the red colours of the Perth regiment.

"Katharine, I want you to stay here with Lady Jean, until you receive word from me," George told her. "We are meeting the

Prince at Scone Castle and then plotting our route to Edinburgh."

"Scone Castle?" she asked.

"Yes, the House of Scone," James interrupted, stepping forward, holding Balgair's reins. "The Prince's father, King James the Eighth, stayed there almost thirty years ago. It is where all our Kings have been crowned for the last five hundred years."

George kissed his sister on the cheek. "I will send word soon," he said. "Stay here until you hear from me."

"I will," she said. "Be safe George, take care of yourself." He nodded and walked towards the brown mare.

James stood before her. "I want to carry something from you into battle with me," he said.

"From me?" Adeena asked, confused.

"Just your words, the ones that live within me," he said. He held a sheaf of paper that he had extracted from his saddlebag. "Give me your mark, Katharine, that I may keep it always close." He handed the paper to her and an inked quill that he must have used for his letters.

Adeena took them and bent over the wooden table that sat beside her. She thought for a moment.

Forever, I will wait for you.

She looked at it and then over at James, now saddled on Balgair. He wanted her 'mark.' She bent over and hesitated, and then signed the note. She looked down at what she had written:

Katharine

Adeena took the paper and handed it to him. He read it slowly, closed his eyes for a long moment and then bowed his head to her. He folded the note, placed it inside his uniform and turned the reins of his horse towards the road.

As she watched him ride away, the morning sun filled her

eyes with a brightness that overwhelmed her. She wondered how long it would be until she saw him again.

The sun grew brighter still until she felt it completely absorb her.

PHILIPPE WANDERED THROUGH THE BYWARD MARKET IN A state of confusion.

He was not used to this feeling. He was usually in control. As a reporter, it was usually him with inside knowledge, or a strong hunch to follow, a puzzle he could solve by following clues, like a scavenger hunt that eventually led to his journalistic prize.

But as he slowly wandered by the clubs and restaurants of the Market, still dressed in his new black shoes, dark suit and purple tie, he felt hopelessly lost. Adeena had told him she needed him, needed him to 'really be with her.'

And yet she had kicked him out of her apartment for the first time in their relationship, and instead of being there to help her, here he was parading around in his silly outfit, dressed up like a monkey with nowhere to go. Adeena was the woman he loved, even if he couldn't always understand her.

He stopped and looked back over his shoulder at the light from her 14th floor condominium window.

'I need you to really be with me.' Her words rang in his ears.

He wondered what true love looks like in this situation. Does he go and get her help? Does he just listen? Or, does he work hard to believe what she was trying to explain, even if it was completely impossible?

Maybe I just need to give her time and space?

Philippe stood thinking for a moment, watching cars flash by, and couples holding hands walking down the street together, looking happy just being with each other. Finally, he turned around and started back to Adeena's condo.

Whatever he should be doing, he knew it didn't involve turning his back on her now.

THE SUN WAS STILL BLINDING ADEENA'S EYES WITH AN impossible brightness. As she tried to shield her eyes, she noticed shadowy figures standing nearby, staring at her.

"Adeena?" spoke one of the figures. *"Belle?"*

The figure came closer. It was her mother.

"Mom?" she replied. "Where am I?"

"In the hospital, at the Civic," her mother responded softly. She closed the blinds a bit to help shade the bright sunlight streaming into the room. "How are you feeling?"

Adeena sat up and looked around. She was in a hospital room. One half of the wall beside her was made up of large windows overlooking Carling Avenue and the open fields of the Central Experimental Farm across the street. Her mother stood beside the bed, a nurse by her side.

"I'm okay," Adeena finally replied. "What happened?"

Her mother sat down on the edge of the bed and took her hand.

"Philippe called me last night," she said. "He was in a bit of a panic. He told me you blacked out, so we called an ambulance and brought you to Emergency here. You were so groggy, we couldn't wake you up."

Adeena felt strange listening to this story. It seemed less real to her than travelling back in time, though much more probable to just about everyone else. "Is Philippe here too?"

"Yes, *belle*," her mother replied. "He just went to get a coffee. He's been here with you all night."

Adeena wondered what he was thinking about all this.

Jackie put her hand on Adeena's forehead. "I called Tara, too. She wants to come and see you."

Adeena closed her eyes.

What have I done to all these people who believe in me?

The nurse stepped forward, a sturdy looking middle-aged woman with a shock of short blonde hair and a blue butterfly tattoo on her neck. "Do you think you can stand up for me?" she asked gently.

Adeena wasn't sure about that, just like everything else in her life. "I don't know," she replied, pulling off the sheet that covered her. She was wearing a thin hospital gown.

The last time she had worn this outfit was in high school when she ended up in the trauma unit after an overdose. For two days she went in and out of touch with the conscious world, coming down from a mix of alcohol, LSD and God knows what else that she had taken at the 'After-Prom' party.

Her bare feet touched the cold tile floor, and though she felt a bit wobbly, the nurse was pleased that she stood up without assistance.

"That's good," she said, locking her arm around Adeena's to make sure she didn't fall over. "Mum, she's going to need to walk. We have to get her moving."

Her mother stepped forward. "Of course. I can take her."

"Thanks," the nurse said, looking down at her charts. She read them over them for a few seconds. "Oh, wait, before you do, Dr. Lochiel has ordered an MRI and I need to ask Adeena a few screening questions."

"Oh, sure," Adeena responded.

"Do you weigh more than 200 kilograms?" the nurse laughed. "Forget that one! Uh, next question. Is there a possibility you may be pregnant?"

Jackie smiled, folded her hands together and raised her eyes, as if praying for an affirmative response.

"No. I am pretty sure I'm not. But..." Adeena hesitated.

"But what?" her mother interjected.

"Well, I haven't had a period, since, uh," Adeena looked at her wrist as if she was wearing a watch. "I guess technically I just missed one, but it feels like it's been a long time for some reason. And I've had some really wicked cramps lately."

The nurse made a note on her chart. "Really? I'll let the doctor know. We're doing some blood work first and we'll find out for sure, one way or the other."

WILLIAM HAD SPENT MOST OF THE MORNING TAKING THE tour of the ornamental gardens at Drummond Castle near Perth.

He was amazed at the complexity and design of the gardens, but his real interest lay inside. He was disappointed to learn that the castle was not open to the public. However, he found out from the guide giving the tour that Drummond Castle was an important landmark in the Scottish Lowlands, and that James Drummond, Third Duke of Perth, was a prominent character in its long, illustrious history.

After the tour, William approached the guide, a wise-cracking retired teacher who had taught both history and geography in secondary schools in Scotland. The man, Daniel, had thick bushy eyebrows and an even thicker moustache set on his long stern face. He wore a bonnet that topped his ceremonial kilt and jacket. At six and a half feet tall, he made an imposing impression.

The two men hit it off at once, with their shared passion for history and interest in understanding the origins of the things around them – little details most just took for granted.

"During the 1745 rising," William asked him, "who was in charge here?"

"The castle, ye mean?" Daniel asked.

"Yes. I know that James Drummond fought in the war, and was a Lieutenant General with Bonnie Prince Charles, as was his brother John," William said. "Their mother, Lady Jean, did she manage the castle during the rising?"

Daniel looked at William closely for a second. "Impressive, laddie. Ye've nae missed a thing, have ye?"

"I've just started doing some reading. I'm interested in the Jacobite risings and I've been looking for a new research project for my graduate students," William explained, thinking that this was going to be his focus for some time to come.

"Then ye know that Lady Jean was sent to Edinburgh and locked up for a lang time, and that she outlived both 'er sons."

William hadn't had time to fully research James Drummond yet. "Oh, interesting. And, when did the Duke of Perth die?"

"James was a brave lad. He was greatly influenced by those around him. He was brilliant, naturally gifted – and would have changed the world had he not died after Culloden," Daniel mused. "Tried to hold up the family honour, be a good Catholic, please his mother, and all his relations. Pleased everyone it seems, except himself, perhaps."

"How did he die?"

"At sea, in the channel, on a French frigate, maybe a few weeks after the slaughter on the moors of Culloden House," Daniel explained. "He was wounded in battle, leading his men till the end. They had nae a hope in hell, and he probably knew it too. Still, he was at the front of the charge, commanding the left wing against the Redcoats."

William was silent. He had heard about the Battle of Culloden, but it had never seemed so personal before. Daniel pointed to a statue. "He was buried at sea, but there's a plaque o'er there, if ye want to see for yerself."

William stared at the inscription on the large sword that served as a tribute to the man.

James Drummond, 3rd Duke of Perth

b. 11 May 1713 / d. 13 May 1746

'Poor as I am, I would rather than a

thousand pounds that my colours are safe'

He looked over at Daniel, who stood watching him. "He never married?"

"No sir, not our poor James," Daniel replied. "I'm afraid duty and honour were his mistress. His mother made sure o' that."

"And so, he died without issue. No children?" William said, still staring at the sword.

"Indeed. That line of Drummond ended with him," Daniel replied, shaking his head.

CHAPTER 19

Adeena listened carefully to the muffled voices outside her hospital room door.

It was quite a gathering, she thought – a clinical psychologist, an investigative reporter and a suspicious administrator – all sharing clues. All that was missing was Colonel Mustard. Hard as she tried, the only word she could make out was 'Adeena.'

A minute later Tara and Philippe walked in. He looked tired while she seemed possessed with enough energy to power the whole neurology ward.

"Oh Dee!" Tara gushed clutching a bouquet of flowers. "Up to your old tricks!"

Adeena brightened. "Your life's too boring when I play by the rules."

"You play by the rules? That's my fantasy."

"Really? Then you need to get an actual life, Tar."

Philippe sat down on the edge of the bed looking lost. Tara bent over and gave Adeena a hug. "Well, I'm glad you're okay. You had me worried, and that doesn't help my beauty rest." She paused a moment and then asked softly. "How are you feeling?"

"I'm fine," Adeena replied, glancing at Philippe, then at Tara and finally over at her mother, who had stepped into the room. "I'm just so sorry to have put you all through this."

Her mother moved closer. "I just had a word with Dr. Lochiel before he got called into surgery."

Adeena pulled herself up higher on the bed. "Really? What did he say?"

"He thinks you might be having 'ocular' migraines."

"Ocular?" Philippe asked. "As in eyes?"

"Oui," Jackie replied. "It's sometimes called a 'silent migraine' because usually there is no pain. But, there can be intense auras with them."

"Auras?" Adeena repeated. "Like seeing things?"

Her mother nodded. "Kind of. It's usually just bright spots and flashing lights, but it can go further. Hallucinations, intense sensory distortion and..." she paused for a moment, pursing her lips as if trying to contain the rest of her thoughts.

Adeena sat frozen, listening to her mother. "What Mom? Is there something else?"

"Well, it seems you've also got symptoms of a hemiplegic migraine. It's actually a neurological disease with prolonged aura and blackouts. It's usually genetic."

The room went quiet. Tara reached for Adeena's hand. But it was Philippe who spoke first.

"So, the doctor's not sure which kind this is?" he started. "They both include auras or visions? And people blackout with the hemi... What did you call it?"

"Hemiplegic migraine. It's rare, but intense. Patients report visual and sensory aura," Jackie replied. "Dr. Lochiel isn't sure himself. He's in touch with a specialist in Toronto apparently, who is doing research on migraines. There are some new theories and an experimental procedure they've been testing."

Adeena couldn't process all of this. Too many medical terms. Everyone trying to explain something that was not meant to be understood. And did her mother say genetic?

"The doctor wants you to get some rest, take it easy Adeena, for a while at least. I thought we could go up to the lake afterwards," her mother said in a gentle tone.

Adeena nodded her head. "As long as I can practice."

"Sure," Jackie said. "We'll bring your cello up with us."

The "c" word jolted the room into silence. A dark look passed between Tara, Adeena and Philippe. No one said a word as the rhythmic beeping of a medical monitor set an eerie mood.

Jackie broke the tension. "Oh, and they're doing a complete physical too, Adeena." The hanging silence seemed to spook her mother.

"You know what?" she announced. "You guys don't need me hanging around." She hugged Adeena and gave her a kiss on each cheek. "Take care, *ma belle.* See you in the morning."

AFTER HER MOTHER LEFT IT WAS OBVIOUS THAT TARA'S MOOD had changed.

"Adeena, there's something we do need to discuss," Tara started.

Oh shit, here it comes.

Adeena pushed her hair back, and squarely faced her accuser, girding herself for what came next. Tara rarely called her anything but *Dee.*

Philippe sitting on the edge of the bed, looked horrified. He suddenly bounced up in front of Tara. "Sorry to interrupt," he said. "Adeena, did they bring your morning pills, the ones you're supposed to take for your blood pressure?"

Adeena looked at him strangely. What was he up to? He winked slyly as Tara glanced down at her cell phone. "Oh, I forgot about those," she said, discreetly pushing the nurse's call button. "Tar, did you see them?"

Tara looked around the room, confused.

Adeena suddenly let out a shriek. "Shit!" She held her forehead, trying to grimace as convincingly as she could. "Ouch! Oh fuck that hurts!" She closed her eyes and let her head drop onto her chest dramatically.

Tara called out, "Dee? What is it?" She touched Adeena's hand. It was limp and there was no response.

Philippe stood up. "Why does this keep happening to her? Tara, we better find a nurse."

THE NEXT MORNING AS ADEENA ATE LUNCH SHE HAD TIME TO think.

She had just survived both an MRI and a complete physical that included a Pap test. She had laid her arm out for so many needles since being in the hospital she felt like a sieve. But in a strange way, this wasn't a bad place to sort things out.

Philippe had been sweet to distract Tara yesterday when she seemed on the verge of interrogating her about the Duncan Cello. Adeena knew Philippe didn't believe her time travelling story. But he seemed determined to be there for her. Knowing there was now a theory about what might be happening, 'migraines with auras,' he probably felt he could rationalize her stories now.

'Migraines with auras.' She turned the phrase over in her head.

Is that all this is? That would be a tidy explanation. She closed her eyes and saw James again, riding away on Balgair. His face filled her mind, as she remembered the warmth of his arms around her. She sank into her bed, holding her arms together reliving the moment.

"Adeena?"

She opened her eyes. There was a bearded, middle-aged man in a white coat at the door.

"I'm Doctor Lochiel."

Adeena let her arms go and sat up. "Hi. Please come in."

The doctor stepped forward. He was a big, burly man. With

his thick, reddish hair, she had the sense he could be a Viking warrior as easily as a neurologist at the Civic Hospital.

"We've gone over all your tests, and I'd like to ask you a few questions," he said, standing beside her bed scanning the various monitors hooked up to her.

"Sure, no problem."

"Have you been mountain climbing, scuba diving, or perhaps, skydiving?" Dr. Lochiel began.

Adeena chuckled. "Oh right. All three, in my spare time!"

"So, I take it, that's a no?"

"Correct. I've been playing my cello and rehearsing with the orchestra, but I've laid off the whole mountain-climbing thing," she smiled. "I don't think I would ever go skydiving, and I'd love to learn scuba diving, but haven't had the chance. Not this week at least."

The doctor was making notes on his clipboard. "There seems to be some sort of trauma happening to you, the type that we've seen when people are exposed to severe changes in temperature, atmospheric pressure, altitude – that sort of thing," he said. "It can lead to blackouts, loss of blood pressure, migraines and..." he hesitated, touching her forehead and then lifting one of her eyelids slightly.

"And what?" she asked.

"Uh... visions, intense dreams, hallucinations," he said, checking her other eye. "We've had patients who think they've gone to other places when they blackout. Your mind is a powerful organ, Adeena."

She looked at him carefully. "What are you saying?"

He returned to writing notes. "Normally I tell patients to stop skydiving or mountain climbing, that sort of thing," he said. "But I'm not sure telling you to stop playing the cello would make any difference!"

Adeena stared at him.

"Just take those pills I prescribed for now, and we'll arrange to do some more tests. I'm also talking to another neurologist about your case. There is a specialist in Toronto who is doing some research on these kinds of cases," he said. The doctor hesitated for a moment, then added. "There is one other thing, too."

Adeena sat waiting for him to continue.

"We did a full body scan MRI, because we were doing both neurological and gynaecological foci," he said. "You'd reported problems with your menses and pain in your pelvis?"

"Yes, so..." she replied. "You found something?"

He tugged his beard before answering. "I'm afraid there seems to be damage to your fallopian tubes. This may affect your ability to conceive, naturally at least."

Adeena said nothing. She looked out the window at the overcast sky. Little beads of rain had formed on the window. She closed her wet eyes.

"I'm sorry, Adeena," the doctor said, laying a hand on her shoulder. "I've sent the scans to gynaecology and I can have them come and talk to you. Is that okay?"

She nodded her head without opening her eyes. "Yeah, sure."

Dr. Lochiel put his hand on her shoulder. "You'll be okay, Adeena. Just get some rest now. You've been through a lot."

He left the room and she scrunched her head into her chest, wetness running down her cheek, wanting nothing more than to completely disappear from the world.

TARA ALWAYS LOOKED FORWARD TO THE ANNUAL CONFERENCE of the Association of Canadian Museum and Gallery Curators. The late October conference moved across Canada, and each year's social evening reflected the unique culture of the area.

She had enjoyed a down-home lobster dinner and Fifties-style 'hop' in Charlottetown, PEI; a hay ride, barbecue and square dancing lessons in Canmore, Alberta. But her favourite social was Québec City. After an authentic French-Canadian baked beans and *tourtière* dinner she had danced like a fool to the spirited music of a local fiddler well into the night with a group of tipsy curators from the across the country.

As her five hour flight from Ottawa to Vancouver reached its cruising altitude, she wondered what this year would be like. The venue was promising – the Whistler resort two hours north of the city by way of the Sea-to-Sky Highway that hugged the Pacific on its way up the Rockies.

Tara was more interested however, in the file that Pablo had given her before she left. He had gathered all the documents, receipts, expenses, press clippings and miscellaneous paperwork for the *Art of Rebellion* exhibit, which continued to draw a steady stream of patrons and critical acclaim.

She had been distracted from doing much investigation while preparing for her featured seminar at this year's conference. Her boss, André, had recommended her after seeing her present to Ottawa-area curators. She was flattered. Now she had to live up to her billing as a young, smart curator with fresh ideas on attracting new visitors to help struggling galleries balance their strained budgets.

As soon as this presentation was over, she was determined to comb through the file Pablo had prepared for her and see if there were any clues that might help confirm or lay to rest, the accusations that Friedrich Lang had hinted at on the opening night of the exhibit.

Was there a chance that the real Duncan Cello was not what they were so proudly displaying at the National Gallery? If so, how was that even possible and who would have switched it?

As she adjusted her seat and pulled out her laptop to go through the slides for her presentation, a face flashed before her.

Adeena.

Tara had a sense that somehow she was involved, and if so, the consequences might be more than their friendship could handle. She hoped she was wrong and that poor, suffering Adeena could just get on with it, become the classical musician she had always dreamed of being, and settle down with Philippe.

As her laptop fired up, she let herself enjoy a little smile. *Philippe.* The one thing Adeena had got right. He would be her rock, with his own impeccable sense of style and adventure.

If only Tara had grabbed him first.

BEING ALONE AT THE LAKE WITH HER PARENTS, ADEENA FELT almost like a kid again.

Her father had arrived from Scotland a few days ago, and now here they were all together up at the place that was tailor-made for unplugging from the world. She had been so happy to see her father. He had so many things he wanted to talk to her about, and some time alone up at Wolfe Lake was the ideal place to talk.

She had actually spent Thanksgiving in the hospital, after her blood pressure had dropped dangerously low, and they decided to keep her under observation for a few more days. Philippe had visited as much as he could until he had to leave on a special assignment to Washington DC.

Before he left they struck a truce.

Adeena stopped talking about travelling back in time. Philippe focused on her health – her migraines in particular. They let the real issues lie, unspoken. She wanted to tell him what Dr. Lochiel had told her about the MRI scan, but she couldn't do it, at least not now. Before she said anything about her fertility, or lack thereof, she wanted to discuss options with her gynaecologist. She better have all the facts and options before she got into that topic with him.

Before they parted, Philippe tried to reconnect.

"Babe," he started, "I am sorry I gave you a hard time. You must have hated me for not believing you."

Adeena listened, unsure how she really felt. "I was disappointed. But you did come back for me. Thank you."

"I had to, Adeena," he said. "What kind of husband would I make if I left my wife when she needed me most?"

She watched him without saying anything. He was a good man. He deserved a good wife. "Philippe, you haven't done anything wrong. You've been there for me. You even saved me from Tara! I should be the one apologizing."

He smiled. "Yeah, you put on a pretty good show for her. I didn't know you were such an actress!"

"I'm a performer. That is what I do!"

He took her hands in his and looked at her seriously. He said nothing for a few moments and they studied each other's face. Finally he spoke, slowly. "And are you still performing? With me?"

Adeena raised her eyebrows. "What do you mean?"

"I don't know," he said quietly. "But something's changed. It feels like, like there is a wall between us, a barrier or something. It's separating you from me and I can't seem to break through it."

Adeena closed her eyes. He wasn't just a good reporter, he knew how to read her. "I don't know. Maybe I just need some time."

"Okay," he said. "Come here." He took her in his arms. "I'm here for you. When you're ready to be with me again, I'll be waiting for you."

WILLIAM WAS GLAD TO BE HOME AGAIN, FINALLY. EACH DAY IN Scotland had been an emotional adventure.

The spirit of Margaret Rose lived deep within him, even though mother and son were worlds apart. He thought of all the people he had met including Fay, his mother's nurse. She had been there until the end, providing his mother with more than just professional nursing. The two were a treat to watch in action, and after his mother died, Fay tearfully confessed she felt "a hole in mah heart wider than th' sea itself."

Besides Fay, there was Murdo, the young sheep farmer who lived next door to his mother's cottage on the North Sea. He had understood Margaret Rose and shown real affection for her. He too was moved to tears after she died. He told William that his own grandmother had passed away when he was 'just a wee brat' and he never got a chance to know her.

Murdo said Margaret Rose was like the grandmother he had always imagined. William later discovered that Murdo used to take her shopping, kept her freezer stocked and dropped by for a dram of Brandy from time to time, loaded with produce, sweets and fresh-cut flowers.

Now that his mother was gone, William could move forward.

He thought back to how his mother had always connected with Adeena, and about Margaret Rose's dying wish – for Adeena 'to save us.' Grandmother and granddaughter developed a bond he had admired, even if it did scare him. Now back home, he had lots of things to talk to his daughter about. While he had fretted over Adeena as a child, his own strained relationship with his mother had occupied too much negative space in his head. Now finally, he could focus.

"Will, are you going to daydream all day? Is that thing going to work?"

He looked up from the tangle of wires before him to Jackie in the kitchen putting the finishing touches on dinner. He was determined to get the satellite feed hooked up to their new flat screen TV. "Yeah, just about done," he called out. He hooked up the last connection and flicked on the power switch.

Four different lights started blinking, all red. He was worried until finally, one started to glow a deep blue and then the other three followed suit, blinking happily to indicate the connection was working.

"I think I got it," William called out. He moved around to the front, clicked on the remote and waited a few seconds until the screen lit up with a signal from the satellite. "There you go. Now we can watch the news and all your cooking shows!"

Jackie smiled from the kitchen. "Good work, Will. Now come and pour me some wine, *tout de suite!*"

He threw the leftover wires and the manual in the box from the satellite converter and put them in the spare room. The door to Adeena's bedroom was open. There was a large cello case next to her.

"Adeena, you want some wine?" he called out. "Come and show us your new cello and I'll pour you a glass."

CHAPTER 20

Adeena's dad watched in awe as she unpacked the Duncan Cello in the great room of the cottage. "I've been waiting to see what all the fuss is about," he said.

She held it upright so he could take a closer look.

"Ohhh, nice" he sighed. "Pure perfection."

Her mother in the kitchen didn't seem impressed. "What's so special about it?"

Adeena looked at her father and smiled. He shrugged. This was one of those things you either felt instinctively or you would never understand. Father and daughter chuckled.

"It's the oldest surviving cello in the UK," William called out. "Almost three hundred years old, and the guy who created it apprenticed with Antonio Stradivari."

"Oh well," Jackie mused. *"Bravo!* An Italian designer. What's he like, Gucci or Armani or something?"

Adeena laughed. "Mom, he didn't make shoes. Or purses!" She noticed her father studying the cello closely.

"I thought this was supposed to be on display at the gallery," he asked without taking his eyes off the instrument. "Didn't the exhibition open already? How'd you get it?"

Her mother looked over at her, smile gone. Adeena knew this

was going to come up. "It needs to be played. I'm the only employee at the gallery who is an actual cellist."

Her mother didn't seem convinced. "What's Tara say about this?"

"She's okay. We got a copy made for the exhibit, so this one can be played."

William choked. "A copy?"

Adeena needed him on her side. "It's done all the time. We got Thomas Peeters in Gatineau to make it. He's copied some of the most valuable cellos and violins in the world, down to the tiniest detail, perfect replicas."

"Yeah, but they're fakes! It's not the same, not even close."

Adeena took the Duncan Cello and held it upright. Maybe it was time to tell them more. "There is something else, and I need you both to believe me." She could feel her pulse racing, but needed to get this out. "This is actually *my* cello."

Her mother, who had been peeling a carrot, put it down and wiped her hands with a towel. She walked over near to where Adeena stood holding the cello upright. "What are you saying, *belle?*"

Her father stared at her. They were making her uncomfortable and suddenly the room seemed warm. "Can you both sit down for a second? And just listen, okay?"

William sat on the edge of the leather sofa in front of the wall of windows looking out over the lake. He seemed worried. Her mother remained standing, arms on hips. "It's okay, tell us."

Adeena closed her eyes and saw James and George. "This cello belonged to Katharine Carnegie in 1745."

Her father stared intently at her. "It did? How do you know?"

"Her brother told me on the way to Drummond Castle." She waited for their reaction. They looked confused.

"I know you're going to have me sent back to the hospital when I tell you this, but no one else believes me. Philippe certainly doesn't." She felt her eyes watering, but blinked the tears away, determined to finish. "Mom, Dad," she took a deep breath, finally saying out loud what she had never spoken before:

"I think Katharine and I are the same person." Adeena couldn't hold back the tears now and started to sob, barely able to continue. "I don't know how it can be, but somehow she's inside me."

Her father stood up and took the Duncan Cello from her. Her mother stepped forward and swept Adeena into her arms.

"It's okay, *ma belle.* It's okay. We're here for you."

She had finally said it.

It was one thing to think that she and Katharine were the same person. It was quite another to say it out loud to someone else, least of all your own parents.

Do they believe me? She pulled away from her mother, searching her face for clues. Adeena couldn't tell, but she could see the concern in her eyes.

Her father wore the same worried expression. "Pumpkin," he began. "This must be killing you, going through this." He hesitated, and she got the sense he was selecting each word carefully. "Your grandmother used to tell me things I couldn't believe. But, lately, I'm just not sure about anything anymore."

It was his turn to give her a hug. "Dad, somehow Katharine and I share a soul or whatever you might call it," Adeena said quietly. "And I found a way to go back and help her."

Her dad nodded his head and held on to her tightly. She felt herself fighting tears. "I don't really know where she begins," she sobbed, "and I end."

ADEENA LAY IN HER BED STARING AT THE CEILING.

She had told her parents everything that happened when she played the Duncan Cello and became Katharine Carnegie. She didn't go into great detail about James Drummond, only that Katharine and James were a couple.

Her dad asked lots of questions, and while he wouldn't confirm he believed that she travelled back in time, he reviewed everything she told them in great detail. He probed, asked all the right questions. What he was really thinking was hard to say. He seemed to be playing the role of professor reviewing a student presentation. But maybe he really wanted to believe her.

She had mentioned her grandmother a few times, and it made him wince each time. Was he worried his daughter was becoming just like his mother? The mother that had caused him pain as a child and so much worry as an adult?

Adeena wondered what her mother was thinking. While her dad asked lots of questions and genuinely seemed like he was trying to help her by sifting through historical facts, her mother stood in stone silence.

Wasn't her job as a psychologist to ask questions? Adeena knew about the research she had completed for her Ph.D. studying autistic children with clairvoyant-like abilities. Was she trying to develop a theory for this, her own daughter's fucked-up psychosis?

What a family! Dad, the historian with a crazy mother. Mom, the psychologist who works with crazy people.

And me? The crazy person.

She smiled, finding some humour in this profile of her nuclear family. The door to her room was slightly ajar, and she could hear her parents still talking about her. They were trying to be quiet, as they discussed the situation in front of a crackling fire.

"You think Tara knows she's got that cello?" her mother asked.

There was a long silence, punctuated by the popping of burning logs in the fireplace. Her father must be thinking about that one. Adeena could see him in her mind, not wanting to believe his daughter was a criminal. "I don't know. I'm really not sure," he finally responded.

"If she's taken it without permission she could be arrested," her mother exclaimed. "God, why can't this ever end?"

Adeena knew they were referring to her teenage years.

"No," her father replied, "this is different. I don't think she's taking drugs, and that Kurt asshole isn't pushing her this time." There was another long pause. "Maybe this is the Stuart curse all over again, like Mum."

"Oh God!" her mother gasped. "I hope not. It haunted her until the very end."

Adeena thought about her grandmother. 'Haunted' was the right word. She now understood her better than anyone else ever could. Somehow, Katharine had been in her grandmother's dreams too. The difference was that Adeena was living the dream *as* Katharine.

Her parents still blamed Kurt for that awful night of the prom.

She went alone, because the day before she had caught him in bed with Brandy, the new girl who had just joined the band. 'Asshole' was right. Adeena and Kurt were not just lovers, they were also a song-writing team. But apparently fucking Brandy was more important than creating music with Adeena.

Adeena had gone to Kurt's house to ask about changing the ending for a song they were working on. She found him on the couch naked between Brandy's legs, fornicating with abandon.

Adeena grabbed his prized Gibson electric guitar. They had used it to write and perform some amazing songs together. Collaborations that fused their creativity and she had thought – their love.

She held the guitar high above her head, brandishing it like a Neanderthal threatening a grizzly bear.

"What're you doing?" Kurt yelled. "You fucking crazy?"

Adeena swung the heavy guitar in a circle over her head. "Maybe I am, asshole!"

The naked Brandy slut screamed as Adeena smashed the

guitar to the floor, and then swung it around and around smashing a lamp. “Stop!” Kurt yelled.

Adeena was wild with rage. She took the guitar, turned and heaved it against the picture window behind her. The glass shattered dramatically.

Without another word she stormed out, leaving behind the boy she had given her heart to for the last three years. And more importantly, the music they had created together. It had elevated their relationship to another level entirely – in her mind, at least.

Adeena rolled over in bed, reliving it all. The very next night she went to the prom, alone. She was still in a daze, drinking and stumbling through the evening. She saw Kurt on the dance floor, with ‘the slut.’ Someone offered her a blue ‘happy-shit’ tab. She didn’t hesitate and dissolved it on her tongue.

It wasn’t simple jealously that drove her. She wanted to blot out the dreams they had created together, the music she and Kurt had worked almost demonically to compose, to perfect and finally, to triumphantly perform.

Why couldn’t she be like other kids? Kids who were happy just enjoying music instead of taking the express train to hell trying to create it?

The prom ended for Adeena at the hospital, with her frightened parents being woken by the police in the middle of the night. It was late the next afternoon when she opened her eyes to find them surrounding her, thankful she had not left this earth.

Now as she lay awake in the cottage listening to their whispers just outside her bedroom door, she thought about how they had always been there for her.

But maybe this time, she was expecting too much of them.

THE NEXT MORNING JACKIE WAS UP EARLY. SHE WANTED THE new TV on while she got set for a day of cooking and baking.

"So that thing works now?" Jackie called out to her husband, as he put on his jacket.

"Should be okay. Just use the remote to pick the channel you want," he responded as put on his jacket. William glanced at the shopping list. "This is everything?"

"I think so, and make sure you get *pastry* flour, not *cake* flour. And pure lard please, not shortening."

He nodded and blew her a kiss before heading out the door. Jackie was in a baking mood with two empty shelves in the freezer reserved for her apple, rhubarb and cherry pies. She would soon fill them again.

It was Monday morning, and it felt strange to still be off work. She had managed to get an extra week off, while William was finishing up his sabbatical. Looking after Adeena was her priority for the week, her sole patient as it were. Jackie needed to come up with a strategy for helping her poor suffering daughter. That along with getting the crust just right on the pastry.

She smiled, thinking there was a better chance of success with the pies. Adeena's emotional revelation last night left Jackie and William at odds. She burned thinking about his reasoning. He argued that the historical facts, the diary he brought from Scotland and of course his family's affinity for ghosts from the past, all pointed to the strong possibility this could really all be happening.

Jackie didn't buy it. She spent three years of her life completing a Ph.D. to prove that the clairvoyance demonstrated by some autistic children had a scientific basis. While there were a few cases that defied easy explanation, almost all the children's 'abilities' were due to factors such as near photographic memories, intuitive reasoning and in some cases perhaps, a type of memory that pre-dated their own birth. She had just read a study with evidence that DNA markers can transmit epigenetic memories across generations.

Did something get passed down to Adeena from the Stuarts? Jackie would figure this out, one way or the other. Sometimes the best way was to get busy with something else, while your mind sifted through options in the background.

Jackie reached for the remote and clicked the red power button. The new flat screen TV in the family room lit up. She poured some coffee and checked on the pea soup she was making. The ham bone and dried yellow peas had come to a boil. She turned the flame down and covered her tall cherry-coloured *Le Creuset* stockpot with its tightly fitted lid.

On the TV, she noticed a preview for an upcoming segment on the morning talk show.

"Adeena!" she called out. "Come and see this! They're doing a thing on the NAC, on the orchestra!"

Jackie carried her mug of coffee into the family room and turned up the volume. As the commercials ended and the next segment on the show began, Adeena emerged from her room, looking like she hadn't slept much.

"Morning," she muttered, shuffling zombie-like to the kitchen.

"Morning, *belle*," Jackie replied in a sing-song voice. "Sleep okay?"

Adeena mumbled something as the sounds of classical music came from the TV. There was an exterior shot of the National Arts Centre, then a close-up of a man sitting at a piano making notes. The caption under him read: "Friedrich Lang, *NACO Music Director.*"

"Adeena! Look! Is that your boss?" Jackie exclaimed.

Adeena stared at the TV, trying to focus. "Yup, that's him. What is this?"

"Not sure, it just started."

The image of the conductor gave way to a pan of the NAC Orchestra in concert and then to some close-up shots of them rehearsing. Adeena walked into the family room from the kitchen, sipping a coffee. "That's our rehearsal," she said. "Oh, that's Southam Hall." Adeena put her drink down and flopped onto the stuffed chair across from where her mother sat the sofa.

The TV scene changed to a live studio interview with one of the program's female hosts seated at a table in front of a stylish wrap-around fireplace in the background. Friedrich Lang sat across from her, smiling, He wore a collarless white shirt.

"Tell us about your composition, Maestro," the host began. "It's brand new, right?"

"Correct," Lang replied. "I call it *Voyage of Destiny.* I've actually been working on it for some time."

Adeena stood up. "Liar! You stole it from me, you bastard."

Jackie looked over at Adeena. "What are you talking about?"

"Just a sec," Adeena snorted. "I want to see what kind of bullshit he feeds her."

The host of the show looked impressed. "It's not often that we have the music director and conductor of our national symphony, who is also a composer. Can you tell us more about your new work?"

Lang smiled. "I have always been drawn to Brahms and Bach naturally, but my hero of course, is Ludwig."

"Beethoven?"

"*Ja.* Naturally, I'm not comparing myself to him, but in Germany where I grew up and studied, he was everywhere. It felt like he was alive, still composing, inspiring me to find *my* voice."

"Fascinating!" the host gushed. "Is your work a tribute somehow, to him? To Ludwig van Beethoven?"

There was a pause as Lang considered the question. "I always wanted to capture his journey, his voyage, painful and difficult as it was, towards his musical destiny."

Adeena grimaced. "What a fucking load of crap!"

"Adeena," Jackie interrupted. "He's your boss."

The interview lasted another few minutes and included cutaway shots of Lang leading the orchestra in rehearsals playing Katharine's score. Adeena grabbed the TV controller as the interview ended and turned the set off with a purposeful *click* as if vanquishing a demon.

"Wow!" she snapped. "I can't believe he is getting away with this! He took the music Grandma sent to me and is trying to claim he wrote it. A tribute to Beethoven? Fuck!"

Jackie got up from her chair to check on the soup. "Are you sure it's the same music?"

"He hasn't changed a single note," Adeena replied. "Mom, it's breaking my heart. I'm so pissed off about this." She walked back into the kitchen. "You know, I almost want to quit, tell the whole world what he's doing."

Jackie was worried. Adeena had always been impulsive and stubborn. "You've worked your whole life for this chance. You told me since you were five that you wanted to play cello with the orchestra. You can't quit now."

"It doesn't bother you? What he's doing here with the music, passing off a composition that's not his?"

Jackie pulled a stool up in front of the island in the kitchen and sat down. "Have some breakfast, Adeena," she said. "I made some carrot muffins. The ones you keep asking me to make all the time?"

"You don't care?"

"I do. But I think you have to be smart about this. You're going to lose your job if you're not careful," Jackie said. "Sit down, put something in your stomach. We'll talk about it."

"Do you have any idea what that music means to me or who really wrote it?"

Jackie rolled her eyes. Why did her daughter have to have such a penchant for melodrama? Okay Jackie, Psych 101. *Listen. Repeat for understanding.* She chose her words carefully. "This music is important to you. You don't believe I understand where it came from?"

"Exactly."

"Well, tell me then. Where did it come from, what does it mean," she paused. "To you?"

Adeena groaned. "Mom, I'm not one of your patients at the hospital."

Jackie chuckled. "I'm sorry, *belle*, you're right." She took a sip of her coffee, recalibrating her approach. "Maybe there is something you can do with your boss, about the music. I just don't want to see you get hurt. You need to *finally* do what you've dreamed of your whole life. I don't want to watch you mess this up."

"I know, I know," Adeena exclaimed. She blew out her frustration with a sigh. "It's just like what I was telling you and dad last night. When I play that music on the Duncan Cello, I . . ." She stopped, unable to finish her sentence.

"Come here. Sit beside me." Jackie patted the stool beside her. Adeena dropped heavily down onto the stool and lowered her head towards her mother. Jackie put her hands on Adeena's shoulders and massaged her daughter's tense muscles. "It's going to be okay, belle. We'll get through this, together."

"Thanks, Mom," she replied, without lifting her head. "I just need someone, anyone, to believe me."

Jackie had heard that statement many times before. Some of her toughest cases went nowhere until the patient felt they had found someone who understood them, someone who believed the truth of what they were experiencing.

"Adeena, I believe that what you told us last night is completely real to you. It's like you and Katharine are the same person. And that cello and that music are some kind of, I don't know, bridge that unites you somehow."

Adeena looked up, her mouth gaping open. "You believe me?"

"Yes. You don't understand how this could be happening and you need to make sense of it."

Adeena stared at Jackie, digesting what she just heard. "Wait, did you say 'completely real to me'? You mean, it's not actually real? It's just real to *me*? Is that what you're saying?"

Jackie sighed. "Adeena, what seems real to you, is real."

"Oh my God! You don't believe me. You're just playing doctor!"

"*Belle,* I'm trying to help you make sense of all this," Jackie replied. "Yeah, I'm a psychologist and I've seen this before. But, I'm your mother first."

"You've *seen* this before?" Adeena stood up, her tone rising in anger. "You've seen patients go back in time, and become another person? Wow! Thanks, Mom! Now I know I'm a fucked-up nut job, just like all your other crazies!"

"They're not 'crazy' and neither are you."

"You don't get it. You're just like Philippe," Adeena exclaimed. She pointed to her bedroom door. "The cello in that room connects me to the past. Not just dreaming about it. Actually *going back,* becoming Katharine Carnegie, the woman who wrote the music that son-of-a-bitch is trying to claim *he* wrote. Katharine, who is falling in love with James Drummond, the Duke of Perth. The same Katharine that Grandma dreamt about for so many years. I am Katharine, or she is me, or..."

Adeena hung her head. She put her hands to her face in frustration. "I don't want any of this. I just want to be who I am. Whoever the hell that is. . ."

DOCTOR BENJAMIN LOCHIEL HAD SEEN PLENTY OF CT SCANS in his twenty-six years as a neurologist.

The tools he used had evolved dramatically during his career. He felt like a pioneer some days as new techniques in X-ray computer tomography were unveiled at an ever accelerating pace. No sooner had he started to understand the latest breakthroughs, than he was called to attend yet another demonstration of an even better imaging technology.

But the series of CT scans he was looking at now just didn't make sense, they were unlike anything he had ever seen. Could it be the new tech he had started using had a bug? Something that would account for what he was seeing on his monitors?

And now his colleague was spouting gibberish.

"Say again?" Benjamin said, as he stared at his high-resolution monitor. Benjamin was on the phone with Dr. Raymond Chung, a neurological researcher from the University of Ottawa, who had helped develop the new CT imaging software. "I didn't get that last part."

"This series of scans shows accelerated rates of neurogenesis from what I see," Dr. Chung said.

"Neurogenesis? New cells?"

"Yes, like in a fetus, generating neurons from neural stem cells," Dr. Chung explained. "At least that's what I'm thinking, looking at these scans. I've been focusing my own research on this area. Adults have a steady rate of new cell generation, but I've never seen this rate of growth in anything but prenatal brains."

Benjamin peered closely at the looping scan sequence on the monitor. He removed his glasses and magnified the resolution. "Hmmm," he said. "Strangest thing, isn't it?"

"How old is this patient?" Dr. Chung inquired.

"Just a sec," Benjamin flipped through his charts. "Let me see here, uh ... twenty-nine."

There was silence at the other end. "Interesting. I want to do some more work on this. I've never heard of this rate of generation in an adult before. I wonder..."

Benjamin waited for him to continue. "Wonder, what?"

"Dr. Lochiel, I should come over and take a look for myself, make sure the system is calibrated correctly. And I also have a new test with a synthetic thymidine agent we're trying to get approved."

"Thanks. Let's set something up for next week."

Benjamin hung up the phone and looked at the scan one more time.

"You've got an amazing cerebrum, Adeena. An impossible, beautiful brain!"

CHAPTER 21

William found history something of a guilty pleasure. There was always something new to discover if you kept poking at it.

"Adeena, listen to this," he called out to his daughter as she took a break from her perpetual music practices. She looked up from her iPhone.

"What is it?"

"The Drummonds. They were always on the wrong side of things."

She smiled. "Dad, don't tease me! What'd you find?"

"You know I went to Drummond Castle looking to find the real story of James, Third Duke of Perth," he said without looking away from his laptop.

Adeena put her phone down and walked over to him. "What about him?"

"Well, we know he died trying to live up to everyone's expectations. But really, his whole family always wanted a king they couldn't have. Each generation kept trying to restore the Stuart line to the throne," William said. "But it always failed. Spectacularly!"

"Yeah, I read about the '45 – the Jacobite rising, and how bad that ended for them," Adeena said, "especially James."

"You're right," William said. "But take a look at what happened in 1501, to his cousin Lady Margaret Drummond who was having breakfast with her two sisters one morning at Drummond Castle. Porridge, apparently, was on the menu."

"Oh? I know exactly where she'd be eating it," Adeena said. "I even know which dishes she'd use."

William looked at her thoughtfully. He wanted to believe everything she told him about becoming Katharine Carnegie, but he still couldn't accept it. "Well, okay. But this was nasty porridge, laced with poison. Lady Margaret and her two sisters died after eating it."

"What? Who poisoned them?"

"Good question. This is where it gets interesting. Lady Margaret Drummond was the King's mistress, his true love they say, and there's speculation they were secretly married. In any case, the King, James the Fourth, was very taken with her."

"Secretly married, why?"

William took a sip from his tea before continuing. "Because there was another Margaret the King was supposed to marry. He was betrothed to twelve-year-old Margaret Tudor, daughter of the King of England, Henry VII. The King of Scotland had no interest in her, even though the marriage arrangement was part of a peace treaty with England. He fell for Margaret Drummond, a commoner his own age."

"How old were they?"

"Let's see," William did a quick calculation. "Both in their twenties. Margaret was twenty-six and the King, uh... twenty-eight."

"So she was poisoned at Drummond Castle," Adeena said slowly, turning her head away. "Pity, such a beautiful place for music, and dancing, and..."

William studied his daughter lost in her thoughts, gazing out the window at the lake. "And what?"

"Oh, sorry. I was thinking about the gardens at the castle and how the moon lights them up so perfectly."

William recalled his own pleasure at seeing the ornamental gardens of Drummond Castle. "You saw them, at night?"

"The night I danced with James."

"Drummond?"

She nodded and held her gaze on William, waiting for his reaction. He remained silent, fighting his skepticism.

"Finish your story, Dad," Adeena said looking away. "Who poisoned Margaret Drummond?"

He welcomed the diversion and turned back to his computer. "Nobody knows for sure. Legend has it that it was somebody who didn't want a Drummond to become Queen, which would have screwed up the peace treaty with England."

"How did Margaret meet the King in the first place?"

William chuckled. "You like the details, don't you? Well, I spent way too much time getting sidetracked on this whole thing, but I did find a letter that says the King met her at Restalrig, a little village near Edinburgh. Quite the ladies man. They say he liked to pretend he was a commoner."

"Really? So what happened?"

"Well, the King saw her at the fair they have in Restalrig every year, right near the huge church he attended each week. There were games and dances, and the two of them kept winning. He was taken with her, and apparently, she with him. She had no idea he was the King. But soon afterwards Margaret got pregnant and found out she was carrying a royal baby!"

JAMES ADMIRED THE RUINED CATHOLIC CHURCH AT RESTALRIG.

Only two walls were left, both soaring high above the surrounding farmer's fields. He could still see the intricate detail that formed the border of an inside window of the taller V-shaped wall rising eternally toward Heaven.

These walls which could still be seen for miles, refused to die. Two hundred years ago, protestant zealots had labelled the ancient church a monument of Catholic idolatry, and ordered the townspeople to cast it down, which they did, stone by stone until it was almost erased from memory.

Only these magnificent walls remained now in modern day 1745, guarding the desolate churchyard and a few old gravestones. James felt a kinship with the stone walls. They were of God. And of all the Scottish kings in the past who had built them, and of all who had resisted the English who now occupied the Kingdom.

He turned Balgair slowly away from the church toward the adjoining village of Lochend. They were on their way to meet Prince Charles.

As James reached the narrow cobblestone lanes of Lochend, the Prince called out to him. "Perth! The King would be pleased to know you hold this parish firmly in your grasp."

"Thank you," James replied as he brought Balgair alongside the Prince's mount. "Our conquest of Edinburgh extends far indeed." James smiled thinking how easy it had been to take the Scottish capital. The English army had been disorganized and the city had welcomed their Bonnie Prince and his colourful army with open arms. The enemy had been quickly vanquished.

The Prince raised a hand to stop the procession of men and horses marching behind him.

Charles seemed in good spirits. He was dressed in a coarse blue grogram coat trimmed with gold lace. Together with his red waistcoat and breeches, a star and garter on his left shoulder and a rich sword belt over his other side, he made a royal impression. Even James felt in awe. But it was the Prince's attitude, not his dress, that gained James' admiration. He had watched the Prince lead the charge, both on foot and on horse many times since he arrived in the Highlands almost ten weeks earlier. And now he demanded a level of military discipline and sacrifice that began with himself. The Prince insisted on daily drills and challenges and sent out orders of the day, every day.

"How many men in your regiment?" the Prince asked.

"Over a thousand make camp here today," James responded. "Good men and strong boys, ready to fight. But most aren't prepared for the strength of body and mind you demand."

Charles nodded his head and looked out toward the village and the smoky grey clouds. It was getting colder with each passing day and the breeze this morning was particularly fresh. "Winter is near, Perth. We need to gather our forces on the Canongate to prepare for battle. We must not get too comfortable with our victory at Edinburgh." He raised a hand and the men on horses behind fell silent.

The Prince pointed toward the town square.*"En avant toutes!"*

James turned Balgair around and trotted beside the Prince's mare. "Any news of Cope?" he asked. James' regiment had been ordered to disperse to the ridge of the 'miry land' as the Prince called the Restalrig area, to prevent spies sent by the English General Cope from learning the true strength of the Prince's army. Over 7,200 infantry and 300 horse from across the Kingdom were now at his command to wrest control of Scotland and depose King George in the process.

"The General has no idea what awaits him," the Prince said. The two horses walked slowly side-by-side along the cobblestone street leading into the village. A few of the townspeople had come to see the Prince's parade, and he bowed his head in a gesture of humility. James noted the warm ways the Prince was greeted here and everywhere he went.

"The Council is still divided on our course," James said as they continued along the street. "You allow them much power over our future."

"Indeed, they slow us down and expose our divisions," Charles responded. "But I give them a voice hoping to ensure their support." He paused a moment. "And you, Perth? What are your thoughts?"

"Your Highness, we can hold Scotland. You have given rebirth to our pride, a pride the King in London tries to kill with noose and musket," James said. "Beating Cope in our *own* Kingdom and holding Edinburgh and Glasgow must be our obsession. The Highlands are with you. Most of the Lowlands from here to Aberdeen have been waiting for this day since my father dared dream of seeing *your* father on the throne again."

The Prince said nothing as the two men rode in silence. Charles Edward did not look pleased though, and tightened the reins to stop his horse. The column behind halted once more. Charles looked sternly at James pulling back hard on Balgair's bridle. The big stallion snorted his objection loudly.

"This will all be for naught if George remains King," the Prince boomed.

James turned in his saddle, still fighting his horse. "I will follow your orders to the death, but I must warn you. Marching on England will leave us weak. It will scatter our forces. We may take Lancashire and the North Country, but we may lose Scotland if we turn our backs on her now."

The Prince sighed. "James, I need your support. I came to restore my father's crown. That is what gives our cause legitimate claim. Indeed, divine blessing. France and her armies will soon be here to support us, a glorious dirk to cut the English throat. And then, the entire island will once more be ruled by a Catholic king."

"And if the Council does not agree?"

"That is why I need you, James. I need you and your passion, your forward views. I need *you* to help persuade the Council to invade England. Ten days from now, we will lead the charge to take back the crown that was stolen from our fathers and from our grandfathers."

ADEENA WAS GLAD TO BE ALONE AGAIN. SHE HAD SPENT THE last few days at the lake with her parents, and they all needed to find a little space.

Her parents were having a hard time with her, and she knew she was probably being difficult. It was a lot for them to make sense of. Hell, it was a lot for her. Her dad seemed like he just might want to believe what she was saying, but her mother? It felt more like she was dealing with Jackie, Ph.D. from the hospital, than with a nurturing parent.

I wish this was a condition that could be treated.

Her parents were gone for the day to shop and have lunch, visiting all the little places around the lake they loved so much, leaving her alone to practice. She had both the Duncan Cello and her own instrument with her. She sat staring at both of them. Her own cello an old friend – reliable, solid and comfortable. While it wasn't full of surprises, she knew how to draw music from it even if it took effort some days to find her motivation.

The Duncan on the other hand, was the gateway to another world. It was a fix for the aching inside of her, a conduit to the musical expression she had searched for her whole life. It may have been built for Katharine, but it gave Adeena the voice she had never found.

She thought of all the bad decisions she made growing up.

None had ever led to what she really wanted, a need that even now she couldn't put into words. A longing. A desire, always unfulfilled lying just beneath the surface. Doing what had already been done held no attraction. Creating something new on the other hand, music that had never been heard before, gave her a maddening drive that never relaxed its grip.

Adeena stood up and touched the Duncan Cello. It felt powerful. Timeless. It fused art and love. It made her whole, even if it meant living as someone else, born three centuries earlier.

Her own cello sat on the corner. Unassuming. Timid.

She closed her eyes and felt bittersweet emotions sweep across her. She shook her head back and forth and began humming in a trance-like moan.

Another bad decision was on the way.

JAMES DRUMMOND KNEW THE *TOLBOOTH* ON HIGH STREET IN Dalkeith well.

His men feared its 'black hole,' the underground dungeon. Poor souls sent there in irons rarely survived the blackness and filth that awaited them. And if they did manage to, they returned missing limbs, ears, blinded or horribly disfigured. It was an image James found useful to conjure at times. Fear was a powerful ally, although he used it sparingly, preferring to inspire his men through examples of bravery.

He turned Balgair toward the markets of Dalkeith, the bustling village a few miles from Edinburgh. It was late October and his officers were busy buying up most of the last of the harvest from the vendors.

James continued to where his men were bivouacked not far away, between Newbattle Water and Melville Burn. The sun was sinking low in the sky and a few of the boys were lighting the evening fires. He halted a moment to watch his men roll one of the heavy twelve pounder cannons towards the camp.

He called out to one of them. "Be quick. The morrow will not wait!"

A sooty-faced man marching in front of the cannon spat without missing a step. "Aye, and nor will I." He raised a hand admonishing the men pushing the cannon behind him to pick up the pace. He directed them to an encampment at the ridge of the berm where another five cannons already sat positioned for the battle to come. "Forward!"

James watched as the cannon procession picked up speed, even as the road ahead steepened. His men were becoming more disciplined with the drills the Prince insisted they practice each day. But they were anxious to march, to move, to fight. The Lowland divisions, like their Highland brethren, were not really an army, but a collection of private regiments, small clans, horses, and guards. They got to drinking, raping and fighting when they were too long in one place. They used their muskets to shoot small game and sometimes after too much drink, each other.

That would change tomorrow. Last night, in a heated meeting of the clan chiefs, lords and dukes from across the Lowlands, the Prince's Council decided by a single vote to invade England. James was reluctant and agreed with those who thought it prudent to secure Scotland, raise funds and wait for help from the French. But when Prince Charles finally persuaded the majority that bold action was needed before the English could organize an effective army, James had accepted the decision.

And sworn his life in allegiance.

Now his men would lead the Lowlanders, providing an army train of heavy cannon and mortar. They were to begin the march west by way of Auchendinny, Peebles and Moffat towards Carlisle in the morn, while the Prince and the lightly-equipped Highlander Division would take a more easterly route.

As James rode ahead, he saw fires lighting up the darkening sky. The glow from the setting sun was just about extinguished and the moon was rising, full and threatening through a gap in the dark clouds. He felt the wind picking up as he looked ahead for his tent. He was surprised to see it lit up. He kicked Balgair hard, but the stallion needed little encouragement to trot quickly towards camp.

As he approached the tent, a soldier came running towards him to take his horse. The man looked wild-eyed at James and was about to say something, pointing toward his tent, when James heard it.

Music.

The music that filled his dreams by night and lifted his heart by day, poured from his tent glowing bright and warm against the dark sky.

ADEENA DREW HER BOW AGAINST THE DUNCAN CELLO.

She was unsure of herself. Unsure of why she needed to do this, to be here and risk everything she wanted. But she was not Katharine. They might share a soul, but they lived in different worlds, in different times. They were loved by different men.

"Katharine!"

Adeena looked up as the canvas door of the tent was torn open and James stood silhouetted before her. She stared at the imposing figure and lowered her head. Wetness stung her eyes. She trembled as she continued playing the song that burned within her.

James rushed to her and took her face in his hands. She peered up through tears at his blurry outline.

"What happened?" He bent down to kiss her head tenderly. "Why have you come here?"

James took the cello, laid it aside and pulled her into his arms. She was frozen at first, unable to speak as she tried to separate herself from Katharine. He held her tightly and she found herself beginning to sob.

"Shhhhhh" James whispered.

She fought for control, finally taking a deep breath. She pulled back and he stood staring at her closely. In his eyes she could see only tenderness. On his face, only compassion.

"Katharine?" he began. "I am with you. No matter what you may have to say to me."

Adeena hesitated. "I know. I know you are James. And Katharine... she loves you, very much."

If he was puzzled by this statement, he did not show it. He fixed his gaze on her with the same intensity he had upon entering the tent. "I have come to warn you about the future," she finally said. "Even if I can't change it, I have to tell you what I know," she paused a moment and then added "to save you."

James did not look worried. In fact, he looked so content to be with her, that it seemed nothing she could say would change his demeanour. He spoke with a strong fortitude. "Katharine, I know for what I live. And I know for what I will die. I only hope by the grace of God, that before I do, I may come to know you. To be with the one I was meant for."

Adeena felt time moving through her. Could she change it? Or could she only observe what was destined to occur, and no matter what she might do, have no effect upon it? "James, I am not who you think I am. I can't explain how, but I know more than Katharine ever could."

At this James began to look confused. "What are you trying to say? Have you seen spirits, had dreams you don't understand? What do you mean 'more than Katharine'?"

Adeena let her head fall.

She wasn't sure of anything anymore. Maybe this was a dream, and she had created a world of characters so real that she could not distinguish them from reality. James put his arms around her again, and she felt his strength radiate through her, his chest rising and falling with hers. His hand touched her head, sending tingles down her spine. She drew herself closer to him. She could feel every muscle in his chest and even, it seemed, each beat of his heart.

"James, you're a good man. You deserve more than what awaits you."

"Be not worried, Katharine. Believe in me, believe that I will come to you when this is over," he said, holding her. They drew each other closer, their bodies merging tightly as he continued in a soft voice. "I fight for us, with your music in my heart and your face in my dreams. It gives me the courage to confront what awaits me."

Outside, the winds grew louder, and the canvas walls of the

tent flapped angrily against the thin wood frame. The lanterns providing a faltering light, struggled to remain lit. She could hear men outside singing. For the sake of them all, she needed to tell him what she knew. Adeena raised her head from his shoulder and looked at James. His eyes were wide, his face full of trust.

"You must listen to me," she said. "You cannot invade England. The Prince's plan is doomed, he will lose everything." She saw she had his full attention as their eyes locked. "And I will lose you."

"That we could lose all may be true," he replied. "But that you will lose me? Never!"

This isn't working.

She had to be more direct. "James, most of your men will die. The Prince will flee back to France in disgrace. The symbols of Scotland will be outlawed, and you..." she hesitated seeing his face grow dark, "you won't live to see another summer."

James pushed her away. "Have you come here to curse me?" he replied tersely. "Are your dreams so full of bitter spirits? Where is the hope that your song speaks of, that your voice inspires me to find?" The lines on his face grew sharp with anger. "I fight for all those who died before me. Those who died *for* me. And Katharine, I fight for us."

She looked down at her feet. Outside it was beginning to rain and she could hear heavy drops spattering against the canvas creating an eerie echo inside the tent. The wind picked up and she felt cold, drawing her arms together with a deep shiver. "James, please..."

"You must not come here, if you are not ready to fight. Stay away from me if you cannot find the strength to believe and to risk everything, no matter what may come," he said. "My whole life has prepared me for this moment. My father, my grandfather, and their fathers before them fought for the Kingdom, for their king. And most importantly, for their family." He paused looking at her sternly. "I can do no different."

"I know," she gasped, "but you can still serve them by staying and fighting here!"

"The Council has decided, even if some of us have our doubts. We must accept the Prince's decision and follow him."

"But he will fail! And you will die!"

"The shadows of my future may be dark, but I have no choice but to follow them. Wherever they lead."

She stared in silence. Maybe time couldn't so easily be deterred from its course. Maybe destiny was written with an ink that forever stains.

But she had to keep trying.

"No! No! No! James, why can't you understand? You deserve more than to die without a country, without a king, and without..." Adeena paused. She and Katharine were not separate. They were the same person. "Without me."

James seemed to be in pain. She had not helped convince him, only given him another burden to carry into battle. He fixed his gaze on her. His caring expression was gone.

Time had won this round.

"You must leave, Katharine," he replied "Go, now! Hope is all that I have to face the morrow, and you have taken even that from me. Be gone! Do not return to me."

He gave her a last look, betrayal written across his face. Then he turned, ripped open the flaps of the tent and stepped out into the driving black rain.

CHAPTER 22

The usually stiff breezes of Wolfe Lake were calm. With autumn shadows growing longer, the lake was a sheet of dark glass. It felt to William that the world itself had stopped spinning.

"The lake is so still," he said to Jackie as they gathered baskets and boxes from the Volvo. They had found some great little local shops and their Coleman cooler was filled with cuts of lamb and beef from farmers around the valley.

"I love it," Jackie replied. "You can almost hear the hummingbirds humming." A loon called out and she smiled. "See? They agree!"

William nodded his head taking the cooler from the trunk and following his wife into the cottage. As they opened the door they called out. "Adeena! We're home."

There was no response. Jackie sat her basket down on the kitchen counter. "Belle?"

No reply.

William was puzzled. "Adeena?" He looked at Jackie. "Maybe she went for a walk?" He noticed the frown on his wife's face. She hurried toward Adeena's room. The door was slightly ajar.

"Adeena?"

William was right behind her. He saw his daughter sitting on a stool in her bedroom. She seemed to be asleep. Her eyes were closed, but she still held her cello. Her head hung limp on her chest.

"Help me!" Jackie said. Together they raised Adeena from the chair and laid her on the bed.

"Adeena?" Jackie whispered, as she took her pulse. "Talk to me, *Belle*." Jackie took her other hand and laid it gently on Adeena's forehead. "I think she's asleep, but..."

"But what?" His wife seemed lost in thought. William looked at Adeena and wondered again about her claim that she became another woman when she played the Duncan Cello. He glanced at the cello sitting in the corner where he had placed it. Katharine Carnegie? What connection was this woman to him? Why did she seem to possess such power over both his mother and his daughter?

"Something is very wrong," Jackie said, looking at him without releasing her hands from Adeena. "This is not just *tired*."

"What do we do?" William asked. "Is she okay?"

"I'm not sure. Let me try Dr. Lochiel at the Civic. See what he thinks," she replied. "I'll call the hospital. Stay with her."

William sat on the edge of the bed as Jackie got up and left the room. He watched Adeena. Sleeping, or... or what? There were many things he could not understand in this world. His mother had been at the top of that list.

But she was now officially replaced.

TARA OPENED THE DOOR TO ADEENA'S EMPTY OFFICE AND FELT like she was doing something wrong.

That didn't really make sense. She was the manager after all, and Adeena a member of her staff. But none of her other staff gave her attitude or created intrigue quite like Dee. Most were content to have a position at the National Gallery, and thankful that Tara was fair and seemed to get her expanding budget approved each year.

But then, Adeena had never wanted to work for Tara. It was a way to pay the rent while she pursued her dreams. Tara sighed. *Dreams.* I wish I had time to live my dreams. Hell, I wish I had time to even have a dream.

She shook her head. *Don't get distracted.*

Tara did not get sidetracked easily. A television crew from the BBC was coming to interview her tomorrow about the exhibit and the Duncan Cello. If Friedrich Lang knew some secret that she hadn't found and word got out that the Gallery was displaying a fake, there would be hell to pay.

That was putting it mildly. Careers would be ruined, starting with her own, and likely her boss. What was the penalty for losing a five-million-dollar artifact?

Tara had a nose for problem solving, and it had led her to Dee's office. If something was amiss, she would find it. The banker's box beside Adeena's desk was a likely source of information. That receipt from the luthier still puzzled Tara.

Five thousand bucks to rent some instruments?

Tara rummaged through the box, looking for the receipt. It wasn't there. There were some sketches of the Duncan Cello, and printouts of online research including *Wikipedia* articles on Scottish dress, customs and figures from the past. She picked up a colour print with a picture of an odd-looking character all wrapped up in flowing red plaid robes: 'James Drummond, 3rd Duke of Perth, 1713-1746.' His eyes seemed fixed on Tara with an innocent boyish smirk.

Cute, she thought. She went through all the papers in the box. Lots of references and photos of the Duncan Cello, some scraps of music notation that seemed to be handwritten, a stack of index cards on each of the artifacts in the exhibit, but the receipt she sought was not among them.

Had Adeena seemed a little flustered about the whole thing? Tara recalled their conversation. Dee said the luthier had things that 'he could adapt to be historically accurate.' She really needed to find that receipt. If it wasn't in the box with the other papers, maybe in Adeena's desk? Tara opened the middle drawer and saw a bewildering assortment of entangled items.

"God! What a mess!" she said out loud, shaking her head.

Artists. They might make us laugh and cry, but they'll *never* run the world, Tara thought. She took out all the junk from the top drawer of Adeena's desk. Cards, papers, wrappers from two packages of sunflower seeds and a few granola bars, along with a half dozen or so teabags, earbud headphones and empty foil packages of Starbucks instant latte mixes. Jeez! How does anyone work like this?

Tara closed the drawer and wondered if she had been duped. And then she noticed it – a book on the Jacobite uprising in Scotland. Sitting on top of the bookcase, like it had been hurriedly shoved there. There was a piece of paper sticking out from it. Tara opened the book and pulled out the missing receipt.

Nice filing system, Dee. Or, was she trying to hide something? Tara couldn't be sure if it was just part of her friend's sloppy manner or something more devious. She scanned the receipt. 'Thomas Peeters, Luthier.' The description read: 'Creation of musical prop. $5,000.'

'Prop?' A single prop? Tara wondered. She thought they were renting a few instruments. This sounded like the vendor had created just one instrument. She looked at the receipt again scanning for the phone number and dialled it from the phone on Adeena's desk. She got a recorded message:

"Hello. You've reached Thomas Peeters. I'm currently out of the country until December 15th. Please leave me a message or visit my website for more information."

Tara put the phone down and studied the receipt. It was time she and Adeena had a talk.

ADEENA COULD HEAR THE DRIVING RAIN. SHE WAS LYING down, her eyes closed, unaware of where or when she was.

Or *who* she was.

Am I Katharine? She let out a deep sigh and felt a jabbing pain, excruciating pressure pushing deep into her skull. Her sigh turned into a cry of agony.

"Adeena?"

The voice was low and deep. It came from someone very close by. She tried to lift the heavy wall that kept her eyelids sealed shut. She was able to crack them open slightly and saw the blurry outline of someone sitting next to her bed.

"Can you hear me, babe?" It was Philippe, talking softly.

"Ohhhh," she murmured. The torture chamber inside her head pounded. Every cell in her brain felt like it was being attacked. "Oh, my God!"

Someone else came into the room in and she felt a gentle hand on her forehead. "Belle? You've been out for hours. Can you open your eyes?"

Adeena fought through the pain, trying to open her eyes enough to see her mother. "It hurts so bad. Ohhhhh..."

"It's okay, *belle.* We're here. I'll get you something for your head. Don't try to move yet."

THIRTY MINUTES LATER, ADEENA MANAGED TO SIT UP IN BED. The pills her mother gave her had helped a bit. Apparently Philippe had been in her room watching her for the last few hours.

"It's killing you," he said staring at the Duncan Cello in the corner of her room. "Your mom and dad are worried." Philippe put both hands over hers. "So am I."

Adeena had so much she wanted to say to him. So many things that she needed to sort out. But she was still feeling groggy. "Philippe, I'm sorry. I didn't want..." She was unable to finish her thought.

He moved closer to her on the bed. "Shhhh. It's okay," She sank back down on the bed and closed her eyes. "Just rest. Turn over and I'll rub your back."

She did as he suggested and rolled over. She felt Philippe's hands on her back as he began to massage, slowly working his way up to her neck and lightly working his fingers over her head. Then he returned to her back releasing some of the tension she felt.

She was growing tired again, and fighting to stay awake. The soothing massage continued until finally she fell into a deep, peaceful sleep.

ADEENA SAW PHILIPPE AND JAMES RUNNING TOWARD HER. SHE was running, too – in the wooded area behind the cottage, up the steep hills, higher and higher. They were getting closer to her until finally she looked back and both were gone.

She opened her eyes with a start.

The light through her window was grey but bright enough to confirm to her it was a new day. Adeena sat up in bed stiffly. The smoky aroma of frying bacon drifted toward her. Her feet touched the coolness of the wooden floor and she stood up, for the first time in the last twenty-four hours. She heard the television.

"Hey," her father said as she ventured out of her room. "How you feeling?" He wrapped his arms around her, squeezing her in an extended hug.

"Better." She lingered in the comfort of his embrace as her mother approached.

"Ma belle."

Adeena let go of her father. Her mother quickly took his place. "You had us so worried."

"I'm fine now. Really. Thank you, both of you."

Her mother smiled. "Come, have some breakfast. You must

be starved – you've been out for nearly a whole day."

Had it been that long?

The last twenty-four hours seemed like one long dream, past and present colliding in pain. She sat on a stool by the island in the kitchen. Her mother placed a mug of steaming coffee before her and poured in a little half-and-half cream. Adeena took a sip and relished the tiny surges of caffeine bliss.

Her phone vibrated on the counter where it was being charged. The familiar alert tone indicated a new message. She put down her coffee after another long sip and went to check.

Hope you're okay. Had to go for a TV interview.

Adeena stared at the phone. "Philippe was here, right? When did he leave?"

Her mother turned from where she stood at the stove. "Yes, most of yesterday and he was still here last night when we went to bed. He said he had to work today and would be leaving before we were up."

Her father, setting the table with dishes for breakfast, nodded without looking up. "He's supposed to be part of a live panel on the news channel, but I haven't seen him yet."

Adeena glanced at the television. There were a few talking heads, with the Parliament buildings in the background, but Philippe wasn't one of them. Her father finished up at the table and went back to his spot on the overstuffed chaise near the fireplace. He picked up a book with a peculiar old-fashioned journal cover and settled into his seat.

"What're you reading, Dad?"

He looked up blankly. "What?"

"That book. Strange cover..."

"It's a journal your grandmother, uh, picked up for me in Scotland when we . . . went to Kinnaird Castle," he said, his words trailing off.

"Kinnaird, are you sure? Can I see that?"

Before he had a chance to reply, Adeena strode towards him. He held the book tightly.

"Can I see it Dad, please?" she asked.

He handed the book to her. She read the cover out loud: "Sixth Earl of Southesk?"

"It's his journal," her dad said. He looked at her nervously.

"His? Who?"

"Sir Carnegie," her father explained in a halting voice. "He was an MP and a Captain for the English during the Jacobite rebellion in 1745."

"Holy shit!" Adeena began to read a passage from the journal, transfixed. Her mouth hung open as she absorbed the words. Her father reached for the leather bound book.

"Adeena, no..." He tried to pull it back from her, but she held on tightly.

"I need to read this!"

Before he could protest, there was a loud banging at the back door.

IT HAD BEEN A WHILE SINCE TARA HAD BEEN UP TO WOLFE Lake.

She and Adeena had often ventured up on their own, sometimes with, but usually without, male companionship. In fact, she thought, the weekends with just the two of them had been the best. Watching old movies, eating junk food, swimming and canoeing, inventing every insane martini combination they could dream up. They'd had some good memories up here – a long time ago.

All that was about to be lost today when Tara retrieved the Duncan Cello from Adeena Stuart. How could Adeena simply steal a priceless artifact from the gallery and think everything would be fine between them?

Tara banged again on the door sharply. She felt the biting

cold on her cheeks as she waited.

Mrs. Stuart appeared with her usual understated elegance.

"Tara, it's been so long!" she said, opening the door and wrapping her arms around Tara. Mrs. Stuart had always treated her like a daughter and that was going to make this even tougher.

"Hi Mrs. Stuart," she responded, taking note of how manicured she looked, even at eight-thirty in the morning. How does she do it? Tara had always wanted to be like Adeena's mom. She somehow managed to juggle a professional career and a family, while seeming to spend all her time shopping and dressing like a modern Grace Kelly.

Let it go, Tara. You're here on business. Bad business. "Is Adeena here? I need to speak with her."

"Yes, she's having coffee with..." Mrs. Stuart hesitated as they entered the kitchen from the front entrance. "Adeena?" she called out toward the bedroom. "Tara's here."

A muffled response came from the bedroom. "Just a sec."

"Tara, have a seat. Would you like a coffee or, wait, you like tea right? Darjeeling?" Mrs. Stuart offered, opening a cupboard and checking her selection of canisters. "I'm sure we've got some here."

"No, it's okay, Mrs. Stuart, but thank you." Why couldn't she just be a bitch like her daughter? It would make this a lot easier.

"Hey Tar, what's the occasion?"

Tara looked over her shoulder as Adeena appeared from the bedroom, in jeans and a checkered flannel shirt. "I need to talk to you. It's important."

Tara was still dressed in her wool coat as she stood in the kitchen. Adeena looked at her without saying a word. "Okay. Why don't we go outside for a walk?"

THE CRUEL WINDS OF NOVEMBER COULD ARRIVE AT ANY TIME in Eastern Ontario. Overnight they returned with a ferocious bite. The lake greeted them with angry white caps forming over the dark waters.

Adeena was glad she had grabbed her wool toque and her lined jacket before she stepped out. As they walked across the yard, towards the menacing blackness of Wolfe Lake, she knew the moment of truth was here.

"Dee, how could you?" Tara said after they had gotten away from the cottage.

"Could I what?"

"Steal a five-million-dollar-cello!"

Adeena stopped walking. The wind, so insistent up until now, was suddenly still. Flakes of snow started to fall.

Tara pulled the collar of her coat higher, trying to cover her ears. "I know you had Thomas Peeters make a copy of it so you could try to fool me!"

"I never meant to get you in trouble."

"Really? My God! Are you for real? You think you can just go around playing stupid games and leaving me to clean up your mess as usual?" Tara was exasperated. "You've gone too far this time. I can't save you." She paused, her tone turning icy. "I'm not even sure I want to."

Adeena absorbed the words and felt even colder. Snowflakes were starting to collect on both of them. "I wish you would let me explain."

"Explain? Explain? Are you totally fucking crazy?" Tara rarely swore. It took something bordering on life-changing for her to use the "f" word. "Where is it, Adeena? Where's the *real* Duncan Cello?"

The two women stood staring at each other. Their steaming breaths visually documenting their exchange. Snow filled the air.

Adeena knew she had lost. What had she been thinking? How in the fuck did she think this was going to end? She would have to hand over the Duncan to Tara. And likely go to jail.

"I... I... don't know what to say, Tar. That cello belonged to Katharine Carnegie, who I think is... well, maybe a distant relation. It's so much more than just a museum artifact. I am not sure I can explain just how important it is..." Adeena paused hoping that somehow she could draw Tara into her reality, "...to me."

"So you do have it? You stole it then?"

This would never work.

Tara would never understand and she would never care. How could she? She lived in the normal world, where people went about their lives, building careers, focusing on the here and now. They didn't struggle to tie together the threads of time. They didn't find themselves drifting between two souls separated by centuries.

"Can I try to explain? You've always been there for me and you've always helped me find my way back." Adeena hung her head before her best friend and waited for a response. The world was turning white, the sharp edges of rocks and trees blending into soft uniformity.

Tara stood before her. She said nothing. It was a standoff. If Adeena had hoped that she would somehow get a sympathetic hearing, there was no indication coming from the other side. Might as well face it. It's over now and time to face the music.

Literally.

"Okay," Adeena finally replied, keeping her head hung low. "I... I..."

The high-pitched ring of a cell phone interrupted them. Both women touched their coat pockets. Another ring and Tara found her phone and pulled it out.

"Hello?" she said in an annoyed tone, holding the phone tightly against her ear. Adeena looked up. Tara stared back with daggers in her eyes.

"What is it, Pablo?" Tara barked. Her expression morphed into confusion as she listened. "What do you mean? I don't get it." Tara's eyes were darting back and forth. Her brows were raised. "The Duncan Cello is sitting in my office?"

CHAPTER 23

The Duke of Perth's steel pistol proved a persuasive negotiating tool.

As James Drummond fully cocked the gun's hammer and pointed the barrel at the head of Carlisle's town clerk, it became even more convincing.

"Tell me again why ye cannot proclaim the new King of England?" James demanded, push his polished Doune pistol against the trembling clerk's forehead.

"I never proclaimed a king before, and know no form for it," John Pearson stammered. He looked uneasily at the three other men in the room who stood behind James like a murder of crows.

"No form for it?" James laughed. "What shall we do?"

"Maybe this'll help," one of the soldiers snorted, unsheathing his dirk and pressing the steel blade to the man's quavering neck.

With a gun at his head and a knife to his throat, clerk Pearson acquiesced. "I think I may be able to come up with a form."

"I thought ye might," James smiled. "You will proclaim as of 17 November 1745, the return of the Stuart monarchy to

England. King James the Third, already proclaimed James the Eighth of Scotland."

"Yes sir," the clerk responded. His eyes darted between James and the soldier holding the knife to his throat. "Shall I start now, sir?"

"Indeed you shall!" James exclaimed, backing away. "Leave him to his work," he told the man holding the knife. The soldier backed away reluctantly. "The Prince will be here on the 'morrow. We have much to finish before then."

As James left the clerk's chamber, he knew what news he would share in tonight's letter to his mother. She had waited all her life for the return of the Catholic monarch to the English throne. And today her wish came true.

If only on paper.

ADEENA SAT CURLED ON THE SOFA, WATCHING HER DAD BUILD a fire. Warmth at last seeped into her as she took another sip of hot tea and watched flames engulf the dry logs.

"Tara left in a hurry," her dad said. "She didn't want to stay? Have lunch with us?"

Adeena chuckled. That would have been interesting. After getting a call from work, Tara stormed away, yelling over her shoulder: "Hope you got a good lawyer!"

Now that she was gone, Adeena speculated how the Duncan Cello got back to the gallery. "Dad, what time did Philippe leave?"

"Last night after we went to bed, I guess," her dad said, closing up the steel mesh that held the dancing licks of fire at bay. "He had to work this morning."

Yeah, he worked alright, Adeena mused. *Worked at saving my butt.* She wondered how he got the Duncan Cello into Tara's office.

Her father sat down on the chaise lounge where he liked to

read. She noticed the journal sitting on the table beside him. "I'd love to read that," Adeena said, pointing to the leather volume.

He sighed. "I know you would. But don't you think it'll just make things worse?"

"Dad, please. Didn't Grandma Stuart give it to *us*?"

"Pumpkin..." he started, but then fell silent.

Adeena recalled her feelings for the Captain she had sparred with a few times. "The prick that wrote that journal is Katharine's brother. He's a real asshole."

Her father studied her for a moment. He nodded slowly before responding. "I did some research before I left Scotland. I couldn't find much on Katharine Carnegie, but I did determine she was a musician."

Adeena lit up. "You found something? Tell me!"

"I went to Drummond Castle and met the guide there, a history teacher. He took me to a private archive in Crieff, and I found correspondence that's never been published – letters from James Drummond."

"Really? How many?" Adeena asked wide-eyed. Her mother watched from the kitchen, frowning.

"A dozen or more to his mother; I, uh – forget her name, I think it's ..."

"Lady Jean," Adeena interjected.

"Yes, that's it."

"She's amazing," Adeena said, recalling the iron-willed woman. "James is afraid of letting her down. I think that's what drives him."

"How do you know all this?" Her dad looked at her strangely.

"Because I spent time with James, and his mother and of course, the asshole Captain."

"Sir James Carnegie? The one who wrote this journal?"

"Yeah, and there is something even stranger."

"Stranger? Stranger than you going back in time and becoming another woman?" Her father had spoken the words, and now her mother stepped forward from the kitchen. She seemed ready to interrupt, but didn't.

"The score, the one you sent to me, that Grandma took from Kinnaird," Adeena explained. "I wrote the first bars myself, when I was a teenager, but I could never finish, hard as I tried. And I had lyrics in my head that didn't make sense, until you sent me that music."

"Are you sure it was the same?" her mother jumped in.

"Yes, I am. When I got the score I couldn't believe that the first eight bars were, note for note, the ones I had written – a song I couldn't finish. And my lyrics, words that just poured from me one day a long time ago and were still stuck in my head – they fit the music perfectly."

Adeena studied the effect of her words on her parents. They looked worried. Her dad spoke first. "There is no record of Katharine Carnegie ever publishing music," he said more to himself than to his wife and his daughter. "In one letter though, James Drummond talks about the music she performed, and the effect on him and the men in his regiment."

"What'd he say?" Adeena and her mother both exclaimed, almost simultaneously.

"Trying to remember," he said, reaching for his iPad. He searched a second. "I took pictures of some of the letters." He tapped the screen and scrolled down until he found it. He read the words aloud:

> "Lady Katharine's song pierced not only my heart, but those of all the men who heard it that evening. Even the Prince is humbled against the power of her instrument, of her words and of her voice. She awoke the passion to fight in every last man gathered at Drummond and I am glad you asked me to thank her afterwards.
>
> Even now, as our situation becomes precarious, I hold her words close."

Adeena closed her eyes. "I remember that night. I played at the ball and afterward James and I danced." She relived the breathless excitement of dancing for what seemed like hours. "He wouldn't let me stop!"

Her mother shook her head and Adeena caught her looking at her. What was she thinking?

As if to answer, her mother bit her lip tersely and walked back toward the kitchen without a word.

"AND YOU EXPECT ME TO BELIEVE THAT?" TARA BARKED.

The young man standing in her office, Michael from security, smiled nervously. "I work the night shift and go to school during the day, I don't get much sleep."

"Oh perfect! That's your excuse for sending up a fake?"

Michael shrugged his shoulders as Pablo tapped on the glass doors of her office holding a cello case. She waved him in.

"Good thing the exhibit is closed today," Tara fumed as Pablo came through the doors. "Let me see!"

Pablo put the case down and opened it up. "This is the cello we have on display." He turned to Michael who stood beside another cello case on a stand. "And *that* we believe is the actual Duncan Cello. It was in the secure area until Michael realized the mix-up and brought it up this morning. I asked him to put it in your office and called you right away."

"Let me see them both," Tara snapped.

Pablo held up both cellos. She could see no obvious differences. They seemed to be identical twins, but upon closer examination the cello that Michael had delivered from storage looked older somehow when she compared the two instruments side by side.

Tara was only an amateur archivist. Her job was to organize exhibits, select works and attract paying customers. She wisely let others handle the meticulous work of restoration and preservation. She was certain they would confirm this instrument, supposedly stored in the basement all this time, to be the actual Duncan Cello. She would have them tag the fake, and increase security on the real one.

Her phone rang. It was André, her boss. She waved Pablo and Michael out of her office. "Close the door, please," she said dropping down on the leather chair behind her desk. She hurriedly gathered her thoughts.

"Good morning André. How are things in London?" She needed time to think. Good thing he was in England, likely calling for an update and to discuss strategy for the auction he would be attending this evening at Harrods.

As they talked, Tara noticed Michael and Pablo outside her office. They seemed to be having a lively exchange, with Pablo doing most of the talking, and Michael shaking his head vigorously. Pablo raised his arms for emphasis and proceeded to use an animated series of arm gestures to reinforce whatever he was saying.

Michael grinned, nodding his head watching Pablo. After a moment they shook hands and patted each other warmly, leaving Tara wondering what in the world they were talking about.

Whatever it was, she didn't like the looks of it.

November of 1745 was darker and colder in Northern England than usual, even for this forlorn month. The sun had been swallowed up, leaving behind only grey gloom and frigid air for both man and beast alike.

Despite their initial success at Carlisle, when the town welcomed the Prince's army, the campaign to return the Stuart monarchy to England was hitting a wall of resistance.

James Drummond struggled to keep his own spirits high, and his men from fleeing back to the comfort of their homes in the Tay Valley. While he favoured inspiration over desperation and praise over punishment, of late he had found more and more that he needed to dispense military justice. Even for a minor infraction, he had made men suffer the bite of a horsewhip or the terror of a freezing night in a black cell without rations.

His regiment moved heavy guns, artillery and supplies to support the Highland regiments led by Prince Charles. When they arrived in an English town that had been surrounded by the Prince and his army, they would help secure rations, brandy, and lodgings before making their camp. The first night often lead to drunken looting and raping, all of which he tried to curtail as much as possible without much success.

Katharine's warning haunted him still. Her words about the Prince echoed in his head. 'His plan is doomed... and you will not live to see another summer.' Her written message inside his tunic kissed his bare chest.

Forever, I will wait for you.

As he opened his tent to greet yet another cold grey morning, her face washed over him. Her eyes, her mouth, her whole countenance – were something he conjured readily. He felt his passion rising, recalling the feeling of her in his arms at Drummond Castle. If she were here now, he would take her as a man does with the woman who is truly made for him. And she would give herself to their holy union. He wanted Katharine flowing through him and he through her. Two united as one.

The bitter chill yanked him from his reverie. The wind blew fiercely this morning and a group of ragged soldiers approached him with a look of desperation.

"Brandy's 'bout done sir," one of them quipped. The boy, no more than ten and five years, held a flask in his hand. "Look!" He turned the bottle upside down.

James knew that men could not be expected to start another wretched day without brandy. "I'll get more for all of you. But here, take this now." He pulled a flask from his vest and offered it to the young man who bowed his head.

"Thank you, sir."

James watched as the boy offered the brandy to his older companion, who stared with hollowed eyes and feeble expression. The old man looked dirty and seemed cold with a chill that must be deep in his bones by now. His hand shook as he raised the vessel to his lips and sucked a heavy dram. The warmth lifted him a little and he sighed his appreciation.

Brandy and oats were all that kept these men from deserting. They were farmers, not soldiers. To raise their spirits, he would search for beef today in the village. A boiled supper tonight, if he could provide it, would give them strength to start the fifty-mile trek to Manchester, a prize the Prince coveted.

James was doubtful. He touched his heart and felt the parchment with Katharine's words upon it press against his breast. He was driven by the Prince, by his mother and the whole of Drummond clan to fight and to face death if necessary.

But it was the thought of Katharine that kept him longing for life.

JACKIE STARED AT THE IMAGES ON DR. LOCHIEL'S HIGH-resolution computer monitors.

"Give me your theory again please," she asked, somewhat overwhelmed with his five-minute explanation about the series of scans he showed her.

"No problem," he said as he clicked the mouse on his laptop and the screen refreshed. "I worked on this with Dr. Chung from the university for quite a while, and even I don't quite get it."

Well at least it's not just me, Jackie smiled. Lately everything she thought she knew was being turned upside down. And her daughter was the biggest mystery of all. Adeena's stories were compelling and William was starting to believe that somehow, impossibly, they were true. He claimed that Adeena was not only connected to a woman from the past, but also that she 'became' her, even though the woman was born almost three-hundred-years earlier.

Father and daughter seemed to feed off each other, but Jackie knew that if she got sucked in, there would be no one left to question the impossibility of the story.

"This is the area we've focused on," Dr. Lochiel said, pointing to a section of a CT scan he had zoomed in on. "And look at this." He clicked a menu on the screen and the screen refreshed again. A three-dimensional image appeared. "You see this area between the lateral and third ventricles?"

Jackie put on her glasses and peered at the screen. She squinted, trying to see what Dr. Lochiel was pointing to.

"Just a second," he said, as he took the mouse and began to draw a red circle on the screen around a small dark area. "Right here. This might look like a tumour, but it's not. It's a collection of nerve cells that are regenerating, at an astounding rate. Dr. Chung has been looking over the scans and wants to come and talk with the patient. He wants to try a new imaging technique he's developing."

"That's my daughter you're talking about," Jackie said curtly. "She's not a guinea pig for you to experiment with."

"Oh, I'm sorry, I didn't mean to make it sound like that," Dr. Lochiel replied, turning his chair towards Jackie. "Your daughter has nerve growth that is normally only present in developing fetuses or newborn babies."

Jackie frowned as she listened. "Go on."

"I know it sounds odd, and that's why this case is...uh..." he paused, looking back at the monitor.

"Case is what?"

"Well, I've never seen anything like this. You know I always try to give you a full range of options for your patients."

"She's my daughter."

"I realize that," he touched his neck and looked down before continuing. "Look, a growth in the brain, of any type is not good. In this case, it seems to be benign neurogenesis. I don't think it's malignant, although we're not sure yet."

Jackie bit her lip. "Okay, so what's the problem?" She studied the doctor, who seemed to be hedging. "Ben, how long have we worked together?"

"Oh, I don't know, maybe ten years?"

"Yeah, so don't hold back here. Adeena has a benign growth in her brain? Are you're worried, or not? I don't understand what you're saying."

"This growth, whatever it is, is pushing against other areas, it's expanding, and..."

"And what? Why can't you give it to me straight?"

Dr. Lochiel looked at Jackie squarely. "Your daughter has new cells growing in her brain. It is like another person is developing inside of her."

WITH THE DUNCAN CELLO GONE, ADEENA POURED HERSELF into the world of practicing and rehearsals, rehearsals and practicing, twelve hours a day. Every day. For almost three weeks now, her days were only about the music.

If not for the composition she and Katharine had created, it would have been a very boring ordeal. But instead, it was the opposite.

The music provided the motivation for her to wake up early. She wrote down all the lyrics she had been nursing since she was fifteen that she sang so powerfully as Katharine. Sometimes when she was alone, she sang them out loud to herself. Her voice didn't have the range it did when she sang as Katharine, but then the circumstances were also much different. She wasn't in a candle-lit castle, backed by live musicians and urged on by a spirited audience.

Adeena closed her eyes recalling those performances. There

was a gestalt created when the music left her lips and vibrated off the strings of her instrument, when it connected with the men and women watching her. It ignited something inside them. An elixir she found nowhere else.

She realized performing in the NAC orchestra wasn't likely to provide that experience to her, but she was determined nonetheless to prove she could play with them. Particularly when they were playing *her* music.

As she was getting set to leave for the afternoon's rehearsal, her cell phone rang.

"Hey you." It was Philippe.

"Hi! Where are you?"

"London, just leaving for Rome with the Prime Minister. I wanted to see how you're doing."

"Tough life, eh?"

"Somebody's gotta do it," he said lightly. "I'd like to be back for your opening. This weekend, right?"

She looked at her watch. "Yup, Saturday night. I reserved some very good seats."

"Need a date?"

"Maybe. Got training as a bodyguard?"

"Is Lang still bothering you?" Philippe asked, his tone growing serious.

"We don't talk to each other, but seeing him take all the credit, and watching his head get bigger by the day, makes me want to cut off his baton arm," Adeena said. "And anything else he might want to wave around."

Philippe laughed. "Could you wait till I'm back before you do something stupid? If there is going to be a mutilation, I need the inside scoop."

"Don't worry, I'll give you an exclusive."

"I'd like an exclusive, with you."

There was a pause in the conversation. Adeena couldn't remember the last time they made love or even just had a fun moment. She was his dark and stormy night, a cliché he should just close the book on. She wanted to feel passion again and be swept away.

"I miss you," she heard herself saying.

"Adeena, I have so much to say to you. I believe in you, what you're doing. That music's inside of you. You belong on a big stage. And..." he hesitated.

"And what?"

"And... you belong with me."

THE HOT BLADE OF A STRAIGHT RAZOR SLOWLY CARVED THE shaving cream from Friedrich Lang's taut throat. He could feel it pull across him smartly, clearing the path ahead like a snowplow.

"Tomorrow, Maestro?" the old barber asked in a thick Slavic accent. "You play new symphony?"

"Ja," Lang replied, looking up at the ceiling, face stiff to get a closer shave.

"Will be good, no?" the barber said, shifting his attention to the back of Lange's neck. He pushed the maestro's head down and gingerly placed a hot towel on his next target.

"Not 'good,' my friend. Magnificent!" Lang chortled.

The barber grunted and without missing a beat began applying shaving cream and preparing his blade for round two. "You play your music, no?"

"Ja." This will be *my* music after tomorrow, Lang thought. For all anyone will ever know, he had created a tribute to the human spirit, to fulfilling one's destiny, no matter the obstacles. If the world wanted to think of it as a tribute to Ludwig, so be it.

"My wife, she see you on TV," the barber continued, a steady patter that Lang usually found annoying, but today judged it to be of much higher quality.

"I did a lot of interviews the last few weeks, even the BBC and Radio Deutschland. They wanted to do a segment on me for their Beethoven retrospective."

"Beethoven? Oh yeah, he's good," the barber chirped.

Lang wondered if the man had ever even heard a Beethoven symphony. Probably he was just very good at engaging his clients. Either way, Friedrich Lang and Ludvig van Beethoven had been used together in the same sentence in most of the stories broadcast or published on the new work.

At last, something was going to happen that he had longed for since trying to compose his first piece of music as a young man. 'Friedrich Lang' would be a name remembered long after he departed this world.

The barber moved on to trimming Lang's sideburns, and tidying up the long ends of his greying mane. The man was a craftsman in own domain, painstakingly trimming and checking each cut. He remained silent, reading Lang's mood, as the maestro slipped into his own thoughts.

Tomorrow, when this work is unveiled to the world, my life will change, he thought. Whether he transcribed the notes on paper or not, this music was his – and he alone would give it life. He saw the effect it had on his own orchestra, and even the bumbling NAC minions who came to watch the rehearsals.

When the two thousand men and women who filled Southam Hall tomorrow evening heard this music, along with the usual horde of music critics, he would become known as the composer of *Voyages of Destiny* and achieve musical reverence. He cared not that the real composer wouldn't share any of the glory. Without Friedrich Lang, this work would have remained unknown. It was his arrangements and his persistence that brought it to the world.

He had known from the first time he played it with Adeena Stuart in his private chambers, that this was no ordinary composition. It had the rare gift of changing those who experienced it.

As the barber finished up and turned him around to see himself in the mirror, he looked at his reflection and saw a composer who was twenty-four hours away from changing the world.

CHAPTER 24

Adeena's black dress felt like it had been created for this moment.

The play of chiffon against skin, the contrast of black fabric on white shoulders and the cascading sheerness wrapped around her all felt so perfect. She was one with it.

Adeena studied her reflection in the mirror with a mixture of happiness and regret, an unsettling feeling of complete calm and absolute terror. She never imagined that the first time she performed with the National Arts Centre Orchestra they would be playing *her* music.

Or would it forever be known as Friedrich Lang's?

Since she lost access to the Duncan Cello nearly three weeks ago, she had begun to accept the inevitable. The music she first scribbled out as a teenager – the same eight bars Katharine Carnegie used as a starting point for her symphonic tour de force and that Adeena raised to perfection with her lyrics, was gone. She might realize her lifelong ambition to become a professional cellist, but Lang would have her music.

She took a deep breath. The dress stared back at her from the mirror.

Let it go, Adeena.

That's what her mother kept telling her. Maybe she was right.

The doorbell rang and Philippe stood posed before her in a crisp tuxedo, holding a sprawling bouquet of red roses.

"You made it!" she exclaimed.

"I wouldn't miss it for all the prime ministers and presidents in the universe," Philippe laughed. He handed her the flowers and cast an appreciative eye over her and the dress. *"Ooh-la-la!"*

They embraced and he held her close. It was good to be wrapped in his arms again. He kissed her cheek and then slowly released her with a whisper, "I missed you."

"Me too. I'm glad you're back."

They enjoyed a moment of silence before he spoke. "Are you ready? I thought this night would never come. Here you are, about to play at the NAC," Philippe said smiling. "I'm so happy for you!"

"Thanks. I'm sorry I've been such a burden to you," she replied, looking down at her feet. "And to everybody else, too."

"Nonsense!" He took her hand and raised her face up before the full-length mirror. "Look at yourself. You've made it through all the crap anyone could throw at you. You're about to step into a whole new world, onto the stage in front of thousands of people. It's where you belong. You've earned it." He paused a moment. "And on top of all that, you're not hard on the eyes!"

She smiled at her reflection and his glowing assessment.

"And after the performance," Philippe continued, "I've got reservations at *Chez Henri* to celebrate!"

"Thanks." She should feel only happiness, but a voice inside her wanted more. She chose her words carefully. "I guess then... you didn't get anywhere, with Lang?"

"Lang?" Philippe repeated. He seemed to deflate a little. "You mean about the score?"

"Yeah, I thought maybe, you..." she stopped. He'd already done so much.

"I tried. Got my editor interested in the story, but there's no way to prove Lang did anything." He turned her around, so he could talk to her face to face. "He even copyrighted it with the Library of Congress and the Songwriters Guild."

Adeena bit her lip and felt wetness cloud her eyes. She didn't want to spoil the evening. But to let go of her creation, and lose the music forever, meant that somehow, she was letting Katharine and James down. And Margaret Rose.

And herself.

She knew that Philippe could see the change in her face. He took her in his arms again. "That music was never published before, there is no record of it, other than those copies you made. Unsigned photocopies unfortunately, don't prove a hell of a lot."

Adeena nodded. He's right. Maybe it's better this way. The Duncan Cello was gone. The music was gone. Katharine and James were dead.

It was time to leave the past behind and find her own future.

William stood beside Jackie, who held a bouquet of carnations and had a smile that he hadn't seen in a long time. He knocked on the door of Adeena's condo.

"She did it," he grinned. "Finally!"

The door opened and Adeena greeted them with a radiance that seemed to light her from within. It reminded William of the little girl who used to take such delight in going to see the symphony with them. She would get all dressed up and just glow for the entire evening, basking in the experience, completely mesmerized by the performances.

"Thank you," Adeena said, before she gave both of them an extra-long hug. "Come on in."

They stepped inside the foyer and Philippe insisted on taking their coats. He looked at his watch. "Come, sit down. We've got lots of time."

Jackie sat beside Adeena. "You look beautiful, *ma belle*." She opened her silver clutch and reached in. "I thought you might want to wear this tonight," she said, opening her hand to reveal a delicate gold cello brooch.

Adeena took the tiny piece of jewelry. "I forgot all about this."

"Remember the last time you wore it?" Jackie asked. "We thought it might bring you luck, again."

"Like my audition, for Canterbury," Adeena mused. "Philippe, I wore this in Grade 8 when I got accepted at the high school for the arts. My grandmother was staying with us then. She gave this to me, said it would give me *sonas*."

"Good fortune," William interjected. "Happiness. Passion."

Philippe grinned. "Well in that case, you must wear it!"

Adeena held the brooch tightly.

"Your grandmother is still smiling on you," William said pointing toward the ceiling. "She always knew you would make it. Told me to have faith in you. She said no force in heaven or on earth could stop you. She was right."

"Grandma was always so good to me," Adeena responded. Her shoulders droopped. "And now I've let her down," she sighed.

"What do you mean, *belle?*" her mother asked, trying to console her. "You're going to make her so proud tonight."

"She sent me the music, because she wanted me to do something with it," Adeena stammered, beginning to dissolve. "Something important. But I've failed her."

William recalled his mother's dying words. 'Adeena needs to save us.' He shivered remembering her insistence on having the score couriered across the Atlantic the same day.

"I'm letting Lang steal that music, right in front of the whole world, in front of my own family," Adeena moaned, starting to shake. "How could I have let this happen? Oh my God!"

Jackie wrapped her arms around her. "Adeena, it's okay."

Philippe sat down across from William. "I tried to expose Lang, but there is no record of that score anywhere. I know he took it from Adeena, but he's made it his own now."

William nodded. "There's no historical record, nothing to point to." He looked at his daughter. "But Pumpkin, I did get some new information from Scotland, from my friend, Daniel, the guide at Drummond Castle."

Adeena stared at him. "What?"

"He sent copies of more letters, and even an old newspaper account. Seems like Katharine Carnegie caused quite a sensation."

"Really?"

"Yeah. Glowing reports of enchanting performances – of the music and of her voice," he continued. "I have to think that if only that score had been published, instead of it being hidden away at Kinnaird for all those years, well, it would have found a place in the historical record."

"Yeah," Philippe nodded, "I think so."

"If I had the Duncan Cello, I could make things right," Adeena said, anger rising in her voice. "Make that bastard pay for stealing our music."

No one knew how to respond.

Silence fell over the room.

A ticking clock methodically recorded the passing seconds like the timer on a bomb about to explode.

WILLIAM HOISTED ADEENA'S WORN LEATHER CELLO CASE INTO the back of his Volvo station wagon. "Are we all going in the same car?" He closed the trunk and looked toward his wife standing near Adeena and Philippe in the brooding light of the parking garage of Adeena's condo.

"Oh, *sacre!*" Jackie cursed. "I got a run in my stocking." She reached down and touched her calf. “Is the Rideau Centre still open?”

William looked at his watch. “I don’t know, but Adeena’s got to be at the NAC...” he said, focusing on his wrist, “...now! They’re on at eight.”

“We’re supposed to be there ninety minutes before,” Adeena confirmed in a small voice.

“Then you’re going to be late, Pumpkin.” William turned to Jackie. “You really need to go to the mall, now?”

Jackie gave him a strange look, silently mouthing ‘Yes’ and nodding, eyebrows raised. He had been married long enough to know this was not the time to argue.

Jackie touched Philippe’s shoulder. “Maybe I can go with him? And you take Adeena?”

“Sure,” Philippe agreed. “My car’s right here.”

TARA WAS HAVING A HARD TIME COMPLETING THE EMAIL TO her boss.

André had been so busy travelling and negotiating three new acquisitions, he had pretty much left things to her. Not that she minded. She felt that really, she was in charge anyway. He was more like a ceremonial monarch. Important perhaps, but not required to run the affairs of state.

It was the model her parents gave her – a strong woman making day to day decisions and keeping all the gears running smoothly. It was in her DNA. But still, she needed to give her director a summary of what had transpired with the Duncan Cello, for the record.

Okay, so when did this all start? She looked over at her desk calendar and saw the little note on today’s date: ‘Dee concert’.

“God,” she said, and whistled. “It’s her big night.”

It should have been an evening to celebrate with her. Help Adeena get ready, support her in any way she could, even if it was only picking out the right shoes. They had been there for each other, for every milestone. Instead, she thought with a pang of guilt, I'm looking for a way to send to her jail.

The fake Duncan Cello, locked away in the basement, was proof to some degree, but she had never actually caught Adeena with the real instrument. Tara knew though, that her troublesome best friend, maddening confidante, and let's face it, surrogate sibling, had done what she had always done. Act first. Think later. Get out of jail free – thanks to big sister Tara.

No wonder Adeena always beat her at *Monopoly*.

Gotta write this email, she thought, trying to focus on what to say to André. As she clicked her mouse to start a new line, there was a tap on the door.

"Tara?" It was Philippe. His head poked through the door. "Working late?"

"Yes, I'm finishing up." She rose from her chair. "Come in."

He stepped through the door wearing a classic tux – a slim black mohair jacket, with narrow lapels and a black tie. His high-shine derby shoes gave him a sleek finish.

"I've got something for you," he said, embracing her and planting a kiss on each cheek, his musky cologne subtly teasing her. He held her a moment longer than usual. "Box seats!" He smiled, presenting her with two tickets. "Show starts at eight. You busy, mademoiselle?

JACKIE WASN'T SURE HOW THIS WAS GOING TO WORK, BUT somehow she had to try.

As she reached the security area of the gallery, using Adeena's security fob that Philippe had given her, she knew she had finally accepted there was something special about William's side of the family. Adeena's stories might be impossible, but maybe, just maybe, not everything could be explained through science. Even as Jackie had delivered her Ph.D thesis debunking clairvoyance among autistic children, a nagging sliver of doubt lingered.

Now she could no longer explain what was happening to her daughter. And sometimes, she thought, a mother just has to do what a mother has to do.

The door to the secure area was open and she heard someone moaning.

Curious, she knocked softly on the open door and proceeded inside slowly. She stopped dead in her tracks as she was confronted with the sight of two men a few feet in front of her. One had his pants down to his ankles while the other was performing fellatio on him with reckless abandon.

"I'm sorry," Jackie blurted out, averting her eyes.

"Fuck!" the man on the receiving end shouted, pushing the other man off him. "Who are you?" He quickly pulled his pants up as his partner scurried behind the desk.

"I'm Jackie. Adeena Stuart's mother?"

The startled man looked pale and trembled as he spoke. "What do you want? With me?"

"Are you Michael?" Jackie inquired, still flushed from the scene she just witnessed.

"Yes," he warbled. "I'm sorry you had to see that."

Jackie smiled. Not something she witnessed every day admittedly, but somehow rather than embarrassing her, it filled her with confidence for the request she was about to make. "That's okay, it doesn't bother me. I'm only here to try and help Adeena."

There was a long moment of silence. "How?"

"I need the Duncan Cello."

The other man who she had just seen on his knees in a rather compromising position with his mouth full of his friend's penis – now popped up from behind the desk. He looked worried as he stared first at Jackie and then at Michael who seemed to be considering her request.

"Pablo," Michael challenged his partner in a measured tone, "we need to help her."

TARA CONTEMPLATED PHILIPPE'S OFFER. "I'D LOVE TO, BUT I'M not sure if I can go to the NAC without having her arrested."

"Arrested? Why?" Philippe repeated, stepping back a bit but remaining close enough that his cologne was still having its way with her.

"You're not aware that she likes to steal precious artifacts?" Tara asked.

"Are you sure about that?"

Tara hesitated. So far, all she had were Lang's comments and an imposter cello locked up downstairs. "No, but I know what she's done. And I know what she's capable of..." She was having a hard time making a convincing case. Philippe's brown eyes were too inviting and his face too handsome.

The room suddenly felt warm. She flushed staring at him.

"She's not perfect," he agreed. "But she's not a criminal."

"Sorry, you're wrong! I've saved her ass so many times, but if she took the Duncan, and I know she did, then even I can't help her this time."

Philippe seemed to be thinking it over. "Whatever she may have done, and you have no real proof of anything," he said, closing the distance between them, "she's still your friend. You two are like family. You even fight like sisters!"

"I know, and it's killing me," Tara replied. "I want so much to help her, but I can't let this one go. It's not some teenage prank. She could go to jail, for a long time." Suddenly the thought of it was too much for her. She had a vision of Adeena in a prison cell, her career and her life ruined.

All thanks to 'sister' Tara.

She felt tears rising to the surface. She struggled to keep them from overflowing. The warring conflicts in her head fought for supremacy. The tears won out and rolled down her cheeks. Philippe put his arms around her. "It's okay Tara." He held her close. "It's okay."

She started sobbing. But the comfort he was bringing her was something she had rarely, if ever, felt before. And she didn't want to let it go.

ADEENA SAT NERVOUSLY ON THE STAGE OF SOUTHAM HALL.

The cavernous theatre was almost full, with only a few of the 2,300 red velvet seats still empty. Yet people kept coming in, all dressed up in high style, hundreds of diamonds twinkling from the necks and wrists of ladies throughout the hall. It was a sell-out for the opening of the new season. The character of the room was changing before her eyes, as the audience transformed the empty space into a living thing that craved musical solace.

Her grandmother would have enjoyed this. But she would have been so disappointed that her granddaughter had let Katharine's music slip away without a fight.

Adeena looked across at the printed score sitting on each musician's stand. That was *her* composition they were about to perform, giving glory to the thief who stole it. All she had left were the lyrics in her head, words that made the music soar even higher.

"Belle!" someone suddenly whispered.

She looked around.

"Belle!" This time the voice was louder.

Adeena glanced to her left.

There, behind the curtain, was her mother.

PHILIPPE COULD FEEL TARA TREMBLING IN HIS ARMS.

He had done his job of distracting her almost too well. And

now he was feeling something unexpected – an electricity running between them that both excited and scared him.

The tighter she held him, the more he felt the powerful rush. Their bodies fit together perfectly, and he was fighting a passion sweeping over him that seemed more than simple lust. He felt physically aroused and emotionally drawn towards the woman he was embracing.

He had known Tara longer than Adeena. But he had never considered her in a romantic fashion, maybe because she was so quick to introduce him to her best friend.

Or had there been little clues all along that Tara had been sending him? Had he missed the obvious all this time?

Philippe could feel her breasts pushing against him and her thighs pressing dangerously close. It was beginning to stimulate him, adding to his confusion. Tara's dark perfume was intoxicating.

He had to stop, not get carried away.

Was she feeling anything? Or was he was only imagining all of this?

THIS CAN'T BE HAPPENING, TARA THOUGHT.

She had to let Philippe go. He had started by comforting her, but this had become something more, at least for her.

Her heart was racing. The tighter she held him, the more he responded, drawing her even closer.

How could she let her feelings get the best of her? She couldn't do this to Dee. It went against everything she believed in.

She lifted her head from Philippe's shoulder and they caught each other's eyes. What was he thinking? His mouth was parted slightly, his eyes open wide, inviting her to enter another world.

Tara raised her arms and placed her hand behind his neck,

gently pulling his face closer. She felt any sense of control slipping away. She had to feel his mouth on hers.

Suddenly there was a knock on the door.

Tara turned to see a uniformed security guard standing before her.

"The Duncan Cello is gone!"

CHAPTER 25

The look on Adeena's face was something coaches of winning athletes liked to see before the big game. Absolute confidence. Fierce pride. The need for revenge.

She sat on stage with the Duncan Cello, a wooden conduit connecting two incarnations of one musical soul. The fact that her mother had brought the precious instrument to Adeena felt even more exhilarating. It filled her with a purpose she had never experienced.

We might all go to jail. But, we'll go as a family!

Adeena clutched her bow like a sword being readied against an invading army. Friedrich Lang sprang onto the stage to thunderous applause and she knew it was time for battle.

Lang acknowledged the warm welcome, bounding onto the conductor's podium. He seemed to bask in the adoration of the audience, primed by the NAC's unrelenting campaign promoting tonight's musical premiere.

She closed her eyes, trying to harness the energy of her pounding heart. She felt her grandmother watching her, smiling, urging her on.

Adeena knew she couldn't let Margaret Rose down this time.

Tara cursed herself as she shifted the Audi into second, racing towards the National Arts Centre just blocks away.

Philippe had played her masterfully. She had relinquished control to her fifteen-year-old self, getting swept away with him in her office like a dewy-eyed teenager, which was obviously part of the plan to keep her occupied.

He had done his job well. There was a spark that had seemed *so* real.

But he was just role playing. Nothing more.

Within seconds of turning the corner at the Chateau Laurier and blasting towards the NAC, the lights of a police cruiser painted her face blue. She had to push Philippe out of her mind.

It was time to put an end to foolish games.

And foolish feelings.

Adeena glanced at Walter beside her with the other cellists and at Maria near the front of the violin section. They smiled weakly, shaking their heads with helpless looks of resignation. It seems they had accepted the situation and were prepared to let Lang get away with grand theft music.

Adeena, however, was not.

Lang tapped his baton on the conductor's rail and all two thousand patrons of Southam Hall fell into hushed silence. The opening piano notes of the ancient score began slowly on the orchestra's polished Steinway.

Adeena waited patiently as the full force of the musical storm to come began with gentle harmonic eddies swirling innocently from the stage.

TARA AND TWO BURLY POLICE OFFICERS BUSTED PAST THE elegantly dressed NAC ushers.

"Police! Let us in!" she yelled, as the officers flashed their badges to the startled ushers and marched past them towards Southam Hall.

"Hurry! Before they start," Tara urged the officers, as they ran down the red carpeted stairs outside the hall. They descended quickly to the bottom, reaching the doors that opened onto the first row in front of the stage.

As they got to the bottom and yanked opened the heavy doors, Tara heard the music begin.

ADEENA'S BOW TOUCHED THE STRINGS OF THE ANCIENT CELLO and began to lovingly coax out the music within. She felt the vibrations in her bones as the mystic tones rose in melancholy exaltation. She was one with the bow and the cello.

And with her music.

Clouds were growing in her mind and she was being swept away as the rest of the cello section joined her lead, mesmerizing every ear in Southam Hall.

Even Lang seemed moved as he gazed upon Adeena, already lost in her own world.

THE STAGE RIGHT DOORS SPRANG OPEN AND TARA LED THE police officers into Southam Hall.

The audience buzzed with the unexpected intrusion as she marched towards the stage, looking for Adeena and the Duncan Cello. Tara was frantic to catch her red-handed with the stolen instrument. Finally, Tara spotted her and raised a hand to point Adeena out to the officers.

With Tara's hand still raised, the music washed over her. It seemed to push her backwards. It took only seconds for her to absorb the power that originated from the stage. She watched Adeena, eyes closed, completely absorbed.

Tara hesitated. A shiver of emotion ran through her and she thought of Philippe in her arms. The music was powerful, unrelenting, and she remained frozen in front of the stage.

Just as the first officer was about to advance, Tara put her arm out to hold him back.

THE HOT LIGHTS OF THE STAGE WERE FADING AWAY AS ADEENA continued to play.

Time was carrying her away and the other instruments faded to nothing. It was just her now, playing in the bleakness of a room she recognized as the one she had performed in at Kinnaird Castle. A few candles and a single hearth provided the only light and warmth.

No matter – Adeena was playing the only way she could, with complete devotion. An aging woman with a grey-haired male companion holding her hand watched intently from their chairs.

Adeena's lyrics ached for release and she felt the need to comply.

TARA WATCHED SPELLBOUND AS ADEENA, TRANCE-LIKE, ROSE from her chair in front of one of the microphones set-up to amplify the instruments. She picked it up and held it close to her mouth. And then with eyes closed, began to sing.

Lang in the conductor's podium looked confused as Adeena's voice resonated across the hall, layered powerfully on top of the orchestra.

Gone is my heart without you,

Now I am lost once again.
Praying for life that grows within,
All I can ask is when?

When will the sword meet the sky?
To show where I belong?
Forever, I will wait for you
Even after I'm gone.

Tara had never heard anything as moving as the song pouring out from the sister she had guided for so long. Adeena's voice enraptured the entire hall and Tara felt herself fighting her own emotions. She looked behind her at the audience who watched in awe, some with mouths open, others holding the hands of loved ones beside them.

John St Clair had not expected old feelings could be so easily reignited.

St Clair listened to the music of Katharine, his new wife's niece. He had heard so much about her but had discarded the praise as patriotic exaggeration.

Yet her music was stirring long dormant feelings within him. She reminded him of why he had tried to stop the Union, that fateful day so long ago as a young man in Edinburgh. And, why he was joining the Jacobite cause once again as an 'old' man.

As Katharine's words echoed through Kinnaird and she stopped playing, he held his breath a moment before shaking his head in wonder. His eyes were moist.

"It's true then, every word yer aunt told me," he said, approaching the young woman who conjured such emotion out of wood and string and whose timeless voice seemed to emanate from another world. "You inspire men, even against their own common sense."

Katharine bowed her head. Margaret embraced her niece. "My husband, the Master of Sinclair, never understood why we need you. I've always known it. But alas," she said with a wink, "he's only a man!"

St Clair laughed, but he knew there was truth to what she said. "Katharine, how can we help you?"

Katharine brightened. "I need to find the score, the music I just performed for you. My brother, the Captain, has hidden it away in the 'keep,' I believe. I can't explain why, but I must find it and get it away from here. I need to get it published in Edinburgh, and in London, too."

Lady Margaret seemed puzzled, but she didn't hesitate. "Your brother is on his way to Kinnaird as we speak, with a proclamation supporting his claim to drive me from my home for good. Your uncle the Earl Carnegie, will roll in his grave if that passes. We must act quickly!"

St Clair stepped forward. "Where is the keep? I will find the score for you, Lady Katharine. But tell me first, why is it so urgent?"

Katharine fixed her gaze upon him, with a force he had rarely encountered from a woman. "It will change our history. It may not return the Kingdom or even this place, but it may help save all of us."

ADEENA WATCHED AS LADY MARGARET SCURRIED AWAY WITH her husband.

She knew it was a long shot, but if they could find the score and get it published, the lost music would find its place in history. Was it possible to change future events? Or would she simply watch as time flowed down the path already travelled?

A clattering of hooves interrupted her analysis. The castle doors sprang open. She recognized the man who stood in the castle's entranceway - the Captain, Katharine's brother, Sir James Carnegie.

He drew back upon seeing her.

"You dare return to this place?" he shouted. "After you have betrayed your king and your country?"

"I've betrayed no one," Adeena replied. She needed to distract him, get him away from here. "I have come to seek your counsel, Brother. Can I show you something?"

The Captain eyed her suspiciously. "You think me a fool, Sister? No, you will come with me, to Lord Greyson. He will sign the orders to lock you away for aiding the rebels."

"She is not going anywhere. And you, sir, are trespassing," Lady Margaret announced, descending the stairs towards them. She carried a leather satchel in her hands and handed it to Adeena.

The Captain looked upon her furiously. "Madam, just as my sister is wont to do now, your late husband supported the rebels. Let me remind you that as a result of his foolishness, my uncle lost not only his title, but this estate through attainder. It is I, dear Aunt, a loyal member of His Majesty's Parliament in London, and not you, who has legitimate claim to Kinnaird."

"That is yet to be settled," Lady Margaret retorted. John St Clair stepped to her side and she turned to him. "Please take Lady Katharine with you Master John, far away from the arrogance standing before me."

St Clair moved forward, but the Captain intervened. "Stay where you are St Clair, or you will be charged with treason too."

St Clair ignored the Captain and moved toward the door. Adeena tried to follow. The Captain blocked their path. "What do you carry there, Sister?" he demanded looking at the satchel she held closely against her bosom.

"Something you took from me," she snapped.

He lunged towards her, grabbing the satchel and trying to wring it from her. They struggled as the Captain tried to pull it away. "Give it to me, you traitor!" he shouted. Adeena refused to release her grip on the leather package until the Captain reached for her neck. He began choking her, until gasping, she let go, releasing the satchel to him.

St Clair tried to intervene and pushed the Captain, still clutching the satchel in one hand, down to the floor. The Captain tried to get up, but St Clair pinned him to the floor with a heavy boot.

"Let me go," the Captain hissed. St Clair pushed down harder as the Captain lay trapped on the wooden floor in front of the hearth.

"Give that to me," St Clair said, pointing to the leather satchel, "or I'll show you the mark a Scottish boot leaves on a coward's face."

The Captain smiled. "I always knew you to be a traitor, and soon we'll be fitting the noose 'round your neck." He held up the leather satchel. "Is this what you want?"

But before St Clair could reach it, the Captain flung the satchel into the flames of the fireplace.

TARA WATCHED AS ADEENA SAT BACK DOWN IN HER CHAIR. The audience, unable to restrain themselves any longer, exploded in applause and cheering, breaking all the rules of orchestral decorum.

Adeena seemed unaffected, with only a blank expression on her face. Tara thought she looked as if she were hypnotized, even as she lifted the Duncan Cello and began to play, leading the other cellists.

The policeman standing beside Tara whispered something in her ear.

"No, wait," she replied.

THE LEATHER SATCHEL SAT IN THE DYING FIRE WITH SMOKE beginning to rise from it.

Adeena raced towards the hearth and tried to save it from catching fire. Just as she was about to grab the satchel, the Captain pushed John St Clair's boot off him and grabbed a fistful of Adeena's long copper hair. She recoiled and tried to push him away.

"Let it burn!" the Captain shouted.

Adeena turned and spat at him. "Let go of me!"

As the two struggled, St Clair swung his arm against the Captain, knocking him away. Adeena broke free from her captor as the Captain slowly rose to face St Clair.

She reached into the fire and pulled out the smoking satchel, just as flames were about to engulf it. St Clair stood guard in front of her as the Captain again tried to lunge towards her. This time St Clair grabbed him and the two men went at each other fiercely.

The Captain quickly got the better of St Clair and broke free. He headed towards Adeena and just before the Captain was about to grab her, Lady Margaret, who had removed a wooden shield from the trophy wall, brought it down hard on her nephew's head.

He staggered, stopped momentarily. "Damn you! Damn all of you!"

But the Captain would not be contained so easily and he tried again to reach Adeena. This time his face met St Clair's fist with a knockout punch.

Lady Margaret rushed towards Adeena. "Did you save it? The music?"

Adeena opened the smouldering satchel and pulled out the score. "Yes, just in time," she said looking over the papers, warm to her touch. "I need you to get this published, before we lose it again." She handed them to St Clair.

He looked at the papers, turning a few pages. "There is no title, no author. You cannot publish it like this."

Lady Margaret pointed to a table where she had been writing letters to her solicitor. "John, give me those papers." He handed them to her and she sat, quill in hand.

"Now Lady Katharine, what do you call your music?"

JOHN ST CLAIR TUCKED THE SCORE INTO HIS SACK FOR THE long ride to Edinburgh. His wife had added the missing cover page in her scrolling calligraphic style.

Song for a Lost Kingdom
Katharine Carnegie
15 December 1745

St Clair flew from Kinnaird on his way to the capital. This time, nothing would stop him from reaching his goal.

ADEENA FELT HER HEAD SPINNING. SHE WAS CAUGHT BETWEEN two worlds and both struggled for possession of her mind and body.

With her eyes still closed, she reached the end of the section as the orchestra launched into the rest of the score. She stood up, trying to focus, unable to understand where or when she was.

She took a few steps forward and then fell from the front of the stage of Southam Hall onto the people seated below.

CHAPTER 26

The machines monitoring Adeena created a symphony of rhythmical beeps in her hospital room. Hour after hour they provided a medical soundscape for the visitors who waited hoping to see her eyes flutter open.

It had been almost thirty-six hours since she had fallen from the stage. Luckily, she sustained only minor bruises, as a man near the stage caught her and she ended up only bumping her head. But she remained unconscious, trapped between past and present, unable to reconnect to either. Forces within her struggled for control.

As the sun began to climb higher in the sky, sunlight filled the room. Brilliant brightness seemed to reach for her. She moved her head slightly and opened her eyes.

"Ohhh..." she moaned.

"Belle?" Her mother came to the edge of the bed, took Adeena's hand in hers and squeezed tightly. "Good morning."

"Ohh..." Adeena whispered, fighting to open her eyes fully against the morning sun. "Too... too bright..."

"Just a sec." Her mother got up and lowered the blinds, then sat on the bed beside her. She laid a hand on Adeena's cheek. "How you feeling?"

"Not sure. What happened?"

Before Jackie could respond her father appeared holding a large coffee and a newspaper. "Pumpkin!" He put the items down on the tray beside Adeena and bent down to touch her face. "You had us worried."

"Sorry." She felt a strange sensation deep in her skull. It wasn't exactly pain, but it felt odd. "My head, it's full of marshmallows... and sticks... or something."

"Does it hurt?" her mother asked.

"A bit. Mostly, it just feels weird."

Her father reached for the newspaper on the tray. "Take a look at this." He held up the front page of the *Ottawa Citizen*. "You did it!"

She read the headline below a picture of Friedrich Lang: 'NACO Conductor Fired'.

"Oh my God," she gasped. "Really?"

"Yup! It happened yesterday," her father answered. "After the story came out about the Carnegie score. The NAC was embarrassed, and they acted. Fast."

A picture of John St Clair riding off with the score filled her mind. Her eyes grew wet and her thoughts turned to her grandmother with feelings both sad and happy in equal parts.

"It's over now," her mother said quietly. Both parents gave her a hug and for the first time in a while, she felt at peace, even as she began to cry.

A FEW HOURS LATER ADEENA SAT UP IN BED. HER PARENTS HAD left for a while. They had both spent another long night with her – hoping, waiting, praying. Someday, she thought, I'll be there for them.

She glanced around her private hospital room. There were flowers by the window ledge and she wondered how many people she'd frightened with her antics.

Antics? Yeah. that's it, she thought. Silly me, travelling back in time and becoming someone else. She closed her eyes and laughed.

Maybe it's over now?

Adeena put her hand on her forehead and massaged it. The words of her song still felt trapped inside, even though she had sung them before thousands of people and helped record them in the annals of history.

Why can't I let it go?

Her mouth felt dry, and she searched for something to drink, looking down at the table beside her bed. A small velvet box sat there, beside a glass of water. She picked it up and opened the case. It was Philippe's diamond ring, a shimmering invitation still sparkling with hope. How had it gotten into her hospital room?

Mom, she thought with a sigh.

Adeena took the ring from its case and held it up. It felt heavy and pure. It dazzled her with its clarity and its perfection. She closed her hand around it, closed her eyes and held it to her heart.

JUST BEFORE NOON THERE WAS A KNOCK ON HER OPEN DOOR.

"Hey you!" It was Philippe. "Your mom told me you woke up. I was so worried. But she knew you'd come back," he said as he bent down and lightly kissed her cheek. "And somehow I did too."

"Thank you," Adeena replied. She noticed he had a copy of the *Ottawa Citizen* tucked under his arm. She could see Friedrich Lang's face above the fold. She pointed to it. "Your story?"

Philippe grinned, opening the newspaper. "Nailed him!"

She nodded, glancing over the article on the front page. "Thank you. How did you do it?"

He sat down beside her on the bed. "Turned out to be so

easy. I found copies of the score, online. You can download it from just about any classical music site. Your dad helped me with the search terms."

"Really? What'd you use?"

"Um, it was a name, I think. Trying to remember..."

"Katharine Carnegie?"

"Yeah, that's it. We put in 'Katharine Carnegie, music, Scotland' and bingo!" he laughed. "There it was. Online, PDF, even a *YouTube* video of a chamber orchestra in New Zealand performing it."

"Wow." Adeena sat stunned, absorbing it all. "Thank you so much."

Somehow, she had changed time. But how? What about James?

Adeena stared at Philippe sitting beside her, so happy, so full of life. He was a good man. He had dreams. He had a future with big plans and grand ambitions. He wanted a family and a partner. But her heart was conflicted. She was caught up in something bigger than herself. She didn't want it, but she couldn't let it go either. She squeezed his hand and wished life could be simpler.

Or at least, that *she* could be simpler. Some people would say she was pretty lucky, and should be happy with everything she had.

There was only one problem with those people. They were normal.

"Dee!" Tara's excited voice broke into Adeena's thoughts. Her old friend strode in through the door holding a bouquet of flowers. "You okay?" she asked as she put her arms around her. Philippe smiled at Tara as he moved over to make space on the bed.

"I'm fine, Tar," Adeena replied. "What about you? You here to arrest me?"

Tara winked, looking over at Philippe. "A big star like you?" she laughed. "No way!"

"Star?"

"You didn't read your reviews?" Tara was smiling. "Philippe, you're not doing your job?"

"Apparently not," he replied with a smile. "But she has been napping a lot."

"I know, I was here yesterday. So boring! I left," Tara joked. She put the flowers on the window ledge and sat on the other side of the bed. She hugged her friend tightly again, holding her for a few seconds before letting her go. "Dee, your performance the other night really blew me away. It was beyond extraordinary. I never knew you had such power, and your voice," She paused a moment, staring. "You have a gift."

"Thanks," Adeena said, sitting in silence for a few seconds. "It means a lot to me, to hear you say that."

Tara gave her another hug. "You're welcome. And not only that, but we've turned this whole cello thing into a win-win!"

"A win-win?"

"Publicity, social media, the exhibit at the Gallery," Tara explained. "You performing with our Duncan Cello, Lang stealing that music and getting fired – thanks to Philippe's story." She paused a moment gathering steam. "Well my dear, everyone, everywhere, wants to come to the National Gallery in Ottawa now to see the 'stolen' Duncan Cello!"

Philippe jumped in. "Your dad and I found out it was originally used in the first public performance of Katharine Carnegie's score. The whole story has gone viral, and Tara's been doing interviews with reporters around the world. Even the museum in Scotland, that owns the Duncan Cello, sent a letter of congratulations!"

"Apparently it is the first time the Carnegie score has been played on the Duncan Cello since the 18th century," Tara added. She paused a moment and then said breathlessly. "And my boss André is moving on to a gallery in New York. They want me to apply for his job. And it's all because of you, Dee!"

Adeena looked at Tara and then over at Philippe. They both had a happy glow. It was long overdue.

"I'm so happy for you, Tar. I know I've been a pain," Adeena smiled. She turned to Philippe, sitting on the other side of her. "And you've been so good to me. You've put up with more than most men would."

"It's okay, Adeena. I'm just glad you're okay now," Philippe said. "And we can move on."

Adeena lowered her head, lost in thought for a moment. She had to release him. She had to find out who she really was. And whether she belonged in the past or the present. It still wasn't over for her, but she couldn't expect him to be part of all that.

"You deserve more, Philippe." She took a deep breath and reached for the velvet box under her sheets. She opened it and removed the diamond ring. "You need someone who can be there for you, completely." Adeena took his hand and opened his fingers. She placed the ring on his palm and closed his fingers around it. "I would have been honoured to be your wife, but..."

Philippe sat in silence. Tara gasped. "Dee... he loves you!"

Adeena felt her conviction rising. A sudden strength surged through her. "I know. I know." Adeena kept her hand closed around his. "But I'm not the one, Philippe. Thank you for loving me – loving me so good. Thank you for believing in me and for everything you've done to try and help me. But, you need someone who will always be there for you and be part of your world."

Philippe said nothing. His eyes were wet, his shoulders sagged. Tara sat dumbstruck, silent.

Suddenly, Adeena's head exploded in excruciating pain.

And then all the light went to blackness.

WILLIAM LISTENED TO THE DOCTOR EXPLAINING THE prognosis one more time. Jackie sat next to him in the doctor's office.

"We think there is ongoing neurogenesis between the lateral

and third ventricles," Dr. Lochiel explained. "We have a series of scans we made the last time she was here, and I'm afraid, things seem to be getting worse."

Jackie flinched. "I shouldn't have gotten her that damn thing. It's killing her."

The doctor looked confused. "What thing?"

William wondered how his wife would respond. She had already gone way beyond her comfort zone in taking the Duncan Cello to Adeena, and seemed to be coming to terms with the idea that her daughter could become another person in the past.

Jackie turned to William. Her eyebrows were raised, and her head cocked to the side. He tried to read her. It was clear she didn't know what to tell the good doctor. She wanted him to reply instead.

"She's been trying to help Adeena deal with all of this," William finally interjected. "It's been a lot for us to go through, all this blacking out and..." He hesitated, not exactly sure how to explain it all.

Dr. Lochiel nodded his head. William knew the doctor had done a lot of work investigating Adeena's condition. She was resting comfortably in her hospital room, sedated and monitored. Apparently for the most part, she was fine, even though she had been sleeping for a few hours.

"Adeena is healthy and in good condition," Dr. Lochiel continued. "But, we are going to do more tests and then we might need to make some decisions."

"Decisions?" William repeated. "What does that mean?"

Jackie straightened up. "Surgery?"

"Possibly," Dr. Lochiel replied. "I am working with Dr. Chung from the University of Ottawa. His research with imaging and laser therapy might be something we could try. He is going to help our radiology department with a new set of ultra high definition scans. He has some new diagnostic software that helps us visualize tumours and growths, and uh..." The doctor seemed reluctant to finish his sentence.

"And what?" William implored. "What is it you're trying to say?"

"Mr. Stuart, I've explained this to Jackie and I'm not sure what she told you, but the growth inside your daughter has some strange features. It's almost like a secondary cortex."

William needed a translation into a language he understood. He looked at Jackie for an explanation.

"It's another brain, dear," she said, staring at the ceiling. "And it's growing inside our daughter."

IT HAD BEEN A LONG WEEK OF MISERY AND THE MORNING WAS shaping up to be worse for James Drummond.

To ensure the size of their regiments remained unknown to English spies, the Prince decided to march by cover of night. In daylight the twenty or even thirty-mile routes they travelled were unfit for cannons and carts, and for the men and horses who slowly dragged them behind. But in the black ink of night, the rutted trail covered deep in snow was sheer torture.

A few days earlier they had trudged ahead, foot by agonizing-foot, in cold quiet suffering until they reached the town of Carlisle. The town surrendered after intense negotiations, and while the men made camp, tried their best to warm themselves and find desperately needed nourishment and rest, the Prince's council gathered in the little nearby village of Carleton.

James was shocked at the vitriol cast his way.

"England is nae place for a Catholic duke," Lord George Murray spat in disgust on the wooden floor. He glared at James in anger. "I'll resign 'afore I fight with him again."

James' religion had not been an issue until now. But Murray was incensed that as instructed, James had helped negotiate the surrender of Carlisle without him. Prince Charles listened carefully.

"You fight to return a Roman Catholic king to the throne, Lord Murray," the prince reminded him.

"Aye, but we're in England now," Murray shot back. "Our army is subject to English laws until we take the crown."

James studied Lord Murray, who was among the most trusted members of the Prince's Council. Why Murray had been left out of the negotiations for the surrender of Carlisle was a mystery, and his rage at not being included was fierce.

"A Catholic duke has no right to negotiate in this country," Murray barked. "I shuid have bin part of that!"

"Indeed," the Prince replied, trying to calm things down, "but you were occupied and Perth was here and agreeable to the task."

"Agreeable?" Murray shouted. "Agreeable? Nae. Ye mean illegal!" He reached for his sword. "I'll no risk men to die for such a travesty, to shed blood for illegitimate contracts." Murray laid his long bone-handled sword on the wooden table before them. "I am finished."

James knew that Lord Murray's departure would spell doom. His men would follow him back to Scotland, and their ranks would dwindle. The English Jacobites were nowhere to be found, and France's armies were promised, but not given.

"Lord Murray," James finally responded to the accusations against him. "I serve as lieutenant general under the grace of our Prince. My only desire is to restore his father as the rightful King."

Murray glared at him, unmoved. "We'll achieve nothing with a Catholic as lieutenant general."

"Then I abdicate, Lord Murray," James announced, "and you must take my place beside Prince Charles. Our cause will fail without you."

Murray stood in silence, teeth clenched.

"Perth, I accept your offer," the Prince said quietly. "You will remain in command of the baggage and artillery columns."

"And nothing more!" Murray added, retrieving his sword. "Nothing more."

WHILE SOME COULD DOUBT THE DUNCAN CELLO WAS A TIME-travelling machine, the evidence in the diary of Katharine Carnegie's brother was more difficult to explain. Confined to her hospital room awaiting more tests, Adeena, wide-eyed and spell-bound, read the journal her father left her. She was drawn more to the long gone world of the Captain than to her own life in the present.

Her dad had brought her the leather-bound diary, probably against his better judgement, she thought. But as her one and only request of him, he must have felt bound to comply. She sat up in bed, reaching for her plastic glass of ice water as she reread the entry for August 6, 1745, laying it down flat on the tray over her bed.

> "When I warned her never to perform the cantata again, lest it embolden the traitors amongst us who would destroy the Union, she refused. In her fury she inquired if I was 'King Kong', a line of royalty I am ignorant of, but I believe was meant as an insult to my person.
>
> I forbade her from ever playing that instrument again and to find something more suitable for a lady - a cittern. I had her score confiscated and placed it in my keep, where it will remain and cause no more harm to the preservation of the Union."

Adeena closed her eyes and replayed the scene from Kinnaird in her mind. She smiled as she remembered calling the Captain 'King Kong.' With a start she opened her eyes and stared again at the pages.

This journal was a record of her travelling to the past, the pages changing whenever she became Katharine. Or at least whenever she interacted as Katharine with her brother, the Captain, Sir James Carnegie. Adeena thought about all the times this had happened. She flipped through the pages, looking for entries for December 1745.

Found it! She read the words slowly:

"16 December 1745

The Master of Sinclair shall be shown no mercy. That he is my aunt's husband matters not. Lady Margaret has conspired with him, and with sister Katharine to pass secrets to the enemy, traitors against the Union. John St Clair will be hunted down as one would a rabid dog.

Alas, I must comply with my forthright orders to join General Cope in England to lend aid in killing the Jacobite incursion. We will cut off the head of the snake, and bring the Young Pretender to the Tower. When it is all over, and the threat to the Union lanced once and for all, I will return to Kinnaird. By then my aunt will be widowed, I pray. And my brother George, joined again to his senses.

As for Katharine, she will either renounce her traitorous love for the swine James Drummond, or she will be disavowed as a Carnegie forever."

Adeena closed the diary. She thought about the story her dad told her of how her grandmother had 'borrowed' this journal from Kinnaird. Adeena chuckled. Her grandmother was a lot like her.

Thinking came long after *doing*.

And Adeena was beginning to realize what she must do.

CHAPTER 27

Jackie looked across the sea of magazines in the hospital gift shop. From the life changing concerns of making your eye shadow last all day to the amazing secret of brownies that don't need butter, she searched for something – anything – that might help her deal with the cards in her hand.

Her daughter had a rare and medically impossible growth in her brain. She had rejected a proposal of marriage from a man Jackie once dreamed would be the father of her grandchildren, a respected professional who proudly shared her French-Canadian heritage. Instead, Adeena was smitten with someone dead for more than two centuries.

And that wasn't the worst of it.

Despite Jackie's reluctance to admit it, somehow it seemed her daughter travelled to the past and embodied another woman, the same one William's poor mother had been haunted by all her life.

And then there was the final straw – learning that Adeena could likely never have children. That was the toughest blow of all.

Brownies? Eye shadow? Yeah. Why not? Might be as good as anything else at this point.

"I don't believe it," her husband sang out from the far end of the magazine rack. "Look at this!"

She turned around and glanced at the cover of the magazine William held up as she moved closer. It was a man in traditional Scottish dress, raising a sword dramatically to the sky while the sun rose boldly behind him. He stood in front of a castle that looked familiar.

William approached her. "Isn't this the guy from Kinnaird? What was his name again?"

Jackie adjusted her reading glasses. *"Sacrement!"* she exclaimed. "That's Angus, from the dinner party." She giggled to herself, recalling her outrageous flirting session with him. He had tied himself in knots while she probed around the edges of his middle-aged fantasies. She had left him with a tiny peck on the cheek and told him to go find 'the one'. He'd looked crushed when she walked away, but perhaps she'd given his ego a boost. He certainly gave hers one.

"And look at this," William said, pointing to a smaller inset picture on the cover of the *History Scotland* magazine he held up. "It's about the Battle of Culloden." He read the subtitle to Jackie. 'Unpacking the Pivotal Battle in a New Light.'

Jackie stared at Angus on the cover, under the headline. 'Castle Economy: Bringing History to Life is Big Business.' The man glared at her, ready to defend his country. She smiled again. He might look tough to the world, but underneath, he was more interested in finding a woman who understood him. Hopefully she'd helped him on his journey.

"Should we get it for Adeena?" William asked as he began leafing through the pages of the glossy magazine.

"Absolutely," she smiled with a twinkle in her eye.

ADEENA WASN'T SURE IF SHE COULD DO ONE MORE DAMN medical test. It's just a simple 'procedure' they would explain, as they injected more dyes into her, strapped her to yet another machine and found new ways to scan, photograph and x-ray her head.

Enough! I'm fine!

She glanced down at her left hand thinking of the diamond ring. Giving it back to Philippe was the last thing she could recall before she woke up. She hadn't heard from him since and wondered how he was doing.

At least now he could find someone who might give him a family. A woman who didn't struggle just to know what century she lived in. The leather-bound journal sat on the nightstand beside her, like a door that opened to her other life. She wanted to let it go, cast it aside and just be content being Adeena Stuart – musician, composer, modern woman. But she was numb inside, and wasn't sure she could feel anything anymore.

She closed her eyes and felt forces struggling within her for control.

"Hey you," a familiar voice rang out. It was Dad, with Mom not far behind. "How you feeling?"

"Fine, but bored out of my skull."

"Well, this might help. We got you some new reading material," her dad said, triumphantly handing some magazines to her. "Look at this!"

Adeena studied the cover of the magazine on top. Was that Kinnaird in the background? "Where'd you get that?"

Her mother sat on the bed. "The gift shop, downstairs." She pointed to the magazine Adeena held. "That's my friend Angus."

"Your boyfriend Angus, you mean," her dad chuckled. "You should have seen your mom flirt with him!"

Adeena smiled. "Really? Mom!"

Her mother batted her eyes in feigned shock. "Hey, I was just doing my job. I needed to keep him distracted so your dad and grandma could steal stuff from the castle."

"I think you might have enjoyed your job a little too much,

my dear," her dad smiled. Her mother was blushing as her dad revved up the story. "That was the night we found the diary and the music Grandma wanted you to have so badly. She seemed to know where it was hidden."

No matter how hard Adeena tried, the past kept intruding. She bit her lip as she started flipping through the pages of the glossy magazine. Seductive images of the Scottish countryside and stunning pictures of medieval castles jumped off the pages. This wasn't helping her stay in the present. This was the past calling her back.

She closed the magazine and set it aside. She let out a long sigh and closed her eyes. "I just want to go home."

Her mother reached for her hand. "Soon, *belle.* Dr. Lochiel has a new test they want to run first."

"Come on!" Adeena exclaimed. "I've had enough damn tests. What're they looking for now?"

Her mom, sitting on the edge of the bed looked worried. Instead of the lecture Adeena was expecting, there was only silence. Her parents looked at each other like they shared some horrible secret.

"Has Dr. Lochiel talked to you?" her mom finally asked, turning back to Adeena.

"Well, yeah. He said I might have a tumour, but they weren't sure." She heard her own words, as if for the first time. *A tumour?* In her brain? Why wasn't she completely freaking out?

Her dad moved closer. "Adeena, something bad is happening when you," he hesitated, "whenever... whenever you play that cello and..." His voice trembled and he seemed unable to finish.

"If you are travelling back and forth somehow," her mother interjected, "to another time and place..." She paused, looking at the monitoring machines, before turning back to Adeena. "Well, it seems to be producing some serious side effects."

"It's killing you!" her dad blurted, choking back a sob.

Adeena knew he was probably right. She closed her eyes and

whispered, more to herself than her parents. "It's because I don't belong in this time."

Her dad looked up, his eye full of tears. "What? Adeena, why do you say that?"

She was hurting him. He displayed his emotions for all to see. Her mother, maybe being in the same hospital she worked in professionally, seemed to handle hers differently.

"Belle," her mother said softly, "what do you really want?"

Good question.

Adeena noticed her mother's eyes were growing wet now. I'm such a wonderful daughter, sharing my joyful existence with my lucky parents, Adeena thought closing her eyes.

What do I want? I wish I knew.

Her dad sat down n the other side of the bed and touched her arm. She opened her eyes and studied his face. It was so earnest, and so sad.

"Pumpkin, you've made Grandma proud," he began quietly. "You've exposed Lang for what he was. And you got the music published. It was lost to the world, and you brought it back. Made it famous – for all time."

For all time. The lost score now had its own history – a record of performances across the centuries. How many musicians had studied it, played it, made it part of their repertoire? How many men and woman had been moved by it, connected to its emotional core?

"I wrote that music," Adeena said. She fought back tears herself, not wanting to cause even more distress. "And I know how crazy and messed up you think I am, but I wrote it as two different people, in two different times."

Her parents nodded. Whether they believed her story or just wanted this all to go away, she could not tell. "There are two versions of me, each one needing the other to complete the music and to..." she stopped as an image of James angrily leaving his tent swept across her mind.

"To what?" her mother asked. Her dad's face contorted into pained confusion.

"To save a good man," she answered. "Someone that doesn't deserve to die. Someone we both love."

"Both?" her parents exclaimed in unison.

"Katharine. Katharine and I. He might be the only one anywhere, in any time, who really gets me," she said looking out the window. "James feels my music, more than any person I've ever known. He gets it even more even than I do. He seems to know where it comes from."

Adeena turned back to her parents. She hung her head slowly and could hold her tears back no longer. They streamed down her face.

"Everything that matters most to me," she sobbed, "is in the past."

WILLIAM WAS BEGINNING TO DREAD ONE OF THE THINGS HE loved most.

History.

Doomed men fighting for lost causes. Bitter rivalries that tore apart families and even nations, now reduced to long-forgotten curiosities. The unfinished tumults of time that had wracked his mother, now threatened his daughter.

"No, Adeena, you're wrong," he said slowly. "Your life is here. It's here and now."

Jackie wrapped her arms around Adeena, trying to console her. William touched his daughter's head, rubbing the back of her neck gently. He whispered "We don't want to lose you." Why couldn't he break this family cycle? "Just let it go."

Adeena released her mother and hung her head. She took a few deep breaths, trying to regain her composure. "There is something wrong," she said in a barely audible tone. "Something I have to fix."

"You can't change the past, Adeena," William pleaded.

"I published the score, didn't I?"

"Yes, but you can't save James Drummond. He's wounded at the Battle of Culloden and dies at sea. Prince Charles is defeated, driven into exile and dies – alone."

Adeena didn't seem convinced. "I know. But that doesn't matter."

Jackie was shaking her head. "Why? Why? Can you please tell us? Your future is not with someone who dies in battle as a young man. Someone who's already been dead a long time."

"I can't explain it," Adeena replied. "Grandma used to tell me stories, about our family. Stories about the pain she went through." She turned to William. "Dad, you told me about those letters you found from your grandmother, Faith. You know how much our whole family has suffered, for so long."

William recalled the letters between his mother and his grandmother. Tales of despair, of crushing poverty, near starvation, and wanton cruelty by a cast of horrible agents. His grandmother Faith claimed it could all be traced back to the 'risings' so long ago. "Those are just stories, Adeena. Most folks lived through hard times back then."

"No, Dad, not like that. We've suffered because our family honour was disgraced," Adeena said. "Grandma knew it. She told me stories, over and over again. I think that's why she sent me that music. She wanted me to make things right."

William had had enough. "Oh my God Adeena! You've already done what you could do. You *have* made a difference. You published the music. That's what she wanted." He softened his tone. "We're here and we're a family that cares about each other. Your grandmother is gone. The past should be studied, not transformed into something it was never meant to be. Something it never can be."

"You're wrong!" Adeena burst out. "I can't live without trying."

"But it's killing you!" Jackie shouted. "How is that making

things right?" She grabbed the leather journal on Adeena's nightstand. "You are not Katharine Carnegie! Let her go!"

TARA TOOK A MOMENT TO GET HER BEARINGS.

The three-hour interview was finally over. She had done well. Extremely well.

To think she was a candidate for the top position at the Gallery was almost more than she could comprehend. The Duncan Cello incident was questioned. However, the committee agreed it was a 'gutsy' idea. What a sensation to have one of the staff members use it without permission! And then to reveal it was the goal all along to highlight the first modern performance of the Carnegie score on the same cello that had been used in its very first premiere in the 18th century. And to use it to bust a plagiarizing composer.

Brilliant! They all agreed.

The free publicity and the viral social media aftermath was more effective than millions of dollars of paid advertising. The exhibit was now the hottest ticket in Ottawa. Tara had propelled the National Gallery to the centre of international media attention and created a sexy profile for the highbrow institution.

They credited her management of the whole affair with the kind of 'new thinking' they wanted more of in their next director. Her parents, career superstars themselves, always told her she was a natural leader and that she should pursue this kind of advancement at all costs.

But was it all coming too fast? So much pressure and responsibility came with the Gallery's top job. Was there more to life than being chained to a big desk? She'd missed out on so many things thanks to the steamroller in her head relentlessly pushing her to reach higher and higher.

Am I doing it for me or for my parents? Am I just rolling mindlessly down the tracks they set for me a long time ago?

As she reached her office her cell phone chimed. She looked at the display: 'Blocked' number.

"Hello?" Tara answered.

"Hey, Tar."

"Dee?" Tara asked, "I was so worried. Are you okay?"

"Yeah, fine. What about you?"

Tara wasn't sure how much to tell her. Their lives seemed to be headed in opposite directions. "Good. You coming home soon?"

There was a pause at the other end. "I don't know. I think they like having me here to practice their torture routines. They have so many of them. They like to call them 'procedures' and I've got another big one tomorrow."

"Well, soon as you're out I'm taking you away. Want to go to New York? My treat."

"That sounds good," Adeena replied without much excitement. She waited a second and then added, "I know this is probably nuts, but I have a favour to ask you."

"Sure, no problem. What do you need?"

"Is there any way..." Adeena hesitated almost a second before continuing, "any way at all, that maybe, you could bring..." Tara could sense the trepidation. "...the Duncan Cello to the hospital?"

Tara took the phone from her ear and looked at it, shaking her head in disbelief. She laughed before putting it back to her head. "Are you completely out of your mind my dear?"

"There's a strong possibility of that," Adeena sighed. There was another long pause before she added, "There's someone who needs my help. Someone I met."

Tara processed the words without understanding what they could possibly mean. The last time she had seen Adeena was when she broke off her engagement with Philippe, handing him back his ring. Tara had seen the pain on his face. "Someone you met? Who?"

"Have you got a few minutes?"

"Sure," Tara said closing the door to her office. She settled herself on a leather chair. "Tell me the whole story. Your life is my favourite reality show."

For the next half hour Tara listened to a story that began to scare her. Adeena had always lived on the edge of the real world, but this was just too much. She travelled back in time and became another woman? She was doing it because of dreams her grandmother had, and only Adeena could ultimately save their family?

Wow! Their worlds were more divergent than she had supposed. Adeena needed help alright, but it would probably involve a SWAT team from a mental institution.

"Dee, wait, wait!" Tara interrupted Adeena's story. "Can I be perfectly honest?

"Of course."

"I am really worried." Tara strung her works together carefully. "You have a rare gift, and when I saw you that night at the NAC, I realized that I never before appreciated your musical talent. Dee, you're an artist and you have a career just waiting for you to claim it. A life on stage, performing. You can go as far as you want. I really mean it. You are totally amazing!"

"Thanks, Tar," Adeena replied in small voice. "So then, why are you worried?"

"Because I think you're losing touch with reality. You threw away a life with Philippe, and now you're going to do the same with your career, your future."

"I wouldn't have made him happy, Tar. I had to set him free, so he has a chance to find someone else."

Tara felt a warmth inside. She dared not think of what might be. Her heart was her weakest organ. "You crushed his dreams, Dee. He loved you so much."

"He'll be okay," Adeena said simply. "But there's another reason I had to break it off, Tar. There's someone else I care about."

Tara's mind raced, fearing the worst. "Not that guy from your dreams, I hope."

There was a pause on the line. "It's not a dream," Adeena said, her voice growing more determined. "I know you have no way of understanding how this could be, and I really don't get it either, but I need to be with him. He sees what's inside me and I know it's probably impossible, but I have to see him again, before it's too late."

Tara listened, fighting the programming in her mind that rejected everything Adeena was telling her. First, that she travelled back in time when she played the Duncan Cello, and second that she had the same soul as a woman in the past who was in love with a doomed man. Can something like that reach across time?

"Tar? You still there?"

"Yeah, Dee. I am." Tara sighed, blowing out her frustration and shaking her head. "Adeena, I really want to believe you. And I want to help you. But I'm just not sure I can."

"Not sure you can believe me?" Adeena asked. "Or help me?"

"Both."

AFTER SHE HUNG UP THE PHONE, TARA SAT STARING BLANKLY, looking around her office. She felt beaten, bruised. The long phone call had taken her from the heights of dizzy excitement about the job interview to the depths of a dark world. Her eyes settled on the cello case in her office. She kept the imposter cello here now, not trusting anyone else to guard it.

It seemed to sit there, smiling back at her.

Tara needed to walk. She wandered down to the *Art of Rebellion* exhibit and watched a crowd admiring the real Duncan Cello. A young couple was taking a selfie with it in the background, and an old man just stood and stared at the old instrument, lost in his private thoughts.

She walked closer as the couple finished with the photo and moved on. She took their place directly in front of the cello. She looked over the old instrument that had become such a central figure in her best friend's life, and curiously had helped propel Tara's career to a zenith.

Was there more to the world than she understood?

CHAPTER 28

The Battle of Culloden was horrific. Its deep scars remained long after the savage fifty-three-minute massacre ended on April 16, 1746.

Adeena shivered as she read the article about the bloody battle from the magazine her parents gave her. She shook her head at gloomy pictures of the marshy ground where over a thousand exhausted men rushed to their deaths, holding only swords and shields to meet the onslaught of British cannon and musket. Why the Prince chose the water-logged moor for his final showdown was mostly unknown and widely debated.

She remembered his boyish charm and naturally commanding presence. To picture him on this tragic day, with James near the front line of death, was something she didn't want to dwell on. But it was impossible for her to let it go. She grew more infuriated as she read how the Jacobites were near starvation – cold, weak and desperate, while the British army dined on beef and brandy the night before, and approached the whole affair after a hearty breakfast as something akin to a leisurely sporting contest.

What a waste! So much blood, shed for nothing. Had

Katharine's music played a part in this? Inciting men to fight when they should have fled?

She closed the magazine, laid back on her hospital bed and closed her eyes. She saw the Prince at the Drummond Castle ball, appointing the eager James as his lieutenant - young, proud and determined.

"Ready, Adeena?"

She opened her eyes to see the new shift nurse she met this morning. "Ready?"

"Your CT scan. It's this morning," the nurse reminded her. "They're running a little late. Just wanted to check on you. Still okay with the IV?"

Adeena looked at her left arm attached to an intravenous tube. "Yeah. It's fine."

"Good. Shouldn't be too much longer. We'll take you down to radiology once I get the word."

"Don't rush on my account," Adeena smiled. "If somebody wants my spot, it's all theirs."

The nurse grinned. "Back soon."

Adeena frowned thinking about the procedure. Her physician, Dr. Lochiel, explained they would be doing another session in that awful machine, the CT scanner. She really didn't like the feeling of lying on the narrow table and being slid into the mouth of the monster.

The doctor mentioned they would use a new dye and a gas that she would inhale while they did the scan. He said it would help them follow the trail of what was going on inside her head, with the growth they still didn't understand.

Must be a regular wonderland in there, she mused. My brain is totally messed up. They must so love using me as a guinea pig. She closed her eyes wishing she could be anywhere else but here.

"Dee!"

Adeena opened her eyes with a start. "Tar?"

"Special delivery," Tara said presenting her with a towering Starbucks latté, topped high with whipped cream and chocolate sprinkles. "Thought you might like a change from hospital dishwater."

Adeena sat up on her bed. "Thanks!" She took the cup from Tara, tasted a bit of the whipped cream with her tongue and took a long sip of the warm coffee. "Oh! Now that's heaven, thanks!"

Tara sat on the edge of the bed. She looked at Adeena strangely. The two women said nothing for a few seconds. But Adeena could see a smile on Tara's face that she hadn't seen in a very long time. "What's with you, Tar? Win the lottery?"

"Nope. Better!"

"Huh?"

Tara couldn't hold it back any longer. "They want me to run the gallery!" she finally burst out. "You're looking at the new Director of the National Gallery of Canada. Well, 'Director-designate' at least."

Adeena was stunned. She put down her coffee to give Tara a hug, but felt the restraint of the IV tube pulling her arm. Tara leaned in and they did their best to embrace each other. "Congratulations, Tar! Glad I didn't screw up your career."

"Not at all! They thought I planned the whole thing. You won't believe what our little escapade has done for the gallery. We're famous!"

Adeena chuckled. "So you're going to be 'she who must be obeyed'. 'Cause of me?"

"Guess so," Tara nodded her head, still smiling. "I suppose I should thank you."

"You really should," Adeena joked before turning serious. "You know I didn't want to lie to you. It's hard to explain why, but I felt it was mine to take, and somehow it would be okay."

Tara only smiled in response, to Adeena's relief. "Tar, you're going to be a great director. The gallery is lucky to have you."

"Thanks, I appreciate that." Tara looked down, gathering her thoughts for a moment. "Something else though, I need to ask you, to make sure you're okay with it."

Adeena took another sip of her coffee. "Okay, with what?"

Before Tara could respond there was a light tap on the door. Adeena looked up and saw Philippe standing just inside the room holding Adeena's Bam cello case.

DR. BENJAMIN LOCHIEL COULDN'T STOP FIDGETING AS HE waited beside Dr. Chung. The imaging system was taking forever to complete its calibration cycle.

"We'll see three dimensional scans building in real-time with this," Dr. Chung said, pointing to a display of progress bars on the flat screen that covered almost the entire wall of the tiny control room. "Once we start scanning, the isotopes in her system and the neural gas she inhales will give us a moving picture of what's happening with the tumour."

Benjamin looked at his watch. These machines opened a window into the brain he could not have imagined when he started his medical career more than twenty years ago. Now in a few minutes, he would get to see the next generation of imaging technology and maybe, understand how the cells of an unexplained secondary cortex were multiplying inside his patient's head.

"You think it's all going to work?" he asked, as Dr. Chung leaned over to start inputting a series of numbers and values into an intimidating-looking screen. There were so many separate windows on the monitor display it looked more like they were attempting to land a man on the moon, than look inside someone's head.

"It should," Chung replied without looking away from the screen. "Give me another few minutes to get this set and then call down for your patient."

PHILIPPE BARRICADED THE DOOR TO ADEENA'S ROOM WITH the back of a chair, as instructed.

Why he was here, involved in all of this, was something he didn't want to dwell on too much. He was still recovering from last night.

Tara had called him, distraught and needing to talk. He met her at the Gallery, inside her office where he had held her in his arms the night of Adeena's debut performance.

"Come in, Philippe," she said. "Thanks for dropping by. I need some advice."

"No problem," he said as Tara moved towards him. He held his breath, admiring her as if they had never met before. She came closer and though they would usually embrace in friendship, she stopped just before reaching him.

"Are you okay?" she asked.

"Yeah," he replied. "I've done a lot of thinking. Adeena's right. I need to let her go."

Tara took his hands in hers. She stared at him and he studied her face. Did her eyes look wet? "You're a good man and I'm so sorry to have to call you with my problems. I have a decision to make, and I just need someone to talk to."

"Tara, it's fine." He wondered if she had felt anything the last time he had been here, in her office, holding and comforting her. It was not something he was proud of, but it was a feeling for her that he had not acknowledged existed within him. Maybe he simply pushed it aside? Or was it just a chemical reaction, a one-sided feeling on his part.

Or maybe, it was nothing.

"Philippe, I..." Tara hesitated, still holding his hands.

Her eyes were wet now. He wanted to hold her. "Shhhh, it's okay." He put his arms around her and she moulded herself against him. He could feel her crying, and he pulled her closer. "Let it out, Tara," he whispered.

She cried and he just held her. Finally, she lifted her head from his shoulder and looked up into his eyes. She whispered, "I care about you. Is that bad?"

"No. No, it's not bad," he said gently. "I have to tell you, I felt something too, last time I was here, in your office."

Her mouth opened and a look came over her he would never forget. It was wonder, joy, hope and regret – all bound together. "I have too, for a long time," she said simply.

Philippe knew it was true.

He just hadn't let it get through his armour. Adeena was the wily woman he tried to fashion into what he longed for in a partner, while Tara was always in the background, trying to help him sort it all out. He was rushing so fast head-long into traffic, he never considered how much better it could be going the other way.

Now it was his turn. His eyes teared up. No words came to him.

No words were necessary.

ADEENA SAT STUNNED IN HER HOSPITAL BED, LOOKING AT Tara and Philippe holding the Bam cello case.

"You brought the Duncan?" she said in disbelief.

Tara smiled. "I finally realized that colouring inside the lines limits your creativity."

Philippe opened the case and gently lifted the Duncan Cello. "Tara called me last night and..." he hesitated a second, as if he wasn't sure how to finish his thought.

Tara jumped in. "And we both agreed that we want to help, even if we don't completely understand it all."

"But, isn't this going to screw things up for you, Tar?" Adeena asked.

"Hey, I'm supposed to be using 'new thinking', remember?" she smiled. "And I also decided last night that I'm taking a holiday before I start my new job. If it gets approved, of course."

"She wants to go to Greece," Philippe added. Adeena looked at her two friends. Were they blushing?

"You're going with her?" Adeena smiled.

"If that's okay with you, Dee?" Tara asked timidly.

"Of course! Yes, yes of course," Adeena replied. She wondered why she felt no jealousy, no regret, not a single negative feeling. There was only happiness that these two had found each other, and in a way, it was because of her. "You guys deserve a break. Together."

Tara and Philippe were glowing, and Adeena could almost feel the heat from her bed. But she had no time to dwell on it. She looked up at the clock on the wall, and then down at the catheter in her arm. "Tar, I need your help to get this off."

Adeena began to pull away at the tape holding the needle. "Just pull this out for me."

Tara looked horrified. Philippe set the cello aside and stood beside Adeena. "Let me."

In one swift motion Adeena pulled the tape off and Philippe removed the needle. "My mom's a nurse," he said. "I was in the hospital a lot as a kid, and she actually showed me how to do this." Adeena put the tape back over the vein where the catheter had been inserted into her arm.

"You missed your calling, Philippe," Adeena grinned. Freed from her restraint, she quickly scrambled from the bed. "I need to play the cello, before they come to get me."

Tara and Philippe hesitated. Adeena could see doubt in their eyes.

Or was it fear?

"Please," Adeena pleaded as she reached in the case for her bow. "I need to play. Right now."

JACKIE WAS STILL UPSET FROM FIGHTING TRAFFIC GETTING TO the hospital this morning. An accident in one lane of the

Queensway backed things up for miles, curious rubberneckers all slowing down to gawk.

She looked at her watch. *Damn!* She wanted to see Adeena before her procedure. Poor kid had been through so much. A mother-daughter spa day would be good for both of them. Jackie was looking forward to seeing the look on Adeena's face when she told her it was all set up for Saturday.

Jackie smiled, thinking about it as she approached the room. And then her smiled turned to confusion. She thought she heard music. Faint at first, it grew louder as she got closer to the end of hall and Adeena's room. Now she could hear it clearly. It was the music Adeena had rehearsed so often at the lake.

As she reached the room, she noticed the door was closed. That's odd, she thought, knocking lightly before trying to open the door. It was stuck.

"It's okay, you can go in," a nurse said as she approached. "We need to take her up to radiology."

"I can't seem to open it," Jackie replied. "It's stuck somehow."

"What?" Now the nurse was confused. She tried but couldn't get the door open. "Ms. Stuart? Can you open the door, please?"

No response. But the music inside the room seemed to grow louder.

The nurse tried the door again, pushing the handle back and forth. "Open the door. Now!"

Adeena was warming up, getting ready to begin her journey.

Tara and Philippe looked on as she played, their faces taut. As Adeena began finally began to play the score, releasing the music inside of her that flowed through every vein, her friends watched carefully. She could see how the music touched them too and she hoped they would find happiness with each other.

Adeena heard muffled voices outside her door. She had to hurry. She closed her eyes and began to play in earnest, concentrating on the movement of her bow across the strings, urging the sound to rise from the cello.

Clouds and fog spun inside her head. The music lifted her from the chair.

And then she was gone...

SFLK, THE PREQUEL

Want to keep reading?

Get the FREE Prequel to the *Song for a Lost Kingdom* series now for Kindle or iBook.

Keep up with latest news on the series at stevemoretti.ca.

If you enjoyed Book I, please consider posting a review, as it is one of the few ways that independent authors can spread the word about their books.

And if you would like to become one of my Advance Readers and get preview copies of all new releases, please send me an email. steve@stevemoretti.ca.

Thank again for reading!

Steve Moretti

ACKNOWLEDGMENTS

There are many people to thank for the book you are reading. This has been a team adventure from the beginning.

What started as an idea for a screenplay and then transformed into a novel, has been a journey of discovery with a long list of supporting characters. My wife Pam has always been there encouraging and supporting me, waiting for "the book" before she would give it a read. That kept me going to get something done and printed to show her. Also my daughter Keera who wanted to read it right from the start and is my first true fan!

To the rest of my family, mom and dad and my sons Phil, Marc, Tyler - thank you for telling me to stay on this road. I hope you enjoy the journey with me. Phil also provided invaluable feedback on some of the historical and technical aspects of the story.

I would also to acknowledge the contributions of many, many advance readers and editors who gave me feedback, suggestions and some brilliant ideas! Your inspirations were truly remarkable and the story would be much poorer without you.

I began the novel in 2014, after developing an extensive outline and having only previous experience with screenplays. One of my first editors was Hannah Lawrence, who was studying in Scotland. Her feedback, inspiration and suggestions were like rocket fuel to me as the first chapters began to emerge from my keyboard. I am extremely grateful for all her guidance and help in getting the first draft done.

A special thank you to Julie Brierley, cellist with the Stratford Symphony Orchestra in Stratford, Ontario. Julie was an early reader and provided technical guidance on music, orchestras and even martinis! Her enthusiasm and encouragement were very much appreciated.

I also received valuable input and feedback from Michelle Brown, Brynn Lucas and Deborah Natelson in the first year of writing. From suggesting changes regarding technical points (engagement rings, sword fighting, horseback riding, etc.) to expressing well-deserved revulsion towards an early draft of the Philippe character, your honest appraisals made such a difference. Thank you!

My researcher was Emily Crouch, who dug up documents from her hangout in France, reaching into digital archives in the UK and Europe that provided new insights and opened up interesting directions to explore.

A very special thank-you to my Ottawa writing group, Peter Smith, Wendy Patterson, Morgan Fortin, Averil Elisa, Eric Adler, Nicole Zkwakrala, Mandy Sheldrake and Ivan Blake, among others. Our monthly critique sessions (that I still attend) added layers of depth to the story, caught more typos and grammatical issues than I thought possible in my wildest nightmares and most importantly, provided whole new perspectives. I enjoyed each and every meeting and I know that you will see some of your feedback reflected in the finished work.

Thank you also to Mark Morey for your analysis and insights, Cat Skinner for your thorough and precise critique and excellent suggestions, Olivia Hauvuy for lifting my spirits while showing me what was broken, and to Keith Oxenrider who operated with the precision of a surgeon opening my manuscript. Asma Al-Naser forced me to ask questions early on and I kept hearing her voice in early drafts. Thank you to Joshua Laurent for a succinct analysis of the completed second draft, with some great ideas for improvement. Thanks to my mom, Irene Moretti and to Sara Sykora for a last minute read to patch spelling mistakes and grammatical holes! Any that got missed are my fault at this point.

I would also like to thank of course, my final editor Penny Fletcher for her unbridled encouragement, enthusiasm and energy. Penny has a sharp red pencil and is a great cheerleader!

Thanks to my mastermind colleagues Andy Statia and Kathi Nidd for practical advice and ongoing suggestions and encouragement.

Finally special thanks to Sarah Penner and Lara Cloudon, who read a nearly final draft and gave me invaluable feedback. They are both writers, with natural gifts for language and storytelling. Their notes, suggestions, questions and encouragement provided me with chocolate for the ego that helped propel me to the finish line. Lara will be working with me closely on Book II. She also edited the Prequel and is another one of my mastermind colleagues.

An extra special shoutout to Phil and Pat Moretti for doing such an exhaustive read, and finding many lingering issues that have been corrected in this updated version. Your attention to detail was fantastic! Likewise the feedback, corrections and encouragement from Jen McCarthy, an author with an eye for detail and storytelling, was extremely helpful. Thanks!

Writing may be a solitary endeavour, but in my case there was a whole team behind the words and story that appears on the page. I am grateful to have met so many truly inspiring people along this way.

Thank you for your guidance and support.

Steve Moretti

Ottawa, October 2018

PREVIEW - SFLK BOOK II

LOVE NEVER SURRENDERS

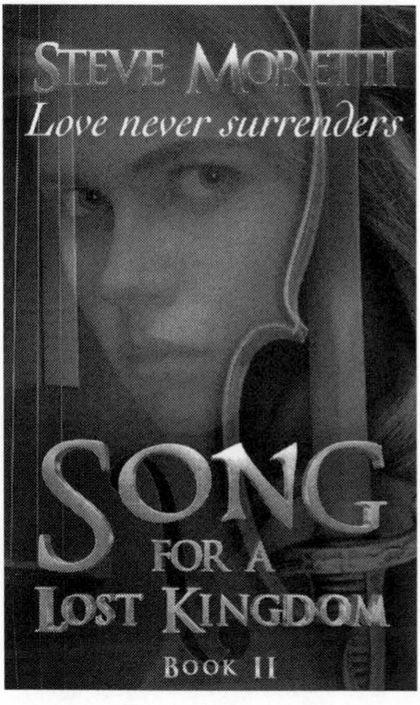

BOOK II - CHAPTER 1

AFTER THREE LONG days and even longer nights of frigid rain, James Drummond had forgotten the feeling of dry.

Warmth seemed but a forgotten reverie. Even the furnace burning inside Balgair, his mount who had endured so much these past eight weeks, seemed unusually distant. The tallest horse in the Prince's army plodded onward through the bitter night.

"We'll be home this eve'," James whispered, patting the stallion's drenched neck as man and beast helped lead a ragged contingent following behind in silent despair. "No wee river can stop us."

The River Esk begged to differ.

It's black waters boiled with demented fury. The winding watery gap between England and Scotland was not to be dismissed lightly. Even the narrow spot below Longtown where James and the rest of the Prince's rebel regiments were headed, was in a spiteful state. While only sixty yards of river separated the two Kingdoms, the Esk was rising fast, already swirling at a depth of more than four feet by the river's edge. No one knew for certain how deep it ran at the centre over its bed of brown shale.

Balgair stopped and slowly raised his massive head. James peered forward, seeing only dimly the shadows before him. He knew the Prince rode in front, on the black mare that had been his mount since the victory at Prestopans almost three months hence. Colonel Gardiner had bequeathed the animal with his dying breath as he lay bloodied and dying on the field of battle, relieved the Prince had won the day against King George's dragoons.

Now suddenly James heard a voice break the silence. "Need th' tallest!"

It was one of the Prince's guides running past the long column. He was seeking out men. James watched him repeat the request over and over as he ran. There were more than a thousand soldiers trekking through the bleak night, and also nearly a dozen women, camp followers, who provided comforts and helped make life somewhat bearable.

James dismounted and two of the women approached him. He recognized both. Colleen and Mary were hard workers who endured suffering better than many of the men he had gotten to know. The two women helped cook and clean, they could mend any material in need of repair, and each was loyal to their man.

But now the poor girls marched alone, burdened with heavy sacks. They set them down and he saw how dirty, wet and exhausted they were from tonight's awful sojourn. And with the angry sound of the River Esk growing ever louder in the distance as if warning them to keep away, they appeared terrified.

"Dinnae let John Daniel dae this!" Mary cried out. "He'll ne'er make it across."

John Daniel was her soldier, a big lad no more than ten and eight years. James touched her wet cheek. It felt like ice as he held her face a moment. "Don't worry, lass. We'll soon be dancing a jig or' the other side. In Scotland!"

He kept his hand on her face and she kissed it. James was

afraid she was right though. The Esk tonight was nae a place for any man. Or any woman.

"Perth!" a voice rang out. It was Prince Charles marching on foot. The two girls bowed their heads as he made his way toward them.

"They're scared," James explained. "Scared we'll send their men into the river."

The Prince studied the two girls, who kept their heads bowed. "Ladies, calm your anxious hearts. I will not use them in this way. I only expect them to follow where I'm willing to lead."

Both girls look relieved. "Thank you, sire," falling to their knees in gratitude.

"Perth, my guides want the tallest men to check the depth," Charles said, turning to James. "But don't you think a man on the tallest horse a more sensible course?"

"Aye," James nodded. A gust of driving rain spat against the Prince's tall frame. He stood firm. The young noble, on the eve of his twenty-fifth birthday, seemed as resolute to James as he had ever seen him over these past months. He expected the Prince to be overcome with discouragement by now.

Only two weeks ago they had been about to seize their prize - the Crown of England. A scant hundred miles from London, in Derby when against both their wishes, it was decided they must turn back. So close James could almost feel it, but the young Prince could not convince the older men on his war council that victory lay within their grasp. He reluctantly ordered a retreat back to Scotland and now here they were, trapped by a few dangerous yards of river, with English cannon and musket closing in quickly.

"My horse is ready, sire. And so am I," James replied with a confidence that masked his real fear.

AT THE WATER'S EDGE, JAMES SENSED BALGAIR'S TREPIDATION. The churning sound of the rushing water warned of the challenge that stretched before the towering brindle-coloured stallion. The inky blackness of a moonless night and the cold unrelenting rain did little to inspire faith in the task ahead.

"Git!" James cried, kicking Balgair hard as the horse hesitated at the edge of the angry river. Balgair reared back and then in a single heartbeat, flung his whole 17 hand high body into the rushing waters. James held on tightly as a torrent of icy spray drenched him.

Balgair struggled to find his footing on the rocky bottom. The strong current pushed hard against him and James knew they would have to move fast or be swept downstream. "Git! Git!" he yelled, digging his boot against his horse's wet abdomen.

They moved forward, each step a struggle as Balgair's hooves slid unsure against the jagged bottom of the river. Freezing water already covered James' boots. As they proceeded deeper into the river, the water rose over the horse's belly threatening to cover the top of his ribs. With each tentative step the water grew deeper, until finally near the middle, it reached the crest of Balgair's neck.

A thousand daggers pierced into James' legs, immersed in icy blackness up to his waist. He fought the pain, urging his mount on, struggling valiantly to progress forward. James prayed with each step forward that they had reached the deepest point of the unforgiving river.

But the level did not recede. Instead, it got deeper and deeper.

Finally, he felt it. A slight incline in their attitude as the Esk reluctantly began to release its watery grip. "Keep going, Balgair!" James cried.

Back on the other side, the Prince with a group of cheering soldiers, watched his lieutenant's passage . Loudly they urged James onward. Balgair sensed progress and fought to move faster, though the water still rose to his shoulders. With each step though, the stallion pushed harder and harder, until finally the water dropped below his thighs. The shore lay just a few glorious steps ahead.

James shouted out triumphantly as they touched Scottish soil again for the first time in months. "We're home!"

A loud howl rose from the men still stranded in England. James drew a deep breath, fighting the aching cold that gripped him. Inhaling the air of his homeland provided a boost to his spirit. He wondered where Katharine was at this very moment.

Had he driven her away forever?

There was no time to linger on his thoughts. He had to help a thousand frightened souls across the river. Most would have to make the crossing on foot. He said a prayer for them and then turned Balgair around, back towards the river.

Without hesitation he kicked the horse gently and began the crossing back to England.

PRINCE CHARLES WATCHED AS THE MEN FORMED A LINE, SIX abreast. It was as if they were preparing to march into battle in tight formation. They waited as James came ashore on his horse. He took a moment to try and vanquish the chill that seemed to reach right into his bones. The men waited for his order.

"Hold each other, by the collar!" James shouted above the rasp of the snarling river. "Don't let go o' each other! God bless ye and may his face shine upon you. Now go!"

The six soldiers let out a ferocious whoop and jumped into the raging water. The man at the end of the formation lost his footing and went under. The others fought desperately to right him, pulling him upright, in a confusion of arms and legs. The man gasped for air, even as the entire group fought the strong current.

"Hold on!" the Prince yelled. "Steady!"

The men held each other by their collars, wrapped tightly together in support. They tried to move forward, but the current was too strong and it was all they could do to turn around and crawl back onto to the rocky shore. They pulled themselves out of the river, choking and defeated.

"Tae no use," one of the men gasped. "Tis pure tough! Too strong!"

The Prince, seated high on his black mare, turned his horse towards the water. "Perth, follow me." Charles urged his mount into the river. James and Balgair followed. "We need to make a dike - slow the current," the Prince shouted above the clamour of the rushing waters.

"With our horses?" James asked, following behind the Prince. He moved Balgair forward, taking his place in front of the Prince's horse. They formed a wall against the fast moving current. On the other side of their horses, the waters slowed just enough that men could advance without being swept away.

"Yes, Perth! We need all the horses in the river, now!"

THE PRINCE'S PLAN WORKED.

The entire calvary formed an unbroken equine dam that slowed the rushing river's flow momentarily so the men could progress without being swept away. The water was so deep, that for the most part, only a solider's head could be seen progressing forward across the river. Wet and nearly frozen, the men cried out in song, trying to dispel the torturous cold that gripped them.

James and Balgair worked in the middle, helping men overcome by fatigue. James pulled eight exhausted men, one-by-one, onto the shore. Nearly frozen to death, they dropped to their knees and kissed the ground in relief. The Prince himself plucked three soldiers from the river, men too weak to complete the crossing, overwhelmed and nearly frozen as they reached the deepest part of rushing river.

James's legs and feet were numb. He felt a chill so deep inside him he imagined no fire could thaw him. But he pushed the pain away, as he watched his men fight for their lives to cross and then celebrate their safe passage to the piper's call on the other side with a spirited jig.

Suddenly he heard shouting. It was a woman's voice. "Help! Help!"

He looked over and saw a group of heads, desperately trying to advance. He turned Balgair around towards them. There was a narrow break in the wall of horses, and the forceful current was pushing the group downstream.

"Hang on!" James shouted, urging his horse toward them. His nearly frozen mount was having difficulty. They had both been in the water a long time now. He knew Balgair's strength must be waning. James kicked anyway, urging his steed forward. The horse slipped on the craggy rocks below and James fought to remain atop his mount, out of the clutches of the merciless river.

"Help us! Please!" It was Mary, yelling hysterically.

"I'm coming," James shouted. "Hold on!"

The current seemed to grow stronger, even as he got closer. He could see Mary and Colleen, trying to find footing, clinging to each other while John Daniel, stood in front, desperate to fight back the entire River Esk himself.

"Hurry!" John pleaded as James tried to close the widening gap between them. The three heads kept getting pushed further away by the strong current. John cried out, "Ah cannae hold 'em much longer!"

The girls were flailing, trying to keep their grip on the beleaguered John Daniel. James could see they were struggling and their only hope was for him to reach them before they were swept away. Only a few more yards and he'd have them.

Suddenly, there was another shriek. "Help!"

John had lost his footing and slipped under the water. Mary and Colleen were frantic, trying to pull him up, but now they were being pushed downstream with the current, even as they splashed and kicked. Finally John's head broke the surface. He was gasping for air, trying to steady himself at the same time.

The rushing water was too strong. Mary was pushed into the

current, even as she tried to reach for John, her hand grasping a clump of his long hair. John reached for her, while Colleen grabbed his arm, tugging hard and throwing him off balance. Suddenly Mary lost her grip and the turbulent waters sprang her loose into the mouth of the furious river, sweeping her away in an instant.

James heard her horrible screams as she disappeared into the black night. He kicked Balgair again.

"I'm coming!" he shouted, trying to close the remaining distance to John, with Colleen still attached to his arm.

"Ah cannae do it!" John cried as he tried to turn into the current, pulling Colleen with him. She was frantic. Her head slipped under the water as John kept trying to regain his footing. "Help!" she screamed in desperation, trying to climb onto John's head.

It was not to be.

Just as James was about to reach them, John slipped beneath the waves. The current ripped Colleen away downstream and her frightened shouts were soon swallowed by the sound of the river's unrelenting fury.

ADEENA WANDERED THROUGH THE CAMP UNDER THE brilliant stars of a December sky. She had been seeking to find James for nearly two days and she was starting to realize that something was different.

After she played the Duncan Cello in the hospital, she found herself performing as Katharine again. This time at Drummond Castle with the Duchess of Perth, Lady Jean, for a group of women raising money for Prince Charles and the rebels. Adeena kept expecting to fall unconscious and wake up in Ottawa, returned to her own time. But instead, each morning she woke as Katharine Carnegie and the world became a little more familiar.

Today, travelling by carriage for more than six hours since dawn and then setting out on foot, she had found her way to the military bivouac near the little village of Ecclefechan where Lady Jean had got word her son lay gripped with fever, fighting for his life. The paths were muddy. Each step was a struggle. It had taken two hours of difficult hiking to get to the camp.

"O'er here, miss," the solider who had been guiding her said, pointing to a large tent pitched on the mossy field. It appeared dimly lit from inside. "That's his tent, th' Duke o' Perth."

"Thank you," she said surveying the front entrance of the canvass shelter. She hesitated, remembering her last encounter with James. He had warned her to stay away. But now he lay sick and his mother had begged her to visit and try to help him.

"Wull' ye be okay?" the soldier asked, as she stood hesitating in front of the tent.

"Yes, thank you, I'm fine." Adeena pulled back the opening of the tent and peered inside. It was hard to seet anything. A candle set on a table, burned low, nearly out of wax. She made her way inside and found a single cot in the middle of the tent, covered with a thin wool blanket, muddy and wet. The cot was empty.

A pair of leather boots sat near it. She looked around for James wondering if he had left somehow, without his boots.

"Ohhh," she heard someone moaning softly. It was him, curled up on the dirt floor, holding his knees together. He was shaking and she rushed to him.

"James, it's me," she said, falling to her knees.

"Kath..." he whispered, unable to draw enough breath to speak her name.

She touched his forehead. He was burning up. His eyes peered dimly out at her and he seemed confused. He was sweating. His lips were crusted, chapped. "I'm here," she said, moving him to a sitting position, pulling him toward her. She placed his head on her lap and tried to soothe him.

He began to cough, trying to say something. His hacking was rough, echoing the congestion inside his chest.

"Shhh. It's okay. Don't talk," she said softly. She touched his head and ran her hand through his long matted hair. The coughing fit finally subsided and he closed his eyes. She could feel the tension in his shoulders and began to massage them slowly. His breathing came in short bursts as he kept trying to clear his lungs, fighting the cough that came in waves of uncontrolled barking and hacking.

"Is there a doctor here?" she asked. He shook his head without opening his eyes.

ADEENA MANAGED TO GET JAMES MOVED TO A TINY INN IN the village the men called 'Fechan'.

The army surgeon was called and prescribed bed rest, soup and brandy, at least twice a day. He left a bottle of Ecclefechan whisky with her and packed up quickly to attend to men in the camp who desperately needed his services.

"He's pure tough, lassie," the aging surgeon told her as he prepared to leave. "But ye must be stronger still."

"Thank you," she said. "I know."

For the next twenty-fours she was the best nurse she could be. She fed him clear broth, and made sure he took the whisky afterwards. Clean linen shirts arrived from the camp and she helped him to change, and to wash his face and hands. By late afternoon, more than a full day since she had brought him to the top floor of the only inn in the village, he remained weak and still confused. His coughing slowed somewhat though, and his chest seemed to be clearing a little.

"We were so close," he said to her, trying to raise his head from the bed. "We should a kept on, to London."

James tried to push himself up, but he couldn't do it and she moved her chair close to the bed. She took his hand. He squeezed it, but just barely. "You're still weak," she whispered.

"I know," he replied, closing his eyes. "But I should be with my men. Some are'nt going to make it."

"I'll take you to them, soon. You can't do anything until you're stronger."

He sighed deeply and closed his eyes. Adeena wondered what was going through his mind. Suddenly he cried out, "I should've saved them!"

She leaned in to him, still holding his hand. She placed her other hand on his forehead, touching him gently. "Who? What do you mean?"

He cried out, "In Kendall, a townsmen shot one of my men in the throat. He bled to death in my arms."

Adeena listened without speaking. She could only imagine the horrors he had seen.

"Then a mob dragged two o' them through the town, tied to a horse. The butchers! Like dogs..." His voice trailed off as he closed his eyes. He was lost in his own torture, his breathing uneven and fitful. He seemed to be reliving the worst moments of the foray into England, and Adeena knew there was nothing she could say that would ease his mind.

She watched him for a few moments, then covered him with a blanket. He opened his eyes to stare at her, and she could see the wetness as he stared back, almost unseeing. There was pain inside him, a darkness she could almost feel. With tears streaming down his face, he raised a hand and touched her face.

She kissed it, trying anyway she could to bring him some small degree of comfort. He closed his eyes again and she could feel him relax a little. She stood up, took off her boots and removed the simple skirt and blouse she was wearing.

And then naked, she slipped into the bed with him. She wrapped him in her arms and held him as he fought the demons torturing him until finally he found the release of sleep.

BOOK II - CHAPTER 2

"C'mon, Nathan. You've got to do better than that."

Jackie couldn't accept what she was being told by Dr. Lochiel and the other doctors standing around her daughter. "Is she in a coma? Is there anything we can do? What are you saying?"

The team looked uneasy. Dr. Lochiel stared at at the EEG monitor. "We're getting mixed readings Jackie. Her GCS score is really low, but her EEG is off the charts."

William standing beside Jackie looked confused. "Can I get that in English?"

"The GCS score is her level of consciousness. Really low means a deep coma," Jackie explained. "And that's not good."

"But her EEG on the other hand," Dr. Lochiel continued, "shows that she's not really in a coma at all. In fact she is..." He paused and looked to the other doctors.

"She is what?" Jackie asked.

"We're not sure," Dr. Lochiel replied. "We really don't understand what's going on here."

A STRANGE SET OF FEELINGS HAD COME OVER TARA DURING the course of the last week.

Her world had changed so much, even as she waited for confirmation of her promotion to Director of the National Gallery. Staff treated her with new reverence. At meetings everyone hung on each word she uttered. It all felt so natural completely in tune with her personality. But she carefully held her authority in restraint, sensing it was a better way to motivate staff and build allegiances. The ocean she now swam in was warm and inviting. She knew this is where she belonged.

Her relationship with Philippe on the other hand made her feel like a freshly caught fish flapping to get away. She had fallen for him hard and wasn't sure how much of herself to let go.

"Tara, what is it?" he asked, as they sat together in the coffee shop at the Civic Hospital. They had just come from seeing Adeena, and she needed to sit and gather her thoughts.

"I don't know how to help," she began, idly stirring the hot cup of tea steaming in front of her. "Not sure what I'm supposed to do this time."

Philippe said nothing as he sipped his coffee. Tara had only been in love once before, and it was a disaster. She had so dominated Greg, her teenage beau, that he had broken things off after a few months with a one line text message. Apparently she was not 'loving' enough for him. She later found out she had been nicknamed 'The Bitch' for her 'attitude'.

"I'm not sure there is much you can do," Philippe offered finally. "You miss her, don't you?"

"Yeah, I do. I've always helped her through things, been there when her world collapsed and found a way to fix it."

"But you can't this time, and you're..." Philippe hesitated. He studied her for a few seconds and then touched her hair. "What are you thinking?"

Tara closed her eyes, fighting the growing moisture in her eyes. She had always known what to do when Adeena was in trouble. Tara had lived much of her life through her best friend, sharing her joys and pain, relishing her adventures, from the giddy feeling of a new love to the heartache of the inevitable break-up. She had been with Adeena through all her struggles and triumphs.

"You're not used to not to this, to not having an answer. Is that it?" Philippe asked.

She opened her eyes. "I think so."

He wiped a tear that was starting to escape down her cheek. "Well, just let me in and we can figure this out together."

THERE WAS NO PLACE THAT FRIEDRICH LANG COULD FIND respite.

He stared out the window at the blackness. The wet pavement from hours of steady rain glistened in its indifference towards him. Cars swept past, red tail lights lingering through the mist. Through blurry, drunken eyes he saw blood flowing in the streets.

There is a cancer growing in this place.

It covers this horrible city where he had been persuaded to come and 'build' an orchestra. He was to be the star, the maestro that would put Ottawa in the spotlight of classical music. He remembered his first interview, the head of the NAC Orchestra selection committee extolling her grand vision and how Friedrich would be at the centre of it all.

Fick dich selbst. Fuck yourself, bitch.

He poured another vodka into his glass and downed it in a single shot. A burning trail blazed deep into his gut.

He closed his eyes, and jabbed them with both hands until they exploded with stars. Why in the fuck had he thought he could take credit for such a well known piece of music? Was he goddamn crazy?

His career was ruined. His reputation destroyed. There was no hope.

No future.

No money.

He'd been dismissed 'with cause' and no severance was due to him. He might even get sued now, lose his house.

A loud *meow* interrupted his darkness. His thin, neglected cat Heinz pawed into the room and rubbed against his leg, meowing for attention. He pushed her away roughly with his foot, flinging the poor creature across the room.

If I am going down, I'm not going alone.

THE MRI PROFILE IMAGE OF HIS PATIENT'S HEAD CREATED A blue glow in Dr. Nathaniel Lochiel's office. He set down his glasses and leaned closer to the 40 inch High Definition monitor on the wall.

He had examined all the scans of Adeena Stuart made since she had slipped into a coma last week. Now, as Dr. Chung worked on starting up his prototype 3-D imaging system, Nathaniel focused on a dark area of the MRI scan.

Was it really growing? Could it really be second cortex developing inside a living person?

"Okay," Dr. Chung called over. "Take a look." He tapped his mouse, plugged a USB cable into his laptop and the HD monitor that Nathaniel had been staring at went black for a second and then completely white.

"Ready?" Dr. Chung asked.

"Yeah, let me see what you got," Nathaniel sighed. This case was starting to overwhelm both of them. Maybe today they would get some answers. The monitor filled with the profile of Adeena's head again, showing her entire face, brain, and neck, in eerie glowing shades of translucent blue.

Dr. Chung clicked his mouse in the middle of the screen. The camera zoomed into the centre of the image, focusing on the darkest areas in the middle of the brain. "Look at this."

The flat image began to rotate, and then morphed into full 3-D. Dr. Chung moved the mouse forward and was now controlling the image on the screen, as if he were navigating through a video game.

"Wow," Nathaniel whispered.

"Thanks. Now that we're inside, I can go anywhere, zoom into anything you want to see."

"Can we compare to previous scans as well? I want to see the growth of this new area."

"Of course." Dr. Chung moved his mouse. "Just give me a sec." A menu came up on the screen, and he changed some numbers, selected a pull-down menu and clicked again.

The image refreshed and now date and time code numbers were overlaid on the screen. A small dark blue area, surrounded by thin veins in a pale tone, came into focus. As the numbers rolled forward, the area began to grow, erratically, but steadily. It doubled in size before the numbers stopped.

"That's all we've got, so far," Dr. Chung said.

Nathaniel wasn't sure how it was possible. But there was no doubt now.

Adeena had a second cortex inside of her, and in was growing steadily.

HE HAD NEVER EXPECTED THEIR WORLDS TO COLLIDE, BUT FOR the first time, William had a sense that the study of history and the science of medicine were forcing he and Jackie to look at the world from each other's perspective.

They sat together in Adeena's hospital room, despondent in their helplessness. The background noise of the monitoring equipment, with its regular and predictable rhythms, created an ambient background soundtrack that reminded him of a Brian Eno album he used to listen when he was completing his PhD.

But in those days, the music helped him get through long

nights of research and writing, imagining the worlds of European history and the characters that shaped it. While he knew they were real, they seemed distant and long dead. He stared at his daughter lying on her bed, tentacled by machines to the miracles of modern medicine while inside of her...

"Will," Jackie interrupted.

"What?" He turned to her, trying to refocus.

"We need to work together."

William sat up and took a deep breath. Jackie rarely asked for help in dealing with anything related to her job. His role was usually to just listen as she reviewed a case, and watch in wonder as she talked through a solution, with him doing nothing more than occasionally nodding in agreement.

"Work together?" he asked.

"I don't think Nathan is telling us everything. Adeena's in a coma, that much I know. But there is something else going on inside her, that worries me." Jackie reached for Adeena's hand and held onto it. "She's gone back, hasn't she? And she's stuck. And..."

She paused unable to complete her thought. The monitoring equipment filled the silence with ambient Eno-like rhythms.

"And, what?" William asked, not sure where his wife was going, but guessing it was a place she'd never been.

"Well, that's where I need you to give me a history lesson."

"How's that going to help Adeena?"

"I'm not sure, Will. But we can't just sit here and wait, doing nothing. There's something gong on inside her head, and somehow the past and present are fighting in there."

She bit her lip and looked at the hospital floor. "And I don't want her to be the victim."

Made in the USA
Middletown, DE
03 March 2021

34700974R00227